MARIE

OR

SLAVERY IN THE UNITED STATES

RACE IN THE AMERICAS

Robert Reid-Pharr, Series Editor

Frank J. Webb, *The Garies and Their Friends*
José Vasconcelos, *The Cosmic Race*
Onoto Watanna, *Miss Numè of Japan: A Japanese-American Romance*
Gustave de Beaumont, *Marie; or, Slavery in the United States: A Novel of Jacksonian America*

M A R I E

OR

SLAVERY IN THE UNITED STATES

A NOVEL OF JACKSONIAN AMERICA

GUSTAVE DE BEAUMONT

Translated from the French by

BARBARA CHAPMAN

With a new introduction by

GERARD FERGERSON

THE JOHNS HOPKINS UNIVERSITY PRESS
Baltimore and London

Hardcover edition published by Stanford University Press, 1958

Printed in the United States of America on acid-free paper

Johns Hopkins Paperbacks edition, 1999
9 8 7 6 5 4 3 2 1

The Johns Hopkins University Press
2715 North Charles Street
Baltimore, Maryland 21218-4363
www.press.jhu.edu

Library of Congress Cataloging-in-Publication Data

Beaumont, Gustave de, 1802–1866.
[Marie. English]
Marie, or, Slavery in the United States : a novel of Jacksonian America / Gustave de Beaumont ; translated from the French by Barbara Chapman ; with a new introduction by Gerard Fergerson.
p. cm. — (Race in the Americas)
Originally published: Stanford, Calif. : Stanford University Press, 1958.
Includes bibliographical references.
ISBN 0-8018-6064-4 (alk. paper)
1. Slavery—United States—History—19th century. 2. Slaves—United States—Social conditions. 3. United States—Race relations. 4. Women slaves—United States—Social conditions. 5. Slavery—United States—History—19th century—Fiction. 6. Slaves—United States—Social conditions—Fiction. 7. United States—Race relations—Fiction. 8. Women slaves—United States—Social conditions—Fiction. I. Title II. Title: Marie. III. Title: Slavery in the United States. IV. Series.
E443.B3713 1999
973′.0496—dc21 98-31234
CIP

A catalog record for this book is available from the British Library.

Contents

Introduction, 1999

In his 1938 biography of M. Alexis de Tocqueville (1805–1859), George Wilson Pierson establishes the powerful influence of Tocqueville's lifelong friend and fellow lawyer, Gustave de Beaumont (1802–1866), on the conclusions advanced in *Democracy in America.* Beaumont and Tocqueville, both prison magistrates under Louis Philippe, came to the United States in 1831 and 1832 in order to examine the American penitentiary system and the then-popular subject of prison reform. Puzzling over the lack of historical recognition and critical attention to Beaumont's 1835 novel, *Marie; or, Slavery in the United States,* a romantic tale about an interracial relationship between a male French traveler and a young woman descended from a "mulatto" and "soiled by a drop of black blood," Pierson attributed the oversight to the novel's being "apparently too romantic, too sentimental and too interrupted, too much concerned with social issues, too little with political."[1]

Beaumont's place in American literary and social history probably has been compromised by the very subject that he wanted to explore in *Marie, ou l'Esclavage aux Etats-Unis, Tableau de moeurs americaines* (originally published in two volumes in France in 1835): the reconciliation of American democratic ideals with racism and slavery. Beaumont warned in his foreword to the novel, set in Jacksonian America, that "all but the form is serious." His announced intention was to explore "the violence of the prejudice which separates the race of slaves from that of the free men, that is, the Negroes from the whites." By the time that the reader confronts the story of how racism and slavery pervades the character of American social and political relations, a revelation is made that the novel will analyze "the condition of the black race in America."

Marie's republication will have significant implications for how historians and literary scholars portray the history of slavery in the United

[1] George Wilson Pierson, *Tocqueville in America* (1938; reprint, Baltimore: Johns Hopkins University Press, 1996), 522.

States. Its exposure of the cruelties of slavery and the assault on Native Americans by President Andrew Jackson and his enthusiasts enables us to critique racial and gender ideologies that supported a stratified social order. Tensions in an evolving political system immersed in vigorous debates about the movement of slavery into the territories, state sovereignty, and the profitability of slavery are also evident.

Though the work exhibited a sensitivity to the oppression of blacks and Native Americans, which translated into several indictments of the gap between equality and the political status of these marginalized groups, Beaumont clearly was a product of his age and viewed slavery and the experiences of increasingly demarcated racial groups as evidence to support his belief that there were stages of civilization in the movement of societies toward democracy. A belief in racial difference and hierarchy was not uncommon among both proslavery and antislavery advocates during the early nineteenth century. Of the progress of civilization that Beaumont and his contemporaries felt touched feudal societies in Europe and that would ultimately free American democracy from slavery, he notes that "it is impossible not to foresee a more or less imminent epoch in which slavery will have completely disappeared from North America" (214).

Even though his analysis of race would not undermine a belief in racial difference and hierarchy, Beaumont fundamentally believed that American slavery contradicted principles of equality and democracy advanced in the United States. This is made clear in the appendixes to *Marie*, where he more boldly declares with respect to slavery and the experience of free blacks that "the laws of the United States guarantee an equality which is not found in reality." Beaumont presented an indictment of American democracy and slavery but not of racial difference and hierarchy, as he revealed what Jacksonian Americans did not feel were contradictory elements in the doctrines that defined liberty and justice.

What happened to *Marie* between 1835 and 1999? The introduction and plot that unfolds in this novel—part ethnography, part fiction—is hardly the type of literature that an American publisher would welcome during the 1830s, when law and public policy increasingly stipulated harsh penalties for trafficking in "incendiary materials," as antislavery tracts and other written attacks on slavery were often designated. Indeed, the choice to expose the cruelties of slavery in the form of a novel probably stemmed from what was a common strategy to protect the lives of those whose experiences were revealed and told without changing basic elements of a story. A lack of protection for those who shared their stories and experiences could expose individuals and have severe implications, for example, for fugitive slaves who could be sold back into slavery and others who might have been "passing" as white in American society. And even if a sympathetic abolitionist had advocated *Marie*'s translation into English and publication in the United States, the book's even-handed indictment of a religion-based abolitionism that fell short of advocating black equality was clearly problematic.

Although the novel progressed through five editions in seven years in France and won some of France's highest literary awards, the first English translation would not appear in the United States (or anywhere else) until 1958. Twenty years after Pierson's authoritative biography lauded the contributions of Beaumont, consensus historians during the 1950s would largely ignore complex representations of difference, identity, and national character and promote, instead, a sanitized version of Tocqueville's meditations on America's evolving democracy.[2] The circulation of the first English translation of *Marie* in this country would also occur four years after the United States Supreme Court had mandated the desegregation of schools in 1954. One year later, the brutal murder of the young Emmit Till in Mississippi, allegedly for whistling at a white woman, signified the broader cultural and political taboos that were explored in this sentimental tale of interracialism. This is not to mention that between 1831, when Beaumont first arrived in the United States, and 1958, which marked the appearance of the first English translation, interracial marriages were illegal in virtually every state in the south.[3]

One cannot understand *Marie*'s importance in American arts and letters without an assessment of the ways in which Beaumont's interest in American slavery intersected with his and Tocqueville's interest in American democratic institutions. Under the impression that America's democratic institutions and practices could provide a crucial model for France and other republics in transition, they sailed to the United States

[2] Please consult Alexis de Tocqueville, *Democracy in America* (New York: Random House, 1981) for more detailed information about the tensions that were exhibited in Tocqueville's use of the concepts of democracy and equality. In his introduction to this work, Thomas Bender also makes several compelling arguments for the enthusiastic support of Tocqueville's work among American intellectual historians.

with the intention to supplement their investigation of prison reform with an exploration of forms of government, civil society, and processes for citizen participation. In the aftermath of the French Revolution's challenge to aristocratic tyranny and religious dominance, they both embodied Enlightenment ideals about liberty, equality, and the "natural rights of man." These ideals pervaded Beaumont's exploration of American slavery. "But here the American," Beaumont notes in an appendix to *Marie*, "does not believe he is violating the principle of equality, since he considers that the Negro belongs to a race inferior to his own . . . a white skin is the mark of nobility for them, and they treat each other with the regard and honor habitual among the members of a privileged class" (231). Beaumont would also exhibit a skepticism about the rationalization of slavery, white privelege, and racial inferiority through religious doctine, a quality that was probably shaped by his upbringing by religious parents and his environment, which had been touched by the Revolution's assault on the Catholic Church and the bourgeoisie in his provincial French community.

Beaumont's interrogation of race, racism, and American discourse on slavery through the words of characters in *Marie* exposes tensions in the evolution of the plantation economy and representative government in Jacksonian America. Though Beaumont and Tocqueville would remain limited in their critiques of the white planter class's dominance of

[3] I imagine, however, that contemporary historians of race and the African American experience will be more attentive to *Marie*'s literary and historical significance, particularly in light of the documentation of plantation life and the lives of free and fugitive black men and women during the past thirty years. The pioneering work of John Blassingame on the importance of slave narratives, as well as the work of other social and literary historians, has transformed the authority and centrality of first-person accounts of enslaved and "free" blacks. See John W. Blassingame, *The Slave Community: Plantation Life in the Antebellum South* (New York: Oxford University Press, 1972); William L. Andrews, *To Tell a Free Story: The First Century of Afro-American Autobiography, 1760–1865* (Urbana: University of Illinois Press, 1986); Robin Blackburn, *The Making of New World Slavery: From the Baroque to the Creole* (New York: Verso, 1997); Hazel Carby, *Reconstructing Womanhood: The Emergence of the Afro-American Woman Novelist* (New York: Oxford University Press, 1987); Eugene D. Genovese, *Roll, Jordan, Roll: The World the Slaves Made* (New York: Pantheon Books, 1974); Brenda E. Stevenson, *Life in Black and White: Family and Community in the Slave South* (New York: Oxford University Press, 1996); Paula Giddings, *When and Where I Enter: The Impact of Black Women on Race and Sex in America* (New York: W. Morrow, 1984).

local politics and the influence that this had on the application of "natural rights" to free and slave black men and women and Native Americans, *Marie* would privilege a discourse on the denial of rights to blacks in American society by positing debates about equality in fictional form. Beaumont confronts the early 1830s movement to colonize African Americans in other areas of the country and Liberia, a development which he thought simultaneously had stiff financial implications and signaled that blacks would never be perceived as the equals of whites. He recognized that colonization and movements to disenfranchise free blacks in the United States fundamentally challenged political rhetoric in America, where Andrew Jackson was an architect of a new Democratic party that would ultimately expand the franchise for white men who did not necessarily own property (and in very limited and short-lived local cases, women) and champion "states' rights" on slavery.

Marie's romantic plot not only confronts whiteness as a sign and marker of privilege in America, but also exposes how the cultural, social, and political positions for antebellum blacks, whites, and Native Americans were sharply demarcated. The central character is Ludovic, a French traveler who lands in Michigan on a journey to find a political career. During his travels to Baltimore to seek a professional career, Ludovic encounters Nelson, a merchant, who then introduces him to his politically engaged son, George, and his daughter, Marie. Ludovic instantly falls in love with Marie, who seems to avoid him, because she is in possession of a dark "mystery." This occurs in the context of his relationship with what readers are told is "an American family." When the mystery is revealed to be that Marie is "colored," and that her father had married an orphan from New Orleans who was discovered to be a descendent of a mulatto, Ludovic finds himself in a bind about love and race in a society wherein he is an interloper. It is only after Nelson and George urge him to travel the United States and observe the impact of race on social and political relations before a proposal of marriage to Marie that he begins to grasp and question the impact of racial oppression in American society. Ludovic's struggles to understand American race relations and slavery dramatically mirror Beaumont's own journey and surviving correspondence. Ludovic travels to Boston, Philadelphia, and New York. In New York, where he and Marie agree to marry, they encounter a "race riot" at the church after it is announced that they will wed, which prevents the marriage from taking place. Subsequently, Ludovic and Marie decide to head to Michigan, where Marie dies from a strange "fever." George, who has joined with Native Americans and escaped slaves to resist "Indian removal," is killed in a battle to prevent westward expansion by the United States government. Nelson embarks on a campaign to spread Christianity among the remaining Native Americans. Ludovic, in grief about Marie's death, retreats to a lonely, isolated existence in the woods.

The character of Marie in particular represents the complex tensions about slavery and race that Beaumont is exploring in his journey around America. Marie's ultimate and strange death from "fever" might be read as a metaphor for the potential of interracialism to fail as long as slavery exists.[4] Cholera had appeared in Europe during 1831 and would appear in America, signifying for many a kind of providence for those with weak moral and physical constitutions. Marie's fate might also be read as the tale of the classic "tragic mulatto" whose death represents the shame of slavery.[5] Just before her sudden death, Marie would relate her growing sickness to her racial identity as "a poor colored girl, scorned by all" and melodramatically assert that "all these ills are nothing compared to the torment that my soul feels" (166). This may be interpreted as a veiled reference to the broader battles between the north and south, free and slave, or black and white.

Beaumont's narrative persistently engages race and racial difference as it explores the political ideology that supports slavery and racial oppression both in the north and south. Embarking upon his travels, Ludovic remarks that the United States "contains people of different races" (23). There are "some whom the polar ice chills, others are warmed by the tropical sun." Doctrines of racial difference and inferiority, *Marie* reveals, are central to the debate about slavery and linked to both proslavery and abolitionist positions. George, Nelson, Marie, and Ludovic explore the meaning of racial categorization in a lively debate about the implications

[4] Charles E. Rosenberg, *The Cholera Years: The United States in 1832, 1849, and 1866* (Chicago: University of Chicago Press, 1987).

[5] Jacquelyn Y. McLendon, *The Politics of Color in the Fiction of Jessie Fauset and Nella Larsen* (Charlottesville: University of Virginia Press, 1995). McLendon and Hazel Carby have some of the most engaging readings on the role of the "tragic mulatto" in sentimental American literature of the nineteenth century. I am particularly drawn to their identification of the body and the notion of "mixed race" as narrative devices used to explore and interpret prevailing naturalist and biological theories of alleged race and gender differences.

of racial difference for strengethening justifications for slavery (59–61). George remarks to his father that the law has established that "a Negro is not a man; he is a chattel, a thing." "Inferior race! So you say! You have measured the Negro brain." Consistent with theories of racial categorization among many Enlightenment and early-nineteenth-century pre-Darwinian naturalists who underscored the primacy of the environment in the development of racial "types," Nelson remarks to his children and Ludovic that freedom is a "fatal gift" for those "whose minds are naturally restricted."[6]

Marie exhibits the various tensions that inform ideas about inherent racial and gender differences, as well as the proposition that blacks and whites have different moral reasoning capacities. The emergence of the "noble savage" in the work of late-eighteenth-century literature exhibited a widespread belief that environment was a key influence in the cause of these alleged racial differences. Such ideas about race and racial difference would be challenged among a new generation of naturalists who questioned the origin of racial types. A process of "degeneration," which seemed to incorporate arguments for stasis and change in the development of human racial types, was increasingly applied in the early nineteenth century to ideas about human racial variation in the work of Buffon (1707–88) and other French naturalists, who drew upon developments in comparative anatomy, for example, to advance more materialist explanations for the development of species or human racial types. Naturalists debated whether races were in fact fixed types who had been stunted in their evolution toward a "most perfect form" or whether they were influenced by more material biological processes influenced by a process of change, as historian Peter J. Bowler has suggested. Curiousity about the biological impact of hybridization—and, in the case of racial types,"miscegenation"—also influenced these discussions.

In their attempts to account for human racial types, Buffon and his

[6] Peter J. Bowler, *Evolution: The History of an Idea*, rev. ed. (Berkeley: University of California Press, 1989), 93; Stephen Jay Gould, *The Mismeasure of Man* (New York: W. W. Norton and Company, 1981); Michael P. Banton, *Racial Theories* (Cambridge: Cambridge University Press, 1987); Nancy Stepan, *The Idea of Race in Science* (New York: Macmillan Publishing Co., Inc., 1982) For a critique of how these scientific ideas intersected with ideas about slavery, see James Oakes, *The Ruling Race: A History of American Slaveholders* (New York: Knopf, 1982); George M. Fredrickson, *The Black Image in the White Mind* (New York: Harper and Row, 1971.)

Enlightenment contemporaries had also wrestled with previously static models of human species as shaped by the biblical story of Creation. God, some declared, might not have played a role in the development of racial types, given the existence of a fossil record which undermined the Biblical timeline. Surely, elements of these latter tensions in early-nineteenth-century naturalist thought appealed to Beaumont, who allowed George to confess during his battle on behalf of Native Americans and escaped slaves that he was "ignorant of God's designs" (166). This implied that change and progress were inevitable, inscribing religious and scientific messages that race and slavery could be interpreted through a broader experience of human progress.

Notions of racial and gender hierarchy are also inscribed in *Marie*'s very gendered discussions of race relations. Indeed, the work is built on many of these intersections. Beaumont employs several literary references both to define (white) womanhood in terms of prevailing conventions of "true womanhood," while revealing the exclusion of black women from prevailing ideologies about whiteness and womanhood. "American women are superior to women of color; they are able to love with reason," Marie tells her father, Nelson (61). One might advance an argument that Marie's words are challenging prevailing constructions of womanhood, given that "reason" was a quality heavily identified with men in work on moral capacity among early-nineteenth-century naturalists, but if this is the case, Beaumont is positing reason solely as an attribute of white women.[7]

Throughout the novel, we are repeatedly told before and after the "mystery" of Marie's ancestry is revealed that "white women of French or American blood have very pure morals" and that they are "virtuous." This discussion of the intersection of gender and racial characteristics in the novel reveals a tension with respect to white womanhood and the maintenance of an order of sexual relations that ensured the oppression of black women under slavery. As cultural critic Hazel Carby has noted, a critical analysis of slavery as a racialized patriarchal system commonly finds that the "cult of true womanhood" and its popular manifestations from the 1820s existed as a "definer of what constituted a woman and womanhood."[8] Black women, who were raped by their white masters to produce marketable commodities—more slaves—existed outside of the

[7] Anne Fausto-Sterling, *Myths of Gender* (New York: Basic Books, 1992).
[8] Carby, *Reconstructing Womanhood,* 24.

normative moral order that defined true womanhood. This is made evident by the violence directed at Marie in several public venues when it is discovered that she is a woman of color. It is also strikingly attested to by Beaumont in his introduction to the novel, wherein a character asks about a woman sitting among "mulattoes" in a balcony at a theater and is apparently horrified that "a woman of English origin could be so lacking in shame as to seat herself among the Africans."

Beaumont, who clearly saw Marie in a more privileged position in relation to representations of womanhood by virtue of her fairer skin in comparison to her darker sisters, also casts Ludovic as at times perplexed about the moral order that differentiates between the rules that govern social standing and morality of black and white women. The tension consuming Ludovic centers on a reconciliation of Marie's position within a very circumscribed political and social space for women and not a dismantling or toppling of the domestic ideal, for example. This is primarily underscored in the second chapter, which is on American women and seems to depart from the rest of the novel as a sociological study, but actually supports the construction of Marie and womanhood through its lamentation on the "masculine behavior among women" in America.

Beaumont well understood that there were sharp demarcations in the social and political world of Jacksonian America based on race and gender distinctions. He also expressed opinions about the mockery of freedom for free blacks, whom historian Barbara Fields has termed "an anomalous adjunct to the slave population."[9] Historians continue to debate the factors that contributed to their aggregate increase between 1800 and 1850, such as natural increase, in-migration, or the influence of a more liberal postrevolutionary period, but they are generally clearer on the violence and marginalization that free blacks encountered both north and south.[10] Of the free black population in New York City, where the novel

[9] Barbara Jeanne Fields, *Slavery and Freedom on the Middle Ground: Maryland during the Nineteenth Century* (New Haven: Yale University Press, 1985), 3. Fields' documentation of demographic shifts among the black population details the limitations of available sources before the 1850 U.S. Census incorporated questions that enabled more extensive research on nativity and residence.

[10] Leonard Curry, *The Free Black in Urban America, 1800–1850: The Shadow of a Dream* (Chicago: University of Chicago Press, 1981), 218–20; Suzanne Lebsock, *The Free Women of Petersburg* (New York: W. W. Norton and Company, 1984), 90–92; Dorothy Sterling, ed., *We Are Your Sisters: Black Women in the Nineteenth Century* (New York: W.W. Norton and Company, 1984); Herbert Aptheker, ed., *Colonial Times through the Civil War*, vol. 1 of *A Documentary History of the Negro People in the United States* (New York: Citadel Press, 1951).

tells us Marie and Ludovic encountered race riots after they announced their marriage, Beaumont writes, "the black population, possessing liberty, aspired also to equality" (234).

Beaumont had already established in the preface to his novel that color and racism determined blacks' marginalized social and political status, as well as their legal separation from whites. During an October 1831 visit to an almshouse in Baltimore, the city with the largest number of free blacks in the United States, he and Tocqueville witnessed public whippings of free and enslaved blacks, as well as segregation of schools, hospitals, theaters, and cemeteries. His use of demographic data, statistics, and excerpts from legal codes in the appendixes is intended to strengthen his argument that blacks, whether slave or free, were not subject to the same democratic principles as whites. Free blacks encountered different laws and public policy with respect to their movement and actions in various northern and southern states. Voting was a rare privilege in parts of the country. Laws in some states stipulated that they had to leave after manumission or emancipation. Free blacks could not practice or hold licenses for certain occupations. In many places, it was also illegal for them to convene without whites. There was also the paramount reality, as several slave narratives underscore, that they might be sold into slavery because of a whim among whites or for the commission of a crime.[11]

Beaumont and Tocqueville's arriving in the United States at the same time that an abolitionist movement gained new momentum surely had an impact on how Beaumont cast abolitionist discourse and rebellion against slavery as themes. He made an important distinction among those who advocated emancipation. Some, he stated, condemned it as "contrary to the Christian religion" but were "full of the prejudices of their race" and eschewed equality, while others cared "as a Christian loves his brother men" and received blacks "with open arms and treat[ed] them as equals" (123). Frederick Douglass, Nancy Prince, and Harriet Wilson would join other black autobiographers in their statements about "freedom" and the equivocal platforms of white abolitionists, and Beaumont's 1835 work spared little in its portrayal of internal divisions among the movement.[12] In 1831 and 1832, the years of his nine-month visit to the United States, antislavery advocates witnessed the publication of the first issue of William Lloyd Garrison's *Liberator*, as well as the emergence of antislav-

[11] Fields, *Slavery and Freedom;* Curry, *The Free Black.*

ery platforms from newly established organizations such as the Afric-American Female Intelligence Society of Boston, the Female Literary Association of Philadelphia, and the New England Anti-Slavery Society. Seemingly sensitive to the development of black civil society and voluntary activism in the United States, Beaumont may have been alluding to the work of leading black abolitionists during the 1830s, including Charlotte Forten and her daughters, Margaretta, Harriet, and Sarah Louise, Bishop Richard Allen, Charles B. Ray, Samuel Cornish, Sarah M. Douglass, and others.

Beaumont remained critical of American abolitionists and their attitudes about race and racism, but he seemed especially troubled by the specter of slaves using violence as a strategy to win emancipation. Three months after Beaumont's arrival in America in May 1831, Nat Turner's rebellion in Southampton County, Virginia generated a political and local backlash against blacks from slaveowners. Turner's killing of his master and other whites put fear in antebellum whites, who wanted to exact vengeance swiftly on many suspected conspirators, undoubtedly because whites were outnumbered by blacks in a great many southern locales. They also responded with harsh laws making it illegal, for example, to teach a slave to read and write and for free blacks to carry or own firearms or buy the freedom of slaves who were not in their families. These changes did not go unnoticed by Beaumont, who allows the characters in *Marie* to debate the feasibility of violence as an end to slavery. Interestingly, Beaumont cautions the reader through Nelson be aware that "revolt will bring their destruction," as he makes a case that the progress of democracy will inevitably result in the end of slavery (61).

Beaumont casts slave revolt as anathema to "the progress of reason," reflecting his belief that slavery would ultimately disappear because it would become unprofitable. He cites the case of Maryland in particular, where a plantation economy initially focused on tobacco gradually yielded to wheat production and urban manufacturing." Beaumont's argument for progress and the imminent demise of slavery, however, would

[12] Henry Louis Gates, Jr., "In Her Own Right," *Collected Black Women's Narratives*, The Schomburg Library of Nineteenth-Century Black Women Writers (New York: Oxford University Press, 1988); Harriet Jacobs, *Incidents in the Life of a Slave Girl* (Boston: self-published, 1861); Frederick Douglass, *Autobiographies* (New York: The Library of America, 1994); Harriet E. Wilson, *Our Nig; or, Sketches from the Life of a Free Black* (Boston: self-published, 1859); Andrews, To Tell, chapter 3, "Experiments in Two Modes, 1810–1840," in particular.

probably have produced a skepticism among the approximately two million slaves in the United States in 1830, when the rising popularity of cotton as a staple of the plantation economy and the expansion of the domestic slave trade (and illicit international trade, outlawed in 1808) precipitated debates about the annexation of new slave territory in the west and limits on the emancipation of blacks.

Even as the imagery of an emergent industrialism that draws upon steam, for example, to aid in the transport and movement of slaves is revealed in the book, Beaumont appears to have underestimated the impact of proslavery thought on the direction of local and national politics in the early 1830s. Though the melodramatic ending of the novel may suggest a degree of uncertainty about the end of slavery in his model of progress and civilization, the twenty-eight-year-old lawyer's focus on the bills calling for abolition of slavery in state legislatures might have made him more optimistic about the path of the debate on emancipation. I am also sure that, for Beaumont, the legacy of violence from the French Revolution had a lasting impact on how he interpreted rebellion among slaves and Native Americans in a slave economy on the verge of greater expansion.

The inevitable progress of civilization is taken as axiomatic in Beaumont's assessment of slavery and other social and political movements, including President Jackson's aggressive policy of Indian removal. Signed into law on May 20, 1830, the Indian Removal Act, together with the 1831 U.S. Supreme Court decision in *Cherokee Nation v. Georgia*, established that Native American tribes were not sovereign nations entitled to the land on which they lived. Beaumont, though horrified by the manner in which whites treated these "savages" (his words in Appendix K of *Marie*), shared his thoughts in a letter to his sister and family in late 1831, declaring that they lived in a "mixed state, between savagery and a civilization not yet in existence."[13] He felt that some Native Americans, such as the Cherokees, who were in treaty negotiations with the government about their lands, could have been incorporated into American "civilization" in a step toward progress. His character Nelson, a representative of this process of "enlightenment," eventually gives up after a struggle to "teach the Indians the principles which are the bases of all civilized societies" (182). Taken together with George's death while defending the land

[13] Pierson, *Tocqueville in America,* 194.

and sovereignty of Native Americans and escaped blacks, the novel's melodramatic ending can be interpreted as Beaumont's rendering of the passage of a difficult but necessary stage in the advance of American civilization.

A critical historical and literary appraisal of *Marie* is long overdue. This provocative novel provides scholars of the African American experience with an additional lens through which to contextualize the evolution of the slave plantation economy of the early nineteenth century. The discourse about American democratic institutions and practices that focus upon race, scientific theories of racial difference, the intersection of racialized and gendered ideologies, public policy, law, and the history of American democratic ideals will surely provide important fodder for enduring debates and questions about the social and political environment of Jacksonian America. What was the link between scientific knowledge and popular ideas about race? How did prevailing racial ideologies intersect with gendered notions of difference? How did early nineteenth-century travelers document differentials in the social status of "free" and enslaved blacks, and between blacks and whites? How did implementation of public policy differ from professed visions of equality under the law, particularly with respect to the experiences of an increasingly urban free black population? How might we join literary history and social history in new and exciting ways to explore the meaning of race?

The appearance of this 1999 edition of *Marie* is taking place as the United States is grappling with a "national conversation about race." In many ways, this event represents a return to the question of how we reconcile a legacy of racism and slavery—vividly revealed in Beaumont's portraits of Jacksonian America—with American democratic ideals. And yet, there is still a great resistance to acknowledge, publicly, the history of slavery and the impact of race on the framing of our history and public policy. There appears to be an even greater societal unwillingness to name the force of racism as a barrier to social mobility, equality, and inclusion in American society.[14] With this historical recovery of *Marie*, Beaumont's observations about race, racism, and slavery offers new evidence of historical tensions in American democratic ideals. *Marie* also has a lot to

[14] See Wahneema Lubiano, ed., *The House That Race Built* (New York: Vintage Books, 1998) for some important meditations on the history and functions of race and racism in contemporary America.

teach us about the illusions of freedom and equality in a society in which race remains a signifier of difference.

GERARD FERGERSON

Publisher's Note

Although written in the form of a novel, this work is being published in its first English translation primarily as a commentary on American society in the age of Jackson. Gustave de Beaumont, remembered chiefly as Alexis de Tocqueville's travel companion and literary executor, was a penetrating observer in his own right. If his work is dated as fiction, it remains fresh and in some ways prophetic as a social commentary. It also gives an important clue to certain still-prevailing European attitudes toward America.

As presented here, the work is slightly abridged, and the order of Beaumont's notes and appendixes has been altered. The text of the novel itself has been cut very slightly, especially in passages of overly florid or sentimental description which have no particular bearing on the theme. The omission of such passages has been indicated by three periods enclosed by brackets.

In its original French edition, *Marie* was published in two volumes. At the end of each volume, Beaumont placed notes amplifying or documenting his observations in the text proper, as well as a number of appendixes. The present translation retains those notes which still may be informative or interesting to the modern reader. The briefer ones appear at the bottom of the pages to which they refer; the longer ones have been placed in the back of the book as appendixes. Of Beaumont's original appendixes, the following have been omitted: "Note sur le mouvement religieux aux Etats-Unis" and Part I of "Note sur l'état ancien et sur la condition présente des tribus indiennes de l'Amérique du Nord." (Part II, on the "present" condition of American Indians, has been retained.)

Except for a small number of supplementary notes added by the translator to Beaumont's own, no critical annotation seemed necessary. The author's own bias is scarcely concealed and is not in need of being pointed out. Readers who wish to compare Beaumont's observations with his actual experiences in the United States are referred to the authoritative work by George W. Pierson, *Tocqueville and Beaumont in America* (Oxford University Press, 1938).

Introduction

In 1835, toward the end of Andrew Jackson's presidency, there appeared in France two striking and prophetic studies of American government and society. The first was Alexis de Tocqueville's *De la Démocratie en Amérique*; the second was Gustave de Beaumont's *Marie, ou l'Esclavage aux Etats-Unis, Tableau de mœurs américaines*, a curious work, half novel and half sociological treatise, having for its theme slavery and racial injustice in the United States.

These books were inseparably related and complementary, even as their two young authors were linked by an *amitié fraternelle.* Side by side, as apprentice magistrates under the Restoration, they had watched Charles X drive the Restoration monarchy headlong to its destruction in the Revolution of 1830. Together, then, as uneasy prison commissioners for the constitutional monarchy of the bourgeois Louis Philippe, they had made an astonishing nine-month visit to the United States and Canada in 1831–32. Returning, they first composed a revealing joint report for their government on the American penitentiary reforms, with Beaumont writing the text and Tocqueville contributing the notes. Now they were reporting to their fellow citizens on the broader meanings of this strange new society across the water. And where Tocqueville chose the democratic institutions of America as his concern, Beaumont focused on our *mœurs*, our manners and customs.

Thenceforward their fates were not equal. Tocqueville's *Démocratie*, quickly translated in England and shortly republished in the United States, almost overnight became a trans-Atlantic masterpiece, a classic of western thought. By contrast, Beaumont's *Marie*, never translated, went through five editions and then disappeared into the limbo of well-intentioned failures from which it is only now, belatedly, being rescued. Yet intrinsically it was and will be recognized today as an important book: for *Marie* explores a timeless and tragic theme, the fate of the slave no longer a slave, of the black no longer a black, of the man or woman not yet recognized as a citizen, in a democratic society of equals.

The plot of *Marie*, as the reader will discover, is the tragic romance of a young Frenchman (who might have been Beaumont himself) seeking liberty and goodness in the new world, and unexpectedly finding love with an American girl, in whose ancestry was a hidden but fatal flaw of Negro blood. After many hardships and persecutions at the hands of the white majority and the race-crazed mob, and after many sometimes favorable but often mordant commentaries by the hero-narrator on the state of American arts and society, on the character of American women, the press, the religious conflicts, and the unfortunate lot of the Indians, the hero and heroine, Ludovic and Marie, are driven to flee into the wilderness of Michigan. There Marie dies tragically and Ludovic is left to his sorrows, a disillusioned exile. In *Marie* the symbolic American venture ends badly, despite all its overtones of romance.

It is not at all improbable that Beaumont chose the romantic novel as a vehicle for his ideas because of the success and influence of Tocqueville's uncle, the Vicomte de Chateaubriand, whose *Atala* and *René* had stressed the "noble savage" and deeply stirred the imagination of the 1820s. In point of fact, nearly all the great novels of that Romantic epoch had been exercises of sentiment tinged with melancholy; lyric confessions coupled with philosophic theses, played out against a background of untamed nature. Certainly the form of *Marie* drew heavily from this fashionable current of inspiration, yet in substance Beaumont's novel went considerably beyond its predecessors in the French literary tradition.

Superficially, Beaumont's tale embodied and continued a long line of anti-slavery thought produced in the eighteenth and nineteenth centuries by some of the best minds of France. Politically, the status of the Negro race had seemed to rise in pace with the emerging doctrine of the rights of man. The Abbé Prévost, Montesquieu, and Voltaire had severely criticized slavery and the slave trade in the colonies. Rousseau, Diderot, Mably, and d'Holbach had loudly protested the evident injustice. In the growing liberalism of the eighteenth century, abolition had occupied an important place along with, if not above, such local and national problems as penology, mendicity, and child welfare. With growing travel to Africa and the colonies, the sweeping wave of humanitarianism also embraced the sordid fate of the black man. The assemblies of the Revolution produced volumes of pamphlets and printed addresses. With the Englishman Clarkson, Mirabeau, the Abbé Grégoire, and other important voices kept the protests echoing. In 1794, finally, the *Société des Amis des Noirs*, whose first members had been such men as Brissot de Warville, Condorcet, and Lafayette, obtained a hard-won decree of abolition. In 1802, the year of Beaumont's birth, Napoleon virtually reinstated slavery in the French colonies. But 1815 saw the slave trade abolished in principle by the Congress of Vienna. About that date, a parade of literary luminaries, including Madame de Staël, Benjamin Constant, and Lamartine, descended into the political arena on the side of Destutt de Tracy, Broglie, Passy, and others to revive the cause of abolition. Yet not until 1848 would the French Negro receive his full share of the fraternal and equalitarian dividends of the Revolution through full emancipation.

Needless to say, slavery had never been purely a political or legal problem in France. Even earlier than the philosopher-statesmen, the fiction writers had seized upon the heroic possibilities of the subject and had portrayed a romanesque kind of natural man. As far back as 1745 Antoine de Laplace had published his translation of *Oroonoko* (written in 1688 by Aphra Behn). This novel, one of the earliest glorifications of natural man, had served to instill in French thinking the noble sentiments of the *bon nègre* in its French translation. Thus was provided the framework and substance for much of the subsequent *littérature négrophile* in France.

The early romantic writers became fond of portraying the Negro as an exalted hero against a backdrop of exoticism and primitivism. Saint-Lambert's hero in *Ziméo* (1769) affirmed this romanesque tradition. Bernardin de Saint-Pierre, in his extraordinarily popular *Paul et Virginie* (1788), presented his two slave characters sympathetically, while assailing the cruelties of bondage. On the eve of the Revolution, and during the years following, the cause of abolition figured heavily in travel literature and in the theatre as well. Poets and playwrights hailed Toussaint L'Ouverture as the noble man of nature incarnate, the avenger of all the wrongs ever committed on the progeny of Oroonoko. But when the excesses committed by the slaves of Santo Domingo became known, French opinion cooled. Chateaubriand himself assailed their barbarity in 1802 in his *Génie du Christianisme.* And it was not until Madame de Staël renewed the tradition of the *philosophes* that the theme of the *nègre généreux* was reinstated.

Under the Restoration the Negro hero regained his former glamorous status. First young Victor Hugo composed *Bug-Jargal* in 1818. His hero, noble of feature and demeanor, was a kind of humble black knight who loved a white girl, Marie, abducted her during a slave revolt, but then heroically gave his own life to save Marie's white lover. Hugo's insistence on the nobility of the slave dramatically reestablished the Romantic tradition of Oroonoko, Ziméo, or the Negro character Imley in Chateaubriand's *Les Natchez.*

In 1823 the Académie Française proposed *The Abolition of the Negro Slave Trade* as the subject for the poetry prize. The next year, when Beaumont was twenty-two, Madame de Duras, an intimate friend of Chateaubriand, published a short psychological novel, *Ourika.* Here was the story of a Senegalese girl who had been raised in a French family as an equal but whose black skin precluded full acceptance into society. Her love, too, was unrequited and she died in a convent, crushed and brokenhearted, after seeing the white man she loved take another as his bride. Goethe became an ardent admirer of this little story, which in its application of socio-psychology preceded and possibly inspired Beaumont's *Marie.*

Beaumont's novel, however, departs markedly from the inherited stereotype; the noble slave heroes of literature. For Beaumont's story turns on the freedman, not the slave, and on the freedman's *de jure* guarantees of free movement and equal treatment. Essentially, it is the tragedy of the *de facto* violation of these guarantees, and of how the soul of a human being is shattered and destroyed by such discriminations. In retrospect, one sees that both the heroines, Ourika and Marie, were disinherited by their societies. Ourika had also fallen victim to the force of public opinion. But Ourika had remained throughout an underling, an African household pet for a French family, dying without ever having her love returned. Beaumont's heroine, by contrast, is born free, and no trace of her African descent marks her noble features, a fact which makes sheer mockery of racial segregation. Marie also is loved and cherished. So, by his choice of a mulatto heroine, the author shows how the scourge of slavery reaches even into that intermediate zone of light skin color and freedom, to plague an innocent being and deprive her of all happiness and even the will to live.

No doubt, the French anti-slavery tradition had left its mark on the young Beaumont. There is, however, another kind of literary genre from which *Marie* also springs. If we look back at Rousseau's Saint-Preux, Chateaubriand's René, and Madame de Staël's Corinne, we see that Beaumont's Ludovic is, in his turn, the very embodiment of what his creator was, or at least of what the author would have wanted man to be. Such heroes are apart from the race of mortals. Sénancour's Obermann had been an agonized hero for whom life was purposeless. In Chateaubriand the heart had been tormented, in Sénancour the intellect. In Beaumont there is a tormented heart, a disillusioned intellect, but also a shocked sense of justice. Beaumont, too, had imbibed the *mal du siècle* of the Romantics; but his compulsive drive to champion the oppressed took him out of the circle of agonized mourners. He was in the pit with a very real demon, the socio-political problem of race relations in a democracy. In short, Beaumont was a writer *engagé, avant la lettre.*

Gustave Auguste de Beaumont de La Bonninière, born on February 6, 1802, had passed his early years in the peaceful calm of the Château de La Borde in Beaumont-la-Chartre (Sarthe). His father, Count Jules de Beaumont (1777–1851), an even-tempered, affable man, for years served as mayor of the commune and studied the passing events under the Empire without becoming involved in the new spirit. His mother, Rose Préau de La Baraudière (1778–1848), was energetic, sensitive, and so compassionate for her charges that she came to be called "La Providence" by the village folk. The Beaumonts proved conscientious parents who, while teaching Latin to young Gustave, also fired him with love for his fellow man and a sense of Christian charity.

His early ambitions led him to Paris in pursuit of a legal career. In 1825, as a young magistrate under Charles X, he met another young magistrate, Alexis de Tocqueville, with whom he immediately formed a rich and deep friendship which was to last their lives through.

At Paris and Versailles, the two friends became anxious witnesses to the onrushing tide of democratic fervor which finally swept the demagogic House of Orleans into power in July 1830. Although they had supported Charles X, they now had to serve Louis Philippe. To escape a turbulent France and an uneasy personal situation, in October 1830 they seized upon prison reform, and the idea of a trip to America. Their proposal of a study of the then famous penitentiary systems of the new republic came at a propitious moment, for France was anxious to learn all she could of the Auburn and Pennsylvania systems. While prison reform was their avowed purpose for visiting America, study of democracy in action was the real purpose of the trip. How, they asked themselves, might the example of America serve as a prescription for a very ill France? Leaves proved difficult to obtain, particularly for Beaumont, whose memoir on political persecutions a short time before had made him too valuable a man to release. However, permission was finally granted on condition that the two young magistrates pay their own expenses.

Armed with seventy-odd letters of introduction to prominent Americans (including one or two from Lafayette), the two friends set sail for the great adventure. Their sojourn in America lasted a brief nine months (May 11, 1831, to February 20, 1832), but it proved extraordinarily rewarding. As has been related in George W. Pierson's *Tocqueville and Beaumont in America* (Oxford University Press, 1938), they made a complete circuit of this country and Canada, covering over seven thousand miles by stagecoach, steamer, on horseback, and on foot. In intervals between visits to penitentiaries, they penetrated deep into the Michigan frontier, purposely taking the overland route from Detroit to Saginaw in order to taste of the virgin forest. They experienced a steamboat wreck on the Ohio, a stagecoach breakdown in Tennessee, and the rigors of a brutal fourteen-degree-below-zero winter as they tried to reach the Mississippi overland. Beaumont, the taller and stronger of the two, bolstered the courage and nursed the health of his weaker friend during these hazardous days. Meanwhile they met and talked with Americans of all levels, took voluminous notes of their constant conversations and observations, and kept pressing on. Many lasting impressions were first gained during this journey. Of particular interest to Beaumont were the diverse opinions expressed by Americans on slavery, Negroes, and the South. Eventually much of this experience was incorporated into the book, *Marie*. How much of this personal material Beaumont used, and he did so with singular faithfulness, can easily be seen by consulting Professor Pierson's book.

The idea of a joint study had been in the minds of the two young travelers from the beginning, but perhaps midway in their journey their interests began to diverge, and in the end they agreed to compose separate legacies.

Beaumont early became fascinated by the problems of colored minorities, the Indian and the Negro. After leaving New York City, the two travelers had sailed up the Hudson to Albany, then pushed on by stage to Schenectady, Utica, and the Finger Lakes country. Where were the Indians? At Oneida Castle, between Syracuse and Utica, they saw their first Indian woman, drunk and degraded. Her ignoble condition belied Chateaubriand's romanticized portrait of the noble savage. Beaumont resolved to devote his attention to this "noble savage" now no longer noble. On the boat from Buffalo to Detroit, they met John Tanner, government Indian interpreter, who had spent thirty years with the Indians, and who gave them a copy of his memoirs which served to supplement their observations.

As their journey took them southward, however, Beaumont's compassionate interest was drawn even more strongly to the Negro. During the week of October 12–18, 1831, the two commissioners found themselves in Philadelphia, a point on the perimeter of the slave states. It was there that the ugly anomaly of the new republic became engraved in Beaumont's mind. Visiting a theatre, they were astonished to notice the audience carefully segregated by race and descent. In Baltimore, Beaumont next saw a Negro caned for being out of his section at the race track, with no protest from the apathetic bystanders. And in an almshouse which they visited, they came upon a foaming-mad black who had been driven insane by his master's cruelty (see Pierson, p. 516, and *Marie*, pp. 45–46, in this translation). To these *expériences vécues* were added many conversations concerning slavery with American leaders. The dominant idea of *Marie* began to crystallize. Here was, for Beaumont, a greater tragedy than that of the Indian, a tragedy which was to become the raw material of his book, while the Indians' sad story would be relegated to an appendix.

The Americans themselves were not unaware of their problem. The year 1831 was a period of great social unrest and of a burning zeal for reform. In the matter of slavery, particularly, it was a moment of transition for both southern and northern attitudes. The international slave trade had been abolished in 1808. There had followed an interval (1808–30) which has been called the "period of stagnation," for no strong anti-slavery sentiment of real importance prevailed. The year 1831, however, saw the uneasy acquiescence shattered by three noteworthy events: the publication of Garrison's *Liberator*, Nat Turner's rebellion in August, and the beginning of the slavery debates in the Virginia legislature.

Turner's abortive insurrection in Southampton, Virginia, left some sixty white people massacred. This fact, coupled with the remembered horrors of Santo Domingo, intensified the fear ever-present in the predominantly slave communities. Together, these threatening omens were sufficient to convince many Southerners that peaceful coexistence could only prevail under a strict master-slave relationship.

The North was less sure, and northern doubts and moral questionings were to contribute no little to Beaumont's social documentation.

While there had existed no great body of literature in America comparable to that of France, there had always been a current of humanitarian idealism which challenged man's cruelty to man and aimed at emancipation. This activity had taken the form of sermons and orations, poems, letters, and even plays. The early crusade had been on moral and religious grounds. Samuel Sewall and Cotton Mather had written prophetic protests. Sporadically, a line of great figures had given of their energy, conscience, and heart to denounce slavery. In due respect we must mention Woolman, Benezet, Rush, Franklin, Jefferson, John Quincy Adams, and Benjamin Lundy. Such young poets as Timothy Dwight (*Greenfield Hill*, 1794), Ralph Waldo Emerson (*Vision of Slavery*, 1822), and William Cullen Bryant (*The African Chief*, 1825) had appealed to anti-slavery sentiments through their songs. But no one had yet attempted a great Negro tragedy. Richard Hildreth's *The Slave: or Memoirs of Archy Moore*, one of the earliest novels to be written by an American, with a tragic hero of part Negro blood, would not appear until 1836. And for *Uncle Tom's Cabin* the conscience of our country would have to wait until 1852.

Marie therefore preceded and marked a great turning. In the developing stream of American anti-slavery literature, it must be accorded a place of signal honor and significance. For not only was Beaumont's romance a pioneer of its kind—the first abolitionist novel based directly on the North American experience—but it treated the whole question of race, as distinguished from that of physical bondage, with an understanding and a psychological prescience far ahead of its day. For Beaumont the black slave was, in a sense, too crude and obvious a vehicle. His sympathetic conscience probed deeper: to the mulattos, to the shadowy borderland of the freedmen, to the fate of men who had been freed but were still (who knew how far?) short of true freedom.

Yet *Marie* deserves attention, and most respectful study, for still a third reason. Beaumont had first been interested, and never ceased to be fascinated, by the American social scene. The peculiar culture of a democracy, the habits and standards, the foibles and prejudices, the code and the tyrannies of mass rule—these also became the preoccupation of his hours, the very warp and woof of his tale. While following the fate of his doomed characters, he never took his eye from the society in which such tragedies could be played out. So *Marie* became a sociological treatise—in some ways a brilliant cultural analysis—while never ceasing to be an idyllic tragedy of love.

Thus there were in this book really two books. And therein lay at once its unique quality and a great weakness. In a sense these contrasting elements grew out of an unreconciled conflict in Beaumont's own nature, half scholar that he was and half poet-reformer. Beaumont was also confessedly aiming at two audiences: at the vast, amusement-seeking public with his novel, and at the thoughtful public with his notes. So he exposed both groups to a double burden —and ultimately perhaps bored or puzzled not a few readers of both kinds. After its publication in 1835, *Marie* went through five editions in seven years, was awarded the Prix Montyon by the Académie Française, and helped get its author elected to the Académie des Sciences Morales et Politiques in 1841; then it was gradually forgotten.

Beaumont himself went on to a liberal and useful career. In June, 1836, he married a distant cousin, Clementine de Lafayette, granddaughter of the General by his son Georges Washington Lafayette. Clémentine, very liberal and an ardent admirer of the *philosophes* (cousin also of the abolitionist Destutt de Tracy), helped, along with Tocqueville, to enlarge Beaumont's horizon.

In 1835 and 1837 he twice journeyed to Ireland, an Ireland which was still under the yoke of England, poverty-stricken, oppressed, the victim of tyranny, violence, and massacre. The English aristocracy had not yet bowed to the great leveling force of modern democracy. Here was a powerful yet noble and worthy adversary for the onrushing popular movement of the age. Beaumont sensed the *devenir* of the Irish who were awakening to the new sounds. They were beginning to threaten that aristocracy which had long been responsible for their misery and persecution. His purpose again was to write a book for the French while injecting into all mankind a sense of justice, a love of liberty, and hatred of tyranny. This purpose was accomplished when, in 1839, his book, *L'Irlande sociale, politique, et religieuse,* was published, and was in turn awarded the Prix Montyon.

Thus Beaumont became a three-time champion of the oppressed. For his three crusades against oppression he used three different types of vehicles: for his Negro and Indian tragedy the novel, for his prisoners a documentary work, for the Irish a history. Of this trilogy *Marie* is the greatest and most interesting work. Despite a certain naïveté of plot and a tendency toward melodrama, it is more sophisticated and on a deeper level of social analysis than its predecessors, on either side of the Ocean, or than *Uncle Tom's Cabin,* which came seventeen years later. *Marie* has never attained the success of the *Démocratie*; but the more one reads it, the more one is brought to realize that *Marie* is the companion book to the *Démocratie.*

For all its old-fashioned and somewhat stilted style, *Marie* was and remains a daring tableau of America. Discreetly, yet firmly, the young Frenchman imparted to his fellow citizens new views and new considerations for which most of them were not prepared. He sought above all to dissect the American organism and to present impartial findings. Though writing a love story, Beaumont searched with a shrewd and probing eye into the major contradiction of the new democracy, the fate of the freedman in a society whose existence rests on freedom, of inequality in a society whose primary maxim is the equality of all.

From a study of social mores, Beaumont's story moves to the tragic fate of the black man, both slave and free, the victim of hateful persecution engendered by passions stronger than law. And in a government run by the people the unleashed tyranny of the majority becomes a frightening thing. This terrifying potential of the mass is the heart problem which, to Beaumont, presaged the eventual disruption of our society. For the reader of today *Marie* remains a very timely study of the American dilemma in its embryonic stage.

Marie issued a warning message to both worlds, old and new, on the devastating character of mob law. In his characteristically sympathetic yet somber tones Beaumont deftly prophesied, more than a century ago, both the racial persecution and the potential tyranny of the majority which continue to haunt us.

ALVIS L. TINNIN

New Haven, July 14, 1958

MARIE

OR

SLAVERY IN THE UNITED STATES

Foreword

I owe the reader some explanation on the form and background of this book.

I warn him first that all but the form is serious. My principal aim was not to write a novel. The tale which serves as a frame for the work is extremely simple. No doubt a skilled and practiced pen would have lent it most interesting and dramatic developments, but I know nothing of the novelist's craft. Therefore one should seek in this book neither a carefully calculated plot, nor artfully manipulated situations, nor complex happenings; in a word, none of the devices commonly used to arouse and sustain interest and create suspense.

During my stay in the United States, I observed a society which harmonizes and contrasts with ours; and it seemed to me that if I could manage to convey the impressions which I received in America, my narrative would not be entirely useless. It is these very real impressions which I have blended with an imagined story.

I fully realize that in offering truth under the veil of fiction I run the risk of pleasing no one. Will not the serious-minded public reject my book because of its title alone? And will not the frivolous reader, attracted by its appearance of light fiction, stop short before its fundamental seriousness? I do not know. All I can say is that my chief aim has been to present a succession of serious observations; that in this work the basis is true, and that there is nothing fictitious in it but the characters; that, finally, I have tried to clothe my work in less severe garb in order to attract that portion of the public which seeks in a book ideas for the intellect and emotions for the heart.

I said just now that I would depict American society; I must now indicate the dimensions of my canvas.

There are two things principally to be observed among a people: its institutions and its customs.

I shall remain silent on the first. At the very moment when my book will be published, another will appear which will shed the most brilliant illumination upon the democratic institutions of the United States. I refer to the work of M. Alexis de Tocqueville, entitled *Democracy in America.*

I regret that I am unable here to express fully my profound admiration for M. de Tocqueville's work; for it would give me pleasure to be the first to proclaim that superior merit which soon will be contested by none. But I am hampered by my friendship. Also I am firmly convinced that after having read that fine, complete work, filled with such lofty judgment, and with a profundity of thought comparable only with its elevation of feeling, everyone will approve of my not having treated the same subject.

It is, therefore, solely the customs of the United States which I propose to describe. Here again I must observe to the reader that he will not find in my work a complete picture of the customs of that country. I have tried to indicate the principal features, but not the whole physiognomy of American society. If this book were received with indulgence, I would later complete the task I have begun. The truth is that a single idea dominates the work and forms the central point around which all the developments are arranged.

The reader is aware that there are still slaves in the United States; their number has grown to more than two million. Surely it is a strange fact that there is so much bondage amid so much liberty; but what is perhaps still more extraordinary is the violence of the prejudice which separates the race of slaves from that of the free men, that is, the Negroes from the whites. For the study of this prejudice, the society of the United States furnishes a double element which it would be hard to find elsewhere. Slavery reigns in the South of this country, while there are no longer slaves in the North. In the Southern states one sees the wounds inflicted by slavery in full force; and, in the North, the consequences of slavery after it has ceased to exist. Slave or free, the Negroes everywhere form a people apart from the whites. To give the reader an idea of the barrier placed between the two races, I believe I should cite an event which I myself witnessed.

The first time I attended a theater in the United States, I was surprised at the careful distinction made between the white spectators and the audience whose faces were black. In the first balcony were whites; in the second, mulattoes; in the third, Negroes. An American, beside whom I was sitting, informed me that the dignity of white blood demanded these classifications. However, my eyes being drawn to the balcony where sat the mulattoes, I perceived a young woman of dazzling beauty, whose complexion, of perfect whiteness, proclaimed the purest European blood. Entering into all the prejudices of my neighbor, I asked him how a woman of English origin could be so lacking in shame as to seat herself among the Africans.

"That woman," he replied, "is colored."

"What? Colored? She is whiter than a lily!"

"She is colored," he repeated coldly; "local tradition has established her ancestry, and everyone knows that she had a mulatto among her forebears."

He pronounced these words without further explanation, as one who states a fact which needs only be voiced to be understood.

At the same moment I made out in the balcony for whites a face which was very dark. I asked for an explanation of this new phenomenon; the American answered:

"The lady who has attracted your attention is white."

"What? White! She is the same color as the mulattoes."

"She is white," he replied; "local tradition affirms that the blood which flows in her veins is Spanish."*

If this blighting viewpoint on the black race and on even those generations in which the color has disappeared gave birth only to a few frivolous distinctions, my study of it would present but a sightseer's interest, but this prejudice is of graver import. Each day it deepens the abyss which separates the two races and pursues them in every phase of social and political life; it governs the mutual relations of the whites and the colored men, corrupting the habits of the first, whom it accustoms to domination and tyranny, and ruling the fate of the Negroes, whom it dooms to the persecution of the whites; and it generates between them hatreds so violent, resentments so

* In January 1832, a Frenchman, a Creole from Santo Domingo, whose skin is rather swarthy, finding himself in New York, went to the theater where he seated himself among the whites. The American audience having taken him for a man of color, requested him to leave and, upon his refusal, ejected him from the hall with violence. I have this from the self-same man to whom the misadventure happened.

lasting, clashes so dangerous, that one may rightly say it will influence the whole future of American society.

It is this prejudice, born of both slavery and the slave race, which forms the principal subject of my book. I wished to show how great are the miseries of slavery, and how deeply it affects traditions, after it has legally ceased to exist. It is, above all, these secondary consequences of an evil whose first cause has disappeared which I have endeavored to develop.

I have appended to this principal subject of my book a large number of diverse observations on American mores; but the condition of the black race in America and its influence on the future of the United States are the true purpose of this book. This is the place in which to inform the *serious* portion of the public I am addressing that at the end of each volume will be found, under the heading of appendices and notes, a considerable quantity of material treated *seriously*, not only in matter but also in manner. Such an appendix is the one treating of the social and political condition of slaves and freed Negroes, also the notes concerning social equality, dueling, religious sects, Indians, etc.; these notes comprise half the book.*

I shall not end this Foreword without asking the reader, and notably American readers (if this book should at any time appear in America), to be advised that the opinions expressed by the characters are not always those of the author. Sometimes I have carefully modified them, and then contradicted them in footnotes. As for the rest, aside from a very small number of exceptions which are indicated by footnotes, the facts set forth in the tale are true, and the impressions recorded are of my own experience. It must not be forgotten that in depicting American society, the author presents only general features; and that side by side with the general rule, the exception, though not explicitly stated, is often to be found. Thus, in one part of the book, I say that neither literature nor fine arts exist in the United States; however, I have met in America distinguished men of letters, skillful artists, brilliant orators. In the same country I saw elegant *salons*, refined circles, truly intellectual societies; I say elsewhere, however, that in America there are neither

* In the present translation, the appendix and notes have been rearranged. See Publisher's Note, p. v .

intellectual societies, nor elegant *salons*, nor refined circles. In these cases, as in many others, my observations apply only to the majority.

I shall conclude with a reflection to which I attach some importance.

M. de Tocqueville and I are publishing each a book at the same time, on subjects as distinct from one another as the government of a people is distinct from its mores.

Those who read these two works will perhaps receive different impressions of America, and may think that we did not form the same judgments on the country we traversed together. Such, however, is not the cause of the apparent dissidence which may be remarked. The true reason is this: M. de Tocqueville has described the institutions; I myself have tried to sketch the customs. Now, in the United States, political life is far finer, and more equitably shared, than civil life. While men may find small enjoyment in family life there and few pleasures in society, citizens enjoy in the world of politics a multitude of rights. Envisaging American society from such diverse viewpoints, we have not been constrained to use the same colors in order to paint it.

1

Prologue

The religious quarrels which, during the sixteenth century, troubled Europe and engendered the persecutions of the following century, peopled North America with its first civilized inhabitants.

Today, peace continues the work of war: when long years of repose followed in the European nations, populations increased out of all measure; the ranks were closed; society was encumbered with idle burdens, disappointed ambitions, precarious careers. Then indigence and pride, the need for bread and moral activity, bodily troubles and tribulations of the soul, hounded the least fortunate from the regions of their unhappiness and drove them, haphazard, across the seas, into regions less crowded with humanity, where they could once more find unoccupied territory and positions to be filled.

The first migrations were of exiles for reasons of conscience; the succeeding ones were of exiles for reasons of common sense. And yet, of those who go today to the United States in search of better conditions, not all find them.

About the year 1831, a Frenchman resolved to go to America with the intention of settling there. His project was inspired by diverse causes.

A recent revolution* had revived in his country political passions which all had believed extinguished: his sympathies and convictions drew him to one party; his family ties held him in another. Thus placed between his principles and his sentiments, he experienced continual distress; to follow the dictates of his heart, he must

* The July Revolution of 1830. Beaumont is alluding to the conflict between his aristocratic background and his liberal convictions. [Translator's note.]

stifle the voice of his reason, and if he remained faithful to his beliefs, he offended those whom he loved best.

Hoping to escape from the vexations of political life, he tried to go into business, but fortune was against him. At the age of twenty-five, he found himself without a career, having nothing to look forward to but a share in a modest patrimony. Therefore, spurning one day his native land, he boarded a vessel at Le Havre which would bear him to New York.

He did not remain long in that city; he stayed there only long enough to inquire as to the best route to follow before going West.

Some advised him to go to Ohio, where, they said, one could live better and more cheaply than in any other state; others recommended Illinois and Indiana, where he could buy, dirt cheap, the most fertile lands in the Mississippi Valley. Another said: "You are French and a Catholic; why not go to Michigan, where the people, who are from Canada, speak your language and practice your religion?"

The traveler found this advice to his liking; to act in accordance with it was the more easy since, to go to Michigan, he had only to follow the flow of European emigration, then moving westward.

He went up the North River, which flows majestically between two mountain ranges, and passed through the infinite number of small towns with great names, such as Rome, Utica, Syracuse, and Waterloo. After traversing Lake Erie, a hundred leagues in length, and passing Detroit, he beheld stretching before him the immense plains surrounding Lake Huron, famous for the purity of its waters and for its islands sacred to the Great Manitou; and, coasting the left bank of this lake, he penetrated the interior of Michigan by way of the great Saginaw Bay, ascending the river from which that bay takes its name.

The banks of the Saginaw are low, as is all the land surrounding the Great Lakes of North America; its waters flow in a slow and peaceful course among the prairies, which they render fertile when they do not transform them into swamps through stagnation. The aspect of this region is cold and severe; the sun's rays, pale as reflections, are feebly projected through a mist-laden atmosphere. Rushes sway above the surface of the waters, innumerable reeds hedge in the banks, and beyond are tall grasses which the scythe has never laid low. Such is the monotonous scene presented to the eye on every side. The undulation of the rushes, the murmur of the reeds, the rustling of the grasses, and the infrequent cry of some diving bird, hidden among the floating plants, comprise the whole movement and life of these wild solitudes. Looking into the highest heavens, one may see an eagle majestically gliding; it follows the traveler's barque; now motionless above it, now swooping in a sublime arc, it seems the king of the wilderness observing the daring stranger who penetrates his empire.

From time to time a savage's hut appears; not far from it stands an Indian, impassive and mute as the trunk of an old oak. [. . .]

At times the river narrows; then along higher banks can be seen vegetation of a poor and stunted sort; a thin stratum of soil covered with immense marble and granite rocks, where yellowing maples, grayish pines, and moss-covered beeches barely exist; their lusterless foliage is not much to look at, the sparsity of their crowns is depressing; they are small as saplings, and half dead with age.

However, sixty miles above its mouth, the river and its surroundings take on another aspect. The air becomes pure, the heavens blue, the soil fertile; the influence of the Great Lakes is no longer felt; the sun regains its power. To the right vast prairies spread into the distance, from which the flooding river withdraws, leaving them fertile; on the left bank rise gigantic trees, with venerable trunks, young and flourishing crowns, a magnificent primeval forest in which numerous clearings attest the presence of civilized man.

There our traveler stopped, not wishing to live in utter solitude but simply to be near the wilderness.

Hardly had he stepped a few paces into the shade of the ancient trees when he perceived traces of habitation; here a field of corn surrounded by a barrier of felled trees; there the charred stumps of pines; farther on the trunks of oak trees chopped off at the height of a man.

Walking on, he noticed the roof of a cottage; the approach was by a narrow path, upon which he distinguished human footprints recently made. Soon a more smiling countryside could be seen; below the dwelling place spread a charming lake bordered on all sides by the forest; it was like a vast mirror framed in verdure; its surface, perfectly calm, gleamed under the warm rays of the sun, and the engirdling land, embellished with all the subtle colors of the foliage, was brilliantly reflected in the crystal waters.

A small, apparently abandoned canoe, made of bark after the Indian fashion, was drawn up on the bank.

The cottage presented a singular combination of elegance in form and crudeness in building material. It was constructed only of a few logs, one laid atop another, but their arrangement revealed something of the taste of the architect. They were placed symmetrically, in such a fashion as to outline a number of Gothic arches; surrounding it one could see the same blending of untamed nature and human industry. Here, a grassy bank; there a rustic chair formed of maple boughs tastefully interlaced; beyond, a flower bed backed by the virgin forest.

The nearer he came to this solitary dwelling, the more puzzled the traveler grew as to its occupant; he was lost in vain conjectures when a man appeared. His dress was European, simple but refined; his face contained much that was noble, though its features were worn; and his brow, still young, bore traces of the sorrows and resignation which are the product of long misfortune and old griefs.

The traveler approached hesitantly.

"God forbid that I should trouble your seclusion," he said to the hermit.

"Welcome, welcome," the dweller in the wilderness courteously replied.

With these few words, each recognized in the other a Frenchman, and tenderness filled their hearts; for it is a great joy to an exile to hear the language of his fatherland in a strange country.

The hermit took the traveler's hand and led him to a small cabin, which stood near the cottage and was more simply constructed; there he seated him, bade him rest a while, served him a frugal repast, and gave him all the attentions of warmhearted hospitality.

Though the forest dweller felt genuine happiness at the presence of the traveler, he lapsed, from time to time, into somber reflection. Everything indicated that there were sad memories in his soul, which sometimes slumbered, but whose reawakening always caused pain.

The two men spoke first of France, and soon were conversing like old friends. "What can possibly have brought you to this wilderness?" asked the hermit.

The Traveler: I am seeking a country which might make me happy. I have just traversed a land which seemed charming to me.

I have seen such splendid lakes, such great forests, and beautiful meadows!

The Hermit: But where are you going?

The Traveler: I do not yet know. This solitude fills me with emotion—I have never seen a more enchanting place—life should flow in sweet peace here. I could be tempted to stay.

The Hermit: With what purpose?

The Traveler: Why, to live here. I could be a neighbor to you.

The Hermit: What! You have renounced France, then? Forever? To live in America? Have you considered this step well?

The Traveler: Yes, it is a subject on which I have long reflected. I like the laws and customs of this country; they are liberal and generous. Every man's rights are protected here.

The Hermit: Are you sure that in this land of liberty there is no tyranny? And that the most sacred rights are not here unrecognized?

The Traveler: There is a simplicity in American customs which pleases me. This is my plan: I will settle on the borderline separating the wilderness from civilized society; I will have on one side the life of the town, on the other, the forest; I will live near enough to the wilderness to enjoy the charms of profound solitude in peace and close enough to the cities to take part in political activities!

The Hermit: There are illusions which sometimes cost us many tears!

The Traveler: Why should I not be happy? You yourself——

The Hermit: Do not take me as an example—and beware of following in my footsteps. I have already spent five years in this wilderness, and the emotion I have just experienced at seeing a Frenchman again is the only pleasure which in all that time has entered the heart of the unhappy Ludovic.

Thus speaking, the hermit rose—his features betrayed an inner struggle. Then the traveler, seeking words which might cheer his host, said: "It would give me great pleasure if you would show me your establishment—the land about it, and the surrounding forest."

This request was agreeable to Ludovic, who hastened to satisfy it and seemed pleased at showing the extent of his holdings to the traveler. The latter had noticed from the first that the hermit carefully avoided approaching the pretty cottage at whose elegant construction he had wondered on his arrival; his curiosity grew.

"Is that cottage a part of your domain?" he asked Ludovic.

"Yes," he replied.

"I have been admiring its tasteful appearance," the traveler continued, "and I would be charmed with a closer view."

"No, no!" replied the hermit quickly. "Never!"

"Is it inhabited, then?"

Ludovic remained silent a moment. "Yes," he answered at last in a sad and mysterious tone. And he led the traveler in the opposite direction.

As they walked on, the two Frenchmen returned to the principal subject of their conversation, America. While the traveler continued to express his admiration of it, the hermit opposed his views with judicious comments, sometimes even with pointed irony. Thus they passed in review all the facets of the American way of life which first attract the foreigner's attention.

"Oh, let us stop here a few moments!" cried the traveler, when they found themselves at the edge of the lake. [. . .] "Who could remain unmoved by this scene? Tell me—speak freely—what more could one desire for happiness if the love of a young American girl should lend its charms and enchantments to this solitary retreat?"

Speaking thus, the traveler seated himself upon the green bank; Ludovic, filled with quite different emotions, took his place beside him.

"In Europe," said the traveler, abandoning himself to his poetic feelings, "all is dirt and corruption! Women there stoop to sell themselves, and the men are stupid enough to buy them. When a young girl marries, she does not seek a tender soul with which hers may unite, she does not ask for a support to her weakness: she marries diamonds, a title, freedom. Not that she is heartless; she may have loved once, but her beloved was not sufficiently rich. They haggled over her; the man could not throw in a carriage with his price; the bargain fell through. Then, they tell the young girl that love is all foolishness; she believes it, and corrects her mistaken notions; she marries a rich idiot. If she has any soul at all, she pines away and dies. Usually she lives happily enough. Such is not the life of a woman in America. Here marriage is not a business, nor is love a commodity. Two beings are not condemned to love or to hate each other because they are united; they join because they love each other. Oh, how attractive these young girls are, with their blue eyes, their ebon eyebrows, their pure, candid souls! How sweet the perfume wafted from their hair, unspoiled by art! What harmony in their gentle voices, which never echo the passion of greed! Here, at least, when you court a young girl, and she responds, it is a meeting through tender sympathy, and not through cold calculation. Would it not be losing an opportunity for tranquil but delicious felicity not to seek the love of an American girl?"

Ludovic listened calmly. When the traveler had ceased speaking, he said, "I pity you for your errors; I will not undertake to correct them, for I know how worthless to one man is another's experience. I am, however, distressed to see you pursuing these chimeras. I might, by a single example, prove to you how misled you are. You have just been praising to me the merits of American women. The picture you have drawn is not entirely false; but your imagination has given it smiling colors which are not there.

"I believe I can easily paint for you, without bias, a faithful portrait of the women of this country; for I have received neither kindness nor abuse from them."

The traveler made a gesture of incredulity; however, out of courtesy to his host, he indicated a desire to know the opinion of the hermit, who, after a reflective pause, expressed himself in the following words.

2

American Women

American women generally have well-informed minds but little imagination, and more reason than sensibility.*

They are pretty; the girls of Baltimore are renowned above all others for their beauty.

Their blue eyes bear witness to their English origin, their dark hair to the influence of hot summers. Their frail and delicate constitutions carry on an unequal struggle against the rigors of a severe climate and the sudden changes in temperature.

One cannot but be saddened by the thought that this beauty, this freshness, and all the graces of youth will wither before their time.

The education of women in the United States differs completely from that of women in our country.

In France a young girl lives, until she marries, in the shadow of her parents. She is placid and trusting, because always at hand there is tender solicitude which watches sleeplessly over her; spared from thinking because others think for her. Doing as her mother does, with her joyful or sad, she is never ahead of life; she follows its current. So the tender vine, attached to the branch which upholds it, receives from it violent jolts or gentle swayings.

In America, she is free before her adolescence; having no guide but herself, she walks aimlessly upon untried paths. Her first steps are not so dangerous; the child sets out on its journey into life as a fragile craft glides unendangered upon a calm sea.

But when the stormy billows of passion roll up, in early youth, what becomes of the frail skiff, with its swelling sails and its inexperienced pilot?

* See Appendix B, pp. 216–17.

American education wards off the danger: at an early age the girl is informed of the traps besetting her path. Her instincts will defend her but poorly; she is taught to place her trust in reason; thus enlightened on the snares which surround her, she depends solely upon herself to avoid them. She is never lacking in prudence.

These guiding torches given to the adolescent girl are a necessary consequence of the liberty she enjoys; but they deprive her of two qualities which are so charming in youth: candor and naïveté.

The American girl needs knowledge to be chaste; she knows too much to be called innocent.

This precocious liberty gives her thoughts a serious turn and stamps her character with a certain masculinity. I remember hearing a girl of twelve discussing and answering the grave question, "Which of all the kinds of government is the best?" She placed the republic above all others.

This coolness of the senses, the supremacy of the mind, this masculine behavior among women, may find favor with one's intellect; but they hardly satisfy the heart. This was my first estimate of American women; however, I did meet a young girl whose character, both impetuous and tender, upset this impression.

Arabella seemed to me gifted with a brilliant vivacity of mind, a touching sensibility of heart, and that noble enthusiasm of soul which attracts and subjugates a man. According to her, she was passionately fond of literature and art; her eyes grew moist with tears when she was but speaking, even theoretically, on the subject of feelings; her love of music was fanatic; her passion for poetry delirious; she spoke of them all with the most exalted admiration—she was Corinne and Sappho united in a single soul. Seduced by so many charms, I denounced the rashness of my first judgment, when a quite natural circumstance dissipated the enchantments of my new idol. We were attending a concert together; just previously she had spoken of music in general terms that enraptured me; but when she critically appraised the performance, I was seized by an astonishment I cannot convey to you. She uttered an inexhaustible flow of eulogies; she extolled the music so much and so loudly that she couldn't possibly hear it: all her praises rang false. Besides, she seemed to have no discernment; she had at her command a fixed quantity of enthusiasm which she lavished at random, indiscriminately, ceasing only when the supply gave out.

This characteristic, which I found later in a great number of

American girls, is not attractive. The women who display this artificial exaltation are as cold as the rest, and the more they promise, the more they deceive you. I reverted to my former opinion, but only to have it upset again.

At the age of eighteen, Alice was not pretty, but she attracted one by her personality; she was negligent in the art of dress; her attire lacked both grace and elegance, and one would have said she was quite without pretension, for she wore spectacles in public. But she was pleasing, and desired to please; her coquetry was entirely intellectual; she charmed with her flashes of natural and vivacious wit. I saw her surrounded by adorers, and I supposed that she was really worthy of the homage being paid her, until I discovered that for a long time she had been secretly *engaged.*

In the United States, when two people realize that they suit each other, they promise to become united to each other, and are what is called *engaged*; it is a sort of unsolemnized betrothal, and has no other binding force than their own sworn word.

This affianced young person, who cared so little about making herself pretty, was more of a coquette than any of the other young ladies, because she was disinterested. That put an end to my admiration. At any rate, excessive flirtatiousness is a characteristic common to all American girls, and is a consequence of their education.

To every girl over sixteen, marriage is the great interest in life. In France, she desires it; in America she hunts it. Since she is so early the mistress of herself and her own conduct, she makes her own choice.*

One can appreciate how delicate and perilous is the young girl's task, trustee of her own destiny; she must have in herself the foresight which in France a father and mother have for their daughter. Generally, one must admit that she fulfills her mission with admirable sagacity. Within this pragmatic society, where everyone is engaged in business, American girls have theirs, too: that of finding a husband. In the United States, men are cold, and tied to their busi-

* Rarely do her parents contradict her on this point; if they have any objections, the girl wins out ordinarily, with a little persistence. Society would blame the father who long resisted the prayers of his children. This does not mean that paternal authority, in this free country, is powerless: the law gives parents the right to disinherit entirely; but they do not avail themselves of it under these circumstances, because custom, always more powerful than law, protects freedom of choice in marriage.

ness affairs; one must either run after them or attract them with powerful allurements. It is no wonder if the girl who lives among them is prodigal with studied smiles and tender glances. Her coquetry is, however, enlightened and prudent; she has taken the measure of her arena, she knows the bounds over which she may not step. If her strategems merit censure, at least their aim is irreproachable, for she wants only marriage.

There is no lack of opportunities for young people to reveal their mutual inclination and tender feelings. It is customary for them to go out together unaccompanied, and in doing this the young men give no offense to decorum. The only formality they must observe is that of walking separately, for a man may offer his arm to a young lady only if he is engaged to her. One may observe the same freedom in the drawing room. Rarely does a mother take part in the conversations of her daughter; the latter receives whom she pleases, entertains him unsupervised, and sometimes invites to her home young men whom she has met elsewhere and who are unacquainted with her parents. There is no impropriety in her acting thus, for these are the customs of the country.

American flirtatiousness has a quite special nature; in France a coquette is less desirous of marrying than of pleasing; in America she is eager to please only in order to marry. In France, flirtation is a passion; in America, it is a calculation. If a young lady who is engaged continues her flirtations, it is more through prudence than inclination; for it has happened that a fiancé breaks his word; sometimes a girl foresees this dread possibility and tries to capture other hearts, not for the sake of possessing several at a time, but in order to have a replacement on hand for the one she risks losing.

In this case, as in all others, she provokes, encourages, or holds off the sighing swains with complete freedom.

In America this freedom is given to a woman only to be snatched away suddenly. In our country, the young girl exchanges the swaddling bands of infancy for the bonds of matrimony; but these new bonds rest lightly upon her. In taking a husband, she gains the right to join the outside world; by engaging herself she becomes free. Then begins the life of parties, pleasures, conquests. In America, on the contrary, the gay life is the young girl's; she retires from worldly pleasures to live among the austere duties of the domestic hearth. A man pays homage to her not because she is a woman, but because she can become a wife. Her coquetry, after catching her a husband, is of no more use, and after she has given herself in marriage, she uses it no more.

In the United States a woman ceases to be free on the day when, in France, she becomes so.

The privileges enjoyed by a young girl, and the early reduction to nonentity of the married woman, greatly increase the number of *engaged* people. In general, the purely ethical contract, which arises from this sort of betrothal, is ratified soon after by marriage, but not infrequently young girls endeavor to postpone the event. Acting thus, they achieve a double goal: engaged, they are sure of marrying, but are not yet wives; the certainty of future wifehood is secured, while the liberty of girlhood is retained.

Nothing, in American women, appeals to one's imagination; there is, however, one side of their character which makes a deep impression on any serious-minded man.

The morality of a population may be judged by that of its women, and one cannot observe the society of the United States without marveling at the respect in which the married state is held. This respect never existed to so high a degree among any of the ancient peoples, and European society, corrupt as it is, cannot conceive of such moral purity.

In America they are no severer than elsewhere toward the irregular life and toward even the debauches of a bachelor; many young men can be found here whose dissoluteness is well known, and whose reputations do not suffer thereby; but their excesses, to be pardoned, must be committed outside the circle of family and friends. While indulgent concerning the pleasures obtainable from prostitutes, society condemns without pity those who obtain them at the expense of conjugal fidelity; it is as inflexible toward the man who incites the transgression as toward the woman who acquiesces. Both are banished from society; and to incur this punishment it is not even necessary to have been guilty; to have aroused the suspicion suffices. The domestic hearth is an inviolable shrine which no breath of impurity must besmirch.

The morality of American women, fruit of a serious and religious upbringing, is protected further for other reasons.

Completely engrossed in practical matters, the American man has neither the time nor the temperament for tender sentiments or gallantry; he is gallant once in his life, when he wishes to marry. He is undertaking a business affair, not a love affair.

He has no leisure to love, still less to make himself loved. The taste for fine arts, which is so closely allied to the pleasures of the heart, is forbidden him. If, emerging from his industrial sphere, a young man displays a passion for Mozart or Michelangelo, he loses public esteem. Fortunes are not made by listening to sounds or looking at colors. And how chain to the accountant's stool one who has once known the charms of a poetic life?

Thus doomed by the traditions of the country to confine themselves to practicality, young Americans are neither preoccupied with pleasing women nor skillful at winning them.

Moreover, there is a corrupt element, influential in European society, which is not to be met with in the United States: this is the idle rich and the soldiers in garrison. The wealthy without professions and the soldiers without glory have nothing to do; their sole pastime is the corruption of women—impetuous, open-handed youth, in need of space and action; comparable to the flood waters of the Mississippi: beneficial when flowing freely, deadly when stagnant.

In America, everyone works, because no one is born rich,* and the dreary idleness of the garrison is unknown there, because the country has no standing army.

Thus, the women escape the perils of seduction; if they are pure, one cannot tell if it is due to their virtue, for this has not been put to the test.

The extreme ease of becoming rich also comes to the aid of upholding morality; money is never an essential consideration in marriages; commerce, industry, the practice of a profession, assure young people of a living and a future. They marry the first woman they fall in love with; and nothing is rarer in the United States than a bachelor of twenty-five. Society thereby gains moral married men in place of licentious bachelors. Finally, the condition of equality protects marriages, while difference in rank obstructs them in our country. In the United States there is only one class; no barrier of social distinction separates the young man and young girl who agree

* It does happen, by accident, that a few young people are conditioned by an inherited fortune and a polite education to gallantries and social intrigues, but they are too few in number to be a nuisance, and if they give the least indication of troubling the peace of a family, they find the American world leagued solidly against them to oppose and crush the common enemy. This explains why American bachelors of wealth and leisure do not stay in the United States but come to live in Europe, where they find men of intellect and corrupt women.

to become united. This equality, propitious to legitimate unions, is highly embarrassing to those which are not. The seducer of a young girl necessarily becomes her husband, whatever the difference in their economic position, because while superiority of fortune exists, there is no difference at all in rank.*

This rectitude of tradition, which applies less to individuals than to society as a whole, gives a serious cast to all American society.

The country is dominated by a public opinion, from whose rule no woman can flee.

Pitiless in Italy toward insincere coquetry, public opinion readily forgives the errors of frailty; in England it demands prudish refinements which it scorns in Spain, and in Madrid it is as indulgent to the sins of the flesh as in London to the vagaries of the heart. In America, this public opinion condemns all passion without pity, and authorizes calculation alone; indifferent to sentiment, it is exacting concerning moral obligation.

Love, the charms of which form the whole life of some European peoples, is not understood in the United States.

If some ardent soul experiences the need to love, and abandons himself to it passionately, it is as rare an accident as the appearance of a roc soaring above the American shore. Woe to that isolated being! He will find no sympathy! Not an echo will reply to him! No sustaining hand will uphold him! In that country they respect only the arithmetical value of things. How reduce into dollars and cents an exalted soul and a throbbing heart?

Perhaps they love in America; but they do not make love there. Women, so tender by nature, take on the imprint of that prosaic, rational world.

You can see, American women merit your esteem, but not your enthusiasm; they can conform to a chilly society, but their hearts are not made for the burning passions of the wilderness.

* Thus, whoever seduces a girl contracts the obligation, by the very deed, to marry her; if he does not, he risks the disapproval of society, and is barred from it.

When, in England, a young man of the aristocracy seduces a young girl of the middle class, his adventure makes little scandal; and the world in which he lives easily forgives him the damage he has done in the inferior class. Things cannot be thus in a society where conditions are equal and where there is no class distinction.

3

Ludovic, or the Departure from Europe

Ludovic's words produced quite an impression on the feelings of the traveler. [. . .]

"You have presented to me," he said to Ludovic, "only a corner of the picture. I admit, like you, that there may be some blemishes, but nonetheless America does contain the essential elements of happiness. There are, in the United States, two things of inestimable price, which cannot be found elsewhere: these are a society which is new yet civilized, and virgin nature. From these two abundant springs flow innumerable material advantages and spiritual pleasures. Moreover, I will admit that the portrait you have just offered to my eyes, true as it may be in general, does not seem to me to resemble all American women. I have seen some whose ardent passions revealed themselves in a burning glance. This country contains people of different races. If there are some whom the polar ice chills, others are warmed by the tropical sun."

At these words, Ludovic's features contracted; he experienced an emotion the traveler could not fathom. The latter continued. "I believe," said he, "that we bring to bear on our opinions of the United States two different ways of thought; I judge the country with seriousness, you with a certain superficiality. You are struck by the ridiculous aspects and lack of elegance of this society, at which you laugh, while I——"

"Stop!" cried Ludovic in a stern voice; "you misunderstand my character, and your error is more cruel than you can know. No, there is nothing gay, nothing frivolous in my thoughts. My lips can still smile . . . but for a long time my heart has known no joy. You believe that I hold aloof from men because my reason does not understand them, or that my heart detests them; you take me for a malevolent or insane man! Don't believe it. My mind is not disordered, and I do not hate my fellow men, far from whom I drag out my unhappy life! To reach the point I have arrived at, I have plumbed the depths of many an abyss. Ah! Would that you better understood my fate for your own sake; the reefs in my life are the same as those on which I see you are about to wreck yourself. Your illusions were mine; they are those which have destroyed me, and which will cause your ruin. It is a strange error to believe that happiness can be found away from trodden paths. This plaguing soul sickness, which follows one everywhere, this spiritual unrest which exiles you from your country, this need of new and exciting sensations, all these ills are within you, and belong no more to one country than to another. Places do not alter the passions of man. I have listened to your admiration of America, of her institutions, her customs, her forest wilderness. I know much more than you think about the subjects of your enthusiasm. If I should tell you the tale of my past, it would be that of your future!"

As he pronounced these words, Ludovic was animated by an extraordinary flame, and the energy of his words rendered only imperfectly the depth of his convictions.

The soul of the traveler responded; understanding all that was serious, mysterious, and moving in the disposition of the hermit, he said to him with great sympathy, "Forgive me if I took your unhappiness for an ordinary misfortune. But what, then, is the secret of this grief which appeared to my eyes in the guise of a happiness which I envied? What strange calamity removed you from the company of the fellow men you love, and keeps you in a solitude for which you have no liking? Alas! that I should come from France to behold a compatriot so world weary! I pray you, share your sorrows with me, and may the concern which you inspire in the traveler bring some consolation to your soul!"

The hermit reflected for a few minutes. "Very well," he said, lifting his head, "I will tell you the story of my life. I know how indifferent men are to the sufferings of others, and I am accustomed to doing without their pity. Thus it is not in order to gain your compassion that I shall give you an account of my misfortunes; it is a duty I must perform." [. . .]

For the rest of the day, Ludovic appeared absorbed in profound meditation; it was easy to judge, by the somber shadows which from time to time beclouded his brow while he reviewed all the phases of his life, that he had had to go through great adversity.

The next day, at dawn, Ludovic and his guest left the cabin; they directed their steps toward an elevated crag which dominated the end of the lake. From this height there sprang a gushing spring, which scattered in its fall thousands of misty droplets of silver. The tranquil lake, the silent forest, the gentle undulation of the waters, soundless as though not to trouble the stillness of the solitude, everything in these surroundings made the soul receptive.

The hermit and the traveler seating themselves at the foot of an ancient cedar, Ludovic recounted in the following words the story of his life.

The great revolutions which tormented whole nations often stirred up in the depths of individual souls profound troubles which persisted long after the surface of society had become tranquil, and calm had reentered the bosom of the masses.

When I was born, a social order which had existed for fifteen centuries had just crumbled. Never had so great a ruin been spread before the eyes of a people—never had so great a reconstruction challenged the genius of men. A new world was rising upon the wreckage of the old; spirits were restless, passions fired, minds in travail; the face of all Europe was changing—opinions, customs, laws were swept into a whirlwind so swift that one could hardly distinguish the new institutions from those which were no more. The sources of sovereignty had been dislocated, the principles of government were altered; a new art of war had been invented, born of a new science; the men were no less extraordinary than the events; the greatest nations of the world took children for their leaders, while old men were thrown out of power; raw troops triumphed over the most well-seasoned armies, generals just out of school overthrew powerful empires, the reign of the people was solemnly announced; and never had such strong and glorious individuals been seen before, each leaping into the arena which fortune had apparently thrown open to all.

I was a child when these events were taking place. A spectacle of misery and grandeur, destruction and creation, struck my youthful gaze; exclamations of surprise, cries of admiration, and sounding brass announcing victories were among the first sounds to reach my ears.

I grew up far from the city, sheltered by the tender, loving care of my parents. The tumult which filled Europe was scarcely audible in that asylum where peace, true happiness, and all the virtues reigned; life flowed gently there, but monotonously; only, from time to time, a newspaper, a letter from a friend, or a soldier returning to his hearth would throw a sudden gleam across our horizon and apprise us of thrones destroyed or elevated.

When these infrequent reverberations came to me, they threw me into bewilderment; they indicated to me that life, so dull around us, presented elsewhere scenes of brilliance; then I would dream of glory, power, grandeur! The tranquillity of our existence seemed to me an accident in the midst of a universal upheaval.

Little by little, in the inmost recesses of my soul, I built up an ideal world, the child of my dreams, my illusions, and impatient desires, a tremendous world which the real world, however big and extraordinary, could never equal.

If I had been closer to the scene, I might have perceived the shadows as well as the light; if I had seen with my own eyes the actions of the men who governed the nations, I might perhaps have been less dazzled by their grandeur, which I would have seen was marred by pettiness. I would have seen that power was surrounded by baseness, and that great shadows appeared on the sun of glory.

But my isolation rendered all these illusions the more seductive, the distant spectacle of the active world more intoxicating, to my imagination. Thus, I could see, on the vast stage where the fate of nations was acted out, only what by contrast made me scorn my quiet corner.

When, still stirred by the tales which had made my heart leap, I had to fall back into the deep calm of our daily life; when, after entertaining vast dreams I was dragged back to the peaceful routine of rural pursuits, I experienced an unbearable boredom and felt a repugnance I could not overcome for the tranquil happiness of which I was witness. Not that I was insensible to the order and rectitude of which such a moving example was offered me by my family. I was often touched by the kindness surrounding me; for never was an unhappy wretch driven from our home, and the poor would go on their way blessing us; but each day I felt the need of something more. I took my father's virtues and the grandeur of the world I glimpsed; I mingled these two qualities and made a delightful, intoxicating combination of them. Soon they were so intermixed in my thoughts that I could not separate them. I would not have wanted glory without virtue, but virtue without glory seemed dull to me.

Finally the gates of the world were opened to me—I hastened into the arena.

Things were already changed. Peace reigned in Europe. It was not the calm of well-being, but the paralysis which follows a violent convulsion. The multitudes were not happy; they were weary, inactive. A few men with great ambitions, impetuous desires, and noble enthusiasms still bestirred themselves on the surface of society, but these moving spirits had no longer any goal. Everything else had dwindled away in the world, things as well as people. One could see that the instruments of power, made for giants, were handled by pygmies; that the traditions of strength were exploited by the irresolute; that attempts at achieving glory were made by mediocrities. Troubled times had succeeded the century of revolutions; self-interest had succeeded noble passion; crime had bred vice; there was cunning in place of genius, words in place of deeds. I found a society where all seemed still in transition, and yet nothing moved; a sort of regulated chaos, a characterless epoch suspended between the glory which had just perished and the liberty as yet unborn. No longer could one attain power at a single bound, as in the time of my childhood; nor could one advance to it by progressive steps as in the preceding centuries; certain regulations existed in the government which thwarted men of talent but yielded easily to petty intrigue. I made my entrance upon this stage, full of great hopes and immense desires: a single glance sufficed to show me how ill I was cast.

My passions were deep and pure; but for thirty years thousands had counterfeited such passions, or exploited those who had them in reality. No one any longer believed in the sincerity of lofty ambitions; everyone feared them. After having nourished unbounded hopes for so long and become dizzy upon them in solitude, I was practically obliged to expose them to view.

I had conceived projects of political reform—but now people had a horror of them.

Though restless minds were troubled by recollections of glory, society—a cold and prudent body—shuddered at the memory of bloodshed; it liked its lethargy, foreseeing that danger lay in awakening, and mortal crises arose from any movement.

Now how was I to exert any influence upon the march of society?

I attempted to employ myself in some sphere where I might attain power—but I soon discovered that this project was vain. To pursue successfully what is known as a career, one must see it as the sole interest of one's existence, not as a means to a more elevated goal. Exercising a profession imposes a thousand petty duties, not to be borne by one who pursues a great thought. Impatience to succeed is sufficient to hinder success.

I know not how to tell you of the torment of my spirit when, filled with vast thoughts, I was doomed to imprison myself in a narrow specialized circle; after long considering things as a whole, I had to delve into a thousand details and consider individual cases, instead of the world-embracing questions on which I had meditated all my life. I made incredible efforts to get a general idea from one fact, but I would lose sight of the fact in the idea, of the application in the theory; I became unfit for my position. Once again, I would enclose my mind within the limits of a particular problem, but then I would feel my faculties shrinking, even as I lost the ability to generalize my thoughts, and I would stop short, fearing to become unworthy of my future progress.

Bored and disgusted, I withdrew from public life; I was inclined to think that in our era steadfastness of heart and fixity of principles were obstacles to success.

The void into which I fell cannot be described. At the very moment when I thought I was about to attain my goal, I saw it once more elude me. But my passions remained; they left me no peace. I considered my surroundings uneasily; I observed the scene, always hoping it would change; but it offered only the monotonous spectacle of petty persons, petty intrigues, petty results.

An unexpected event suddenly reanimated my languishing energy and smiled on my imagination. It was the year 1825; liberty was astir in enslaved Greece—here was the cause of civilization against barbarism!

Filled with pious enthusiasm, I rushed to the fatherland of Homer. Poetic stirrings of a young soul! How noble and impetuous! Alas! why is it that these sublime aspirations meet only deception and lies? I shed my blood in the cause of liberty. I saw the Greeks triumphant, and to this day I know not which is baser, the victors or the vanquished. The Greeks are no longer slaves to the Moslems, but, still doomed to servitude, they have gained only the sad privilege of choosing their own masters and tyrants.

What could I do in that land of memories and tombs? What could I ask of the ruins of Athens and Sparta? [. . .]

Indifferent, without thought or aim, I directed my steps at random. [. . .] My pilgrimage was not of long duration. . . . Europe bores the traveler because it has been well traveled for two thousand years.

In vain I visited the most picturesque places, the wildest retreats, the most marvelous palaces. I was seeing only what other thousands had seen before me. There was no country that had not been trodden by many feet, no beauty of nature that had not been analyzed; no masterwork of art that had not excited admiration. The traveler in our days has nothing left to do, nothing left to think; his opinions and his sentiments are decided for him in advance. Here, he should weep; a little further on, he should be seized with raptures; thus he follows the well-worn path of his predecessors, among a multitude of worn-out impressions and conventional emotions.

I met with nothing among the other peoples of Europe which could hold me in their midst; they were as stale as we are, and even more corrupt.

Returning to France, I experienced again the old difficulties. What could I do? Where could I go? Return to the paternal roof? I was less fit than ever to enjoy happiness, for the obstacles in my path, far from disillusioning me, had only stimulated my longings.

Must I live forever in a society where I was sure I could never find the life of which I dreamed?

Then I conceived the idea of going to America. I knew little of this country; but each day I heard praise for the rationality of its institutions, its love of liberty, the prodigies of its industry, the greatness of its future. It was from the Occident, they said, that light henceforth would come; and then I thought, like you, "Two things can be found in America which cannot be met with elsewhere: a society which is new yet civilized, and virgin nature." I considered this new project as a divine inspiration, sent to aid me in my adversity.

How sweet was the light that penetrated my soul, that would reveal to me a world equaling my most beautiful dreams!

With what eagerness I jumped at this opportunity! My despondency became energy in an instant, and I felt the rebirth of all my moral strength, caused by the unexpected rekindling of abandoned hope.

A month later I was in Baltimore.

4

An American Family

I chose Baltimore in preference to other American cities, since I knew that I would find there a friend, one Daniel Nelson, to whom my family had rendered some service on an important occasion.

The day I entered the Nelsons' home was the day that decided my fate. I must therefore acquaint you with this American.

At first sight, he did not make an agreeable impression: severe of bearing, cold of speech, brusque of manner—such were his outward characteristics. But this rough shell hid virtues of great worth: he was just to his fellow men, charitable to the unfortunate, and endowed with a strength of spirit which I have never encountered in another man. He possessed yet another quality which I wondered at the more in America since I had met with little of it in France: that of saying nothing without due reflection, and of never speaking on subjects of which he was ignorant.

Habitually calm in conversation, Nelson had a few strong emotions under whose influence his reserve would thaw. The first was a national pride pushed to the limit of delirium; he spoke only in superlatives on the wisdom and greatness of the American people. The second was a hatred: he detested the English.* Finally, an ardent supporter of the Presbyterian Church, Nelson cherished in his soul a feeling akin to enmity against the Catholics and the Unitarians, accusing the former of believing everything, and the latter of believing nothing.

I was struck by another trait in Nelson's character: although he

* See Appendix C, pp. 217–19.

lived in a society where everyone kept slaves, he would never consent to keep any himself; he had bought two Negroes in Virginia, whom he immediately freed upon their arrival in Maryland, and whom he had made his domestic servants. One of them, Ovasco by name, displayed an attachment for his master that amounted to worship, the effect of which, at a later time, caused me to marvel.

Having fixed his dwelling for several years in Baltimore, Nelson occupied a high social place in that city; he had, moreover, found in trade a fertile source of wealth and credit. He lived in brilliant style; on his handsome carriage was painted his coat of arms, with this device: *Ubi libertas, ibi patria.* The same inscription was engraved upon the ring with which he sealed all his letters, and on which also appeared "John Nelson, 1631." This was the name of the head of his family, and the date of his emigration to America. Nelson enjoyed speaking of his ancient origin, and about those of his forebears whose names were remembered with honor among Americans.

However, ambitious ideas had entered his head: he eschewed all appearance of luxury and wealth in order to make himself popular, and was elected to the legislature of Maryland; he obtained successively all the honorific titles to which an influential citizen of the United States can aspire: he was a member of the Historical Society, president of the Bible Society, the Temperance Society, the Colonization Society, Inspector of Prisons and Asylums, and he was, besides, an anti-Mason.

For a long time he had hoped to be a member of Congress; but having been defeated in the last elections, he suddenly abandoned all his political pretentions and, turning in another direction, was ordained a minister in the Presbyterian Church.

When I arrived at Nelson's house, I found him with his two children, George and Marie.

The first, about twenty years of age, bore upon his lofty brow the mark of a firm and noble character; his upright soul revealed itself through the frankness of his gaze. From the first, I felt drawn toward him, and he toward me. Soon a strong friendship justified our sympathy.

His sister, younger than he, appeared to me a dazzling beauty; but at the time of my arrival in Baltimore I only noticed her briefly. She did not go out in society, where I went unceasingly—I hardly saw her at the house of her father, whose company I at first avoided.

Later, I came to value Nelson and his family; but I admit that at first the rigidity of his principles estranged me from him: he preserved in all their austerity the customs of the New England Puritans.* Morning and evening, his children and servants assembled and they prayed together; every meal was preceded by an invocation in which he asked Heaven to bless the food.

When Sunday came,† it was devoted entirely to silent reflection and piety. The simplest amusements were forbidden, and the time not spent in church was passed quietly in reading and meditation on the Bible. This rigid observance of the Sabbath was the same throughout the city; however, Nelson always accused Baltimore of being irreligious and ungodly. "Maryland," he would say, "is far from equaling New England, that home of morality and religion. Yet moral principles become more lax every day in this country, and New England itself cannot resist the general corruption. Would you believe it," he would say to me in a profoundly grieved tone,

* This austerity appears not only in daily habits but in laws as well: drunkenness, games of chance, fornication, blasphemy, nonobservance of the Sabbath are, in Massachusetts, misdemeanors punishable by imprisonment or fine. Puritanism, dominant in New England, influences nearly all the states of the Union: thus, the penal code of Ohio punishes with imprisonment any intimacy between unmarried men and women. In Cincinnati I saw persons sentenced for this misdemeanor and locked in a foul cell, where the outside air never penetrated.

In New York, all games of chance, such as cards, dice, billiards, are forbidden in public places—inns, taverns, steamboats, etc.—on pain of ten dollars fine against the innkeepers and the masters of the steamboats. Any person gaining a sum of money at a game of chance is liable to a fine five times the amount won; anyone winning or losing a sum of twenty-five dollars through a game or wager is declared guilty of a misdemeanor, liable to a fine not less than five times the sum gained or lost. (See Revised Statutes of the State of New York, Vol. I, Part 1, Title 8, chap. 20, art. 2 and 3, pp. 661 and 662.) In the same state the law punishes swearing and blasphemy (*ibid.*, art. 6, p. 673) and forbids the sale of liquor in the vicinity of a church, unless it is at least two miles distant (*ibid.*, art. 7, p. 674). Pennsylvania law contains similar dispositions. (See Purdon's Digest, *s.v.* "Gaming and Lotteries," p. 344 ff.) There are fines and imprisonment for drunkenness, and loss of license for the innkeeper on whose premises infractions take place. If a person is known to be a habitual drunkard, a guardian or legal counselor is appointed for him, as though he were mentally incompetent, and whoever sells him hard liquor or wine—innkeeper, distiller, or grocer—is liable to a fine of ten dollars. (*Ibid.*, *s.v.* "Drunkards," p. 223, sec. 6.)

† See Appendix D, pp. 219–20.

"they no longer arrest people who travel on Sundays,* and even the mail coach, carrying government dispatches, goes its rounds on the day of the Lord? If this disastrous trend is not stopped, all is over, not only with our private morality, but with public morality too; there is no morality without religion! No liberty without Christianity!"

As he could see much less indignation than astonishment in my expression, he said, "I know that France is an immoral country; all that can be blamed on popery. The Catholics have surrounded Christianity with so much formal ritual that they have lost sight of the moral principle which is its soul. But the work of the Reformation will be accomplished: France will become religious when she becomes Protestant."†

This ardent zeal which Nelson applied to the unmaterial he applied also to sentiments of a quite different nature. His love of money was incontestable; it was rarely that, after discoursing to us on the affairs of his church and on his religious meditations, he did not launch into a discussion of the ideal banking system, of discounts, the tariff laws, or canals and railways. His language, his recollections on commerce and wealth, denoted a passion for riches which, beyond a certain point, could be called cupidity—a singular mixture of noble inclinations and base attachments! I found this contrast all over the United States: these two opposed principles clash incessantly in American society; the one, a source of honesty, the other, of bad faith. However, they produce the same result, that of making men *serious*.

My first reaction to ideas and feelings so new to me was one of repugnance; and, persuaded that so restricted a view was not giving me the whole character of American society, I resolved, a few days after my arrival, to see Nelson as rarely as I could without being discourteous, and to seek more agreeable contacts in the world of fashion, which I would try to enter. Nelson's son, George, who alone of that household had won my heart on the first day, introduced me into the houses of the most eminent citizens of the city. During the day we toured the public buildings and monuments of

* See Appendix D, p. 220.

† It is a widespread opinion among the Presbyterians of the United States that the irreligion of France is due to Catholicism, and that Protestantism will restore the religious zeal she has lost.

the town together, we attended political meetings, we went to clubs; the environs of the city furnished delightful walks; I liked especially the bay of Baltimore, which reminded me of the Bay of Naples; here, every view gave me something to remember. [. . .]

As day declined, George and I sought distraction and pleasure in the brilliant assemblies of the fashionable world. It was the gay season: balls and concerts succeeded each other without interruption.

I looked with eager impatience upon this society, of which they spoke so much in Europe and knew so little! I believe I saw at one glance that I would find there nothing of what I sought.

The United States is, perhaps of all nations, the one where ruling gives least glory to the rulers. No single person is responsible for its leadership; the country runs itself. Management of government affairs does not depend on a few men; it is the work of all. Here, everyone has a hand in it, and any individual effort hinders the functioning of the whole. In this country, political skill consists not in action but in abstaining from action. It is a great sight to see a people who act on their own initiative and govern themselves; but nowhere do individuals count for so little.

I believe also that no country is so much a stranger to those great political enterprises and crises which show up a man's merits, genius, and superiority over his fellow citizens. The Americans do not have to wage war, for they have no neighbors, and there are no internal disturbances, for there are no political parties.*

What chances of glory are left to a man, when he need not save his country from anarchy, nor protect its independence against foreign attack?

The United States is, nevertheless, doing great things: its inhabitants are clearing the forests of America, thus spreading European civilization into the depths of the wildest solitudes; they have

* There are no political parties in the sense that everyone is agreed upon the fundamental principle of government, which is popular sovereignty, and on its form, which is the republic. So one does not see, in America, anything resembling what we see in Europe, where some want despotism, some constitutional monarchy, still others a republic. However, parties are formed in the United States on the consequences and applications of one principle recognized by all. These are basically personal quarrels, but private interests have to be hidden under the cloak of the general welfare. The subject "Of Political Parties in America" is treated in the work on democracy in America, to be brought out by M. de Tocqueville. (See Vol. II, chap. 2.)

spread over half the hemisphere; their vessels carry their name and their wealth to every shore. But these great achievements are due to a thousand combined efforts which no superior power directs, to a thousand undistinguished minds who do not seek help from a higher intelligence.

This uniformity, which reigns in the world of politics, reigns also in civil life. Relationships among men have a single object, money; a single purpose, to become rich. The passion for money is born in Americans along with their intelligence, bringing in its wake cold calculation and dry digits; it grows and develops, taking root in their souls, and its unceasing torment, like a burning fever, excites and devours the sickly body it takes over. Money is the god of the United States, as glory is the god of France, and love, that of Italy.

But there is no moral sentiment to be found in this violent passion. Reduced to business contacts, American society is serious without having the dignity of virtue. It inspires no respect; it chills enthusiasm.

Hardly attracted by this first impression, I withdrew from the world of fashion and its assemblies; I resolved to investigate at a distance the customs and institutions of a people who revealed only their superficialities in their drawing rooms. Weary of noise and movement, I felt myself drawn again to Nelson by that same austerity which had made me flee from him.

At the very instant when I was thrown into despondency by my reflections on America, finding myself mistaken anew, and when I saw the goal in which I had put my last hope once more evading me, a new passion, of which I had never suspected the power, took possession of my soul.

In Europe I had never fallen in love, and after having seen the women of America, I no longer feared being enslaved by that sentiment I had always considered a weakness and an obstacle to great achievements. But a tender fondness was to knit up the broken threads of my existence and was to become the sole concern of my life.

5

Marie

Since my arrival in Baltimore I had seen Nelson's daughter each day, but I knew her only slightly. Though a witness of her beauty, I knew nothing of her heart; I had hardly heard her voice. She treated me with a reticence which seemed to me to go beyond the modesty of her sex; however I could take no offense at it, seeing that she was equally indifferent to the world and its affairs. Endowed with all the physical charms which give women their power, she did not attempt to exploit them. There was meekness in her reserve, almost humility, and if innocence had not clearly shone from her features, one might have thought that the hidden work of some remorse on her conscience gave her a sense of secret inferiority.

Upon leaving the drawing rooms of American society, I was so wearied of coquetry that it was easy for a simple, uncalculating woman to charm me. In my eyes, her most potent charm in the art of pleasing me lay in her evincing no desire to do so; soon my awakened attention discovered in her talents and virtues so rare that I could not understand my first feeling of indifference, and, in discovering beneath the roof of my host this treasure which I had almost overlooked, I began to pity the man who pursues afar the happiness whose source is close at hand.

Nelson and his son devoted all the daylight hours to business matters; Marie spent them in some secret occupation, whose mystery I was a long time in penetrating. At teatime we were always reunited; then Nelson would read aloud to us, with emphasis, those articles in the newspaper in which America was praised out of all measure; I heard him reiterate every day that General Jackson was the greatest man of the century, New York the most beautiful city in the world, the Capitol the most magnificent palace in the universe, the Americans the finest people on earth. Because he had read these exaggerations so often, he ended by believing them.*

Every American is surrounded by flatterers; he is flattered because he is the ruler; he thrives on flattery because he is of the people. His perennial sycophants are those who, at election time, praise him to obtain favors and positions; his daily flatterers are the newspapers, which, to gain subscriptions and money, retail to him every morning the most monstrous praises.

In conversing I had more than one occasion to realize that an American, however fulsome the adulation given to his country, is never completely satisfied; in his eyes any carefully considered approbation is a criticism; any restrained commendation is an insult; to do the country justice, one must disregard truth.

These conversations, in which I could never meet the demands of American national pride, always embarrassed me; I was most anxious to have them over with, because they were usually followed by more agreeable conversation, but sometimes the end was long in coming. People do not chat in the United States as they do in France; the American always argues; he has no knowledge of that light fashion of skimming the surface of a subject in a circle of several persons, where each can put in a word, witty or trite, weighty or light; where one will finish a phrase begun by another, and in which everything is touched on but nothing too deeply. In America, they do not aim at liveliness, they reason; thus the conversation is never general, it is always a dialogue. Following this custom, Marie and

* I deplore that blind national pride in Americans which makes them marvel at everything that happens in their country, but I like even less the inclination of the inhabitants of certain European countries to find fault with everything in their own land. These two contrary tendencies, equally exaggerated, are understandable in the light of diverse political institutions: in the United States the people, doing everything themselves, feel that they cannot overpraise their own works; in the countries of Europe, where on the contrary they do nothing, they cannot satirize enough the acts of the governing minority.

Writers desirous of finding American readers are obliged to laud everything American, even their rigorous climate, about which certainly they can do nothing. For this reason Washington Irving, despite his acute perception, feels obliged to comment admiringly upon the temperate warmth of North American summers and the mildness of its winters.

George were left out of my discussions with Nelson, just as he was never a party to my talks with George or Marie. Nelson was in the habit of commencing the evening by asking his daughter if any new books had come out; for, in the United States, men read nothing; they haven't the time; the women are charged with this duty, and they report on all political and literary publications to either their fathers or their husbands, and so inform them that they may discuss these works as if they knew them. Then Nelson would request his daughter to play some music.

The young girl showed some embarrassment at my presence; however, since her father never listened to her playing, she assumed that I would be no more attentive. Now, generally, in American drawing rooms, when the music begins it is a signal for conversation. I admit that at first I had very little curiosity about how Marie would perform. Most American girls are automatons at the piano; they take lessons for three months and memorize one waltz and one contradance; when one asks them to play, they rush to the piano and, without any warming up, dash through their little repertory like children who know a story and babble it to all comers without understanding a word.

All the women of this country learn music, but hardly one has a feeling for it; they do this because it is fashionable, not because they like it. "We love music as children love noise," one American told me. [. . .]

What was my surprise, then, when I heard Marie's voice, appealing and melodious, accompanied sometimes by the brilliant notes of the harp, sometimes by the soft modulations of the piano; when I saw her fingers playing lightly and gracefully over the strings of the one and the ivory keys of the other!

After traversing wild and dreary lands, wide sandy deserts under a blazing sun, the wanderer comes perchance upon a cool valley, where murmurous waters flow, where verdure smiles before his eyes and spreads cool shade above him. He halts enchanted in this charming spot and rests with delight. Feeling his strength returning to his limbs and joy to his heart, he believes he has found all the treasures and beauties of nature united in this haven.

Such was my experience when, in the cold society of America, I heard a lovely melody ringing forth.

Beautiful music contains all things: imagination, poetry, enthusiasm, sensibility, power of spirit, tenderness of heart, songs of glory, sighs of love!

Harmony makes one dream, but not empty dreams. . . . The sounds which struck my ears were ethereal, something more than thought, different from words; a mysterious voice speaking only to the soul. What means its language? I cannot say, but I understand it. [. . .]

Sometimes she would improvise: then I know not what extraordinary faculty was revealed in her. This young girl, so simple and so modest, became suddenly great and commanding; she ruled the emotion with which she was animated; she and her instrument were but one being; the notes seemed the sighing of her voice. I feared she would breathe out her soul in a burst of rapture. She united in herself the genius of creation, the gift of performance, and the grace adorning them.

In listening to Marie, I felt that there yet existed in my heart a spring of sweet joy which until then had been unknown to me.

As soon as I could escape from Nelson, I approached his daughter. Not far from her sat George, silently contemplating her in an ecstasy of tenderness and wonder; his love of his sister was touching, and he loved her above all others.

For a long time Marie appeared to be disquieted by the relationship established between herself and me; she was adroit at breaking off our talks and making them few; she was especially troubled at my expressions of admiration. The confusion she showed was not a trick of false modesty, which rejects one compliment in order to draw forth more; her distress was too deep to be feigned. While I praised her, her look seemed to say: Your admiration would soon cease if you knew what I am.

How can I make you understand the emotions I felt during those evenings, which flowed quietly and calmly in the modest bosom of a virtuous family, when I was aware of the birth in me of the most violent and the sweetest passion that ever ruled my soul?

Marie had just reached her eighteenth birthday; the whole of her character was a charming harmony, combining the tones of strength and of gentleness, in which the sweet notes predominated. Her glance was melancholy and moving as a dream of love; yet one could see shining in her great dark eyes a flash of that ardent light which scorches the Antilles; her brow would bend, weighted by an indefinable sadness; her graceful figure was upheld by her natural dignity, as the light frigate sways gently over the upholding billows.

She united in her person all that was seductive in American women, with none of the faults which overshadow the light of their good qualities. One would have thought her a European girl, with ardent passions, a lively imagination, with Italian sensuousness and a French heart; and this girl, American by reason of her mind, lived in the midst of a moral and religious world!

I have sometimes seen her eyes filling with tears on hearing of a generous action, on hearing the pitiful voice of an unfortunate, at the sound of a charming melody; but only a fortunate accident was to reveal to me all the goodness of her heart.

6

The Baltimore Almshouse

I noticed that often, at the same hour of the day, Marie would go out alone. This fact in itself did not surprise me; custom permitted young girls to go about the city unaccompanied, either for the sake of walking or to visit their friends. But Marie did not frequent the public promenades; I never saw her there; and as she never received callers it seemed unlikely that she was paying calls. Reflecting upon the long hours of her absence, I could not help suspecting that they were devoted to some affair of the heart. My love for Marie was revealed to me by a pang of jealousy.

One day, having seen her leave at the accustomed hour, I experienced an agitation of heart which I took for a voice of dire warning: where is the man so strong that, in the torments of love, he has never yielded to the weakness of a superstitious impulse? I imagined that the secret trouble in my soul warned me of a frightful and immediate misfortune; with my head full of fancies and my heart of passion, I followed in Marie's footsteps, but already she had disappeared. I halted, wondering and uneasy. I was ashamed at this base spying; instead of searching farther in the city I entered the first street that led outside its walls, walking rapidly like a malefactor who flees the scene of his crime.

I had gone about a mile along a road bordered on each side by tall forests, when I perceived, at my right, a vast edifice, over whose portal was written "Almshouse." In Baltimore I had often heard this charitable establishment praised; I felt no curiosity at that moment to inspect it; however, some hidden instinct drew me toward that refuge of sufferers, as though the sight of others' sorrows might assuage my own. I entered—and what did I see? Heaven! Nelson's daughter, giving her attentions to the unfortunates! "What! It is here that Marie——" This exclamation escaped me, in my remorse, for the cause of those mysterious absences was revealed to my eyes. However, my shame at the odious suspicions I had entertained was dispelled in the joy I felt that they had been unfounded. Upon seeing me, Marie blushed charmingly.

"Yes," cried a feeble, plaintive voice, "Marie Nelson is our good angel; she knows the secret of healing the wounds of the spirit; her name is blessed among us."

These words went to my heart. I said to Marie: "I would like to see the hospital. Will you consent to serve me as guide through the miseries of humanity?" She gave a sign of assent.

I understood then how easy it is to be good when one is happy. In my distress, I had thought that the misfortunes of others would distract me from my own; delivered from my pain, I saw these less fortunate ones and felt compassion toward them. Now I knew what filled those long hours that had so troubled my heart. Nelson's daughter went about the rooms, corridors, and wards of the building as though that house of charity were her daily dwelling; all the turnings were familiar to her; all the guards inclined their heads to her; all sorrows were stilled at her appearance.

There are two sorts of public charity in the United States. One is the English type, where everyone who is unemployed, or pretends to be, has the right to public relief, a system by virtue of which all idlers become beggars and find in the imprudent providence of the law more material aid than they could hope to obtain by their hardest work; they live upon alms, degrading themselves and ruining society. Such is the system which flourishes in New York, in Boston, and throughout New England.

The other is the system of charitable institutions, which the indigent have no legal right to enter, but where they are admitted at the good pleasure of the officers of public authority. Following this system, society is not obliged to support all the weaklings; it relieves only as many as possible. Since assistance can be refused to the poor, no one feigns poverty, being sure of the disgrace without being sure of the relief. This system, in use in France, is followed also in Maryland.

The Baltimore Almshouse contains three categories of unfortunates: the poor, the ill, and the mad.

Marie met among them only love, respect, and gratitude.

"Look," she said to me, "at that young woman with the pale, hollow cheeks, her eyes bedimmed. She was once beautiful, and supported her poor children by her work; now she is wasting away, and soon she will die, cut down by that deadly illness which reaps so many young lives in this country."

However, she approached the bedside of the consumptive, took her hand and dropped a tear upon it.

"Do not weep, dear young lady," said the poor woman. "Since I have seen you this morning, I will be happy for the rest of the day."

Next Marie stopped beside a young girl. "This one," she told me, "has been blind and a deaf-mute since birth. Though lacking the principal senses through which we receive our ideas, she is gifted with great intelligence, experiences vivid impressions, and succeeds in communicating them. Doubtless, the lack of those missing senses renders still finer and stronger those she possesses, those of touch and smell. See how she recognizes me by my hands, my clothing! how tenderly she kisses me! how happy she is to press me to her heart!"

And the poor girl trembled in Marie's arms, giving her a thousand caresses. The unfortunate creature, who knew none of the joys of the world, nevertheless rejoiced; her face was all alight, and her lips showed an expression of contentment which she could not have imitated from another. [. . .]

Nelson's daughter received a thousand blessings as she went her way. [. . .] I marveled, on this occasion, at how superior to us are women in the exercise of charity. Their good works are never a burden, because, with them, as it is the heart which gives, so it is the heart which receives. Contrarily, the humane deeds of men come almost always from the mind. This sort of charity is hard for the sufferer to take; in other words, if reason dictates that the rich should help the poor, it follows that he who receives is inferior to the giver, as the poor man is inferior to the rich. It is not thus according to the laws of the heart and religion; when the poorest is the equal of the wealthiest man, the same gratitude is felt by the bestower of charity as is felt by the receiver, who gives the rich man the happiness of giving. Man protects with his strength; woman, despite her weakness, brings consolation.

However, lamentable outcries now reached my ears. "That," said Marie to me, "is the wailing of the poor people who have lost their reason."

Two among them caught my attention and pity at once; they had reached madness by opposite paths.

The first, condemned to solitary confinement for murder, had gone mad in his cell, and had been transferred from the prison to the hospital. His madness was as cruel as his crime; he dreamed at night that an eagle hovered over his head, awaiting the moment when he should fall asleep to tear out his heart; during the day he was haunted by bloody phantoms, and when I saw him he addressed his jailers with this strange reproach—looking at me as though asking confirmation: "How barbarous!" he cried, "I had a butterfly as a companion in my cell, and the brutes have killed it!"

Marie assured me that there was no truth in these words—the imagined death of an insect had become the torment of this man who had murdered a fellow man!

The other was a perfectly beautiful young girl whose religious fervor, pushed to the extreme, had robbed her of her reason. Her brow gave evidence of her purity; in her lovely dark eyes, which she kept continually raised to the heavens, one could see her feeling of beatitude; nothing terrestrial could catch her attention, nothing disturbed her ecstasy. She was truly an angel: living already in Heaven, she understood nothing in this world; therefore she was mad.

Thus from two contrary starting points these two had arrived together at the same destination, the one through crime, the other through innocence! These are the mysteries of humankind; the same refuge protected that pure and candid soul, dreaming on earth of the joys of Heaven, and the cruel creature who had found his joy in the blood of men; society banished both from its midst, seemingly unable to admit of extreme goodness or extreme evil.

I was lost in these sad reflections when I heard frightful shrieks. A guard informed me that these were the cries of a furiously demented Negro; the cause of his madness was this: there lived in Maryland a professional slave dealer named Wolfolk. He made a big business of this and was, perhaps, the foremost dealer in human flesh in the United States; all the colored population knew and abhorred him; it seemed that all the vileness of slavery was personified in him. This poor Negro had been taken by Wolfolk from Virginia to Maryland to be sold, and on the way was subjected to such brutalities that his reason had snapped. Since then, one fixed idea had possessed him, never giving him an instant's rest: he believed his mortal enemy was constantly at his side, awaiting the moment when he could cut out from his body strips of flesh for which he hungered. His frenzy was so terrible that none dared approach him; he took anyone he saw for Wolfolk; only one person had any power over him; his cries would die away when he beheld Marie Nelson. I do not know by what tender compassion, by what charm possessed by women alone, she had found access to his heart; he was, of all the wretches confined within those walls, the one for whom she showed the greatest sympathy; and this I could not understand, for after all he was only a Negro!

We approached the cell whence issued those furious howls. "Look!" said the jailer, opening the door.

I saw a tall Negro, with a strong, manly face; nobility was stamped upon his visage and his limbs were muscular; his mouth foamed with rage, his eyes emitted flashes of indignant lightning. At sight of me, he struck a defensive attitude, using as a weapon the chains with which he was loaded. "Monster!" he cried, "You thirst for my blood! But come no closer!" And so saying he bared his teeth, white as ivory inlaid in ebony, indicating that he would devour me if I took one step toward him.

Then Marie, taking my place, said to him, "My friend, it is I." These few words magically put an end to his transports. "Ah," he responded in a gentle voice, "I am not afraid when I see you; everyone wants to kill me but you."

Marie endeavored to persuade him that no one there wished to kill him. When she left him, I wished to judge the power of her words; I looked back at the Negro, whose frenzy came once more upon him.

His madness presented a horrifying spectacle and made a painful impression upon me; however, it was softened by the memory of Marie's compassion for him. Never, since I had been in America, had I seen a white person take pity on a Negro; I had heard it constantly said that colored people were not worthy of commiseration, deserving nothing but contempt; Nelson's daughter, at least, did not share this hateful prejudice.

I returned to the city alone, Marie not having wished me to accompany her. "Perhaps, one day," she said to me, "you will be grateful that I refused." I could make no sense of these words.

I left the Almshouse with mixed emotions. One cannot behold without a cruel pang all the infirmities of our poor nature gathered in one place; but there is never a sad memory without the germ of a sweet thought; each of the sufferers I remembered brought to mind that angel of consolation.

Shall I confess it to you? I retained, from that visit to the asylum of miseries, an impression of personal happiness, for which I have often reproached myself. My pity for unhappiness was sincere, but that was not the only sentiment in my heart. I was still selfish enough to think that none of those afflictions touched my existence. The proximity of Marie, the grace of her person, enhanced by the radiance of her charity; the promise of happiness which I found in loving her; a delightful future opening before me—these smiling images contrasted in my thoughts with the abject, wretched lives of those outcast beings: the shame of nature, a reproach to society, doomed from birth to opprobrium, to illness, to all the sufferings of body and soul! And I secretly rejoiced at the comparison, believing I was superior because I was more fortunate. Alas! what would have been my dismay if, chastising my proud passions, a voice from Heaven had announced to my spirit that I would one day suffer anguish unknown to all those poor wretches!

However, the memory of the Almshouse and the compassionate young girl I had found there never left me.

Thus, not family affection, nor love of my fatherland, nor the wonders of nature, but a woman appeased my restless ambitions and checked my footloose humor. I could see no other possible future but to love Marie forever. I aspired to a single joy, to be loved by her.

I had come to America seeking the cure for an insatiable need of violent emotions and noble aspirations, and a sentiment full of gentleness brought peace to my troubled soul, calming the erratic impulses of my heart.

I came to observe the development of a great nation, its institutions, its customs, its marvelous prosperity, and a woman became the sole object worthy of my wonder and admiration.

7

The Mystery

I avowed my love to Marie, my desires, and my hopes—but she received the revelations of my heart in a peculiar way.

A joyful radiance in her beautiful eyes was almost at once extinguished by a cloud of sadness.

She avoided my presence, though she seemed happy at seeing me; her eyes still met mine but as though in spite of herself; her voice, naturally sweet, was altered; her lips still smiled, but her eyelids were shadowed with melancholy, which became deeper each day.

I would often ask her what caused her distress. She told me, "All your words promise me joy, and my destiny condemns me to an unhappy life; you see what an abyss separates us."

If I pursued my questions further, she would respond only with a dejected silence and a heartrending gaze.

From that moment I was constantly with Nelson and his children. [. . .]

Marie's reticence, the vagueness of her words, tormented me more each day; I prayed unceasingly to Heaven to dissipate this mysterious cloud. I would not so ardently have desired that the shadow be lifted, could I have foreseen how fatal would be the enlightenment.

I was in the habit of walking about near the column erected as a memorial to Washington; this is a lonely place, and it is surprising to find, adjacent to a monument destined to be the finest ornament of the city, a wild forest, the beginning of the wilderness, as it were.

It was there that I collected my thoughts and passed my impressions in review; I found a great charm in these silent meditations.

One day I pursued the course of my reveries, wandering into the forest, with only the caprice of my thoughts as guide, strolling on aimlessly, without any other care but to avoid the trees or becoming entangled in the vines. In this free movement of the body, I felt my thoughts freer, my soul unfettered, my imagination bolder in its flights. [. . .] Ah, how violently, in profound isolation, does an impression of grief seize upon one's senses! Remembering Marie, so beautiful and in such distress, I felt my heart swell with sorrow and love. Oh you, whose souls are troubled, do not absent yourselves from the world, for in the silence of solitude one hears the voices of passion more clearly; the calmness of nature makes one feel the more keenly the agitations of the spirit, and the wilderness seems a void that the heart of man must fill. [. . .]

I had never yet so strongly felt the full force of my love for Marie. The image of her sorrow came to my thoughts like remorse; if I was innocent of causing her pain, I was guilty in not healing it. Love, who frets at pleasures of which he is not the author, is jealous even of tears he has not caused to flow, and which he cannot dry.

A cardinal, flitting among the magnolias, startled my eyes with his glowing plumage, interrupting my meditations. I realized that I had lost my way.

I attempted to retrace my steps, but I had left so dim a trail that I could not find it again.

I calculated, from the sun's position, where I was and the direction I should take to return to Baltimore; but in a forest the slightest deviation from a straight line throws one off the track, and after a thousand blunders, a thousand vain attempts to find my way, I halted, panting; my knees buckled, and I fell at the foot of a cedar half uprooted by some storm.

The forest grew more and more silent; shadows grew long about me, and the mockingbird saluted with a final call the last rays of the sun, dying on the crests of the tall pines. My strength was spent; sleep overcame my senses.

My presence in the forest at the approach of night and the slumber into which I fell were not unattended by danger. The last gleams of twilight are always followed, in the South, by a cold, penetrating dampness; this sudden moisture, exhaled from the earth, is pernicious, and I was to feel its baneful result.

However, this peril was far from my thoughts. My heart was

filled with the emotions which had been stirring me. The image of Marie was always before me; I fell asleep with it; drifting thoughts of her love floated about me and filled my eyes with a thousand enchanting pictures; I seemed to see Nelson's daughter sitting at my side. Her beauty and grace intoxicated me, but her mysterious sadness troubled my joy. I said to her, "Marie! Why do you weep? What secret torment tears your heart? Gentle angel of kindness, are you here on earth to suffer—you, whose mere look enchants and consoles? If you are unhappy, why do you not unburden your heart to the heart of a friend? Alas! you do not know how much Ludovic loves you. You alone have rekindled with your eyes the wan and dying fires of my life, and my starving, insatiable soul now rejoices in the one sentiment which overflows it." And I heard her sweet voice respond in tender, melancholy accents. I took her hand and pressed it to my heart; I covered it with kisses and watered it with my tears.

Of a sudden I awoke—I felt a hand glide softly across my brow—I half opened my eyes—what was this I saw? Heavens, Marie! Marie, kneeling beside me, raising her hands in entreaty toward Heaven. [. . .]

At first I was speechless in the presence of her who was all my life; for I knew not but that some dream deceived my senses. I believed I was awake, but might this not be the beginning of a vision?

"Oh, dear God! Ludovic!" she said, "let us flee from this place: soon night will fall; a mortal chill will succeed the burning heat of day."

"Marie!" I cried. "Are you the good angel, the guardian spirit of my destiny? Whence have you come, delusive sylph, to deceive my senses and mock my sorrow?"

"I have never deceived you, Ludovic," replied the maiden, with a charming betrayal of emotion, "I am a girl with a simple and truthful heart. I saw you, Ludovic, entering the forest, and, as you had not returned at the decline of the day, I feared for your life. I thought you might have lost your way, and I trembled at the thought of the peril that threatened you."

"Oh, my beloved! How unselfish is your devotion! But you are risking the same dangers!"

"Fear nothing," she replied. "I know all the devious paths in this forest; there is not a tuft of moss I have not trodden, not a tree whose shadows I do not know, by morning or evening light! The women of Baltimore show themselves off in the public squares; while I love these solitary retreats, or at least——" She stopped a moment, pensive. "Let us make haste," she added. So saying, she started off, beckoning me after her. I would have seized her hand; my tears flowed, I experienced a thousand feelings I could not utter. However, I said to her, "Marie, before I knew whether or not I was loved by you, I felt a burning fire devouring my heart; the tenderest feelings mingled in me with bitter torment and cruel agitation—but you have just shown me that you love me, and I feel an inconceivably sweet emotion penetrating my soul—my love is more ardent than ever, but serene! Oh, I beg you, abandon yourself, like me, to the charm of this pure feeling! But one vexation remains; I see your sadness. Marie, you are hiding some grief from me. Then you do not believe in my love! Alas! why does no echo in this forest tell you the feelings I confided to the wilderness?"

"Would to God I had not heard those solitary revelations!" said Marie. "Ludovic, as you slept, your voice murmured words of enchantment, which filled the measure of my unhappiness. Alas! ——"

She did not finish. I saw her press her hand to her throbbing heart; her eyes filled with suppressed tears.

"What, then, is this mystery?" I cried vehemently. "Marie, I entreat you, open your soul to me, that I may know your sorrow as you know my love! Each of your lamentations would be laid to rest in my heart. Grief is not like sound, which grows with echoing; it ceases when it finds an echo. My beloved! Incline your head toward mine, let me support your weakness; the perfume of the sweetest flowers is less delicate than the mingling of two loving sighs, and you do not know what strength can come from the union of two breasts that breathe together. Hear me! Whatever may be your destiny, you cannot be happier with my protection than I will be proud of your love! Marie! Be my love, be my cherished bride! If on this earth doomed to storms, you should be bowed by the hurricane, you will find at least a shelter wherein to rest; your bitterest tears will be softened when mingled with those of a friend, and if, from the heart of a somber cloud, a thunderbolt should be hurled to strike us, close enlaced, heart upon heart, it will be sweet to die together and to render up in each other's arms our last sigh of life and love!"

Thus I spoke. Marie remained silent; however, we walked steadily on, and approached Baltimore, alas! too quickly. How I would have blessed the heavens if we should have lost our way! What intoxication in all my being! What delirium in my heart!

These vivid impressions, dazzling events, are engraved in lines of fire in my memory—my impassioned soliloquy in solitude, the secrets of my love confided to the wilds and surprised in my sleep; so much joy succeeding my danger; Marie, my rescuer, my guide and companion, our voices together, our arms interlaced, our walk in the silent evening, and, as day ended, the gentle light of the moon bringing a host of tender dreams—a universe of feeling, ideas, passions, which made my heart whirl amid the silence of slumbering nature.

I questioned Marie again, saying, "Why do you suppress the smile which tries to touch your lips? Listen, can you not hear my heart beating in time to yours? Can you not feel my soul merging with yours? They are one, no power can separate them more. Woe to him who would try to break this sacred bond!"

"Stop!" cried Marie; after a moment's silence, "Ludovic," she continued, "I shall not try to tell you of the feelings that fill my soul—you have spoken to me in a language which I understand because it is that of the heart—but the words I cannot understand. Ah, pray cease these speeches which intoxicate and desolate me! The thought of happiness is too cruel for one who can never be happy. You love me, Ludovic—heavens! That love, which would be my joy, only proves a measure of my misfortune. Oh, my fate is terrible! Still one more day—and you will know my secret."

We had now reached the edge of the city. "Remain here," she said, imperiously. "Here is the city—I must be alone." With these words she left me, filled with deep distress. [. . .]

The next morning, an irresistible power led me back to the lonely forest. Perhaps Nelson's daughter would come back to give me the promised revelation. [. . .]

I wished to see all the places we had traversed the evening before. Arrived at the place where I had beheld Marie upon her knees in prayer, I flung myself face down upon the earth and covered with kisses the moss she had watered with her tears.

I stayed long in that solitude; Marie did not appear, and each instant I thought I saw or heard her. At the slightest murmur of the wind in the pines my heart beat violently. I started at everything—the fall of a leaf, the flight of a bird, the stirring of an insect in the grass.

But I found in the forest only memories and new agitation—Marie did not come.

On my return to the house of my host, I found an atmosphere of general sadness and mourning. Nelson paced his room solemnly, raising his eyes to Heaven and letting fall an occasional sententious word; the servants, seeing their masters distressed, shared their sadness uncomprehendingly.

Marie was not to be seen the whole day. When evening came, Nelson, George, and I were seated in the parlor, taking tea, as was our custom; each was silent; I dared not infringe upon a silence the more difficult to break the longer it lasted, but how could I longer support the torments of my uncertainty?

At last Marie entered, with pallid face and faltering steps; she came with lowered eyes and placed herself beside her father. After several minutes, Nelson raised his voice and said to me:

"My young friend, I know your feelings; I believe them to be pure, and I esteem you. But you are in ignorance of our misfortune: you shall know it and pity us.

8

The Revelation

"New England, my native country, is not the place where my children were born; George and Marie were born in Louisiana. Alas! Would to God I had never left the place of my birth! My father, a Boston trader, made a fortune; upon his death, the inheritance was divided equally among his children, and barely supplied their needs. I had two brothers: the elder left for India, whence he brought back great wealth; the other went West; today he owns two thousand acres of land and several factories in Illinois. I was undecided; some said, 'Go to New Orleans—if you don't die of yellow fever you will make a fortune.' The choice did not deter me—I followed that advice. Alas! I suffered less from the insalubrious climate than from human corruption.

"Wherever society is divided between free men and slaves, one can count on seeing tyranny on one side and servility on the other; contempt for the oppressed, hate for the oppressors; abuse of power, and vengeance.

"But—what an accursed country, oh God! What depravity! What cynical immorality! And what scorn of the word of God in a Christian society!

"However, in that land of vice and impiety, I noticed a young orphan girl, innocent and beautiful, whose thoughts were pure, and whose religious faith was fervent; she was of Creole background.

"I joined my destiny with that of Theresa Spencer. At first the heavens smiled upon us; within a few years the births of George and Marie were a double proof of our love. I had undertaken large commercial enterprises; they prospered according to all my hopes. Alas! Our happiness was as fleeting as that of the wicked! I am not impious—but I was struck down by the thunderbolt of a vengeful God.

"Before her marriage, Theresa Spencer had attracted the eye of a young Spaniard, Don Fernando d'Almanza, of a very wealthy family whose fortune had been made while Louisiana was a Spanish colony. There was no one more charming than this young man; his intelligence was as noble as his birth; the distinction of his manners equaled the handsomeness of his face. However, Theresa avoided him. I know not what inner sense caused her to feel that the man who declared the tenderest love for her was an enemy.

"We have since learned that he hoped to gain her love without becoming her husband.

"Theresa's inflexibility irritated him in the extreme, and later the spectacle of our felicity undoubtedly rendered the pangs of his wounded vanity all the more keen, for he conceived and soon executed the most execrable vengeance.

"Secretly he spread the rumor that Theresa was, through her great-grandmother, a mulatto; he brought proofs to this allegation which could justify it, naming all the forebears of Marie back to her whose impure blood had, he said, tainted the whole family.

"His denunciation was hateful, but it was true. The stain upon Theresa Spencer's origins had been lost in the night of time. At Fernando's voice, sleeping memories reawoke—the memory of man is long when it comes to the misfortunes of others! Public opinion was in a turmoil; a sort of inquest was held; the oldest inhabitants were consulted, and it was found that a century before, Theresa Spencer's family had been soiled by a drop of black blood.

"In following generations this admixture had become imperceptible. The whiteness of Theresa's complexion was dazzling; nothing in her features disclosed the flaw in her origin; but tradition condemned her.

"From that day on, our life, which had flowed with such peaceful sweetness, became bitter and cruel. The more highly we had been respected by the world, the more shattering was the shame of our fall from grace. Soon I saw that the friendships I had considered the most solid were tottering. A single friend, faithful in adversity, did not blush to own my affection.

"That generous friend, related to you by ties of blood, had, as a Frenchman, more friendliness toward the black race, and less prejudice against it, than one ordinarily finds among Americans.

He alone, in our dark days, extended a helping hand and preserved me from the opprobrium of bankruptcy. The blow to my social position had struck my credit as well. The men of this country, so indulgent toward a bankrupt, are pitiless toward a misalliance! *

"The evil was, however, without remedy. I struggled against my fate, because it is our habit never to despair; but the obstacles were too much for human strength.

"Theresa blamed herself cruelly for the calamity, of which she was innocent. Orphaned at a tender age, she had never known the secrets of her family. Her grief was so profound that she could not survive it; she died in my arms, worn out by her tears and despair.

"When she was snatched from my love, so young in years and so aged by grief, so pure and so unhappy, I misdoubted Providence and my own courage for the first time. It was wrong to doubt thus; for I have found the strength to bear my sufferings, and Heaven has not abandoned me.

"I left New Orleans, where I was exposed to too many evil passions, torn by too many cruel memories. I fixed my residence in Baltimore, where no one knew of the stain of my alliance, nor the blemish which marked my children.

"For ten years I have lived in this city; I have formed new relationships, built up my credit, found wealth again—without happiness, which can no more exist for me.

"We live here in outward tranquillity: the trouble is in our hearts alone.

"Not a soul knows the shame of my children; but it might be discovered any day. We are loved and honored, because no one knows who we are. One word from a well-informed enemy could ruin us: we are like a guilty man whom society believes innocent, not daring to accept a prominent position because too overwhelming a disgrace would follow the revelation of his crime.

"George, whose proud and noble nature is roused to indignation by the world's injustice, believes he is the equal of any American; and if I had not beseeched him in the name of his sister, whom he passionately loves, to remain silent, he would have revealed his origin a hundred times and braved public opinion.

"Marie, on the contrary, submissive and resigned to her destiny,

* See Appendix E, pp. 221–22.

seeks the shadow of isolation. This is the secret of her aversion to society. Ah, yes—indeed she surpasses all the women of Baltimore in intelligence, talent, and goodness; but she is not their equal.

"I owed to you, my young friend, this confession of our misfortune. Hospitality demanded it of me. You seek happiness upon the earth—alas! you will not find it among us—the joys of the world are elsewhere; here, sorrow and sacrifice!"

These were Nelson's words. During his recital his austere face had sometimes worked with emotion. George quivered on his chair; his silent anger was shown in his brusque gestures and his flashing eyes. Marie, head bowed on her breast, hid her face from all eyes.

As for me, I listened, uncertain whether I grasped the strange words which assailed my ears, although there was nothing unclear in the speech I had just heard.

My heart and my reason rebelled.

"So this is the land of the free—who cannot do without slaves!" I cried. "America is the cradle of equality, and no country in Europe contains so much servitude! Now I understand you egotistical Americans. You love liberty for yourselves. A race of merchants, you sell the liberty of others!"

Hardly had I pronounced these words when I wished I could call them back; because I feared I had offended Marie's father.

Indignation had seized all my being. Nelson's daughter, seeing me at first aroused and then abstracted, misunderstood the sentiments which moved me.

"Ludovic," she said in a half-smothered voice, "Why do you grieve? Did I not tell you that I am unworthy of your love?"

I replied, "Marie, you mistake what is passing in the depths of my heart. It is true that my feeling for you is no longer the same—I know you are unhappy; my love is only the greater!"

"Generous friend!" cried George, holding out his hand to me. "You speak nobly!" And a ray of joy suddenly shone upon that somber brow.

But Nelson remained impassive. When he saw that our emotions had become somewhat calmer, he said to me, "Your ardor leads you astray, my friend; beware of the consequences of a generous emotion. If you contemplated reality with a less prejudiced eye, you could not endure the sight, and you would realize that a white man can never marry a woman of color."

I cannot tell you how these words troubled my heart. A strange situation! As Nelson spoke to me thus, there sat Marie, whose complexion was even whiter than the swans of the Great Lakes!

I said, "What, then, is the origin, among a people exempt from prejudice and passion, of this false idea which makes a sin of misfortune, and of this pitiless hatred which pursues a whole race of men from generation to generation?"

Nelson reflected a moment, then held the following conversation with me, whose exact words time can never efface from my memory:

Nelson: The black race is despised in America because it is a race of slaves; it is hated because it aspires to liberty.

Common practice and law alike say the Negro is not a man, he is a thing.

He is an article of trade, superior to other merchandise; a Negro is worth ten acres of well-cultivated land.

For the slave, there is neither birth, marriage, nor death.

The child of a slave belongs to the slave's master, as the fruits of the soil belong to the owner of the land. The loves of a slave leave no more trace on society than does the breeding of plants on our gardens; and when he dies, the only thought is to replace him, as one replaces a fruitful tree destroyed by a storm.

Ludovic: Thus your laws forbid Negro slaves to have filial respect, paternal love, and conjugal tenderness. Then what is left to them in common with mankind?

Nelson: The principle once admitted, these consequences follow: The child born in slavery knows no more of family life than does an animal. The maternal bosom nourishes him as the teat of the wild beast feeds her young. The touching relationships of mother with child, of child with father, of brother with sister, have neither sense nor moral value to him, and he does not marry, because, belonging to someone else, he cannot give himself to anyone.

Ludovic: But why do not the American people, enlightened and religious, recoil in horror from an institution which offends the laws of nature, morality, and humanity? Are not all men created equal?

Nelson: No people are more attached than we to the principles of equality; but we will not allow a race inferior to ours to share in our rights.

At these words I saw the red color mount to George's features, and his lips trembled on the verge of uttering a cry of indignation, but he made a powerful effort and succeeded in restraining his wrath.

I replied to Nelson: "In the United States they believe that the blacks are inferior to the whites; is it because the whites generally show more intelligence than the Negroes? But how can one compare a race of men brought up in slavery, who transmit through generations a tradition of misery and brutishness, with people who can look back on fifteen centuries of uninterrupted civilization and who give their children an education that commences with the cradle and develops all their natural abilities? In Europe we have not the prejudices found in America, and we believe that all humanity forms but one family, of which all members are equals."

Nelson: No doubt, slavery offends the laws of morality and of God. However, do not judge the American people too severely. Greece had her helots, Rome her slaves, the Middle Ages their serfs; nowadays there are Negroes; and these Negroes, whose minds are naturally restricted, attach little value to liberty; for the most part emancipation is a fatal gift. Ask them—they will all tell you that they were happier slave than free. Left to their own resources, they do not know how to support themselves, and there die in our cities half again as many freedmen as slaves.*

Ludovic: It is natural that the slave who suddenly becomes free does not know how to use or enjoy independence. Like a man whose legs have been bound from childhood, who is told suddenly to walk, he staggers at every step. Liberty is a deadly weapon in his hands, with which he wounds all about him; and most often he is his own first victim. But should one conclude that slavery, once established, should be respected? Of course not. Only it is just to say that the generation which receives its freedom is not the generation to enjoy it: the benefits of liberty are reaped only by the following gen-

* This is a constant number. Thus, during the years 1828, 1829, and 1830 there died in Baltimore one out of every 28 freed Negroes, and one out of every 45 Negro slaves. [But the freed Negroes probably were older, on the average, than the slaves; thus the significance of their higher mortality rate is not necessarily the one Beaumont implies. Translator's note.]

erations. I will never recognize those so-called laws of necessity, which tend to justify tyranny and oppression.

Nelson: I think as you do; however, do not make the mistake of believing that Negroes are treated with the inhumanity of which all slave owners are commonly accused; most of them are better clothed, better fed, and happier than your free peasants in Europe.

"Stop!" cried George violently (for at this moment his anger became stronger than his filial respect). "This talk is iniquitous and cruel! It is true that you take as much care of your Negroes as you do of your beasts of burden! Better, even, because a Negro brings in more for his master than a horse or a mule. When you beat your Negroes, I know, you do not kill them: a Negro is worth three hundred dollars. But don't boast about the humanity of the masters toward their slaves—the unthinking cruelty that kills is far better than the calculated cruelty that leaves one to suffer a horrible life! It is true that according to law a Negro is not a man; he is a chattel, a thing. Yes, but you will see that he is a thinking thing, an acting thing, that can hold a dagger! Inferior race! So you say! You have measured the Negro brain and said 'There is no room in that narrow skull for anything but grief!' and you have condemned him to suffer eternally. You are mistaken; your measurements were wrong; in that brutish head there is a compartment that contains a powerful faculty, that of revenge—an implacable vengeance, horrible but intelligent. If he hates you, it is because his body is mangled by your blows, his soul is crushed by your injustice. Is he stupid to hate you? The best of animals loves the cruel hand that beats him, and rejoices in his servitude; the most stupid among men, the brutalized Negro, even when chained like a wild beast, is free to think, and his suffering soul is as noble as that of God who died to free the world. He submits, but he is conscious of his oppression; his body alone obeys; his soul is in revolt. He grovels! Yes, for two centuries he has groveled at your feet—some day he will stand up and look you in the eye, and kill you. You will say he is cruel! But will you have forgotten that he has spent his life in suffering and hating? He has but one thought: vengeance, because he has but one feeling—misery."

As he spoke, George was illuminated by an almost superhuman flame, and his eyes emitted sparks of hate and indignation.

"My boy," Nelson responded calmly, "do you believe that my heart has not bled in judging as I have the race to which your mother was related?"

"Oh, Father," cried George, "you were first an American, then a husband!"

Marie here threw a beseeching look at her brother, saying, "George, why are you so carried away?"

Then, turning to Nelson: "Father, you are right. American women are superior to women of color; they are able to love with their reason; I know how to love only with my heart."

In pronouncing these words, she threw herself into his arms, as though to hide the blush of shame upon her cheek.

George went on: "My sister blushes at her African origin—as for me, I am proud of it. The men of the North can pride themselves only upon their intellects, which are cold as their climate, but we owe the warmth of our spirits and the ardor of our hearts to the hot sun of our fathers." He was silent a moment, then added with a bitter smile, "The Americans are a free and mercantile people, but let them beware, soon one branch of industry will be lacking. Soon they will lose the privilege of buying and selling men: American soil will not support slaves for long."

Nelson: Yes, I can see, with joy, that slavery is every day decreasing; and its complete disappearance will be only a matter of time.

George: And if the slaves grow tired of waiting?

Nelson: Woe be to them! If they have recourse to violence to become free, that they will never be; their revolt will bring their destruction. It is true that the number of blacks in the South will soon exceed that of the whites; but all the Central and Northern states will make common cause with the Americans of the South to exterminate the rebelling slaves. Any appeal to violence will be their ruin: let them have faith in the progress of reason.

Already in the North, slavery has been abolished; and the Southern states can hear the murmurs of liberty. Not long ago, prompt punishment would have strangled the voice bold enough to demand, in the South, the freedom of the Negroes; today this question is being debated in Virginia, in the very heart of its legislature. It seems that each year the ideas of universal liberty win another degree of latitude—the north wind spreads them. Now they are flourishing in Maryland; it is New England, my birthplace, which is spreading its enlightenment, its customs, and its civilization throughout the Union.

Ludovic: There is such power in an immutable moral principle!

George: And above all in self-interest. Do you know why Americans are tempted to abolish slavery? Because they are beginning to think that slavery is harmful to industry.

They see that the slave states are poor and the free states are rich; so they condemn slavery.

They say that the free laborer, working for himself, works better than the slave; and it is more profitable to pay a good worker than to feed a lazy slave. And so they condemn slavery.

They say, again, that labor is the source of wealth, but that slavery makes a dishonorable thing of labor; the whites will be idle so long as there are slaves—and so they condemn slavery.

Their self-interest is in accord with their pride—the emancipation of the blacks will make them free only in name—the free Negro will never become a rival to the American in industry or commerce. He can be one of two things: a beggar or a menial; other careers are closed to him by tradition. To free the Negroes in the United States is to create an inferior class, and whoever is a pure-blooded white belongs to a privileged class. A white skin is a mark of nobility."

"My friend," I said, addressing George, "you must not believe that these prejudices are destined to live forever! According to Nature's laws one man's freedom cannot be in the hands of another." [. . .]

Turning to Nelson, I went on: "Does American society try at least to cure this festering sore of slavery? Is it preparing a transition for two million men from the state of slavery to that of liberty?"

Nelson: No one, alas! is agreed on this subject. Some want all the Negroes to be freed at a single stroke; others want all children born of slaves to be declared free. One group says: before granting freedom to the blacks they must be educated. Another group replies: it is dangerous to educate slaves.

Not knowing which remedy to apply, they leave the evil to cure itself. Each day the situation changes, but the law is not changed:

the same punishment is meted out to the master who teaches his slave to write as to the master who kills his slave; and the poor Negro guilty of opening a book risks a flogging.

Ludovic: How cruel! I can understand that you will not free all Negroes in haste, but how is it possible that you stigmatize with such contempt those to whom you have already given their liberty?

Nelson: The black who is no longer a slave has been one; and, if he is born free, everyone knows that his father was not.

Ludovic: I can understand, further, the opprobrium which follows a Negro or mulatto, even after affranchisement, because his color is a constant reminder of his servitude. But what I can't understand is that the same stigma attaches to colored people who have become white and whose whole crime is that they count a black or a mulatto among their ancestors.

Nelson: This inflexibility in public opinion is doubtless unjust; but it is essential to the very dignity of the American people. Confronted with two races different from his own, the Indians and the Negroes, the American has mixed with neither. He has kept the blood of his forebears pure. In order to prevent all contact with these races, he must stigmatize them in the public opinion. The stigma remains, though the color can no longer be seen.

Ludovic: In the present state of your laws and customs you do not recognize hereditary nobility?

Nelson: No, of course not. Reason rejects all distinction which might be accorded to birth and not to personal merit.

Ludovic: If your custom is not to admit the transmission of honors by blood, then why does it sanction inherited infamy? One is not born noble, but one is born ignominious! Now, you must admit that these are horrid prejudices!

However, a white man, if such was his wish, could marry a free woman of color.

Nelson: No, my friend, you are mistaken.

Ludovic: What power could hinder him?

Nelson: The law. It contains an express prohibition, and declares such a marriage null.

Ludovic: A hateful law! But I shall defy that law.

Nelson: There is a more serious obstacle than the law itself, that is, tradition. You are ignorant of the condition of women of color in American society. You must know (I blush to say it, for it is a disgrace to my country) that in Louisiana the highest position that can be held by a free woman of color is that of a prostitute to white men.

New Orleans is largely populated by Americans from the North who have come to make their fortunes, and leave as soon as they have made them. Rarely do these transients marry; and this the obstacle that hinders them:

Each summer, New Orleans is ravaged by yellow fever. At this time, all those who can, quit the city, go up the Mississippi and Ohio Rivers, and seek in the Northern or Central states, at Philadelphia or Boston, a more salubrious climate. When the hot season is over, they return to the South and resume their business. These annual migrations are easy for bachelors, but they would be inconvenienced by a family. The American man avoids all vexation by not marrying, and by taking an unlawful companion; he always chooses one from among the free women of color and gives her a sort of dowry. The young girl is honored by a union which brings her together with a white man; she knows she cannot marry him; it is much in her eyes to be loved by him. She might, according to law, have married a mulatto, but such an alliance would not raise her out of her class. Also, the mulatto has no power to protect her; in marrying a man of color she perpetuates her degradation; she raises herself by prostituting herself to the white man. All young girls of color are brought up with these prejudices, and from the earliest age their parents mold them to the end of corruption. There are balls where none are admitted but white men and women of color; the husbands or brothers of the latter are not received; their mothers customarily attend and are witness to the attentions paid to their daughters, encourage them, and rejoice in them. When an American man's fancy is caught by a young girl, he approaches her mother—who bargains shrewdly, demanding more or less as a price according to whether her daughter is more or less of a novice. All this goes on quite openly; these monstrous unions have not even the decency of vice, which hides itself in shame, as does virtue for modesty's sake; they parade undisguised before all eyes, and no infamy or blame is attached to the men who form them. When the American from the North has made his fortune, he has achieved his goal. One fine day he leaves New Orleans and never returns. His children, and she who for ten years has lived as his wife, are nothing to him. Then the girl of color sells herself to another man. And that is the fate of women of the African race in Louisiana.

Thus saying, Nelson gave vent to a sigh. One could see that he had imposed upon himself a painful task, and that the feeling of having to fulfill a duty had alone sustained his voice.

Plunged in a somber reverie, George seemed to pay no attention to this recital. Marie, in her profound sadness, presented a pitiful sight. Thus one sees during the storm a tender flower bowing its head; weak but pliant, it bends to the gusts of the tempest, and when the hurricane has passed, drooping and beaten down, it can no longer raise its bruised stem.

So, while Nelson spoke, Marie, a reed swayed by the storms of the heart, had trembled again and again; each revelation had been a painful blow to her; an instinct of modesty discovered to her the meaning of the words she heard; she felt her humiliation without understanding it; and with innocence in her heart, she bore on her brow the blush of guilt.

As for me, unable longer to bear the emotions in this scene, I cried: "Your customs and laws horrify me; I will never submit to them. Ah, if Marie does not fear to link her destiny with mine, we will leave this country of odious prejudices together; flee the land of slavery and shadows and go to the land of liberty and light—that New England which advances with so firm and quick a step on the road of civilization!"

"Alas, my friend!" replied Nelson, "prejudice against the colored population is, to be sure, less powerful in Boston than in New Orleans, but nowhere is it dead."

"Well, then," I answered, "I scorn those prejudices and know how to brave them; it is infamous cowardice to hold aloof from those whose misfortunes are undeserved."

At this moment Marie seemed to emerge from her despondency. She raised her eyes and, in a voice which betrayed deep emotion, said to me: "How does it happen that you commiserate with us after what you have heard? Man's pity is for passing ills; but a sorrow which, like ours, will never end, wearies and discourages the most compassionate hearts.

"My friend," she added in an almost solemn tone, "you understand nothing of my fate on earth; because my heart can love, you believe that I am worthy of love; because my brow is white, you think that I am pure. But no; my blood contains a stain which renders me unworthy of esteem or affection. Yes! my birth condemned me to the contempt of men. Without doubt this decree of destiny is deserved. The decrees of God, though sometimes cruel, are always just."

Then, finding me unshakable in my sentiments—"You do not know," she said, "that you are dishonoring yourself in speaking to me? If you were seen with me in public, people would say, 'That man has lost all decency; he is going about with a woman of color.' Alas, Ludovic! consider the sad reality dispassionately: to join your life with that of a poor creature like me is to embrace a condition worse than death!

"Doubt not," she added in an inspired tone, "that God himself separated the white from the black. This separation is found everywhere: in hospitals where humans suffer, in the churches where they pray, in the prisons where they repent, in the cemeteries where they sleep the eternal sleep."

"What!" I cried, "even unto the day of death——"

"Yes," she replied in grave and melancholy accents, "when I die, men will remember that, a hundred years before, there was a mulatto in my family; and if my body is borne to consecrated ground, it will not be admitted there, for fear that contact with it might soil the bones of a privileged race. Alas, my friend, our mortal remains cannot mingle in the earth; is that not a sign that our souls cannot be united in Heaven?"

"Cease!" I cried, "Oh, my beloved, cease, I adjure you, this language which rends my heart! Why this shame? Why these tears? Shame is for the wicked, who make the innocent weep! And if you love me, the source of these tears will soon be dried. Let my love protect you. You fear disgrace for me! Marie! You do not know how proud I am of you. You cannot understand how much pride I would take in appearing everywhere, adorned by your love, your beauty, your sadness! Let these noble traders, with their brilliant armorial bearings and their pure blood, say one word to me—how I will revel in their insolence! What shall I not do for you in Europe, Marie! There, everyone will kneel at your feet, angel of grace and goodness; they will gather around you to receive the blessing of your smile; what man would not wish for the glory of protecting your innocence and helplessness? Here they reject and dishonor you—ah, how I thank you, you cold, indifferent Americans, for your scorn and injustice! You have cut down her whom I love, but you will see her lovely head raised again! You will pay homage to her, you noble lords of the counting house! You sun-browned white men will bow your heads before the lily whiteness of the colored girl—I will make you respect her! Marie will hold first place among your women!"

Thus saying, I cast myself at Marie's feet, as an indication of the worship I deemed worthy of my idol. Nelson's daughter wept with joy; she took my hands in hers, shed tears upon them, and laid her head upon them, showing thus that she accepted my support. These tears, falling upon a strong man from the eyes of a tender woman, doubtless signified that all my power would not preserve us from the tempest!

However, George, who was moved in the extreme, threw himself into my arms. He pressed me close to his breast: the only language his heart could find.

Nelson, impassive, preserving his calm, cold attitude in the midst of the violent passions which shook us, resembled one of those ancient ruins one sees on a rocky promontory, immobile while everything crumbles about it, remaining erect despite the hurricane unchained about its head, and the waves in fury roaring at its feet. Our passions had not touched him, nor had any of our words provoked him.

"My friend," he said, after a short silence, "your generous heart leads you astray. My reason will come to the aid of yours; you do not know what a task you undertake when you wish to combat the prejudices of an entire people, to live in a society with whose opinions and feelings you would clash daily! No, I shall not consent to your union with my daughter. However, I shall not oppose your wishes forever. Journey through America; observe the world in which you intend to live; study its passions and prejudices; measure the strength of the enemy you defy; and once you have discovered the fate of the black population in the slave states and even in the states where slavery has been abolished, then you may form a more enlightened resolution. I most firmly believe that no human strength can resist the impressions you will receive. But if the sight of frightful misery does not shake your courage nor dishearten you, do you think that I would hesitate to accept for my dear Marie the generous protection that you have just offered her?"

Nelson's firm response, whose tone showed a determined will, dismayed me.

"I insist," he added, "that you pass at least six months in observing the ways of this country. This time of trial will doubtless suffice."

In the impatience of my love, I replied, "We are unhappy in the United States—your children because of their birth, you and I because of the misfortune of your children. Let us leave this country and go to France. There we shall find no prejudice against families of color."

I was surprised to see George give no sign of agreement with these words, for my advice seemed to me likely to win his approval; however, he remained silently thoughtful.

"You hesitate," I said to him.

"No," replied George, "no—I have no hesitation. I will never leave America."

Nelson made a gesture of approval, and Marie gave a sigh.

"I am a victim of oppression in this country," George continued, "but America is my native land. Is one to be a good citizen only on condition that he is happy? Strong ties hold me here; the majority of men are held here by self-interest; I am bound to the country by duty. It is ignoble to flee from persecution! Ah, if I alone were unfortunate! Perhaps I should run away—but my destiny is that of a whole race of men. How cowardly it would be to withdraw from the common misery to seek a happy life alone! And then, duty is not the only tie that binds me; I may still enjoy some happiness. Our degradation will not be everlasting. Perhaps we shall be forced to seize by violence that equality now refused us! Glorious the day of just vengeance! No, I shall not flee America. But, Ludovic," he added, "if you must go to France to make my sister, my dear Marie, happy, ah, go!—in spite of——"

He could not finish; a tear fell from his eye.

"Ah, my brother, I shall never part from you," cried Marie fondly.

Nelson, meanwhile, had been reflecting.

"Heaven forbid," he said to me at last, "that we should follow your advice. I know how corrupt are the ways of France; and if my daughter hearkens to my words, she will never breathe the infected air of that accursed society in which morality is incessantly outraged, where conjugal fidelity is ridiculed, and the most odious vice is an excusable weakness."

I pointed out to Nelson that today the ways of women in France were no longer what they had been in the last century.* But as I spoke, he murmured under his breath the words: "France! Impious country! Accursed land!"

He continued aloud: "As for me, I shall never leave my country. The Americans of the United States are a great people. My forefathers left Europe's persecutions—I shall not return to the source of their misfortunes."

I begged Nelson to spare me a time of trial which would be useless, but my prayer was in vain.

* It is a widely held opinion in the United States that the customs of France are still those of the eighteenth century; a great number of people believe that vice is still the fashion, that the time is passed in gallantries to the ladies, in drawing-room intrigues and frivolity. This opinon among Americans is due mainly to the influence of a number of English novelists widely read in the United States, who, knowing nothing of France themselves save through books, are half a century behind the times.

9

The Test

Nelson was inflexible. I could understand his fears, and I had no choice but to obey his wishes. I consoled myself by thinking that this obstacle was only a postponement of my happiness. Was I not sure of Marie's heart? And Nelson had promised that upon my return, if my intentions were unchanged, he would cease to oppose them. [. . .]

On the day of my departure, when I went to the bay of Baltimore to take the steamship that would bear me to New York, and at the moment when the landing boat began to pull away from the dock, Marie, who had already bidden me farewell, raised her hands toward me from the shore. "Ludovic!" she cried. "Your vows! You cannot keep them! I release you!"

I made a movement toward her, but I was on my way. I shouted into the wind; already I was too far away to be heard. [. . .]

Here Ludovic stopped; his face took on a more somber aspect, his gaze was fixed and his lips immobile, as though they refused to utter a grievous confession.

"I pray you," cried the traveler, "continue the story, which is both instructive and moving! I am eager to know your fate. Speak, I beg of you."

"I have not yet told half of my sorrows; and what interest——"

"The liveliest interest," replied the traveler, "renders me attentive to your words. You are telling me your troubles; these fascinate me. I have never sought the joys of the world, but have always felt drawn toward misfortune. The happiness of men is so mixed with pride and egotism that it bores and disgusts me; but a sweet sensation long remains in my spirit after I have wept with the unhappy."

Alas!—Ludovic went on, after a short pause—this was the era of my life of which I have the bitterest memories; it was the time when I felt that the vows which united me with my love were uncertain in my heart. Today I blush at my weakness. Heaven! Through what unhappiness I must have passed to have such criminal doubts!

With all sincerity in my heart, I had sworn to Marie that I would love her forever. The obstacle set in the way of my love, however serious it was made to appear, seemed trifling and paltry to me. What did I care for a social prejudice when I had Marie's heart for my own? But when I had reentered the world of society, with its vexations, I found myself faced by that prejudice, powerful, inflexible, widespread in all classes, which dominates America, with no voice raised against it; crushing its victims without reserve, pity, or remorse. When I saw, in the free states, the black population covered with disgrace perhaps worse than slavery; all people of color branded by public contempt, overwhelmed with abuse, more degraded by shame even than by misery: then I felt terrible conflicts stir within me. At times seized with indignation and horror, I believed I was strong enough to fight alone against all; it pleased my pride to have as adversary an entire people, the whole world! But after these noble dreams I would awaken to a thousand discouraging realities and ask myself what would be my fate, what that of Marie herself, in the midst of such bitterness and ignominy! I hesitated—that was my crime. However, my heart was not duped by the sophisms of my reason. Marie, I would tell myself, would be unhappy when we were united; but would she not be more so if our union was never formed? Would she cease to be a poor colored girl because I had broken my faith with her? Would the world stop heaping scorn upon her because she had lost the support of the only being capable of making her respected?

I took my doubts and anguish with me from city to city, to New York, Boston, Philadelphia. . . .

Here the traveler interrupted his host, for he no longer understood his meaning.

"Just now," he said, "you spoke of the fate of the black race in the Southern states, and I deplored with you the sad condition of the slaves. But, leaving Baltimore, you went to other cities in the Union, where slavery has been abolished. There a different spectacle must have offered itself to your eyes. I know very well that even in the Northern states the prejudice attaching to a man's color is not entirely crushed; but I believed it nearly extinguished."

"Do not deceive yourself," replied Ludovic, with spirit; "that prejudice has kept all its potency. In this case custom must be distinguished from law."

According to law [Ludovic continued], the Negro is equal in all points to the white; he has the same civil and political rights; he could become President of the United States; but in reality he is denied the exercise of all these rights, and only with great difficulty can he achieve a social position above that of a domestic.

In the supposedly free states, the Negro is no longer a slave, but he is a free man in name only.

I am not sure that his new condition is not worse than servitude: as a slave, he had no place in human society; now he is counted among men, but as the last.

It is not rare, in the South, to see whites who are kindly toward Negroes. Since the distance between them is immense and unchallenged, free Americans have no fear, in approaching the slave, of raising him to their level or of descending to his.

In the North, on the contrary, where equality of all is proclaimed, the whites keep their distance from the Negroes, so as not to be confused with them; they avoid them with a sort of horror, and relentlessly ostracize them as a protest against an assimilation which would humiliate them, thus maintaining by custom the distinction which the law no longer makes.

Perhaps also the oppression weighing on a whole race appears the more odious and revolting, the more free is the administration of the country in which it is encountered.

In the Orient there are barbaric lands where the caprice of a tyrant makes sport with the lives of men, where public power manifests itself in extortion and the submission of the populace in servility; where force takes the place of law, a man's whim that of justice, self-interest that of morality, universal misery that of comfort. There, each man bears his life as predestined: oppressor or oppressed, eunuch or sultan, victim or executioner. Nowhere is there good and evil; there is only good fortune or ill fortune; crime and virtue are matters of chance.

Should I be astonished to find, in such baneful lands, millions of men doomed to slavery? No; I would hardly notice that offense to morality in a society founded on contempt for all the laws of nature and humanity; there, each vice of society is a principle, not an abuse; it is necessary to the over-all harmony.

I receive a different impression when, among a free people, I encounter slaves; when I see, in the midst of a civilized Christian society, a class of people for whom that society has made a set of laws and customs apart from their own; for some, a lenient legislation, for others a bloody code; on one side, the supremacy of law, on the other, arbitrariness; for the whites the theory of equality, for the blacks the system of servitude; two contrary codes of morals: one for the free, the other for the oppressed; two sorts of public ethics: these—mild, humane, and liberal; those—cruel, barbaric, and tyrannical.

Here vice shocks me much more, because it stands out against the background of virtue—but this background of light, which renders the shadow the more salient, renders it also the more ill-placed in my sight.

Tyrants perhaps speak in good faith when they say that men cannot be ruled without cruel laws; they know no others; and these words may be believed by peoples who have known nothing but tyranny.

But such an excuse cannot be used by a nation possessing free institutions; they know that slavery is evil, because they enjoy liberty; they should detest injustice and persecution, since they practice justice, charity, and tolerance daily.

In a barbaric country, one has but one hate in the presence of the greatest misery—hate against the despot. To him alone belongs all the power; through him alone comes all the evil; against him alone are aimed all imprecations. But in a land of equality all citizens are responsible for social injustices; each is a party to them. Not a white man exists in America who is not a barbarous, iniquitous persecutor of the black race.

In Turkey, there is but one tyrant responsible for the most frightful distress; in the United States, there are, for each act of tyranny, ten million tyrants.

Such reflections were unceasingly present in my mind, and I felt a profound hatred germinating in my soul against all Americans; for Marie's unhappy lot was the work of their barbarous laws and hateful prejudices. Each of them was an enemy in my eyes.

I saw that attempts were made by a number of noble men to remedy the evil; but this evil is one of those which can be cured only by the passage of centuries.

In a society where everyone suffers equal misery, a general feeling grows up which leads to revolt, and sometimes liberty emerges from excessive oppression.

But in a country where only a fraction of society is oppressed, while the rest is quite comfortable, the majority manages to live at ease at the expense of the smaller number; everything is in order and well regulated: well-being on the one hand, abject suffering on the other. The unfortunate may complain, but they are not feared, and the disease, however revolting it may be, is not cured because it only grows deeper without spreading.

The misery of the black people oppressed by American society cannot be compared with that of any of the unfortunate classes among other peoples. Everywhere there exists hostility between the rich and the proletariat; however, the two classes are not separated by any insurmountable barrier: the poor become rich, the rich poor; that is enough to temper the oppression of the one by the other. But when the American crushes the black population with such contempt, he knows that he need never fear to experience the fate reserved for the Negro.

I was continually witnessing some sad happening which revealed to me the profound hatred of the Americans for the blacks.

One day in New York I attended a session in court. Among those awaiting trial sat a young mulatto accused by an American of acts of violence. "A white man beaten by a colored man! What an outrage! What viciousness!" voices cried out everywhere. The public, the jurors themselves were indignant at the accused man, without knowing whether he was guilty. I do not know how to tell you how distressing was my impression as he came to trial—each time the poor mulatto wished to speak, his voice was drowned out, either by the judge or by the noise of the crowd. All the witnesses damned him; the most favorable were those who said nothing actually against him. The friends of the plaintiff had good memories; those to whom the defendant appealed remembered nothing. He was found guilty without any deliberation on the part of the jury. A quiver of joy went through the crowd: a murmur a thousand times more cruel to the heart of the unhappy man than the judge's sentence; for the judge was paid for his task, while the hate of the people was gratuitous. Perhaps he was guilty; but, innocent, would he not have suffered the same fate?

However, the laws of New York State recognize only free men, equal unto each other! What worth has a legal principle when it is warped by custom? Alas! the justice which a man of color finds in America is like that which, in our country, the vanquished find at the hands of the victors after a civil war.

Negroes equal to whites! A lie! I saw, in the heart of the law courts, Americans segregated from the blacks: the former had the best seats; at the back of the room the Negro spectators were squeezed together into a narrow gallery. Why is this barrier placed between them, as if to oppose their fusing?

In Philadelphia there is a sort of asylum where boys and girls are sent who have been guilty of behavior somewhere between a misdemeanor and a crime: family influence is not strong enough, prison punishment is too rigorous for them; this asylum, severer than the one and less cruel than the other, is intended for these delinquents, who are precocious in crime but not hardened to it. Visiting this establishment one day, I was surprised to find there not one child of the black race. I inquired the reason for this of the director, who replied: "It would degrade white children to allow them to associate with creatures held in contempt by the public."

At another time, I expressed my astonishment that the children of Negroes were excluded from public schools; they told me that no American would wish to send his child to a school where there was a single black.

Then I recalled the words Marie had uttered in her despair: "The separation of Negroes from whites is found everywhere: in the churches where humans pray; in hospitals where they suffer; in the cemetery, where they sleep the eternal sleep." The picture was true, though I had regarded it as an exaggeration due to grief.

Hospitals and jails contained separate sections, where invalids and criminals were classified according to color; everywhere the whites were the object of care and solicitude which the poor Negroes could not hope for.

I saw also in every town two separate cemeteries: one for the whites, the other for colored people. A strange manifestation of human vanity! When nothing is left of men but dust and corruption, their pride cannot die, persisting still in the oblivion of the tomb! [. . .]

But what caused me the greatest wonder was to find this segregation in churches. Who would have believed it? Rank and privilege in Christian churches! The blacks are either relegated to some dark corner of the building or completely excluded.

Consider the annoyance of a select company if it were necessary that they mingle with gross and ill-clad persons. The only diversion allowed on Sundays is church attendance. For American society, gathering at the church equals attending the concert, the ball, or the theater; women appear in their most elegant dress. The Protestant church is a drawing room where one prays to God. The Americans cannot bear to encounter creatures of low degree in that place; is it not just as vexing as though the hideous sight of a black face should mar the aspect of a brilliant assembly? The majority of a meeting must agree that the doors be closed against people of color; the greater number wishes it thus—nothing can hinder them.

The Catholic churches are the only ones that will allow neither privilege nor exclusion; the black population may enter there like the whites. This tolerance on the part of Catholicism, and the rigid policing on the part of the Protestants, is no accident but is due to the very nature of the two cults.

The minister of a Protestant congregation owes his office to elections, and to keep his position he must remain in favor with the majority of his constituents; his dependence is thus complete. He must perforce, on pain of disgrace, uphold those prejudices and passions which he should combat without mercy.

On the contrary, the Catholic priest is absolute master in his church; he is answerable to none save his bishop, who in turn recognizes only the pope's authority. Leading a congregation of which he is independent, he worries little about displeasing them as he censures their errors and vices; he guides his flock according to his faith, while the Protestant minister governs his according to his own interests. A chosen few are admitted into the temple of one sect; the other opens its church to all men; the first conforms to the law, the second imposes it.

Behold the Protestant minister, docile and obsequious toward those who have allowed him to represent them; and the Catholic priest, representative of God alone, speaking with authority to men whose duty it is to obey him.

The prideful passions of the whites demand that the Protestant pastor reject the unfortunate beings from the temple, and the Negroes are excluded. But these Negroes, who are men, enter the Catholic church, because there it is not human pride which rules; the servant of Christ is the commander.

Considering this, I was struck by a sad truth: public opinion, so charitable when it protects, is the cruelest of tyrants when it persecutes. Public opinion, all-powerful in the United States, desires the oppression of a detested race, and nothing can thwart its hatred.

In general it is the function of the legislators' wisdom to modify custom by laws, which in turn are modified by custom. This moderating power does not exist in the American government. The people who hate the Negroes are those who make the laws; it is they who appoint the magistrates, and to please them every office holder must share in their passions. The impetus of popular sovereignty is irresistible; its least desires are commands; it does not give a second chance to a wayward agent—it breaks him. Thus, the people, with its passions, is the ruler; in America, the black race submits to the sovereignty of hatred and scorn.

Everywhere, I found this tyranny of the people's will. Ah, it is a strange and cruel fate for an entire people to be transplanted in a world which rejects them!

The aversion and contempt in which they are held is shown in a thousand ways. I have seen a whole family of Negroes threatened with death by starvation because of a debt of one dollar. In the United States, the law gives a creditor the right to imprison his debtor for the smallest sum; and the creditor's word is always believed. One day, I was airing my melancholy in New York when lamentable cries caught my attention. It was a poor Negro whom they were taking to prison; a black woman followed him, all in tears, with her children. Overcome by pity, I approached the Negress and asked the cause of her tears. Her glance at me was both woeful and defiant, as though she felt my question was only mockery and a cowardly jeer at her misery—a Negro in the United States has no faith in the pity of the whites; however, I repeated my question in a tone of voice which revealed my deep emotion. Then the poor woman told me that her husband was being dragged off to prison for not having the price of a few pounds of bread. "Not a single shopkeeper," she added, "will give us credit, and we've found no one who will lend us a penny!"

The pitiless creditor, who for a trifle caused so much distress, had, it is true, the letter of the law on his side, and that law was as applicable to [white] Americans as to colored people. But, though the law applied to all, its execution was not the same for all. Public mercy, which tempers the rigor of the strictest laws, is all in favor of the whites.

You can see by this one example the rank enjoyed by Negroes in public esteem: even prostitutes turn away from them; they believe that in accepting the caresses of a black they would lower the dignity of the white race! One ignominy these ignominious women will not face—that of loving a man of color.

And do not think that in the free states of the North the origin of colored people who have become white by the mixture of the races is forgotten or lost to view.

Tradition there is as severe as in the South. In vain, to baffle his enemies, does the colored man with a white face leave the country where the taint in his blood is known and go to another state to seek a new life in a new society; the mystery of his emigration is soon discovered. Public opinion, so indulgent to adventurers who hide their names and antecedents, searches pitilessly for proofs of African ancestry.

A Massachusetts bankrupt can find honor and fortune in Louisiana, where there is no inquiry into the ruin he experienced elsewhere. A New Yorker, bored by the ties of a first marriage, can desert his wife on the left bank of the Hudson and go take another on the right bank, in New Jersey, where he lives in undisturbed bigamy. A thief and forger who has flouted the severe laws of Rhode Island easily finds work and esteem in Connecticut. There is but one crime from which the guilty can nowhere escape punishment and infamy: it is that of belonging to a family reputed to be *colored*. The color may be blotted out; the stain remains. It seems that people find it out even when it is invisible; there is no refuge secret enough, no retreat obscure enough, to hide it.

Such was the land where my destiny led me! This was the world wherein I would pass my days with Nelson's daughter! In the midst of such hatred, was not all hope of happiness chimerical? Oh, how my heart ached at this injustice, the full weight of which fell upon Marie! What mighty indignation seized upon my spirit! And what bitterness grew in the depths of my soul!

10

Continuation of the Test

From that moment, I confess, American society lost its prestige in my eyes. Nature itself, which at first had seemed so brilliant, seemed faded; the loveliest days, like the loveliest places, could not charm me. All outward things become indifferent to one tormented by a secret woe. I never felt this truth more strongly than when, one day as I strolled about New York, I found myself watching a sublime spectacle without emotion.

Opposite me the rich meadows of New Jersey rolled afar, dazzling with flowers and a golden harvest. At my feet spread a majestic bay, brimming with waters from two sources worthy of its grandeur, the Hudson and the ocean; a thousand ships asail or at anchor filled the port; flags of every color flew from the mastheads, representing a great congress of all the world's nations; sails swelled, filled by the breeze; the steamboat left far behind both wind and sails; the movement of trade, the noise of industry, the activity of humanity rivaled nature in brilliance and variety; and as a background to this magnificent picture, there were the blue crests of the mountains bordering the North River. Here, at a single glance, I could see the threefold marvel of fertile nature, industrial riches, and picturesque beauty; on land, the laborer with his wagon; on the waters the merchant and his ships; in the sky the lofty peaks with their eagles: triple symbol of the needs of man, the conditions of his happiness and the daring of his spirit. Turning my gaze to the left, I perceived in the distance the cliffs of Sandy Hook:* it is from there you can see the ships coming from Europe, and from

* It must have been a very clear day. [Translator's note.]

Maryland—France and Baltimore—my father, and Marie!—my homeland and my love! And I was lost in one of those reveries, sweeter to the senses than to the soul, where, beholding the spectacle of brilliant and fertile nature, rich and prosperous humanity, calm sea and smiling sky, the unhappy dreamer still suffers at heart. The air I breathed was pure and wholesome, a thousand sights smiled before my eyes and imagination, a thousand delightful sensations besieged my being—I was happy, but only superficially. Impressions merely touched me: their attempts to penetrate my breast were vain. There is, alas! no profound joy for the man who mourns for his far-off country, who is troubled for his love and uncertain of his future.

I do not know how long my melancholy meditations would have lasted: suddenly someone seized my hand; I turned quickly and found myself embraced by George—George whom I loved so tenderly—for in him I loved a generous man and the brother of Marie. Most people avoid an unhappy man, but misfortune draws a friend closer to one.

George had just come from Baltimore; he apprised me of sad events which had occurred during my absence, which proved to me how relentless was misfortune's pursuit of his family.

In Georgia at that time there still existed some remnants of an Indian tribe called the Cherokees; faithful to their native forests, these savages refused to quit them, and on several occasions the United States government had solemnly declared that it would maintain them there. However, the Georgian American cast a jealous eye upon the Indians' fertile lands which, to yield rich harvests, demanded but little cultivation; he undertook to expel them from their domain, and his cupidity invented a thousand ways to stir up strife.

The Indians' cause should have been held doubly sacred, for it was the cause of justice as well as misfortune. These poor savages, in their great simplicity, believed they had assured their rights by saying, "We will die on our savannas because we were born here; all America belonged to our fathers, we have only a fraction left to us; let us keep it. You reproach us for our ignorance and the scarcity of produce we grow in fertile soil. But why should it matter to you? We do not understand your way of building cities and cultivating the land; we have no desire for your industries; we prefer our unspoiled forests which give us game to live on, a green roof to shelter us—and besides, we cannot leave them because they contain the bones of our fathers."

Thus spoke Mohawtan, the Indian chief, famed for his wisdom in council and his valor in combat. The Georgian American listened uncomprehendingly to his words, because they were words from the heart. He replied:

"Why live in these forests, if we give you other places? Go farther away—across the Mississippi, into Arkansas territory, or into Michigan around the Great Lakes; there you will find cool shade, wide prairies, forests full of deer and bison; the term "fatherland" has no meaning when the country of exile is worth far more than the native land."

The Indians could not comprehend this language because it was that of corruption.

The government of Georgia, faithfully representing the greedy passion of the few, first employed every kind of trickery and breach of faith to obtain the voluntary removal of the Indians. They said that the country where the Indians would live would be theirs in perpetuity; they offered them gold for the land they would abandon, and, so as to tempt them further, promised to pay them with firewater.

But the Indian chief had the good sense to reply: "We will follow the example of our fathers who did not give in to the white man. Though these built their cabins near our forests, they agreed not to trouble us; how does it happen that today they want us to leave? Already we have sold much of our land; they told us that money would make our lives easier and happier, but it slipped from our hands as they were taking over our forests, and our ways have not changed. You offer us firewater, which we like; I do not know how it happens that what is so good causes evil, but since we have learned to enjoy that delicious liquor, quarrels, brawls, and murders abound among us. White men! I know no reply to your words, except to say that we are always the more unhappy after listening to them."

Seeing that they would obtain nothing by cunning and ruse, the Americans resorted to violence, not that of arms but that of decrees; for these lawmakers, faced with ignorant savages, engaged them in a lawyers' war;* and, to hide their iniquity under a semblance of justice, expelled them from their lands *in due form.* The legislature of Georgia decreed that the Indians were not landowners but merely usufructuaries; that it was in the province of the national sovereignty to fix the duration of this enjoyment of rights; declaring that the term was up, it authorized the Americans to take over the Indians' territory. The Indians, unversed in the distinctions between tenant and owner under law, understood the decree not at all, except that they were hunted out of their homes; they raised one more protest. The quarrel was referred to the United States Supreme Court; this august tribunal at the top of the social ladder, in an atmosphere inaccessible to mass hysteria, solemnly pronounced in favor of the natives and declared that no one had the right to dispossess them. The question seemed to be closed. However, since businessmen are never at a loss for legal excuses, even for breaking the law, the Georgians contemptuously disregarded the Supreme Court ruling, saying that the question was not within the sphere of that tribunal's action. This was not a declaration of war, but it rendered war inevitable.

These events took place shortly after my departure from Baltimore; they excited lively indignation in all generous souls. Nelson, who all his life had deeply sympathized with the unfortunate Indians, at these new developments could not control his zealous ardor. "These unfortunates," he cried, "will evoke some pity in New England, but not one Southerner will lift a finger against oppression; only a short distance lies between me and them; I owe them my support; I will stand up for their rights, and will prove whether justice and law have become empty words in a country where once they reigned supreme."

So Nelson traveled to Virginia, and thence into the Cherokee country, leaving George with Marie. He at once gained the confidence of the Indians by speaking to them of religion, and tried appealing to the Georgians through the language of reason and justice. His words influenced both sides; they inspired the Cherokees to the defense of their rights and shook the convictions of a number of Americans—until then strongly opposed to the Indians—

* See the footnote on pp. 84–85 below.

who suspected for the first time that their hatred might be as unjust as it was cruel. However, the majority of Georgians persisted in their covetousness, and Nelson's conduct irritated them to such a degree that the legislature, instrument of their passions, ordered the Presbyterian minister thrown into jail as an instigator of civil war. This violent reaction caused great unrest among the Indians and their partisans. A regiment of the United States Army was sent by the President to lend support to the decree of the Supreme Court, whose authority the Georgians had disregarded. These, on their side, defied the Federal government and called up the State militia. Everything pointed toward an immediate and violent clash, when, yielding either through fear or through weariness of a life incessantly vexed by chicanery and bad faith, half the Cherokees resolved upon exile and, without any formality, gave up to the Americans the lands which were the object of their greed. After two months' imprisonment, Nelson was released from his cell; he returned to Baltimore, counting for very little the barbarities he had suffered himself but pierced to the heart by the misfortunes he had witnessed and tried vainly to alleviate. As soon as Nelson had arrived in Baltimore, George had left for New York.*

* After innumerable attempts by the people of Georgia to seize the lands of the Cherokees, the Cherokees asked the Federal government to intervene in their behalf. The government of the United States at first gave them its support and tried to safeguard them within limits guaranteed by the treaties; but as the disputes continued and became increasingly violent, the President ended up by declaring to the Cherokees that he had no wish to intervene in their quarrels with Georgia and that they should come to terms as best they could with the government of that State. He added that to facilitate an agreement he offered to move them at the expense of the Federal government to the right bank of the Mississippi. After this declaration, the Georgians intensified their vexations and their persecution of the Indians, in order to make the President's offer more tempting to them. They had noticed that the Indians' resistance was due mainly to the advice they received from the missionaries who had come to convert them to Christianity and who believed, quite correctly, that it would be futile to attempt to civilize savages without first settling them permanently on their land. As a result, the government of Georgia passed a law which forbade all whites whatsoever to settle permanently on Cherokee territory under the penalty of a fine and of imprisonment. These legal threats notwithstanding, two missionaries persisted in remaining with the Indians, and the government of Georgia had them arrested. They were tried and sentenced to prison. They appealed to the Supreme Court of the United States. That tribunal, fearing

After telling me of these sad happenings, George spoke of his sister. I listened and questioned eagerly. He told me such moving things of Marie that I was ashamed of my uncertainties. I forgot my dreary doubts of the future, to think of nothing but my love. How strong a force is the respect of a friend! George, by his sincerity and his confidence in my feelings toward his sister, strengthened me more by his uprightness than he could ever have done by cunning or deception.

I soon noticed something unusual in George's countenance; his words—frank and natural when he spoke of his family—became mysterious and embarrassed when our conversation took a more general turn. Reticences, brief exclamations, suddenly restrained gestures announced that some deep feeling was at work within him which he tried vainly to suppress. It was not long before I understood that his agitation was connected with his condition as a man of color. Several of my remarks upon the misery of the blacks had caused him to shudder, and while I railed with some feeling against the injustices I had noticed in American society, I perceived the shadow of a smile playing across his lips, and, seizing my hand, he said firmly, "Courage, friend, we shall see better times—the dawn of liberty is not far off. The oppression weighing on our brothers in Virginia has reached full measure—the same tyranny will engender revolt among the Indians; soon——" And as though he regretted having said these words he checked himself; his face darkened, his look became terrible. He had ceased speaking, but his thoughts continued in their course. I questioned him. "The future," he replied in a mysterious tone, "the near future will answer you." These words, and the voice in which he pronounced them, disquieted me; but George dismissed the subject.

---

that by finding in favor of the defendants it might provoke Georgia into seceding from the Union, was genuinely embarrassed. To break out of this impasse, a compromise was reached. The Supreme Court postponed its decision; in the meantime, the government of Georgia pardoned the two condemned men, and the appeal of the two defendants was not given a hearing.

Such, in brief outline, was the dispute between the Cherokees and Georgia. Whatever in this book does not accord with these facts has been modified only to maintain the interest of the narrative. Let us add that the migration of part of the Indians—a consequence of this dispute—and the officious assistance the Federal government gave the emigrants are equally well-established facts.

Then we abandoned ourselves to that delightful conversation known to friendship alone, of which only love can form the text. It is so rarely one finds a friend who understands the mysteries of one's heart!

George was not an everyday confidant: the fact that he was the brother of the woman I loved gave to my friendship for him all the charms of a more tender sentiment; in his soul there was a little of Marie's soul—he cherished her whom I adored—and in his naïve confidence he loved in me the future husband of his sister.

As we unbosomed ourselves we went where chance led our steps. We approached the New York Theater, where a crowd was milling about, and I heard several voices pronounce these words: "Napoleon at Schoenbrunn and at Saint Helena." It was the announcement of this play which had drawn the crowd to the theater, ordinarily empty, and roused the Americans from their accustomed indifference.

The name of Napoleon is great the world over! There is no land so distant that it has not heard of his glory; no earth so firm that it did not tremble at his fall. A Frenchman can travel in all countries without fear of scorn or insult; he will find welcoming faces everywhere; as a Frenchman he is always received with honor.

The American from Louisiana and the Englishman from Canada do not identify themselves with the unfortunate and humbled France of today; but when you speak with them about Napoleon they suddenly remember that their forebears were French.

I dragged George toward the theater, drawn myself much less by a wish for amusement than by the instinct of national pride. Alas! Could I have but foreseen that the evening would bring a bitter close to a day which had not been without sweetness!

I keenly enjoyed the play, which I had seen a year before in France. The costume, the gestures, the curt speeches, and the silence of the Man of the Century held as powerful a sway over the American audience as over an assembly of Frenchmen; to tell the truth, the name of Napoleon carried the whole play, for the majority of the audience understood not a word of our language. However, the enthusiasm was general; liberty applauded glory.

At last I felt happiness enter my heart, but my ears were struck by noisy shouts arising from the audience; I looked about me and saw a thousand insulting fingers pointed toward the seats that George and I occupied. We heard cries of "Throw him out! He is a colored man!" All eyes were fixed upon us. The shouting died away at times, but soon recommenced louder than before; the crowd was alternately calmed and aroused, as though what vexed them was sometimes in doubt, sometimes a certainty. I distinguished in the crowd a single man who appeared to be directing them and who made great efforts to communicate to everyone his real or feigned indignation. "Disgraceful!" he cried. "There's a mulatto among us!" And he pointed out George. Then the general cry arose, "Throw him out! He is a colored man!"

I realized at the beginning of this scene the disastrous possibilities, and my heart contracted. George remained motionless and silent; his eyes snapped sparks of fury. The shouting grew constantly more clamorous; there was a general stamping sound. Then a man rose and made signs that he wished to speak. Everyone quieted.

"Why," said this American, whose name I never knew, and who, from his philanthropy, seemed to be a Quaker—except that Quakers do not go to the theater—"why evict this man? There is no indication that he is of the black race: someone accuses him of being colored, but he cannot prove it." These words, calmly spoken, were greeted by a murmur of approval. No voice was raised in contradiction; the instigator of the disturbance was no longer in the place where I had noticed him. Calm, which exerts so powerful a hold on Americans that it almost resembles a violent passion, suddenly resumed its sway; a terrible storm had been averted, when George, whose long suppressed anger must needs explode, cried out in a terrible voice, "Yes! Yes—I am a colored man!" And he gazed at the assembly defiantly. A thunder of shouts met this declaration. "Get out! Wretch! Scoundrel!" sounded from every side. Nelson's son remained impassive. The wrath of the multitude reached full pitch; they were shouting the grossest insults. Rising from his seat with a gesture of scorn, George cried: "Cowards! You are a thousand to one, and I defy you all! I demand satisfaction for your affronts!"

This brave speech stirred up mutterings and hoots of laughter.

"This man is disrupting the show," said an American near me, stolidly. "He is a colored man, and he persists in staying here."

As he said this he indicated George to some policemen who had turned up to carry out the orders of the public.

"This is shameful!" I cried, turning to the American, whose

calm hostility irritated me more than the noisy hatred of the mob. "I am happy," I said, "to distinguish an enemy among the general confusion; the man you are insulting is as dear to me as a brother, and I demand that you make amends for these insults to my friend."

"Your friend? Then you are a colored man too?"

"If I were, I would not be ashamed of it, but you are mistaken, and if you refuse to give satisfaction to people of African blood, you will doubtless not refuse it to a Frenchman."

The American answered coolly, "I came here to see the play, not to fight a duel. No, I will not fight. Because this mulatto obstinately sits here, do I have to kill you or be killed by you?"

"What a coward!" I cried, in furious indignation, and I would have struck his face, but that I saw George struggling with the police, who had dragged him from his seat; perhaps it was the sight of this violence which calmed me; I sensed the further dangers in this already serious conflict; I seized George and drew him outside the theater, saying the all-powerful words, "Think of Marie!" I hastened to propitiate the authorities; we went before an alderman, to whom I gave my pledge for the good conduct of George and myself. We were soon restored to liberty.

In the United States, as in England, money is a universal passport, and there is hardly a penal law which cannot be circumvented by paying. This phenomenon is conceivable in an aristocracy like England; but it is hardly understandable in a democracy which does not recognize superiority through riches.

The next day George had passed from the most violent exasperation to a somber, silent fury; his silence frightened me more than his outbursts of anger; I heard him muttering these words: "What a fate—to have to bear insults and not avenge them!"

"Friend," I said, interrupting him, "do not breathe that complaint in my presence: because I am happy—it is I who will avenge the insult; the proud American will be forced to make to me the amends he has refused to your blood." As we spoke thus, on the public street, our attention was attracted by a lively conversation, in which several people were taking part. The quarrel at the theater was the subject of their argument. One of them was saying, "The audacity of colored people is a strange thing."

"What did you think of that Frenchman," said another, "who challenged the Bostonian to a duel? They say the Yankee got hit in the face; well, the man who hit him will have a lawsuit on his hands!"

"Just listen to them!" cried George contemptuously, and we went on our way.

This, indeed, is the general procedure in the Northern states. All quarrels end in the law courts; they rigidly follow the principle that no one should take the law into his own hands; everyone appeals to the law.

It is not thus in all the Southern and Western states. There dueling is still found—or something that resembles it.

It is no longer the polite contest of courtesy and chivalry, in which two intrepid champions stand face to face, eager more for honor than for blood, fearing almost as much to be victors as vanquished; and who, more rivals than enemies, more bound by a principle than a passion, aspire less to triumph by force or skill than to vie with one another in generosity.

In America, the duel is always fought over a serious matter and almost always ends in a fatality; they give or accept a challenge not in order to comply with polite custom, but to advertise their rancor. The duel is not a formal custom, a tradition; it is the means of taking the life of one's enemy. Among us, the most serious duel usually ends with the first blood drawn; in America it rarely ceases before the death of one of the combatants.

In the American character there is a mixture of coldness and violence which lends a somber and cruel aspect to their passions; when he fights a duel, the American does not yield to impulse; he calculates his hatred, deliberates on his hostility, ponders his vengeance.

In the West there are semicivilized states, where the duel, in its barbaric form, comes near being assassination; and even in the Southern states, where manners are more polished, they fight much less for the sake of honor than for the sake of killing.

At any rate, the barbarity of the American duel is the surest guarantee of its approaching disappearance; it cannot withstand the influence of advancing civilization; on the contrary, the duel persists despite the light of civilization in countries where the very refinement of its ritual preserves it, where it is deeply rooted in a tradition of elegance and an exalted conception of honor.

The episode at the theater had thrown George into an indescribable state of demoralization; his spirit was deeply troubled, and violent feelings doubtless fermented within him; he seemed the master of his rage; resignation was discernible in his anger. George's self-control frightened me; it appeared to me that he was revolving some momentous scheme, that he resisted being overruled by his strong feelings only because he was under the yoke of a powerful idea; he passed his nights in meditation, and during the day had unaccountable conversations with colored people of whom he had never told me. Fearing for him because of his impetuosity and his wounded soul, I forced Marie's brother to listen to all the advice which the tenderest friendship could inspire. Twenty times I thought the secret would burst from his heart—but at the instant when his lips were about to reveal it, he would clap his hand to his mouth almost convulsively and force back into his bosom the mystery he had so nearly allowed to escape.

However, to forestall any more regrettable consequences, I hastened to make a few overtures to the New York authorities. I visited the governor of the State, the lieutenant governor, the mayor, and the keeper of the city's public records; I found in these officials a simplicity which surprised me; a kindliness which was touching: no luxury in their houses, no affectation in their manners, no haughtiness, nothing which would declare them to be men of power. Since rank does not exist in the United States, there are no upstarts, and consequently no insolence. Then, public officials are changed so often, and know so well that their tenure is brief, that they remain simple citizens to save themselves the trouble of constant change.

Each of them was astonished at my interest in a man of color; however, not one censured me; they even approved of my conduct, regarded in a philosophical light.

I had been introduced to the governor by one of his friends; he listened to me without once interrupting (a strange thing on the part of a public official). When I had finished, he reflected, and told me: "I will fix up this business." I told him that it was already in process of law. "That makes no difference," he replied. The very next day he let me know that no proceedings would be directed against either George or myself.

In a republic, officials have less definite power than in a monarchy, and more discretionary authority. The people are always wary of delegating too much of their sovereignty; they grant little power to their agents but allow them to do a great deal when they see that their actions are in accord with public sentiment. The theater audience had expressed the wish that George be expelled from the room, but the governor rightly thought that no one would insist on his being brought to judgment. So justice had nothing more to do with it. The public official is not, in the United States, as he is in France, zealous to establish himself as the redresser of all wrongs and the avenger of private injuries. Among us, he follows the law; in America, public opinion.

I regarded it as unexpected good fortune to have escaped the difficulties George's violence might have brought upon us. He paid scant attention to the happy issue of my proceedings; he noticed the good deeds of the magistrates only to be irritated by them, for nothing is harder to bear than good will on the part of an enemy. A few days later, he left me to return to Baltimore. I had not discovered his motive in coming to New York. Alas! I would have redoubled my advice and questions, had I guessed the object of his journey, had I foreseen the evils which were to follow.

11

The Test: Episode of Onéda

George's departure cast me once again into despondency and disgust with life: a friend who leaves us in time of misfortune is a support which fails us—the ray of light, the only solace in the dungeon, which, fading, leaves the captive to the horrors of darkness.

The time of trial was almost up; in two months I would once more see Nelson's daughter. But how my state of mind had changed since my departure from Baltimore! My love for Marie was still the great interest in my life, but no longer did it alone fill my soul. I still believed in a happy future, but no longer in that future of immense happiness of which George's sister had caused me to dream. In the love of a young heart there is a fine hopeful faith, which laughs at storms, and which a breath of adversity can dissipate. At the time when I still had my illusions, I would hardly admit that in the delicious cup of life there could be a little bitterness; now I was willing to give thanks to God if, in the bitter chalice of existence, I could find a few drops of felicity.

My heart was full of Marie; but my love for her was inseparable from the too-well-founded fear of the evils which threatened us. My apprehensions became more sharp, my sorrow more cruel, and even my hesitations dared to come into the open.

Something strange was taking place within me: the approach of my reunion with her whom I loved terrified me, although these last two months of my trial weighed upon me with crushing heaviness. [. . .]

With my eyes fixed on a shadowy future, I endeavored to penetrate its mysteries, but in vain. The greatest effort of foresight showed me even in the dim distance that mixture of good and ill. I could not love Marie without happiness, nor live in the society of Americans with a colored wife without frightful sufferings; but what would be the sum of the pain? and the sum of the pleasure? [. . .] Would not the misfortunes exceed our strength of resistance? Would Heaven send us, at least occasionally, a calm and sunny day to dry the tempest's floods?

And, gazing beyond the horizon, which my revery had widened, I sought a few gentle rays of light; but most often, alas! I could see naught but sad and somber clouds. At one time in my weakness, I would bow under discouragement; at another, proudly raising my head, I would tell myself that these threats in the future could be exorcized.

In the midst of these alternations of strength and weakness, courage and despair, a great thought came to me, presenting itself like a light to my spirit, and filled me with enthusiasm by rekindling in my breast the dying flames of my first hopes.

I had seen American society dominated by a prejudice which offended against my reason, my interests, and my heart. Could this prejudice endure forever? I could not believe it. I continued to hear each day that public opinion became more enlightened on this point. Was it then impossible to speed the progress of opinion? What glory to the man summoned by his destiny or his genius to redress so tragic a wrong! If I should be that man! If I should annihilate this blind and cruel hatred among the Americans! I would have not only the merit and joy of a noble action; I would receive happiness, too, as my reward! The odious prejudice blighting the black race would be corrected; Marie no longer would be an outcast among women! Very well, I would undertake the great labor! I would shine in literature and the arts! My ambition would be unlimited, because the goal was immense! One success would be the measure of the next. If I could rise to celebrity! If, in this uninitiated country, I, as an inspired poet, could cause untouched spirits to vibrate with enthusiasm! Then I should become a powerful man in this land where public opinion was sovereign! Then I would proclaim to a world accustomed to listening to me: "There is a woman whom you hate; I love her. You reject her with scorn; I surround her with adoration. A colored woman, you call her. No, you are wrong; this is no woman, she is an angel. No human creature is the equal of Marie. Marie is beautiful, and so much modesty adorns her beauty! She is brilliant, and nature has mingled such graces with her talents to make them pleasing! She is unhappy; and how sweet is the perfume of sadness in the tears she sheds!"

If there should be souls insensible of my voice, I would seize the chisel of Phidias and display to all eyes the charming features of my love, and I would say: "Behold that lovely head! Is not her brow that of a pure and candid maiden? What blemish dishonors her beauty? Where is the stain with which you reproach her? This marble dazzles your sight, but the countenance of Marie surpasses it in whiteness!"

And the world, led by my songs of praise, would prostrate itself at the feet of my idol!

Such was my plan; it was a bold thought indeed! But it was generous and beautiful. How admirable a goal to strive for! What glory if I succeeded! How rich a prize the reward! To be happy, I must become a famous artist or an illustrious poet. By being a genius I would find my way to happiness! Marie would be honored among women, if I should become great among men! My heart leaped at this sublime allurement, so impatient it was to pour through my soul the noble inspirations which the mind alone cannot supply.

Alas! Why do I tell you more of a plan which was yet another illusion in my life, and which I must needs abandon before even undertaking it? My error was perhaps excusable; had I not been led to believe that in America I would find people with a taste for literature and the fine arts?

These great forests adjacent to the cities; these deep, eternal solitudes, where the spirit of the primeval ages still resides; these Indians, simple of soul but strong of heart, subjected to great hardship but rejoicing in their wild liberty; these beautiful skies; these gigantic rivers, torrents, cataracts; this land between two oceans; these huge lakes, seas in themselves—all the poetry of nature had made me think that there was poetry, too, in the hearts of men! I was soon disenchanted.

Here Ludovic ceased as though his tale were done, but his last words had greatly excited the curiosity of the traveler, who spoke these words:

"My indignation is as strong as yours at this poisonous prejudice of which you were the victim—for all my sympathy, like yours, is with the unfortunate race. Since you were ready to attempt the rehabilitation of the blacks in America through the influence of reason and spirit, I would have given my hearty approval to this noble enterprise. How then could you so quickly have abandoned such a splendid plan?"

"You would not understand," Ludovic replied, "the obstacle which abruptly arrested my course; to attain my end, I would have had to rely upon poetry, the fine arts, upon imagination and enthusiasm; as though these had any power over a practical, commercial, industrial people!"

"But," the traveler went on, "this nation is not the cradle of Fulton only; cannot its literary spirit pride itself upon bringing into the world Franklin, Irving, Cooper?"

"No," said Ludovic sharply. "You are uninformed about this country—I must open your eyes."

As the hermit uttered these words, his ears and the traveler's were struck by sorrowful sounds which echoed from above; raising their eyes to the summit of the rock at the foot of which they were seated, they perceived several Indian women who, gathered in a circle, were preparing for a funeral ceremony. The interest of the traveler was aroused; he rose. Ludovic's tale was broken off; and both went in silence toward the scene.

The tears and lamentations of these women, and the pious duty they performed, had as object the commemoration of a recent tragedy in that wilderness, the circumstances of which are such as to arouse pity.

Not far from Ludovic's cottage lived Mantéo, an Indian hunter of the Ottawa tribe; he had married while yet at a tender age a young girl named Onéda. She was remarkable for the beauty of her features, and even more so for the goodness of her heart; nothing could equal her tenderness toward her husband, who himself loved and cherished none but her, despite the custom among the Indians of taking several wives.*

Several years passed, during which nothing troubled the peace

* See Appendix F, pp. 222–23.

of that happy marriage; never had life in the wilderness rendered two beings more happy than were Onéda and Mantéo.

Mantéo was renowned in his tribe as a skillful hunter and an intrepid warrior; there was not an Indian girl who did not cast a jealous eye upon Onéda's happiness, and not a mother but wished that her daughter might have such a protector as Mantéo. Those who were in a position to hope for such an alliance told him that a great future was in store for him and that the Ottawa tribe was on the point of electing him their chief, but that his exclusive attachment to Onéda was an obstacle to his fortune: a warrior as powerful as he, said the mothers, needed several wives to entertain worthily the numerous guests who came to him because of his fame.

This talk having swelled his pride and kindled his ambition, he contracted a new marriage with the daughter of an Indian chief; but he said nothing beforehand to Onéda about this union, because he feared her just reproaches; to prepare her for her unhappiness he merely announced one day his intention to take a second wife: he had conceived the plan, he said, in Onéda's interest alone, for the burdens of the household were overwhelming her, and she needed help.

Onéda received this declaration with all the marks of the liveliest grief; to oppose Mantéo's plan she used words so touching, and at the same time so emphatic, that he saw at once that he would never obtain her consent.

Then, rending the veil which hid half the truth from Onéda's eyes, Mantéo declared that resistance on her part was in vain; that he had long since made his choice, and that the very next day he would lead his new wife to his dwelling. On hearing these words, Onéda was struck with amazement. "You will drive me to despair," she said to Mantéo, and she cried bitterly.

Disregarding these portents of grief, the Indian proclaimed his new marriage, and had a great feast prepared to which he invited the whole tribe. The following day, when preparations for the banquet had begun, Onéda left her hut and seated herself at a distance. Pensive and desolate, she seemed a stranger to all that passed about her; her fixed and somber gaze showed that she was contemplating some dire plan.

All the Indians having assembled, Mantéo, his betrothed, and their families arrived, and were met with cries of joy. A single note of sadness would have been out of place amid this gaiety; no one thought of Onéda, save perhaps Mantéo, who stifled his thoughts of her as though they were a hidden guilt.

However, in the midst of the festivities with their noisy outbursts, a young woman could be seen, slowly climbing the path which led to the crest of the rock. Soon they recognized her for Onéda, who, reaching the summit, called upon Mantéo aloud, deploring his inconstancy and cruelty; the light wind carried her words to the scene of the feast. Then they heard her singing a lament for the happiness she had enjoyed while she possessed the undivided love of her husband. They soon realized that this was her death song. Those sweet memories, carried by the breeze to Mantéo's soul, the sound of that still dear voice, the contrast of those foreboding tones with the joyous songs of the feast, gripped the Indian with profound emotion and searing remorse. He flung himself toward the rock, calling Onéda, swearing that he loved and would love none but her. As he spoke thus, his feet hardly touched the earth, scaling the precipitous rock. All the guests followed; pity and terror filled every soul. The Indian men, who had guessed the young woman's fatal intention, hastened to the foot of the cliff to catch her in their arms. Each one cried out to her, and begged her, in terms of touching entreaty, not to carry out her plan. Already Mantéo had reached the summit of the rock.

"Onéda! Onéda!" he cried.

"Mantéo is a traitor!" replied the Indian girl.

"Have mercy, my beloved! My heart is yours alone—oh, wait! Yet an instant——"

And as Mantéo, panting, was about to seize his wife and imprison her in his arms, Onéda, who had just uttered the last words of her funeral hymn, flung herself from the top of the rock into the lake, where she perished before the eyes of all.

This tragic event had spread mourning among the Ottawas; among the women especially it caused the keenest sorrow, and they dug a grave on the rock itself, scene of the tragedy. Each day since the funeral rites, the Indian women gathered in that place to weep for poor Onéda. It was the third time that they had come to pay their tribute of tears to her memory when they were heard by Ludovic and the traveler. The latter, who had approached them, saw the women light a fire over the tomb and prepare the feast of the dead. Each of them threw into the flames a few sweet-scented grains, hoping to attract the spirit of the unhappy wife by the perfume they breathed into the air; they sang in turn the stanzas of a funeral hymn, repeating the chorus in unison:

"Weep for Onéda: she loved Mantéo, ah, too well! Mantéo loved her not." [. . .]

And the Indian girls, after repeating the ritual feast for the dead, retired in silence.

Ludovic had already witnessed one of these scenes of mourning, which varied only in form; but all was new to the traveler, who was surprised to find among savages such sorrowful lamentations for such a tragedy.

This incident having suspended Ludovic's story, he led the traveler back to the cabin.

The following day, the traveler reminded his host of his promise; and, as they strolled beneath the forest vault, still filled with the impressions of the previous evening, the traveler said:

"Everything in America offends your eyes and wounds your heart! How does it happen that I am enchanted and filled with sweet emotions by this virgin soil? Those Indian women, with their naïve ceremonies and their devout grief, presented a picture of primitive innocence; thus, after seeing among the Americans all the marvels that ingenuity can invent, I find on the same soil the most moving spectacles of nature. Ah! I understand—you must have been unhappy, for you are unjust."

Ludovic listened to these words without replying; he led the traveler to the waterfall where they had sat the evening before; he reflected for some moments, his head upon his knees, then spoke.

You believe that I am unjust to America, and you, my friend, are unjust to me. Ah! you do not know how sincere was my admiration for this country, and I could never tell you all that my disillusionment cost me in tears and sorrow. During the first months that followed my departure from Baltimore, preoccupied as I was with a single thought, I admit that I saw in American society nothing but the relationship between the whites and the colored people; and the shocking injustice of the Americans toward an unfortunate race, I avow, inspired in me a general prejudice against them.

But, after my imagination had conceived those glorious plans, after I realized that, in order to secure for Marie the dignity and rank that were hers by right, I must first mingle with the men of this country, I ceased to see American society from a single point of view, and soon the illusion born of a new hope changed the prism's facets before my eyes. I saw among the Americans virtues instead of vices and, in place of shadows, brilliant light.

Though this impression was fleeting, it has not been effaced entirely, and while the American character no longer dazzles me, I can still see it surrounded by a softening light.

How I marveled at American sociability! * Owing to the absence of class and rank, there is no aristocratic pride or lower-class insolence in this country.

Here, all men being equals, they are always ready to render each other mutual services, and the benefactor does not inquire beforehand into the rank and fortune of his debtor.

Nothing is more favorable to sociability than middling circumstances. Neither the poor nor the rich are sociable: the first because they need everyone's help without being able to render any service; the second because they need no one's help: since they pay for all services they render none.

In every country where rank is distinctly marked, the aristocracy and the lowest class are perpetually at war: the one armed with its luxury and arrogance, the other with its misery and hatred, each with its own pride. An inferior who tries vainly to raise himself hurls insults at the goal he cannot achieve; he has all the injustice of the oppressed, all the violence of the weak. A man of the upper classes falls into the same excesses, impelled by a different cause. When he treats as equals his inferiors, they believe he is afraid of them; he is forced to be haughty, under pain of passing for a dolt. This struggle is still bitterer in those countries where privilege is threatened by the rise of democracy. There the triumph of the people shows all the characteristics of vengeance, and the mighty

* See Appendix G, pp. 223–25.

who succumb could not fall with dignity unless they preserved all their aristocratic arrogance.

In the United States one meets with neither the haughtiness of the one class nor the anger of the other.

Not that the Americans have polished manners; the majority show neither elegance nor gentility. But their rudeness is never intentional, and it comes not from pride but from a defective education.* No one is less touchy than an American: he never thinks anyone intends to offend him.

When a Frenchman is rude, it is because he means to be so; the American would always be polite, if he knew how.

I swear I found these relationships of perfect equality delightful. It is so painful in Europe to be incessantly running the risk of ranking oneself too high or too low; to come up against the disdain of some or the envy of others! Here everyone is sure of assuming his proper place; the social ladder has but one rung, universal equality.†

Nevertheless, there are rich and poor people in the United States, but few of either; and, by the very nature of the political institutions, the rich have such need of the poor that, if there is a preeminence, one cannot tell on which side it lies. The rich make the poor work in their factories, but the poor cast their votes for or against the rich in elections.

Certainly, the masses, placed between the two extremes—the rich and the poor—model themselves more on the second than on the first.

I remember seeing Mr. Henry Clay, General Jackson's redoubtable opponent in the contest for the Presidency of the United States, traveling all over the country in an old hat and a coat full of holes. He was paying court to the common people.

Each regime has its oddities, and every sovereign his whims. To please Louis XIV one had to be polished to the point of ceremoniousness; to please the American people one must be simple to the point of coarseness.

In England, where birth and wealth are everything, the upper classes, with their elegant manners, barely tolerate the common

* See Appendix H, pp. 225–26.

† See Appendix I, pp. 226–31.

ways of the bourgeois and the proletariat; the latter feel they must make excuses for their condition. In America, the rich are the ones who are apologetic for their luxury and politeness. In England, authority comes from above; in the United States, from below.

What makes Americans eminently sociable is perhaps the same thing that prevents them from having fine manners: there are no privileges to arouse envy, but also no upper classes whose elegance could serve as a model for others.

As for me, I admit I like the involuntary rudeness of the plebeian better than the insolent politeness of the courtier.

Again, I admired in the Americans a quality which is valuable among a free people, that of good sense. I believe that in no other country in the world does there exist so much reason, universally widespread, as in the United States.

There are certain countries in Europe where the same moral or political problem receives a thousand different and contradictory solutions. One is sure, on the contrary, of finding the Americans agreed on almost every principle concerning public and private life. You will not meet with one who would deny the usefulness of religious belief and the necessity to be law-abiding.

Every one of them knows everything that is happening in his country, judges it with wisdom, and speaks of it only with caution and after due reflection.

Americans are accustomed to traveling and have a liking for it; almost every one has, at least once in his life, traversed the area between the frontiers of Canada and the Gulf of Mexico. Thus experience reinforces their natural common sense. Among them one finds neither an exclusive admiration for objects of antiquity, nor foolish wonder at novel things, nor inveterate prejudices, nor absurd superstitions.*

* In many European countries, it is argued that there is a degree of perfection for all the moral and political sciences and even the arts, which has already been reached, and beyond which nothing remains to be discovered. That is why all creations of art and industry are stamped with a definitely splendid and durable character. Everything—laws, constitutions, monuments—has been made with a view to eternity. Quite the contrary in the United States. There is nothing they believe to be definitely set. The loftiest sciences, the most sensible laws, the most marvelous inventions, are considered only as experiments. Thus everything they do is of a provisional nature.

They construct a building which will last for twenty years; who knows

The excellence of their good sense is due, perhaps, to the small range of their passions; what makes me believe this is that when they abandon themselves to their national pride, the most exalted of all their sentiments, they lose all reason entirely.

Their limited taste for poetry, for the fine arts, and for the speculative sciences favors them still more in this respect. A man does not go so far astray in his chosen path when he follows neither swift flights of fancy nor dazzling flashes of inspiration.

The meditating philosopher, the savant whose eyes are constantly gazing toward Heaven, those who are moved by an appealing harmony in nature, hardly understand the practical things in life.

This power of reason, the preeminence of common sense over the passions, serves to explain the admirable composure of the Americans.* Insensible to great joys, the American remains unshaken by any misfortune. The most unexpected blow, the most imminent peril, finds him impassive. Strange contrast! He pursues fortune with extreme ardor, and calmly bears all adversity. Nothing stops him in his undertakings; nothing discourages his efforts; when faced by an obstacle, no matter how great, he will never say, "I cannot." Bold, patient, indefatigable, he tries again. This people is steadfastly faithful to its origins; for it was born of exiles, and men who will travel three thousand miles across the sea in search of a new fatherland must needs have a fund of energy in their souls.

Ah! No one, I swear, admires the people of the United States more than I do on this score; it is this same good judgment, this practical common sense and daring enterprise, which have given

---

whether in twenty years there will not be a better way of building? A law is adopted which may be obscure, carelessly drawn up; what is the use of elaborating on it? Perhaps next year they will have recognized its faults.

* I have had, during my stay in America, a thousand occasions to judge the Americans' coolheadedness. I will cite but one example. As I was going down the Ohio River on a steamboat, on which several merchants were traveling with their goods, our boat, named *The Fourth of July*, struck a reef called the Burlington Bar, about five miles below Wheeling, and broke up. This is not the place to relate the circumstances of that accident, or those perils one may assume are always augmented by the imagination or memory of the voyager. I will confine myself to saying that, the boat having sunk, all the goods it contained were destroyed or damaged, and that in the face of the fact that for some this meant considerable loss and for others complete ruin, the American merchants uttered not a single cry of grief or despair.

birth to American industry, whose marvels astonish us. Look at those canals, rivaling rivers, whose destiny it is one day to join the Pacific to the Atlantic; those railroads which penetrate the hearts of mountains, and along which steam power hurls itself faster and more mightily than across the level unity of the waters; the factories which spring up everywhere, the businesses which enrich the commerce of all the nations; the ports where thousands of vessels cross paths; everywhere wealth and plenty; in place of wild forests, fertile fields; instead of deserts, magnificent cities and smiling villages, sprung from the soil by I know not what magic, as if the old earth of America, wild and savage for so long, were pregnant at last with a civilized future, her fertile bosom engendering crops without cultivation and cities without labor, as she used to bring forth forests.

A witness of this prosperity, unrivaled among other peoples, I wondered at it, and wonder still; but it is all material, and it was a world of the spirit that I missed!

Ah! Why have the Americans less heart than head? Why so much intelligence without spirit, so much wealth without resplendence, so much strength without grandeur, so many unpoetic marvels?

Perhaps the industrial quality which characterizes that society arises from the very order that regulates the destiny of nations.

Here Ludovic stopped; but at the instant his voice became mute, his glance appeared more expressive. It was easy to see that he was led by his unspoken thoughts into profound meditation. Finally, in a voice which presaged utterances both poetic and inspired, he let fall the following words in the silence of that lonely place.

12

The Test: Literature and Fine Arts

When one considers the past, three great epochs appear in the life of mankind:

The first is antiquity—the age of Sappho and Aspasia, Horace and Lucullus, Alcibiades and Caesar; a brilliant epoch, the senses being supreme.

The second is Christianity—the time of Saints Augustine and Athanasius, of Saint Louis and of Du Guesclin, of Pascal and Bossuet; a moral epoch, the soul being supreme.

The third begins with the century of Voltaire and Helvétius, Condillac and Adam Smith, Bentham and Fulton; a practical epoch, intelligence being supreme.

First, the age of pleasure; second, the age of feeling; third, the age of self-interest. [. . .]

Material practicality: this is the goal to which all modern societies tend. But in Europe it means a struggle against memory, habit, and custom. The present still submits to the influence of the past. We are not religious, but we have magnificent churches; despite our new matter-of-factness we still house our libraries, museums, and colleges in splendid palaces. The most ordinary spirits, the idlest minds, in our country, pay homage to genius and quality. Even now, the man who has forfeited his own honor bows before the statue of Bayard.

America has no knowledge of these shackles; she advances on the highway of material interests without being hindered by prejudices or troubled by passions.

Do not look for poetry, literature, or fine arts in this country. The universal equality of conditions spreads a monotonous tint over all society. No one is completely ignorant, and no one knows very much; what is duller than mediocrity! There is no poetry but in extremes: great riches or deep misery, heavenly light or infernal night, the life of kings or the funerals of paupers.

In American society there is neither shade nor light, neither heights nor depths. This is the proof of its materialism: wherever the spirit is supreme, one sees it either soaring or falling. Brilliant genius glitters high above dull intelligence, ardent hearts rise above torpid souls. Solid matter is the only basis for a dead level.

Is the world of the spirit subject to the same laws as physical nature? That great minds may appear, is it necessary that the masses be ignorant to serve as their shadow? Do not great personalities shine above the vulgar as high mountains, their crests glittering with snow and light, tower over dark precipices?

There is poetry in the ignorant: when Dante was achieving immortality through a book, Du Guesclin appeared, who "knew nothing of letters." When the Commander in Chief of the French Armies made a treaty, he signed nothing, not knowing how; but he bound himself by his honor, which was held to be enough.

This rude ignorance cannot be found in the United States, whose inhabitants, numbering twelve millions, all know how to read, write, and compute.

In America, great characters lack both stage and spectators to show their brilliance. If countries with an aristocracy are rich in brilliant and poetic persons, it is because the upper classes furnish the actors and the theater: the play is performed before the people, who are the audience and watch the scene only from a distance.

The Roman aristocracy played its role to the world; Louis XIV to Europe. When the classes mingle, individuals are seen close at hand and diminish in stature; there are still actors, but characters no longer; an arena, but no longer a theater.

Every society harbors in its midst childish vanities, enormous pride, ambition, intrigue, rivalry—but these passions rise or fall, are great or petty, according to the conditions and temperament of the people. Turenne was almost as proud of his birth as of his glory; Ninon was a prostitute; the great Bossuet was jealous of Fénelon.

The Americans covet wealth, are proud of wealth, jealous of wealth. And if some New York merchant gives himself over to libertinism, what does his name mean to the world? What effect will his love affairs have on the future?

To tell the truth, there does exist in America something similar to feudal aristocracy.

The factory is the manor; the manufacturer the overlord; the workers are the serfs; but what kind of glory shines from this industrial feudalism? The crenelated castle, with its deep moats, the lady of the castle and the faithful knight, were not unpoetic.

What harmonies can the modern poet get out of cash drawers, distilleries, steam engines, and paper money?

In America the masses are everywhere and always supreme, jealous of any superiority which may appear, and prompt to crush those who raise themselves; for mediocre intelligences repulse superior spirits, as weak eyes, familiar with darkness, have a horror of full daylight. Do not look there for monuments raised to the memory of illustrious men. I know that this people has its heroes; but nowhere have I seen their statues. To Washington alone are there busts, inscriptions, a column; this is because Washington, in America, is not a man but a god.

The American people seem condemned from birth to be devoid of poetry. There is something of a fabulous nature in the shadows surrounding the cradle of a nation, which encourages boldness of imagination. Those obscure ages are always the heroic ages: in antiquity there was the Trojan War; in the Middle Ages, the Crusades. Since peoples have become enlightened, there are no more demigods. The Americans of the United States are perhaps the only ones among all the nations who have had no mysterious infancy. Surrounded at birth by the light of the age of maturity, they have themselves written the history of their first days: and the press, which was born before them, is charged with recording the least whimpers of this infant in swaddling clothes.

Poetry began in France with the songs of the trouvères and with chivalrous love. Such could never be its origin in the United States. The men of this country, whose respect for women is profound, scorn all outward show of gallantry. A woman alone among several men, having lost her way, or been abandoned on a ship, need fear no harm; but she will get no homage. In America they know the merit of women; they do not sing of it.

Hardly was the American nation born when public and industrial life absorbed all its moral energy. Its institutions, rich in liberty, recognize the rights of all. The Americans have too many political interests to trouble themselves with literary ones. When, toward the end of the last century, twenty-five million Frenchmen were governed according to the whims of a prostitute, they could, with their minds at rest on the affairs of the country, amuse themselves with trifles and devote themselves body and soul to the quarrel of two musicians.*

Having little confidence in men of power, the Americans govern themselves; public life is not to be found at the opera and in drawing rooms, but in the courthouse and in clubs.

When there is a pause in political life, commercial life takes over: in the United States everyone is in business because it is everyone's necessity. In a society of perfect equality, work is the common condition; each works to live, none lives to think. There are no privileged classes who with a monopoly on riches have also a monopoly on leisure.

Everyone works! But the life of a worker is essentially material. His soul sleeps while his body is at work; but his spirit does not become active when his body is at rest. Work for him is a punish-

* Gluck and Piccini. "As for me," one Frenchman said, "I will not tip my hat to anyone who does not like Gluck."

ment; its reward is idleness; he knows nothing of leisure. Learning to enjoy the life of the spirit is a science. Nature does not give us this faculty, which is the product only of education and of living a broad life. One should not think that after having amassed silver and gold one can say all at once: "Now I am going to live an intellectual life." No, man is not made thus. The reptile belongs to the earth, and the eagle to the sky. If one is born to think, he thinks; if he is born to make money, he does not think.

There is no lack of authors in the United States, but the authors lack a public.

One can find writers to produce books, because writing is work; it is readers who are lacking, because reading demands leisure.

The public influences the author, and you will never see an author obstinately producing literary works when the public does not want them.

Imagine an inspired poet, born accidentally into this society of businessmen: could he earn his living by his talent? No, genius itself is ruled by the atmosphere of its environment. Nothing can communicate enthusiasm to insensitive beings; one soon ceases to sing to deaf men. The ardor of the poet and the inspiration of the writer, which sympathy keeps alight, are frozen by indifference and insincerity.

Everyone being engaged in industry, the most highly regarded among the professions is the one at which one can make the most money. The writer's trade, being the least lucrative, is beneath all others. Say to an American that it is finer to pursue literary fame than fortune, and he will give you the pitying smile one accords the chatter of a madman. Extol in his presence the glory of Homer—of Tasso—and he will reply that Homer and Tasso died poor. Away with the talent that produces no wealth!

In America, the sciences are valued only for their applied uses. They study the useful arts but not the fine arts.

Theories are invented in Germany and France; in the United States they are put into practice. Americans do not dream; they act.

Everybody aspires to the same goal, material well-being; and since money is its source, it is only money they seek.

If there is literary production in this country, it is nevertheless an industry. There is neither a classical school nor a romantic school. They know only the commercial school, that of writers who edit newspapers, pamphlets, advertisements, and who sell ideas as others sell cloth. Their desk is a counter, their spirit is yard goods; each article has its price; they will tell you exactly what a printed inspiration costs.

These brain merchants live on very good terms with each other. One upholds the political principles of Mr. Henry Clay, another, those of General Jackson; the first is a Unitarian, the second a Presbyterian; this one is a Democrat, that one a Federalist, a third is an ardent defender of religious morality; still another stands up for the philosophical morality of Miss Wright.*

They are all mutual friends; they quarrel sometimes over personalities, never over principles.

Has not each one the right to exercise his profession? Congress's latest law seems sensible to you: all very good. As for me I find it mad. You maintain that our President is a great politician, that's fine; I am about to demonstrate that he is an ignoramus in the art of government. You are pushing for democracy, I am pulling against it. Is society progressing toward perfection? Or is it decaying? Let each of us choose what he likes among these conflicting assertions. They are the various branches of industry; one can even take on several at a time: writing pro in one journal and con in another—contradiction doesn't matter. Shouldn't ideas reach all minds? In either case, one is serving a social need.

It happens sometimes in a political revolution that, virtue becoming a crime and crime a virtue, one sees men of absolutely opposite principles condemned in turn to death. Do the headsman and his assistants stop their work because the crimes are in doubt? Of

* Frances Wright (1795–1852), who with Robert Dale Owen founded and edited the *Free Enquirer*. [Translator's note.]

course not; they continue in their profession. So do writers; they do not work on bodies but on ideas—sometimes on one, sometimes on its opposite. Asking them to adhere to one theory would be demanding that they have opinions, beliefs, exclusive convictions; it would restrict within definite bounds their industry, which, by its nature, is boundless as thought, from which it emanates.

The business of ideas being the last of all, it follows that one is a writer because he has nothing better to do. Anyone who feels he has some talent sells it; the incapable take refuge in the petty trade of letters. They willingly leave the care of writing verse and books to women; it is a frivolous activity which they leave to the weaker sex; they allow them to waste time in writing.

You will find in all American cities a considerable number of bluestockings. Several have acquired a deserved reputation through their works,* but most of them are chilly and pedantic. Nothing could be less poetic than these overseas Muses; do not look for them in the depths of the wilderness, by the torrents and cataracts, or on the mountain heights: no, you will see them plodding in the mud of city streets, wearing buskins on their feet and spectacles on their noses.

Though there are few authors in America, more matter is printed here than in any other country in the world. Each county has its daily newspaper; newspapers are in truth the only literature of the country.† Businessmen and those of modest means need quick, cheap reading. On the other hand there is an enormous consumption of

* Among others Miss [Catherine Maria] Sedgwick, the author of several very pleasing novels.

† The number of daily newspapers at present published in the United States is estimated at more than 1200, not counting other periodical publications. In the state of New York alone, at the beginning of 1833, there were 263 newspapers (for two million inhabitants). Every county, with two exceptions, Putnam and Rockland, publishes its papers within its own borders.

New York City itself has 65 papers, including magazines. Of this number, 13 are dailies, 30 are weeklies, 9 are monthlies, 10 are published twice a week, and 5 twice a month.

The price of an annual subscription to the daily papers of New York is ten dollars. The total of all subscriptions to the different papers in the state of New York is estimated at $750,000. This sum does not include the price of adver-

books for primary and religious education! It is more bookstore stuff than literature. The instruction given to children is purely utilitarian; its aim is not the development of lofty faculties in soul and mind: it molds the proper kind of men for the affairs of daily life.

American literature is entirely lacking in good taste—that refined, subtle restraint, that delicate sentiment which results from the mixture of passion and cool judgment, enthusiasm and reason, spontaneity and design, which prevails in literary composition in Europe. To have elegance in taste, one must first have elegant customs.

Style is not treated as an art, either in the newspapers or on the speaker's platform. Everyone writes or speaks with pretentiousness, but without talent.* This is not the fault only of the orators and writers. The latter, when using a brilliant and classical style, endanger their popularity: the people do not ask of their reporters any

---

tisements. At the same time, Boston had 45 newspapers and 38 periodicals published at intervals of less than a year. (See *American Almanac, 1834*, pp. 95, 96, and *Williams Register, 1833*, p. 124.)

* The reader will readily believe that here I do not agree with the dogmatic language of the person speaking in the story. Would I say that no one writes with talent in the country that has given us Washington Irving, whose works combine grace and style, delicacy of ideas, and fine perceptions; Cooper, whose genius Europe marvels at; Edward Livingston, at once statesman and profound philosopher; Robert Walsh, who combines prodigious facility of style with the charms of a conversation sparkling with wit; Jared Sparks, author of the remarkable *Life of Gouverneur Morris*, and many others I do not name? Would I say that everyone speaks without talent in the United States where I met Daniel Webster, whose parliamentary discourses, models of style and logic, disclose a soul both elevated and patriotic; Henry Clay, remarkable on the rostrum for brillant elocution and an extraordinary gift for improvisation; Edward Everett, whose speeches in the House of Representatives recall the Roman school and the style of antiquity; Channing, in whose sermons one finds much of the style and wit of Fénèlon; etc., etc.?

Finally, would I say that in America no one can be a political figure with literary or oratorical gifts when I saw John Quincy Adams, more versed, perhaps, in literature ancient and modern than any European; Albert Gallatin, whose well-furnished mind and immense capabilities have not prevented him from being entrusted by his country with the highest diplomatic functions; etc., etc.?

As for the rest, one must not forget that the man who is speaking is expressing ideas which, as generalizations, might be true, without prejudice to the

more, in a literary way, than is barely necessary to make things understandable; anything above that is aristocracy.

Thus literature and the arts, instead of being invoked by the passions, come only to the aid of necessity; or, if some leaning toward the fine arts is revealed, one may be sure of finding it marred by triviality. For example, in the United States there is one type of painting that flourishes—portrait painting; but its prosperity is due not to love of art but to self-love.

You may occasionally come across, in this vulgar industrial society, a circle of polished, brilliant persons, among whom works of art are appreciated with taste, and works of genius admired with enthusiasm; it is like an oasis in the burning sands of Africa. Here and there you may find an ardent imagination, a thoughtful mind; but a single poet in a country no more makes it a poetic nation than a fair sky over the valley of the Thames gives it the climate of Italy.

Though literature, properly speaking, does not exist in the United States, do not imagine that Americans are without literary pride. It is a rather strange phenomenon: you will find among their authors none of that monstrous vanity which among us accompanies mediocrity, and sometimes even genius. The writers are conscious that they are exercising an inferior profession.

In America, not the authors, but the nation, has literary pride. Literature is an industry in which the Americans claim to excel as in all the others.

And do not try to please them by saying that the identity of language unites all the fine minds of England with those of America; they will reply that English literature has nothing whatever in common with American literature.

The antipoetic character of the Americans has deep roots in their way of life.

Since they are always in pursuit of money, they never seek for pleasure. Religion and, more than that, their austerity, forbids games, amusements, and plays.

---

exceptions. Without doubt, in general one finds in the United States not orators, but lawyers; not writers, but journalists.

Each great city has its theater,* but the wealthy, who are always one step ahead of corruption, try in vain to make it fashionable. Plays are not a popular pleasure in America. Tragedy, comedy, Italian music are aristocratic diversions by nature; they demand good taste and money from the spectators, two things the majority lacks. Circuses and amphitheaters demand many passions, and North America has none to give.

If large theaters are rare, small ones are unknown. This absence of liking for the drama is doubtless part of morality for American society, who, having no theaters, do not go each evening to laugh at cuckolded husbands, to applaud happy lovers, and to look with indulgence on adulterous wives. The Americans are moral because they have no plays; they have no plays because of their morality. This is cause and effect in one.

It is not only through love of morality that Americans shun the theater, for many who do not attend indulge at home in ignoble pleasures. The play is an amusement for which they have no inborn taste. They derive this antipathy from their English ancestors and are still subject to the Puritan influence of the first American colonists. The English theater has never been anything but an upper-class fashion or a lower-class spree; and it is the middle classes of that country who have peopled America. Whatever the cause, the result is indubitable: the poetic spirit is, in the United States, despoiled of its finest attribute. Deprive France of its theater, and where are its poets?

Religion, so rich in the stuff of poetry, brings to the American heart neither inspiration nor enthusiasm. The American likes his religion to speak not to his soul but to his reason; he likes it as an ordering principle, not as a source of sweet emotion. The Italian is artistically religious; the American is tidily religious.

Besides, there are too many Christian sects in America to furnish subjects of general interest for the fine arts. The Quakers, simple and modest, build no sumptuous palaces. What do the Methodists

* See Appendix J, pp. 231–32.

care for the admirable sermons of Mr. Channing, who is a Unitarian? If the Baptist communion erected a monument of some sort to their faith, of what interest would it be to the Presbyterians?

Instead of the religious unity which has reigned in France for fifteen centuries, imagine a thousand dissident sects: you would have today neither great churches nor great Christian orators, neither Notre Dame nor Bossuet.

Protestant congregations do not gather in magnificent temples decorated with statues and pictures; they meet in simple houses built without luxury and at small expense. The most splendid of their religious edifices is supported by a few columns of painted wood: this is their Parthenon. Take away the Americans' Capitol building, the poetic expression of their national pride, and the Bank of the United States, the poetic expression of their passion for money, and there would remain not a single building in the country which presents the aspect of a monument.

Everything in the United States has its rise in industry, and goes back into it, but, unlike blood which warms itself in the heart, all life which reaches industry becomes cold in that icy heart of American society.

"Let this society grow," say some, "and you will see illustrious men in literature and the arts. Early Rome did not hear the songs of Horace and Virgil, and France needed fourteen centuries to produce Racine and Corneille."

Those who speak thus confuse two distinct things: political society and civilization. America's society is young; it is not yet two centuries old. Her civilization, on the contrary, is old as that of England, from which it comes. The first is progressing; the second declining. England's political society is regenerating itself in American democracy: her civilization is dying there.

The industrial spirit makes society materialistic by reducing all men's relationships to utilitarian ends.

Noble passions enrich the soul; self-interest besmirches and withers it. It seems as though greed were blowing a deadly wind upon America, which, attacking man's intellectual qualities, fells genius, extinguishes enthusiasm, penetrates the depths of the heart to dry up the wellspring of noble inspirations and generous impulses.

Look at the French peasant who, with cheerful humor, serene brow, and laughing lips, sings beneath the thatch which hides his poverty and, without a care for yesterday nor a thought for the morrow, dances joyously in the village square.

They know nothing of this happy poverty in America. Absorbed in schemes, the country dweller of the United States wastes no time in pleasures; the fields say nothing to his heart; the sun which blesses his hillsides does not warm his soul. He regards the soil as the material of industry and lives in his cottage as in a factory.

No one in America understands that completely intellectual life which sets itself up beyond the realm of the practical world and feeds on dreams, speculations, and abstractions; that nonobjective existence which shuns business affairs, for which meditation is a necessity, science a duty, literary creation a delightful pastime, and which, seizing upon both the riches of antiquity and the treasures of today, taking a leaf from the laurels of Milton as from those of Virgil, makes the genius and glory of all the ages enhance its own richness.

In this country they are unaware of the existence of the modest savant who, a stranger to the events of the political world and the vexations of greedy passion, gives himself entirely to study, loves it for its own sake, rejoices in its noble leisure.

America knows nothing of the bright arenas where imagination leaps upon the wings of genius and glory: nor of those courts of love where grace, spirit, and gallantry interplay; nor of the almost celestial harmony which comes of the union of letters and fine arts; nor of the perfume of poetry, history, and memory which breathes so softly from a classic earth to ascend to a serene sky.

The Europe that admires Cooper believes that America too worships him; it is not so. The American Walter Scott finds neither fortune nor fame in his own country. He earns less by his books than a cloth merchant; consequently, the cloth merchant is superior to the idea-peddler. The reasoning is unanswerable.

At first incredulous at this phenomenon, I supposed that Cooper had painted the customs of the Indians in false colors, and that the Americans, judges of a picture whose original was before their eyes, condemned him for unfaithful representation of local reality. Later I realized my error: I have seen the Indians, and I was reassured that Cooper's portraits are striking likenesses.

But the Americans ask what use it is to know what the Indians have done, or what they are still doing; how they live in their forests, how they die. The savages are poor people from whom one can get nothing, neither wealth nor lessons in industry. You can take their forests, that is all, seize them, not to make poetry, but to cut them down and to plow the trunks under.

These beautiful forests, magnificent solitudes, splendid palaces of wild nature, need a divine bard! They cannot fall beneath the ax of the industrialist without having been celebrated by the lyre of the poet. That poet is not to be found in America. But, leaping the Atlantic, the angel of poetry has transported on wings of flame the French Homer to the banks of the Mississippi.

All the worlds are the domain of genius! The universe itself contains barely enough air to fill his great breast. Some years later, the guest of the savages went as an inspired poet, to sing his memories on the shores of the Eurotas and, as a devout pilgrim, to worship God on the banks of the Jordan!

Atala, René, the Natchez, were born in America, children of the wilderness. The New World inspired them, old Europe alone has understood them.

When the Americans read Chateaubriand, as when they see the marvel of Niagara, they say, "And what does that prove?"

Such is the people on whom I hoped to exercise a poetic influence!

Oh cruel disenchantment! Thus was broken in my hands the supporting branch to which I had trusted my last chance of safety in the wreck!

13

The Riot

Thus vanished my dream of literary renown and the future I had built upon it! Any other means to fame was denied me. If the United States had been engaged in a war, I would have tried to enter the ranks of the American army; but in time of peace there is no military glory. The soldiers of the country are reduced to a few thousand men, stationed on the frontiers of the Western states, where their only mission is to keep in check the hordes of Indian savages.

I had fallen into the deep dejection which follows the extinction of the last ray of the last hope, when I received a letter from Nelson announcing his departure from Baltimore and his imminent arrival in New York with Marie; he entered into no details. "You shall know," he wrote, "the cause of this removal and the new blow which has struck us." He made no mention of George.

After a day of waiting and torment, I saw Nelson and Marie arrive. Sorrow showed heavy and stern upon the brow of the father, eloquent and tender in the eyes of the young girl.

My anxiety restrained the first transports of my love.

"What are these new misfortunes," I cried, "with which I see you burdened?"

After several moments of gloomy silence, Nelson said: "A week has passed since elections were held in Baltimore for a member of Congress. George and I went to vote, according to our custom. I am used to seeing the intrigues that go on on these occasions; but I found political passions in a state of excitement such as I had never seen before.

"The struggle was between two candidates: the first, remarkable for his talents, but a *Federalist*; the second, less distinguished, but a *Jacksonian.* After numerous speeches, some followed by hoots and some by cheers, all accompanied by violent quarrels among the electors of the opposed parties, they counted the votes, and the candidate for whom George and I had cast our ballots carried the election by one vote. Suddenly a great tumult burst out in the gathering; first one exclamation, then another, then a thousand could be heard; the disturbance, beginning in one corner, spread suddenly throughout the room, as the buzzing of one disturbed bee in his cell will communicate itself to the whole hive. Finally I heard the electors of the vanquished party cry out: 'The balloting is void; George Nelson is a colored man. Hurrah! hurrah! throw him out—the election must be held over again!'

"Loud applause followed these words. Those of our party remained in gloomy silence; then one of them asked George if the imputation were true. 'Yes,' he replied. Then our friends themselves uttered angry imprecations, and drew away from us. In that moment I felt less embarrassment than fear; because I foresaw George's fury and the terrible outbursts to which he would give vent. I saw him blanch with anger; but strangely enough he suddenly regained his senses and remained calm.

"The objection of our adversaries was valid, the law of Maryland excluding all colored people from the right to vote, even those who have long had their liberty. I did not protest. Drawing George, whose fits of passion frightened me, out of the room, I thanked Heaven that he was calm. As we went out, we noticed a person who was zealously directing public attention to the humiliation of our withdrawal. George looked him in the face and recognized in him Fernando d'Almanza, that American who by his perfidious revelations had caused the mother of my children to die of grief. I had no doubt that the first cry of denunciation had come from his lips; and George surmised rightly that that man was the same who, in the New York theater, had aroused against you and him the hatred of the crowd.

"George's first movement was toward the author of the affront, to avenge with a single blow both the old and the new injury; but I saw him almost at once repress his resentment. He muttered broken phrases in a low voice, of which I could make no sense. 'The great day is coming,' he said; 'vengeance will be sweeter!'

"Persuaded that he hid an important secret in his soul, I pressed him to confide in me. 'It is cowardice,' he said, 'to allow oneself to be crushed with a bowed head. I know that an insurrection is being planned in the South; the Negroes of Virginia and the two Carolinas wish to join with the Indians in Georgia to shake off the American yoke; I am going to their aid.'

"Appalled by this plan, I tried every means to show George its madness and uselessness. Perhaps I did so in words that were too severe, but such a scheme seemed to me fraught with so many dangers! To my remonstrances, Marie joined her prayers and tears. George remained silent. Then I thought that reason had entered his heart.

"We agreed to leave Baltimore, where we could not stay longer; but where should we seek refuge? I suggested to my children that we take our misfortunes to New York, where a highly respected Presbyterian, James Williams, whom I had formerly known in Boston, would give us temporary asylum. Once there, we might deliberate upon the choice of a retreat. As I spoke, George seemed deeply preoccupied; however, he offered not a word to recall his ill-starred plan. That evening when the hour for retiring had come, he overwhelmed us with signs of the most touching affection; he had never shown himself so loving to me, so tender to his sister. He would start out of deep thought to speak sweet words to us. Alas! the next day he was beyond reach of our embraces—he had left Baltimore and had written to me a letter in which he begged us to forgive his clandestine departure.

" 'Never,' he wrote, 'could I have resisted the commands of my father, the tears of my sister; a single look from Marie would have overcome me. But my duty demands that I aid my unfortunate brothers. My father, my dear sister,' he added, 'we will meet again in a happier time. If men are not equal upon earth, at least they are in Heaven.'

"I will not tell you how great was Marie's grief on hearing these last words of the brother she adored.

"George, in his letter, urged us to follow my first plan, that of asking hospitality from James Williams, to whom he would apply later to learn our whereabouts."

Thus Nelson spoke; his voice at the end shook slightly. He then said, in accents of devout resignation, "The more powerful the hand that strikes one, the more should one worship it. My friend," he added, "you may judge now if I deceived you when I told you of the horrible conditions under which people of color live in the United States. Unable to dispel your illusions, I imposed upon your love a time of trial. The term has not yet expired, but undoubtedly your opinion has anticipated it, and what you know of our fortune should suffice to enlighten you."

As I kept silence, under the impress of deep concern and the anxiety that George's fate had inspired in me, Marie, taking my uneasiness for indecision, said in a voice choked with tears, "Ludovic, my heart is grateful for the generous effort you have made to love an unfortunate girl; but, pray, cease to struggle against inflexible destiny. You see, we are bound to our misfortunes as we are to life itself. My fate is forever fixed; I shall drag my wretched existence from city to city; hunted from one place by spite, from another by hate; everywhere outcast by men because I was cursed in my mother's womb!"

I call on Heaven to witness that in the presence of such moving grief my heart faltered not an instant; to be faithful to sorrow I had no need to make a struggle. I felt the tie which bound me to Marie strengthened in my soul. This uprush of tenderness and love mingled with an indignation so deep against the authors of this evil, whose victim was before my eyes, that I could not repress the outburst of this latter feeling.

"So this," I cried, "is the nation that has been the object of my admiration and fellow feeling! Obsessed with liberty, while human bondage abounds! Discoursing on equality, among three million slaves; forbidding distinctions among men, and proud to be white, as of a mark of nobility; with strong and philosophical mind condemning the privilege of birth, and with stupidity maintaining the privilege of color! In the North, proud to work, in the South, glorying in idleness; uniting in itself, in a monstrous alliance, the most incompatible virtues and vices, moral purity and base self-interest, religion and thirst for gold, morality and bankruptcy!

"Race of businessmen who consider themselves honest because what they do is legal; prudent and virtuous because it is politic to be so! Their integrity is trickery countenanced by law, usurpation without violence, unscrupulousness without crime! You will not see them armed with murderous daggers; their weapons are guile, fraud, and bad faith, with which they enrich themselves. They speak of honor and loyalty as merchants speak of their goods! But look at the hypocrisy even in their good deeds! They offer independence to a whole unhappy race; and on those Negroes whom they free they inflict, after striking off their chains, a persecution more cruel than slavery!"

Thus my anger flared up; I checked its outburst at sight of Marie, whose despondency was extreme. After the bitterness had erupted from my heart, there remained only love, and I felt I could express it no better than by addressing these few words to Nelson: "The time of trial is not yet over; I pray you, absolve me from the remainder of it, and let me become Marie's husband."

"Almighty God!" cried the American, not without some emotion, "how great is Thy goodness, in preserving to us the heart of this worthy young man!"

My words threw Marie into a state impossible to describe. The expression of my grievances against American society had apprised her of the change in my sentiments; and when my last words had revealed to her the sole desire of my heart, I saw her pass suddenly from extreme sadness to that excess of joy which also reveals itself in tears; falling on her knees she gave thanks to God, in the attitude of the criminal who, having received an unhoped-for pardon, joins his hands and gazes Heavenward.

Nelson added, "Generous friend, it is the mark of a great and strong soul to be drawn to misfortune. I will no longer oppose your noble impulses; I admire your fine qualities and consider myself unworthy to direct them." Thus saying, he threw himself into my arms and pressed me closely to his heart; then, taking my hand and that of Marie, "My daughter," he said, uniting them, "Ludovic shall be your husband." "Oh, dear God!" cried that lovely girl, "is not such happiness but a dream?" She added nothing to these words, leaned for support on Nelson's arm, and seemed to collect her feelings in an ecstasy of felicity.

However, impatient to fulfill my dearest wishes, I begged Nelson to fix the day for my union with his daughter. "In a few days," he said, "I shall call you my son. There was a time, not long ago, when according to the laws of the State of New York, the marriage of a white man to a colored woman was impossible; but today the prohibition no longer exists: such alliances are made sometimes.

"A friend of our host, the Reverend John Mulon, a Catholic priest, whose philanthropy toward the black race has made him dear to the Presbyterians themselves, will marry you first, in accordance with the rites of the Roman Church, to which you belong; then James Williams, the Presbyterian minister, will give to your union the sanction of the religion whose beliefs my daughter professes. Time was when marriages of this kind excited loud protests among the American people, but the general state of mind grows more enlightened day by day, and hatred dies with prejudice. Perhaps, my children, we would do well, when your union is sanctified, not to leave New York. There is no more good will in this city than in others toward people of color; but in a large city it is easier than elsewhere to live unknown and obscure."

I did not think to inquire at that moment whether Nelson was the victim of some illusion; the contentment of my heart was extreme; all my anxieties vanished; I forgot my past vexations and even their causes; and, believing the well of my misfortunes forever dried up, I saw for the future only promises of happiness.

This feeling was not dispelled by Marie's sorrow; she, after the first intoxication of joy, had fallen back into melancholy. "My friend," she said to me, "it is in vain that you seek to deceive me—your love for me has become a sacrifice.

"When you see my tears, do not blame my love; I weep because I see what your fate will be if our union takes place. The scorn of which I have been the object will be reflected upon you. You are not accustomed to live without respect; and lack of it would cause you to suffer frightful torments. It is not in your power to hide from me the secret wounds of your heart. Ludovic, I should die of grief if I knew you were unhappy."

I set at naught her scruples as unrealities, her fears as chimeras.

The day of our wedding, so longed for, arrived. I was filled with love; never had my heart been open to so much hope; however, I felt a secret displeasure at seeing Marie's brow clouded by a veil of sadness which was not pierced by my joy; I did not know then that there are sensitive, mysterious souls whose sorrow is an omen, and who suffer instinctively, because they have foreseen great misfortunes to come.

However, since morning she had worn the white bridal wreath; her grace and natural beauty were full of secret enchantment, and

I am not sure that her bridal attire was not made the lovelier by the mourning in her eyes. A peaceful, religious joy was apparent on Nelson's countenance; and when John Mulon and James Williams announced that the hour had come to go to the church for the ceremony, I felt myself pierced by a holy and sweet emotion.

Nevertheless, at the moment when our tranquil souls were filled with hopes of happiness, great trouble was brewing in New York, and a terrible storm was ready to burst over our heads.*

In New York, as in all North American cities, there are two distinct parties among the friends of the black race.

The first, judging slavery an evil for their country and perhaps also condemning it as contrary to the Christian religion, demand the emancipation of the black population, but, full of the prejudices of their race, do not consider freed Negroes to be the equals of the whites; they therefore wish to deport colored people as soon as they are liberated; and they hold them to a state of degradation and inferiority as long as they remain among the Americans. A large number of these friends of the Negroes are against slavery only because of national pride; it is distressing to them to be blamed for it by foreigners, and to hear it said that slavery is a relic of barbarism. Some attack the evil for the sole reason that they cannot bear to see it: these, while working for emancipation, accomplish little; they would destroy slavery without offering liberty. They are ridding themselves of an annoyance, an embarrassment, a wound to their vanity, but they are not healing the wounds of others; they have worked for themselves, not for the slaves. Freed from bondage, the latter are denied entrance into free society.

The other partisans of the Negroes are those who sincerely love them, as a Christian loves his brother men; who not only desire the abolition of slavery but also receive the freed men with open arms and treat them as equals.

These zealous friends of the black population are rare, but their ardor is indefatigable; for a long time it was fruitless, but some prejudices have vanished through their efforts, and white men have been known to marry women of color.

As long as philanthropy on behalf of the Negroes had resulted in nothing but useless declamation, the Americans tolerated it with-

* See Appendix L, pp. 243–52.

out difficulty; it mattered little to them that the equality of the Negroes should be proclaimed in theory, so long as in fact they remained inferior to the whites. But on the day when an American took a colored woman to wife, the attempt to mix the two races took on a practical character. It was an insult directed against the dignity of the whites; American pride was completely up in arms. This was the general state of mind in the city of New York at the time of my wedding with Marie.

On our way to the Catholic church, I noticed an unaccustomed restlessness in the city. It was not the regular activity of an industrial and commercial population: ill-dressed men of the working class roamed the streets at an hour when they were usually at work. They could be seen, scorning their habitual calm coolness, walking quickly, colliding with each other, accosting each other mysteriously, forming animated groups, and separating suddenly in contrary directions.

Full of an immense matter that occupied all my thoughts, I paid but scant attention to this outward disturbance; however, from that moment I was surprised to see in the streets neither Negroes nor nor mulattoes.

Nelson asked a passerby the cause of the tumult. "Oh," said he, "the amalgamists* are making the trouble; they want the Negroes to be the equals of the whites; so the whites are forced to revolt."

Another man, asked the same question, replied, "If the Negroes get killed, it's their own fault; how do the wretches dare to raise themselves to the rank of Americans?"

A third man gave a different answer: "They are going to tear down the blacks' houses and rid our city of their ugly faces! Though the whites are wrong to act like this, they acted wrongly in the first place: why did they give the Negroes their freedom?"

While we listened to these deplorable statements, a frightful spectacle struck our eyes.

We were in Leonard Street. Several poor mulattoes happening to pass at that moment, we heard at once a thousand infuriated voices shouting: "Down with the Negroes! Kill them! Kill them!" At the same instant, a hail of stones, flung by the crowd, fell upon the colored people; Americans armed with clubs flung themselves

* See Appendix L, p. 244.

on the poor creatures and beat them pitilessly. Overwhelmed by this treatment, as cruel as it was unexpected, the mulattoes made no resistance, and seemed dazed at the sight of the angry crowd; their eyes, raised to Heaven, seemed to ask God whence came the wrath of a society whose laws they respected.

Soon an even more grievous scene was offered to our eyes. The hapless mulattoes, pursued by a blind vengeance, took refuge in the friendly houses of some colored people. I thought they had escaped the danger; but, once aroused, the popular tide does not so easily recede. Windows were shattered, doors broken, walls torn down. At that moment I ceased to see the people's work: Marie was frozen with terror. "My friends," said Nelson, without agitation, "let us withdraw; this barbaric violence confounds my reason; it reveals a deadly hatred against the colored people. Great danger threatens us if we should be discovered. Let us make haste to the holy temple; we will be protected from all injury within the sanctuary of the church; the American people would sooner die than lose respect for holy things. . . . My children," Nelson went on, as he drew us on toward the church, "as soon as your marriage has been performed, we will quit this city, where evil passions reign that I had believed to be stilled."

In a few minutes we had arrived at the church of John Mulon. Many colored people had sought refuge there.

On entering the holy sanctuary I felt my hope and strength revive. The tumult of the rebellion, the cries of the multitude, its fury and the voices of its victims, all these earthly sounds ceased to beat upon my ears, and the resentment left my heart. I loved Nelson's daughter, and I prayed to God.

Soon the ceremony began. I knelt beside Marie, whose pallor was extreme. During the scenes of horror which we had witnessed not a single plaint had escaped her; only her grieving look seemed to say to me: "Are these, then, our wedding rites?" Since we had entered the sacred precincts, I had seen calm and serenity return to her countenance; but her trust in God was more that of resignation than of hope.

As for me, I allowed free rein to my feelings of joy. After many storms, I had come to land. My past sorrows served as a contrast to my happiness, and I almost blessed the persecutions of fortune, without which I could not have been so happy. If fate had smiled upon my first ambitions for glory and power, I would never have left Europe, and I would not have been today Marie's husband! Henceforth, what were the world's injustices to me? We would be two to bear them, and a woman's tears are so sweet that they mingle a secret charm with the bitterest sorrows.

Thus a thousand radiant thoughts of the future appeared to my mind, while, bowing before the altar, Marie and I received the benediction of the Church. At the moment when the holy priest, after a moving prayer, took our hands to unite them, a great tumult burst out suddenly at the door of the church. "The rioters!" cried an apprehensive voice. The cry flew from mouth to mouth; then a dismal silence fell below the sacred vault. The noise of a disorderly multitude could be heard without, sounding like the rumblings of an approaching storm. Driven by an impetuous wind the thundercloud sweeps on, and already the lighting is upon our heads! "Death to the colored people! To the church! To the church!" These terrible shouts reechoed from all about; terror seized the assembled faithful; the priest grew pale, his knees failed him, the ring that was to unite us fell from his hand! Marie, paralyzed with fear, became insensible and reeled; I gave to the swooning maiden the support of that arm which an instant later would have embraced my beloved wife.

Several intrepid Negroes had rushed to the doors of the church to defend them against the invasion, but soon a thousand missiles fell crashing upon the consecrated building; one could hear the doors groaning on their hinges—the attackers cheered each other on to violence; each success was greeted with tumultuous applause; the blows redoubled, the walls shook, the floor trembled. Already the mob, that worker of prodigious destruction, had irrupted into the outer sanctuary; the interior of the church presented a scene of frightful disorder and confusion; children shrieked piercingly, women uttered woeful cries. At the idea of a general massacre, horror entered every heart; for the populace is the same in every country—stupid, blind, and cruel. Men, or rather monsters, without respect for the sanctity of the place, pitiless to the weakness of sex or age, threw themselves upon the devout gathering and committed acts of the most brutal violence, sparing neither women, old men, nor children.

My anguish was extreme. Nelson, stunned by this spectacle of vandalism and ungodliness, was torn between paternal solicitude and his national pride. "Oh, my God!" he cried; "Oh, profanation! Oh, shame for my country!"

The peril was imminent and terrible. I said to Nelson, "I entreat you, leave the care of protecting Marie to my love." Speaking thus, I took her in my arms. Oh, with what strength I seized my beloved! How powerful I felt in bearing her upon my heart! But hardly had I lifted my precious burden than I heard a number of voices shouting, "John Mulon! John Mulon! Death to the Catholic who marries colored women to white men!" At the same time all eyes were turned upon us; I knew we were betrayed, and that frightful danger menaced us. How could I save Marie? How could I burst through the ranks of our enemies in the midst of so much unleashed passion?

A gleam of hope met my eyes: "The militia! The militia!" cried some of the rioters.

"What do we care?" answered others, "The militia won't dare to fire on Americans!"

A body of militiamen had, in fact, arrived to establish order; but it was made up entirely of white men, who cared little for colored people. Instead of checking the popular fury, they stood by and watched its excesses. Their impassive presence only encouraged the fury of the attackers, who overran the inside of the church, breaking and overturning everything—the furniture, the sacred ornaments, the pulpit, the altar itself. All the exits were guarded, so that none could escape from their violence. In this extremity, recommending the cause of innocence and misfortune to Heaven, I leaped through the midst of the frenzied multitude, hearing a thousand cries of pain and vengeance, holding Marie in my arms, pale and disheveled, having no other protection than the strength of my will, the power of my love, and my faith in the justice of God. Ah! I was daring and strong! I do not know whether it was the effect of my boldness or of Heavenly protection; but a passage opened before me. Marie was so beautiful in her terror that I at first attributed the confusion of our enemies to the fascination of her charms. But what respect could the most noble creature inspire in the impious wretch who outrages God in His temple? I had only the last door to gain: it was the most dangerous passage. Shaken by a thousand terrors, caught between the obstacles before me and the impossibility of standing still, finding nothing but danger about me, I threw myself forward. At that moment I saw the arms of the murderers raised—Marie would be dashed down by their blows. Then it seemed that the vault of Heaven collapsed upon me, at the same time that the earth opened to engulf me. However, my impetus carried me on; I could not hold back, and with that impulse of my body I felt that in wishing to save a beloved life I was delivering it up to the executioners!

Oh God, Thy power and mercy were great on that day! At the moment when I felt I was flinging my treasure into the abyss, a young man came up, threw himself between us and our enemies, whose fury he braved, made a rampart of his body, advanced into the terrible passage, attacked those guarding the door, disarmed, overthrew, and crushed all those who resisted him. Preceded by his protecting might, I moved unhindered; I shielded Marie from harm, protected her from all violence, and experienced the sweetest joy that could be given to a man, in escaping fearful peril and in seeing the charming object of my love revive in my arms.

A few moments later we were rejoined by Nelson, James Williams, and John Mulon, who, despite the struggle they had had to make, had never lost us to view.

"Ludovic! Oh Heavens! Where are we?" cried Marie, opening the lovely eyes which terror had closed, and seeming to awaken from a long sleep. "Where is the church, the holy priest, my father, the crowd?" And she gazed about her. "My beloved," she went on, "I know nothing but that you have saved my life." Then, seeing Nelson: "My father! Ah, I trembled for your life—speak—what has happened since our wedding ring fell from the hands of the priest? I had a terrible dream! Visions of blood! Death cries! George, George, where is he?"

"He is there," replied Nelson.

"Oh, my God! He has lost his life!" cried Marie.

"No, my daughter, he has saved yours."

Nelson told us that in fact George was the brave young man who at the moment of greatest peril had suddenly appeared and had delivered us by prodigies of valor and daring.

"My friends," said Nelson, "Heaven is testing us by cruel misfortunes; however, Providence, who, in permitting a great evil, has miraculously preserved us from yet greater evils, is still generous to us."

"How did George come here?" asked Marie, "and why is he not with us?"

"George," replied Nelson, "came to us like one of those benevolent spirits who descend to earth only to dry the tears of men and who, after consoling them, return to their Heavenly home. I saw him, burning and impetuous, fling himself to the defense of his sister and overthrow his enemies. Soon he came to me. 'Follow Marie,' he said; 'watch over her. Make haste, my father, to leave this impious city.' And as I took his arm to pull him with us, he said, with energy, 'I am not free; my duty calls me elsewhere. I love my sister more than life, but not so much as honor. I am going away from you, I flee from my dear sister, in order not to falter. Let Marie marry Ludovic; he is worthy of her, and she of him. Good-by, James Williams,' he said, leaving us; 'Go to your brother Lewis—you must all find a new refuge, for your house no longer exists.'"

Indeed, we found a mass of ruins in place of our host's dwelling. The doors were broken, the walls demolished, the furniture destroyed; the debris had been piled in heaps on the public square; they had set fire to it for a celebration, and we, upon our return, came upon the last embers of the fire that had consumed all. A number of houses belonging to colored people and to whites who were their friends had met the same fate, and four churches of the black population had succumbed like that of John Mulon to violence and profanation.

Toward evening the rioting died down; the philanthropic society established in New York for the liberation of the Negroes published a declaration which attempted to calm the passions of the Americans against the colored people. It said, "We never conceived the insane project of mingling the two races; in this regard we could not fail to recognize the dignity of the whites; we respect the laws which uphold slavery in the Southern states."

Oh, shame! Who then are these free people, among whom one is not allowed to hate slavery? The Negroes in New York are not demanding liberty for themselves—they are all free; they appeal to the Americans to pity their brothers in slavery, and their prayers, and those of their friends, are crimes for which they must ask forgiveness!

However, the city was still disturbed by that superficial unrest which usually follows the crises of civil war. Fathers were searching for their children; sisters were seeking their brothers; wives, their husbands. They paused to make inquiries of each other and to exchange exaggerated tales; at sight of the ruined churches and the still smoldering ashes they stopped to gaze upon the work of the populace, as they would contemplate uprooted trees and blasted crops after a hurricane. The heroes and fighters rested and returned home; the cowards and intriguers ruled the day.

Everyone, after the event, condemned the rioters and their excesses. Most people, while deploring the wretchedness of the blacks, experienced a secret joy. However, I saw several good citizens, sincere friends to their country, who shed tears at the memory of that dreadful day; they saw, in that act of tyranny exercised by the majority on a weak minority, the most shameful abuse of strength, and they wondered if a people whose evil passions were stronger than the law could long remain free.

At the very hour when the uprising had subsided, we were told that the next day there would be another, the preparations for which were terrible.

Only one course was possible for stopping the insurrection at its beginning: the militia would have to be given orders to fire upon the people; but this order could come only from the mayor of the city. His most sensible councilors advised this measure, but, as a magistrate born of the people, he dared not repudiate his constituents. In vain they told him that the insurgents were the rabble, and not the people. In times of civil discord there comes a moment when it is a vexatious problem to distinguish the one from the other. The mayor heeded the advice of the moderates, who wanted the militia only to threaten the multitude with bayonets. This display of the militia under arms could only be, in truth, a vain demonstration if they were not permitted to break resistance by force; but there are cases where reason goes unheeded because it opposes certain hidden feelings which one hardly admits to oneself. This secret voice said to the Americans, "After all, would the evil be so great should the colored people and their friends perish in a popular uprising?"

Judge of our amazement on learning that the announcement of my union with Marie had been, if not the cause, at least the pretext of the insurrection! At this news all the ill-feeling which had been roused by several preceding marriages between white men and colored women had reawakened. The enlightened part of the populace, without sharing in the violence of these passions, sympathized with them; they had not stirred up the revolt but they allowed the rebels to do as they liked, and I do not know if they would ever have checked their excesses were it not for the fear they felt for themselves of the frenzied mob, drunk with disorder and greedy for destruction.

14

Departure from Civilized America

Nelson remarked to me, "Only this last experience was lacking in your trial."

"I pray you," I cried, "do not offend my heart by questioning it. But tell me, when shall I be united to her who is a thousand times dearer to me than ever before?"

"Alas, my friend," replied Nelson after a long silence, "there are obstacles wherever we turn; unhappiness and hindrances surround us. I am certain only of the necessity of our leaving New York without the slightest delay."

We all shared his thought. But where should we go? Nelson wanted to take us to Ohio, where the American population, composed of totally new elements, paid no heed to people's antecedents or family traditions. He was drawn to that country, moreover, because of the fertility of the soil and the industrious spirit of its inhabitants. But as we were about to agree upon this project, our new host, Lewis Williams, to whose home his brother had conducted us, informed us that the Ohio legislature had just passed a law forbidding all colored people to enter the state.

This new evidence of tyranny, along with the other misfortunes that had befallen us, reawakened in my soul the hatred which my transitory rapture had lulled to sleep.

I said to Marie: "My beloved, let us fly from this persecution; it is too difficult to find happiness among the wicked; for us all men are wicked; believe me, we must renounce this cruel world. Will you come with me to the wilderness? The western United States is a great expanse where Europeans have never penetrated! That shall be our refuge."

Where is the man who, under the spell of clement weather, traveling in beautiful solitudes, in the midst of a deep and untamed forest, where the living waters flow beneath the trembling foliage, where the sunlight plays among the rustling leaves, where all is secret and mysterious, where nature enfolds the soul in calm and the senses in voluptuous freshness—where is he, I repeat, who under the sway of these impressions, has not dreamed of happiness in a dwelling far from the world; and who has not, on the wings of his imagination, suddenly transported to this solitary place a beloved person with whom he can forget the rest of mankind amid all the delights of love and the enchantments of nature?

Those in whom radiant illusions have not inspired this beautiful dream have perhaps indulged in it in moments of sad reality or boredom; discouragement and sorrow give to the unhappy a hope of finding happiness wherever men are not.

The idea of the wilderness came to me through melancholy, but it offered my soul an image of sweet felicity.

I told Marie of this dream with a flow of feeling and tenderness which I would try in vain to convey to you; in its efforts to inspire hope the heart finds expressions beyond human speech, but the fire of this divine language is extinguished when the soul falls back from the celestial Eden to which it aspires into the vale of tears.

While I spoke, Marie listened with rapture; our hearts were as one, and her mind understood mine. When I spoke the words, "Will you come with me into the wilderness?" she cried, "Oh, my love, how sweetly and tranquilly life would flow for me, in any place where I would see none but you!" And, as though remorse had entered her soul, she went on, "Solitude is fitting for me, wretched girl accursed by man and God; but for you, Ludovic, is it not too great a sacrifice to leave the world behind?"

Then I tried to assure Marie of how little I would lose by removing myself from society. To pass my days with her alone, far from the crowd I hated, seemed to me a happiness that left nothing to be desired. To allay her doubts I made no exaggeration of my love; I laid my heart bare to her. "You believe, oh my beloved, that I am making a sacrifice for you—you are wrong. This flight into the lonely forest where we will enjoy such sweet happiness is not only in accord with my heart's desire; my reason too approves. I am disgusted with European men and their civilization. In the wilds where we will go, we shall find other men who are neither polished nor learned, but neither do they practice the arts of oppression and tyranny. We call the Indians savages because they have none of our skills; but what name can those who are without our vices give to us? It is in the heart of their forests that we may behold man in his primitive dignity." [. . .]

"Ah, yes!" cried Marie, yielding to my convictions, "but my father!"

I replied, "Nelson loves us tenderly; wherever we go his blessing and prayers will follow us. Besides, ill-fated himself, will he not wish to share our seclusion?"

Nelson listened without a sign of emotion to my projects; he reflected deeply and then said to me, "The resolution you propose is extreme, but so is our position; I shall not leave you, my children. While you are occupied with your happiness in the wilderness, I shall have other duties to fulfill. I have always sympathized with the Indians in their misfortunes; their ignorance is their weakness; a great number of us harshly persecute these unfortunates. Heaven, which does not permit me to enjoy well-being and security here, thereby warns me that my place is elsewhere, and I can still be useful to my country in working to repair its injustices."

He reflected anew, and continued thus: "We will set out for the West and cross vast territories. The wilderness is far away today, American civilization grows so fast and expands so rapidly. If we seek but fertile soil and beautiful surroundings, we should choose our refuge in the Mississippi Valley, on the right bank, where as yet there are few inhabitants; but the waters of the great river, which in flood enriches the bordering land, are also, through their contact with vegetable matter, the source of effluvia fatal to the life of man. We would do better to turn our steps toward the shores of the Great Lakes, where one breathes air that is always pure. Michigan is famous for its salubrious climate; it contains but one town (Detroit), huge forests, and the Ottawa nation."

The next day, the first day of May in the year 1827, Nelson, Marie, and I went up the Hudson to reach Albany, to go from there to Buffalo, a little town upon the edge of Lake Erie. Nelson would have liked to take no servants with him; I myself wished to do likewise; but the faithful Ovasco begged so earnestly to come with us and evinced such sorrow at the idea of being separated from his kind mistress that we yielded to his prayers.

Thus we left, hunted by persecution and reduced to seeking sanctuary among the savages. Oh, I did not complain of the hardness of my fate. That departure with the beloved object, the ravishing scenes the North River offered us upon either bank—which two can admire so much better than one—the adventurous journey into unknown country; even the obduracy of the misfortunes following our course; all awakened enthusiasm and vigor in me.

Hardly had we gone ten miles up the Hudson when, gazing back at New York, that vast city which once had been the goal of my illusions and which now I quitted without regret, I perceived in the distance, at several different points, flames leaping into the air. "Those," a local resident explained, "are the churches of the blacks and their public schools which are burning." This destruction had been announced the evening before. Thus we beheld once more the hatred of our enemies, when we were beyond reach of their blows. Such was our farewell to civilized America.

Soon we saw no more than the vast sheets of water, mountains, and forests; yet we were still not in the wilds of America. These intermediate lands which separate civilization from the wilderness were calculated to impress us mournfully. I cannot express the pang I felt when, on leaving Albany and coasting the banks of the Mohawk, I saw several Indians dressed like beggars. Less than a century ago, the savages living in these parts were a formidable nation; their warrior tribes, their power, their glory, filled the forests of the New World. What is left of their grandeur? Even their name has disappeared from this earth. The people who have replaced them never even wonder if others have been there before them, and the stranger who passes through the countryside may question them and evoke no memories. Caring little about the future, the American knows nothing of the past. Doubtless the United States will become a great nation; but then, who will take their place upon earth? And will their name also be forgotten by their successors?

However, these regions invaded by European civilization will keep their wild aspect for a long time. Villages and towns are to be found here and there; but there is always the forest.* The ax re-

* The Americans regard the forest as a symbol of the wilderness, and consequently of backwardness; so it is against the trees that they direct their onslaughts. In Europe trees are cut down to be used; in America, to be destroyed. The man who lives in the country spends half his life in fighting his natural enemy, the forest; he goes at it without respite; at an early age his

sounds incessantly; there is constant burning; but one can see hardly a clearing—the feeble conquests of man over a powerful vegetation, which, falling before iron and flames, will not admit itself vanquished and vigorously grows again in spite of its destroyers. [. . .]

But other emotions stirred my heart. Each time I saw a dark forest, a pretty valley, a lake and its charming shores, I was tempted to stop there. "Here," I would say to Marie, "I could live happily. Why go farther?"

One day, passing along Lake Oneida, not far from Syracuse and Cicero, I saw an islet whose aspect made my heart tremble. It was in the middle of the lake; big enough to serve as a refuge for one family, it would not hold two; one could thus be assured of isolation. It seemed to me that nature had never offered so ravishing a sight. The island enchanted my eyes with the freshness of its vegetation, the richness and variety of its foliage; and the surrounding waters reflected in their silvery crystal, on a background of blue sky, its graceful contours, its clumps of flowering trees, and its green groves. "That is Frenchman's Island," I was told.* Was this not

---

children learn to handle the billhook and hatchet. Thus the European who admires beautiful forests is much surprised to find that the American has a deep hatred for trees. They carry this hatred so far that, in order to make their country houses pleasant, they root out the trees and greenery which surround them, and can imagine nothing more beautiful than a house situated in a bare plain where not a tree can be seen. It does not matter to them that they are scorched by the sun, without shelter from its rays: the absence of trees is, to their eyes, the sign of civilization, as their presence indicates barbarity. Nothing could be less lovely to them than a forest; on the other hand, there is nothing they admire more than a field of wheat.

* This is actually the name of that island, and my description of it in the text is perfectly accurate. I was curious enough to visit it, and wandered over its entire extent. The name it bears is due to the long residence there of a French family, who took refuge in the United States after the Revolution of 1789. At that time the shores of the lake were entirely wild, and inhabited by a tribe of the Oneida Indians, from which the lake derives its name. Local tradition says that this unfortunate family, who had fled human society, had to undergo great hardships in the heart of their solitary retreat. I found the site of their dwelling in the eastern part of the island. It was recognizable by several mounds and the presence of fruit trees not to be found in the wilderness.

Need I justify myself for having enjoyed roaming a deserted island, exploring its details, and here setting down an account of my excursion? Despite its natural beauty, the island interested me but little on its own account, but a man had lived there, and that man was French, ill-fated, and an exile!

the retreat I sought? No: the shores of the lake were overrun with Europeans. No more hospitable Indians, but American innkeepers. They had Negro servants; and these Negroes, who are doomed to public contempt because domestic service is their only livelihood, are there to remind one, even on the edge of the wilderness, of the existence of the prejudice of which they are the victims, and the eternal barrier between the two races.

The proximity of men drove us away: we had to push on.

Arriving at Buffalo, we learned of an event which filled Nelson's heart with joy. They told us that at the port, ready to embark for Michigan, there were six hundred Indians newly arrived from Georgia. They were of the Cherokee tribe; a government agent accompanied them, charged with leading them to their new lands. Nelson was not long in recognizing in them the unfortunate people for whom he had so recently forfeited his liberty, those whom American cupidity had condemned to exile, at the same time that cruel prejudice had constrained him and his family to leave Baltimore. The chiefs among the Indians had seen Nelson in Georgia, and all remembered his generous devotion. They were touchingly grateful, and this was an occasion of joy for the whole tribe. Nelson saw in this meeting a sort of providential arrangement, and told us, "Heaven has heard my prayers; it has sent to meet me the poor people to whom I was going. Do I not owe to this shining evidence of all-powerful God the happiness of finding once more the unhappy people from whom a shameful prejudice had separated me? Misfortune reunites us—now we shall not leave each other; a common adversity forms a stronger bond than a common prosperity."

But our interest in the poor exiles grew when we heard some of the reflections their departure inspired in the Americans.

"At last," said one, "these wretches are going away! We've stood them among us all too long. What did they ever make of the fertile lands they are leaving? The most skillful of them never worked in a factory, and all of them prefer forests to fields of grain!"

Another replied, "Happily, American common sense won out over the fine speeches of the philanthropists—the Quakers and Presbyterians."

A third added: "Aren't these savages all too happy? They are going to find rich land in Michigan, wide prairies and huge forests; and all that is given to them forever!"

As we listened to these saddening remarks, we witnessed a still more sorrowful spectacle: the Indians' preparations for departure. The shore of Lake Erie was crowded with half-naked Indians, small, long-maned horses, semiwild hunting dogs, long carbines, and old clothes; all these scattered pell-mell on the beach.

There is something profoundly sad in the farewell of a man to his fatherland; but an entire people leaving for exile presents a scene at once sorrowful and solemn.

The faces of these unhappy people were impassive; but one could guess at their sense of great misfortune.

As the signal to leave was given, we noticed advancing toward the waterfront a group of Indians who were even more grave and silent than the others and who walked with slower steps. One of them was bowed as though he bore a heavy burden. At his approach, all drew back to make his passage easier. Then we distinguished in the crowd a decrepit old man, bent with the weight of his years; his hairless brow, withered arms, and trembling body gave him the look of a specter rather than a living being. Two old men supported him on one side; their sagging shoulders seemed less fit to give support than to receive it; on the other side he leaned upon two women; the first white-haired, the second younger, with a child at her breast. He was the patriarch of the tribe; he had lived a hundred and twenty years. Strange and cruel fate! That man, so near the sepulcher, could not leave his bones among the bones of his fathers and, a venerable outcast, was going, at the brink of death, in search of a fatherland and a grave. Five generations surrounded and accompanied him. The misfortunes of all the others were not equal to his. What does exile mean to the newborn babe? For one with a future, a new world is a fatherland.

There was no regular communication between Buffalo and Michigan. It was therefore a doubly fortunate coincidence for us to meet the Indians who were friends to Nelson and to find a steamboat ready to leave for the very place we had chosen as our destination.

We took our places on the boat among the Cherokees. During the journey from Buffalo to Detroit, Nelson conversed at length with me upon the fate of these tribes, formerly so powerful, today fallen so low; he spoke without the enthusiasm for them expressed by European men, yet without any of the American prejudice against them. Among his words, I will always remember these: "People believe," he told me, "that we are exterminating the savage tribes of the West by the sword; they are mistaken; we are using a surer means of destruction, much less dangerous to him who employs it. In exchange for rich sables and beaver skins, we give them cheap whisky; the uncouth Indian so abuses this drink that he dies of it. This trading enriches the American and kills off his enemies. A few courageous voices have been raised among us condemning this infamous traffic, but in vain; sordid gain fascinates the eyes of the majority.

"There are those who to justify an outrage blame the victim. The Americans accuse the Indians of being worthless and degraded. Perhaps they are; but were they before they knew us? When our fathers came among them, these savages showed them a character not without greatness, a natural and true dignity; as much moral force as physical strength. These virtues are lost to them today: through whom? At that time they knew nothing of drunkenness, debauchery, begging misery, the greedy passions which engender the wish for possessions. All these vices have taken possession of their race; from whom did they come?

"I know," continued Nelson, "how difficult it is to polish their manners, to change their barbaric customs, to break them to the double yolk of a stationary and an agricultural life—prerequisite conditions of all civilization. The obstacle lies in their passionate love of wild liberty.

"But what have we done to overcome this obstacle? Do we work to civilize them or to degrade them? And if that degradation is our work, shall we find in their debasement an excuse for our transgressions?

"The Indians were powerful in this land when a handful of exiles came to seek refuge in their forests; they were hospitable and kind. Now they are told, 'Be off! You are not worth the soil you stand on and do not know how to cultivate it; go and live or die far away.' This language is not in accordance with godliness. If the Indians refuse to learn the useful arts which make for well-being in this life, let us instruct them in religion, the source of happiness in the other life; we will no longer be troubled by our consciences if we make Christians of them."

Thus spoke Nelson, and I listened to him in respectful silence, for his words were those of a just man.

"You, who sympathize with their sorrows," he went on, "make haste to see them and commiserate with them, for they will soon have disappeared from the earth. 'The forests of Michigan are given to them in perpetuity'—yes, these are the terms of the treaty; but what a mockery! The land they occupied formerly, from which they have been thrown out, had also been given to them 'forever.' Their new haven will be respected just so long as it does not excite the envy of their enemies; but the day when the American population finds itself too crowded in the East, it will remember that northern Michigan is a rich and beautiful country. Then a new treaty will be concluded between the United States and the Indians, and it will be demonstrated to the latter that of course it is in their interest to abandon their new retreat and go find another even farther away. But by going West they will reach the Pacific Ocean: that will be the end of their road; there they will stop, as one is stopped by the grave. How many days' march must they make to reach the fatal goal? I do not know, but they are already numbered. Each boatload of emigrants, spewed forth by a Europe gorged with population, swells the ranks of the advancing enemy, speeds its drive, hastens the flight of the vanquished, and brings nearer the hour of catastrophe. After having stayed in Michigan, these Indians will be driven beyond the Rocky Mountains; that will be their second halting place, and when, ever growing, the European flood will have burst that last dam, the Indian, caught between civilization and the ocean, will have a choice between two destructions: the one by man, who will kill him, the other in the abyss, which will swallow him up."

While Nelson and I theorized upon the Indians and their sad fate, Marie took but little interest in our conversation, but at sight of their unhappiness she was much more moved than we. We reasoned; she wept.

My interest in this talk at first distracted my attention from the new scenery that appeared before my eyes.

However, after we crossed Lake Erie and entered the Detroit River, so named because its waters, flowing from the higher lakes, are narrowly confined between its banks, an imposing scene struck my view and left a vivid impression upon my mind.

The farther we ascended the river, the more we saw of the natives, attracted by the noise of the steamboat. For the first time they saw a boat without sails or oars. Nothing can describe the wonder and amazement of the wilderness dweller at this sight.

It was for him and for ourselves a magnificent spectacle—this floating house, propelling itself with such speed against the swift current, without the aid of any visible power, between the jeweled banks of the meadows which were so close together that we seemed to glide upon the grass; the incessant grumbling thunder of the steam, bringing city noise into the profound solitudes; this masterpiece of human industry, marvel of modern civilization, set as contrast here to the primitive beauty of untamed nature.

We were shown on the left bank a long row of painted wooden houses, of new and elegant construction, and exactly like the buildings of all little American towns. This was the city of Detroit: no one knows whether it is named for the river, or the river for it; it was founded by the French Canadians, when France was a power in both worlds. [. . .]

Detroit is the last city in the Northwest; the wilderness begins after that. Thus the city forms the link between the civilized world and untamed nature; it is the place where American society ends and the Indian world begins.

In this spot the two worlds meet face to face; they touch, and have nothing in common.

I had always thought that in leaving big cities to reach the lonely forests I would see civilization decreasing gradually, and little by little tapering off, linking itself by an ever more tenuous chain to a primitive life that would resemble the starting point of society, whose progress or fulfillment would be our learning and mode of living. But between New York and the Great Lakes, I looked in vain for intermediate degrees in American society. Everywhere were the same men, the same passions and way of life; everywhere the same enlightenment and the same darkness.* It is a strange thing that the American nation is made up of all the peoples of the earth, and no nation presents as a whole such uniform characteristics.†

* In 1830, a bear that had lost its way traversed the whole length of the main street of Detroit. The inhabitant of this wilderness town is, however, in every respect the counterpart of the New Yorker.

† One of the principal causes of the uniformity of customs among the Americans is the enterprising spirit of the New Englanders, who, spreading

Up to this time Marie had borne up on the journey with no complaint of fatigue; but when we arrived at Detroit her face showed signs of a weakening which it was impossible for her to hide; she admitted to us that she was in need of rest, so we disembarked.

The steamboat, however, had docked only to take on more provisions and wood, and already the warning bell could be heard. Nelson said to us, "My children, stay here, take all the time necessary to let Marie regain her strength; keep Ovasco with you, whose services will be of help. I will precede you by a few days in Saginaw. The land which bears this name is pleasant and fertile, they say, but it is still wild. I will prepare your refuge there, and the day of your arrival will be the day of your marriage; I will unite you myself, since our laws give me the power to do so. There, at least, my dear Ludovic, you will be able to love the poor colored girl without fear of perfidious revelations, without risking contempt and hatred."

Thus spoke Nelson; these words were moving, and each of us was touched. Nelson said to me on leaving us: "I confide to your honor my beloved daughter Marie; she dares not claim your love; but she has a right to your respect. Your union was blessed by a priest of your sect; but the Catholic religion is not that of Marie; and besides, you know what frightful catastrophe occurred in the holy temple itself, to interrupt the solemn act about to be consummated. Good-by, my son, be a father to Marie until the day when I shall call you her husband." Nelson could judge by my deep emotion that the memory of his counsels would not leave my heart.

A moment later we watched the boat leave, carrying Nelson and the Indians, and we were left alone, Marie and I, amid the Great Lakes of America, between a world left without regret and a wilderness full of hope.

---

through all the Union, are the boldest and most tireless of the pioneers, and thus bring the same type of civilization everywhere.

When one thinks of the divers tribes of Africa and Asia, isolated though in contact, separated by a mountain, a valley, a river, each keeping its different customs and its particular character, one is struck by the contrast of a single people of 12 million men who are scattered over a country which could hold 150 million, and who present a uniform aspect, who perpetually intermingle, and who, by the complete similarity of their tastes, passions, and habits, seem to make up but a single family; so powerful over customs and the destiny of men is the bond of a common origin and language, the same religion and political institutions.

15

The Virgin Forest and the Wilderness

Strangely enough, Nelson's departure grieved me deeply. His wise words and his moving farewell stayed in my heart. But, shall I admit it?—after his leaving, when I was alone with Marie, I found myself happier. I swear that my soul was pure of any sinful hopes. But from that moment, Marie had no other protector than myself; I was the only being near her whom she loved; my heart rejoiced at being no longer distracted by friendship. Such is love—the most generous and the most selfish of all sentiments.

Marie's condition was nothing alarming; with Ovasco to help me I heaped a thousand unnecessary attentions upon her. She needed only quiet and repose. A two-day trip upon Lake Erie, whose waters heave like those of the sea, the constant noise of the steam, which sometimes rumbled and roared and sometimes escaped in piercing shrieks; the perpetual movement and tumult of life aboard ship, had been hard on Marie and brought her to a state near nervous collapse. Several nights of peaceful sleep would restore her lost strength. Then we would think of leaving; but an obstacle arose which we had never foreseen.

We had thought that it would be easy to reach Saginaw by water if we took a small boat at Detroit. Since our arrival in Detroit we had seen numerous schooners, sloops, and canoes, which we were told were always ready to go upstream, to Green Bay, Saginaw, or Sault Sainte Marie, but when I thought to make a choice among the boats, our departure having been resolved upon, my astonishment was extreme at finding not a single one in the port. Their absence was due to an event which was recounted to me in the following manner:

Every year at the same time, Indians come from far-off regions to the frontiers of Canada to obtain arms, ammunition, and clothing, which the English give them. This free distribution, contrived by a treacherous policy,* takes place not far from Detroit; the savage tribes who live around Lake Superior, Green Bay, and Saginaw had flocked in this year according to their custom; they had just left to return home, and a great number who had come down the river in their bark canoes had taken all the sail boats they could find to go upstream against the rapid current.

This circumstance threw us into a great quandary. To await the return of the boatmen, who could not reach home for several days, was more than we could bear; in our impatience to reach our longed-for goal any delay was odious to us. We were plunged into the cruelest perplexity, when we were told of a way overland to Saginaw. "By taking that path," they told us, "you will have half as far to go. True, the route is little used. Several obstacles might crop up, but easily surmounted ones." I believed these words; I did not know then that such bold enterprises are not frightening to an American; I did not know that his dauntless spirit stops only at absolute impossibilities.

They told us we would be able to make the land journey without fatigue in three days—that fur traders who barter with the Indians sometimes make it in one day. We would reach Pontiac first; on the second day we would see the Au Sable River, and on the third we would be at Saginaw.

On the fifteenth day of May, on one of those balmy days that the season of flowers gives us, Marie and I, accompanied by Ovasco, followed the route from Detroit to Pontiac in a little cart, which carried much love and much hope. Oh, how sweet it is, in the age of impetuous desires, to set out toward an unknown world, when one can press the hand of one he loves, and breathe, held against her breast!

* The apparent aim of the English is to keep the friendship of the tribes next door to Canada. Their real but unavowed reason is to supply the natural enemies of the Americans with arms and keep them on England's side in case of war with the United States.

I was astonished by the phenomenon of so handsome, wide, and well-marked a road in the midst of a wild forest.* This forest was not, however, entirely unfrequented; here and there we found a few wooden cabins, where dwelt American pioneers. Caring little for unspoiled nature, the industrious land clearers do not seek a tranquil life of retirement in these silent places; they come to seize the outposts of the wilderness, serving as innkeepers to new arrivals, putting under cultivation lands which they will resell at a profit; then they go farther, ever onward to the West, where they start again the same way of life and the same work. At Pontiac the road ended suddenly. There, on all sides, our eyes met a thick forest through which it was impossible to continue our journey as we had begun it.

Marie was accustomed to horseback riding; we were therefore able, without being foolhardy, to resort to this means of transportation.

I learned at Pontiac that henceforward we would have to follow the windings of a narrow trail through the forest, known to a handful of Americans, and which only the Indians knew well. We would have to have a guide: to obtain one I applied to an American trader who, I was told, made a business of rendering services of this nature to travelers. This man soon had at his disposal an Indian from the Ottawa tribe. It was agreed that I should pay two dollars, one for the guide, the other for the man who had procured him for me. This seemed fair enough to me; but the trader, to whom I gave the money, kept it all for himself, and compensated the Indian with a remnant of old cloth, a sort of tattered rag, with which the savage seemed quite satisfied. After that, deny if you will the superiority of the whites over the red man! As far as Pontiac a few murmurs of civilization still come from far away to trouble the silence of the solitudes, but there begins the absolute power of the untamed forest.

One cannot enter this new world without experiencing a secret terror. No more villages, no more houses, no more cabins, wagon tracks, or marked paths. The hatchet and billhook have never laid low the vegetation which spreads over all the land and hides the sky from all eyes; human industry has not desecrated this virgin nature.

* The Americans do not wait for the land to be inhabited before building roads across it. They begin by establishing roads; these bring the inhabitants.

At each step one stumbles over fallen trees; this is the work of time. In our European forests the old trees are still young; they are not given time to die, they are cut down in the prime of life. Their corpses, being useful to man, soon disappear and do not sadden the eye. The primeval forests of America are not like this. There one finds the living generations together with the dead; above our heads sways the verdure symbolic of life; at our feet lie broken branches, wormeaten trunks, the debris of death. Thus men will go forward, among unburied bones; the sanctity of a grave makes the lives of children less sad by hiding the annihilation of their ancestors.

We proceeded among the forest trees without being able to distinguish the path which we followed on the word of a savage. Onitou (that was our guide's name) bore upon his countenance the harsh, grim expression common to his race; he was the master of our existence. He could betray us, execute some fell scheme; it was enough for him to escape our eyes and leave us to ourselves for us to be lost.

However, these sinister impressions were not of long duration. After traveling for several hours, during which our horses hardly equaled the speed of the Indian, the latter stopped. I offered him a little of that whisky which the men of his race, in their picturesque language, call firewater. He drank some, and his face all at once took on such a benevolent expression and his naturally stern look became so gentle that I was completely reassured. The forest itself lost its terrors and showed itself to us in its most pleasant aspect. Several miles beyond Pontiac, there begins a delightful country: a thousand low hills form as many valleys in which a multitude of lakes breathe forth eternal coolness and present the loveliest landscape to the eye.

As we wended our way through these beautiful forests, so full of life, so impressive with age, so near the civilized world, I seemed to hear mysterious echoes which recounted their past grandeur, and foretold their coming destruction.

Oh, how can I tell you of the enthusiasm that seized my spirits? We went on, Marie and I, in receptive silence, aware of every beauty nature offered by the thousand, holding fast to all our emotions to enjoy each to the full. I was near enough to Marie so that I could press her hand; thus we went into the wilderness leaning upon each other, she upon my strength and I on her love, divided between the sensations aroused by the sublime surroundings and our tender feelings, augmented by the spectacles of nature. What ravishing sights we saw! What delicious agitation in our souls! How the sweet aspect of the present accorded with our enchanting dreams of the future! As soon as we should reach Saginaw, Marie would be my dear wife. And so my beloved would come to the marriage altar, under my protection, through a thousand flowers blooming beneath our footsteps, a thousand leaves rustling over our heads, under a roof of sunlight, shadow, and verdure. Happy our lot—alas! that the horizon was hidden from us! For doubtless it was stormy! [. . .]

I feared the fatigues of the journey for Marie: but she opposed my uneasiness with words of inexpressible charm. "My dear," she said, "I feel strong because I am going toward unhoped-for happiness." She said again, "This lonely retreat to which we are going has been the object of my most ardent desires and the goal of all my ambitions: but, Ludovic, have you no regrets?

And I answered her, "My beloved, for a long time I knew no purpose in life, and I often reproached God for the uselessness of the days he imposed upon me; only your love revealed the secret of life to me.

"In my liveliest enthusiasm for glory I was uncertain if I was not pursuing a chimera. . . . What is glory? The greatness bestowed upon a man by his fellows. But who bestows it? Only posterity.

"Glory is sunlight for the soul; it does not shine until after the death of the body; its divine light gladdens only our shades.

"My dearest, love does not deceive us so: your sweet voice, which enchants me, is not a lie; your glance, which intoxicates me with pleasure, is no illusion; your hand locked in mine is not a dream. Oh, Marie! Love can deceive our hearts too, but only to give them a joy so great that they know not how to contain it!"

Such was our conversation beneath those leafy porticoes, until our eyes were suddenly struck by a brilliant shaft of sunlight; the farther we advanced, the brighter grew the daylight until finally the shade disappeared with the last tree of the forest—we found ourselves at the edge of a vast prairie where nature at her most varied, her richest, and most gracious dazzled our eyes with a torrent of light.

The Indian let us know by signs that here was a halting place.

We had anticipated his advice. Seized with wonder at this new scene we had stopped short, Marie and I, with one accord, as though halted by a simultaneous understanding.

While Onitou and Ovasco led our horses to a nearby spring, well known to the Indian, Marie seated herself next to me. [. . .] Our backs were to the forest, and the prairie that spread before us displayed all its magnificence.

When a beautiful woman, living, ardent, and passionate, appears to you suddenly in a dream of love, her charming features, the sweet melody of her voice, the still sweeter harmony of the graces which adorn her, the enchantment that comes from her balmy breath, her floating hair, her burning glance—all is music, perfume, voluptuousness.

So the wild prairie appeared to my eyes.

Against a background of verdure shaded with innumerable tints, thousands of insects with wings of purple and gold, variegated butterflies, hummingbirds with throats of ruby, topaz, and emerald passed and repassed, skimming the prairie and mingling with the flowers, sometimes alighting on a frail stem, sometimes tilting into a fragrant calyx. Some were tender creatures who live for a day, some counted years of happiness; all were full of life and love; here fleeing to invite capture, there flying conjoined and loving even high in the sky, as though to bear their joys to God; an atmosphere almost enervating in its sweetness, all bestrewn with sparkling creatures which seemed like myriad flowers and jewels dancing in the air.

Such was the scene spread before our eyes. From every side came sweet warblings, tender sighs, happy murmurs. It seemed that in this fortunate spot everything rejoiced with one voice. The smallest caterpillar rippled with joy, each branch in the forest echoed happiness, each zephyr bore a whisper of love.

Amid this magic of nature untamed, intoxicated by the breath of Marie who lay against my heart, by the perfume of her hair over which I bowed, possessed by the irresistible enchantment of this solitude where everything lived to love, I leaned over Marie, and my lips met her sweet lips, and I clung to that chalice of honey and delight. Silent joy! ravishing ecstasy! heavenly voluptuousness, yet incomplete! For a scorching wind passed over my soul and enkindled impetuous desires! Confident in my love, the pure virgin had no thought of resisting me. Then began a terrible struggle in the depths of my heart. A thousand flames consumed it, and my blood leaped boiling in my veins. Oh, my beloved! Your beauty itself, which inspired these transports, and your innocence, which would render my victory so easy, saved me from weakness and remorse. In that moment of wild passion and fascination, in the midst of the dazzlement which possessed my entire being, you appeared to me as an enchanting vision, painted in my imagination in a blue sky among rosy clouds, you appeared, lovely being, with the misty features of a celestial spirit; it was you, Marie, but you more beautiful still, with more seductive grace, innocence, and purity. I saw you through the transparent veil of a future only a few days distant, in our blessed sanctuary in Saginaw, amid even more bountiful nature, more love-inspiring solitude; as my adored wife you rested on my heart, entwined in my arms, lavishing upon me without fear a thousand tender caresses which I received without remorse—and I shuddered to think that I had been about to stain that white flower, to rob it of its innocent sweetness, to pollute with vice and bitterness the pure well of delight! I did not think of Nelson, his counsels, the shame of betraying his trust. Oh, my love, Heaven is witness that in tearing myself from your arms where I was fainting with joy, I yielded only to our love!

At that moment a confused noise struck my ears: the voices of men, neighing horses, barking dogs could be heard. Soon we perceived a band of Indians approaching, following the path we had traveled. My first reaction was one of fear. Who were these Indians? Whence did they come? How did they come to be between us and the village we had left that same morning? Was our guide faithful? Was not the halt he had advised part of a plot? If the Indians attacked, what resistance could I offer? How could I protect Marie? Caught between these savages and the unknown plains, flight was impossible; the direst thoughts filled my mind. My fears increased when I saw Onitou talking familiarly with those who walked at the head of the band. Soon a whole tribe of Indians revealed themselves: men, women, children, baggage, hearth and home—they had everything with them.

A young woman carrying her child came up behind us; another separated from the crowd and, seated at the foot of an old oak, gave her breast to her newborn babe; here and there the men slipped like lithe animals among the vines, seeking wild fruits; others stopped before us and, with the prairie as a banquet hall, seated themselves around a fire, hastily started, over which they hung the still quivering meat of a buck and a moose. As they passed close to Marie I looked at them with the forced smile born of fear when it pretends to be confidence. All of them wore grim, fierce expressions. Most of them pretended not to see us. Some glanced at us with haughty contempt. Only one smiled graciously at us, but that was a fleeting glance. His face suddenly resumed its harsh severity.

I learned later that these Indians, a tribe of Ottawas who lived in northern Michigan, had come to Detroit to go on to Canada; that there, having heard of the arrival of the Cherokees, they had suddenly set out again so as to precede the newcomers to their destination and observe the invasion.

We continued our journey without hindrance, and I learned to travel among the savages of the New World with more security than I could have among many European peoples, long civilized. The day was declining; our shadows and those of our horses lengthened at our right. At the end of the prairie we found more forest. Shortly afterward we were on the south bank of the Au Sable River; it was the opposite bank which was to furnish us with shelter for the night; the next day we would leave for Saginaw. Led by Ovasco and Onitou, our horses swam across the river; I put Marie into a bark canoe which we found on the bank; I got in close to her and, as well as I could, paddled the little boat which carried an adored being, my hopes, and all my future. I shall always recall with delight that short moment of happiness: the hour when day has left and night has not yet come; when the birds of the day have ended their concerts and those of the shadows have not yet begun their lugubrious chants; when, after the heat of the sun that awakens and enlivens all things, the orb of night pours its muted beams over sleeping nature.

A wonderful contrast! The innumerable voices, songs, murmurs, all the harmonies of day, were succeeded by a profound silence; all was hushed around us; no distant sound reached our ears; flies with wings of flame sparkled in the air as they danced, a thousand burning flashes, which one might have taken for sparks from a vast conflagration were it not for the delicious coolness which spread around us. Filled with the calm air we breathed, unable to speak a word, we held our breath for fear of troubling the silence of nature; we remained motionless and our canoe drifted with the current. Already, above the tall crests of the pines, the moon bathed us in its mysterious light, reflecting its trembling rays on the surface of the waters, gently rippled by our frail barque; the peaceful atmosphere entered our souls, and we no longer thought; our hearts were full; our happiness tranquillized like nature itself; just now so lively, ardent, and animated, now calmed and still. It was evening, tender twilight of the wilderness and of the emotions, sweet dew come to refresh our souls parched by the passions of the day.

As I took up the paddle to direct our canoe to the shore, "Oh, my love, how sad!" cried Marie in a low voice. "Are we already there? Why could we not follow this current that carries us on so gently? How easily one can breathe here! How pure is this air which the breath of the wicked has not tainted! Oh, must we leave this place so soon? Where could we find more serenity, more sweet emotions, more tranquil happiness?" And the charming girl leaned toward me, held my arm, and said, "How sweet it would be! Abandoning ourselves to this almost celestial dream, trustfully following the waters of this river, which rocks us so gently; how sweet it would be, oh my love, to die together with ecstasy in our hearts, and rise to Heaven with one leap of our souls toward God! We would only be changing our dwelling place. Could the happiness of angels surpass what we feel now? Could we have such felicity here below?"

I steered for the shore and said, "Marie, I do not know if you are an earthly creature; for your voice, your words, all of you, are full of a divine charm. When I see your tears flowing I take you for the angel of melancholy aspiring to ascend again to Heaven, where innocence no longer weeps; but when your voice enchants and calms me with tones of happiness, I no longer know what to think of the superhuman being who, knowing the joys of Heaven, does not scorn the joys of the earth. My beloved, trust in my love; a sweeter, purer air, a still more smiling land, a yet lovelier nature await us yonder; we shall be better off than here, for we shall be farther still from the world we hate. See how happiness reveals itself more and more to us, the farther we flee."

Upon what shore would the next day's dawn have found us if, yielding to Marie's voice and the slumber which held all nature captive, I had surrendered our boat to the will of the stream? I do not know. Is the shelter our reason selects as safe as that chosen for us by the caprice of the wind, the drift of the waters, the shadows of the night?

Our shelter that night was a little log cabin, the dwelling of a New Englander who had settled near the Indians to deal in furs.

Upon our arrival our horses were turned loose in a narrow enclosure near the house. Our host hastened on foot to cut fodder for them in an oat field; then, taking an ax, he cut down a tree in the forest, with which he built a fire to keep us from the chill of the night. The logs of which the cabin was built let in the outside air through a thousand openings, and the damp mist from the river could already be felt. Soon a crackling fire, fed with pine cones, lit up the shadowy dwelling, and let us look about the hut, cramped but remarkably clean. A woman with a pale, thin face appeared; she was our host's wife, and around her flocked several young children. A crudely painted picture of General Washington was hung above the fireplace. In the United States, Washington is god in the cottage as in the Capitol! On a table in the middle of the room were scattered several pages of a fairly recent New York paper. Everything in our host's house suggested material comfort rather than happiness. Their manners were polite without elegance, their speech correct without refinement, their knowledge accurate but limited—all this showed that they were not born in the wilderness and that they belonged to the middle class of a civilized society. Their sole aim, their fixed idea, was to make their fortunes; they were like all other Americans.

The woman prepared us a modest meal; tea was served in the wilderness hut. This odd situation would not have been without its charms for me, if Marie had been able to enjoy it herself; but she was unwell. A long day of traveling had weakened her; she did not partake of the repast which would have mended her strength. I took great pains to prepare a place for her to rest in; a buffalo hide served as a bed; I covered her feet with my cloak, and then, overcome with weariness, Marie took one of my hands as a token of security, and, leaning against me, fell asleep. Soon everyone slept quietly about me; I alone kept watch within, hearing the least sounds without; an impressive vigil in the depths of the wild forest, in a solitary cabin where a few gleaming flames flickered—the sole movement in my surroundings; a silent vigil which brought before my eyes, like phantoms, the memories of my youth, my ambitions, my vast plans, the triumphs and failures of my life, my illusions and disillusions, my loves and hopes—an almost feverish vigil, in which my imagination wandered continually between the past and the future, from despair to happiness, from wisdom to folly, never stopping until, dominated by an irresistible power, my thoughts wavered, sank by degrees, resumed with an effort, and then fell back and died away in the depths of slumber.

Before my eyelids succumbed I had noticed that Marie's repose was troubled with sudden movements, tremblings, and broken murmurs. In the morning she awoke with a start. Her first movement was to seize my hand again, which she had let fall in her sleep. This gesture roused me from my drowsiness, and, seeing Marie again, over whom I had not had the strength to watch for a whole night, I understood the powerlessness of the will.

Marie was sad and pensive. "My love," she said, "if I were not close to you I would fear great misfortunes, for I have had terrible dreams."

I saw with concern that the night had brought her no rest, and the rapidity of her pulse made me think that she had been seized by a fever. What could we do? Remain in that lonely cabin? Stop so close to our goal? We need travel but one more day. In the evening we would reach Saginaw, to stay there for always. Should we not, at any cost, reach that place of rest, which would restore Marie to herself, and see the commencement of our happiness? I spoke my thoughts to Marie. "Yes," she replied, "Oh, yes! Let us go quickly to Saginaw—there we shall find happiness—you promised me."

We left at dawn. [. . .] A new landscape and new impressions were in store for us. Before reaching the Au Sable River, we had traversed wild solitudes; after leaving it, we truly entered the wilderness. We went on without hearing the song of a single bird, the hum of a single insect, the movement of a single living being. It was no longer the silence of nature at rest after the songs of the day, when one hears her breathing as she sleeps; it was the gloomy silence of nothingness. The only sounds were the steps of our guide and our horses, a regular noise which added to the monotony of the place. No more valleys, no more echoes, no prairie, no sky; everywhere the same forest, everywhere the same trees, everywhere the level earth; at each step we found the same places we had just left. We seemed to walk without advancing, playthings of an invisible power, that gave us the illusion of movement and paralyzed our effort. We went on and on, and the scene never changed! Where were we? Were we on the right track? Where was the North, toward which we should be going? the South, which we should be fleeing? I believed we were going in circles. How huge that forest was! And suppose it should never end? It became more and more dense, its shadows deeper, its hushed vaults more silent, terrifying, and mysterious, so that one felt caught in a labyrinth and lost amid its turnings.

These impressions were the stronger upon us in contrast with the emotions of the day before—some so passionate and others so gentle. I felt a chill enter my soul, and a leaden lump weigh down my heart.

"Oh God!" said Marie, coming close and seizing my hand, "how deep and terrible is this loneliness!" And as her spirit was so receptive to dire omens, she said, "My love, you may be sure that today is a fateful day—I do not know why the thought of George is ever with me; doubtless there has been some frightful calamity——"

She could not continue: a tear completed her thought. I endeavored to reassure her and to give her more confidence than I felt myself. But I was keenly struck by her exhaustion, marked in all her features. I thought a short rest would relieve her, and ordered our little caravan to halt.

During this halt I asked Onitou by signs if we were nearing Saginaw. He quite understood my question, and marking two points in the earth, one representing Saginaw and the other the Au Sable River, he drew a line between them, and on that line marked a third point, indicating where we were; this point showed that we were but one third of the way on our journey. A moment later, while we were seated beneath a catalpa tree, we saw the Indian rise and start off before us, lighter than a deer, crying, "Saginaw! Saginaw!" and pointing to the sun, already straight overhead.

Then Marie made a brave effort to rise; and we continued our wilderness journey. I could soon tell from Marie's voice that her strength was steadily declining. After long hours of travel, I ordered our guide once more to stop, but at my call he redoubled his pace, indicating by an eloquent gesture that the sun was already descending into the bosom of the earth and that the forest would soon be lost in shadows. But the wilds showed themselves in a more and more fearsome aspect. The path we followed was so narrow that Marie and I could no longer go side by side; it was barely discernible; we continually lost it to view and then felt that we were going completely at random across the forest. Night having fallen, the silence ceased, but the loneliness had taken on a voice that was terrible and mournful. We could hear the growling of bears and the sinister notes of night birds. The moon, which lends charm to the gloomiest nights, as the love of a beautiful woman fills an unhappy life with secret enchantments, was not yet visible. [. . .]

The hours flowed by, the night advanced, our horses slowed their pace, a damp chill arose from the earth. Marie remained silent, which increased my desperate anxiety. I took her hand: I found it burning hot. "My dear," she said in a faint voice, "let us not go on—I think I am dying."

At these words my heart broke; I know not what mad resolve would have been born of my despair, when our guide stopped suddenly, and cried three times, "Saginaw!" That cry, thrown to the wilderness, reached afar, and came back to us repeated by a thousand echoes, the first tumultuous, the next less strong, the following ones more and more faint. The forest ended abruptly, and we emerged upon a prairie. We continued on it for a time, descending a gradual slope. At last we came to the shore of a wide river. That river was the Saginaw; and the opposite shore the refuge we sought.

16

The Tragedy

"Oh, Heaven! What joy!" cried Marie on seeing the river bank. Her moral courage would have been incapable of a longer effort. I took her in my arms and placed her in an Indian canoe; I seated myself near her as I had in crossing the Au Sable River. "My love," said Marie to me then, "forgive me—I have distressed you—I believed all through that journey that a malignant fate was against our coming to this place. I was wrong; for you are my good angel and have guided me. Oh! I felt my body failing and my spirit breaking, but I no longer suffer, and I have only happy thoughts."

These words filled my heart with joy, and I steered for the opposite bank as for the end of all our trials.

"Look," said Marie, pointing to our future empire, "see how happy we shall be in that far-off land. Yes, the waters of the Saginaw are still purer and more peaceful than those of the Au Sable; the air is sweeter here, the earth more fragrant; and there the orb of night, our guardian spirit of the wilderness, rises in all its splendor."

Speaking thus, Marie lifted her gaze to the heavens. "Oh, God!" she cried suddenly in a terrified voice, and hid her eyes in her hands.

At that moment the red and flaming disk of the moon emerged from the shadows of the forest and seemed, as it rose, to be poised on the treetops. We watched it rise and swell, as it advanced upon us like a bloody specter.

That terrible image had struck Marie's spirit, and the cry of fright she vainly tried to hold back was again the voice of sinister foreboding.

Even as she reached the long-desired goal, Marie had felt the resurgence of a supernatural energy, which was not of long duration. I know not if her strength waned at the same time with her faith in the future, but I saw her almost at once sink into a great despondency.

I found myself from that moment a prey to unimaginable distress.

Nelson was not at Saginaw. The boat which bore both him and the Cherokees had not yet appeared, and the Ottawa Indians, native to that country, assured me that no stranger had come to these lands for a very long time.

This mischance was for Marie and me a source of pain and uneasiness. It made our situation more difficult. Nelson was to have prepared a shelter for us, which we needed. I set to work at it at once. But I do not know what our fate would have been if, while waiting for our cottage to be built, we had not found the shelter of a hospitable roof.

Saginaw, where you now see two dwellings built with some care, then boasted but one, of rude construction, which we found occupied by an American of Canadian origin. This man appeared overjoyed to see us, and recognizing me by that family resemblance all Frenchmen bear, he said to me, "You come from the old country?" He had been born among the Indians, nearly all of whose customs he had adopted. Hunting and fishing satisfied his needs; and he found great pleasure in a life of completely wild freedom.

As we arrived he was on the point of leaving; he was going to the vicinity of Fort Gratiot to hunt wood pigeons. He offered us his cabin and begged us to stay there until I should have built another. I proposed to buy it from him, leaving it to him to fix the price; but he would not hear of this and replied that he loved the place, had been born there, and would pass the rest of his days there.

Thus can one find in the heart of the wilderness the very character of a nation. The American of English extraction follows no bent but that of self-interest; nothing binds him to the place where he lives, neither family nor tender feelings. Always ready to leave his dwelling for another, he sells it to anyone who will give him a dollar's profit.

Next door to him you may see the man of French origin, attached to his birthplace, cherishing the land where his fathers have lived, loving the objects about him for themselves, and preferring these things with a purely ideal value to the cold pleasures of wealth.

I accepted his offer, and could not persuade him to take a reward for the service he rendered.

We had a shelter, but there were still obstacles and hardships all around us.

Marie was stricken on the first day with a fever peculiar to that country, which new arrivals rarely escape. I must needs divide my time between the care so necessary to my love and the work necessary to the building of our dwelling. The Canadian's cabin, invaluable as it was in our time of need, offered but imperfect refuge; it was built of logs with gaps between, through which the chill of night penetrated as did the heat of day. Insects swarmed in: some, invisible, betrayed their presence by their painful bites; others danced in clouds revealing their slim bodies to be armed with long stingers, and wearying our ears with their perpetual humming; they kept us in continual, pitiless warfare against them and cruelly troubled Marie's repose.

The rude fare to which we were reduced would have been nothing to trouble a man in full health; but Marie's weakness, her illness, and her former way of life made necessary more delicate nourishment, which we completely lacked.

We lacked everything in these wilds: the nearest doctor was in Detroit; and I saw Marie languishing without being able to offer the least alleviation for her pain.

However, we could not think of leaving the place; we would have had to retrace our steps to Detroit to find help; we had no means of returning by water, and it would have been madness to attempt a second time the long trip whose fatigues Marie had had such difficulty in overcoming. [. . .]

Whatever my concern, my heart refused to harbor great uneasiness. Nelson would arrive soon; soon, too, Marie would have a home with better protection against the discomforts of the out-of-doors. Her illness proceeded doubtless from a succession of days without rest or sleep, and would yield to several nights of complete peace, and then, how happy we would be! [. . .]

I considered the obstacles I would have to vanquish, and armed myself to fight them with that moral energy which only confidence in success can give. I worked at our cottage the whole of the time that I did not pass at Marie's side.

I was aided in my task by Ovasco, whose devotion defies description. That faithful servant seemed to multiply himself to cope with all difficulties.

In the midst of the rough work and the sweat it cost me, I took a secret delight in thinking that everything in our happiness would be the work of my own hands.

However, great as were my efforts, the work I had undertaken demanded more time than I had thought. Marie's condition became more alarming; her pulse indicated increasing disturbance. She made not a single complaint; but under the smile wavering upon her lips it was easy to see a deep distress.

She said to me tenderly one day, "Ludovic, you are taking such pains at building our home!" Another time: "You leave me to work on the cottage—ah, I beg you, stay beside me! Who knows the future?" I rejected the frightening thought underlying these words. But the advancing season increased my uneasiness and distress. About ten days had passed since our arrival at Saginaw, and the heat of June began to make itself felt. Penetrated by the rays of the burning sun, assailed by clouds of flies, of which the blazing temperature seemed to augment the number and malignity, our little cabin became the scene of such miserable discomfort as I cannot describe. I made vain attempts to keep away the innumerable enemies that buzzed around Marie; they multiplied more quickly than I could annihilate them; and I saw my love's fair brow bleed from the bites of these vile insects. I passed whole days and nights thus, watching over my beloved, and trying by my care to ease her vexations and pain.

During this time Ovasco worked without respite at the cottage, which was nearly completed. To crown our misfortunes, he himself was stricken with the local fever, so that I found myself alone, without help, surrounded by sickness which I must watch ceaselessly and could not ease.

For a long time my mind had been impervious to any sense of frightful catastrophe. Strange!—when one possesses something dearer than life, and is enjoying it in peace, he is quick to conjure up chimerical fears; and if he is in great danger of losing it, he tries as hard to blind himself to the real peril as he tried before to anticipate imaginary ones. Such is the justice of Heaven. The happy man's joy is troubled by fear of misfortune, and the unhappy man's misery is assuaged by dreams of felicity!

Nevertheless, Marie's words, which kept returning to my memory, the sight of the suffering she underwent before my eyes, and perhaps, too, the obduracy of fate in upsetting all my plans, cast trouble into my soul. I saw a spectral light—and my whole body was covered with an icy sweat. I made an effort to recall my wits, which I felt were going astray, and said to Marie:

"My beloved, in a few days our new home will be ready to receive you; then only Nelson's presence will be lacking to our happiness. If he had left for these parts without a guide, we might justly be very uneasy; but what can we fear, knowing that he is surrounded by Indians who love him, revere him, and find the wildest country the most beautiful? Let us hope that he will soon be restored to us. But, my love, I ask Heaven for one thing more, which is dearer to me than all the good things of this world, and that is the end of your sufferings. We do not know the remedy to cure you; a doctor's aid is necessary. I shall go and seek it at Detroit; I will be there in two days, and two days later I will be here again, bringing with me the man whose skill will save you. During my absence our faithful Ovasco will stay with you; though ill himself he will find strength to care for his kind mistress."

Ovasco, who was there, could not hear these words without tears; Marie listened with every sign of deep emotion. She was silent, appeared to think earnestly, and then said in a weak voice, "My love, do not leave me, I pray you—four days' absence—it is very long! No—Ludovic—no—you must stay." And her gaze, fixed upon me, took on an ineffable tenderness and melancholy.

I tried to make her understand how foolish it was to yield to a momentary weakness which might ruin our future, while the sacrifice of a few days would assure our happiness.

But I found in her an instinctive resistance, against which my reason was powerless.

"My beloved," she said, "I beg you, do not abandon me; you know how fragile is the vine when it is separated from the limb which supports it. Ludovic, far from you I shall be more feeble still—your presence alone sustains me—if you go away I shall break." The tone in which she pronounced these words was heartrending.

Stirred by her speech, the more afflicting since it contained all the bitterness of despair without the violence that would exaggerate it, I fell on my knees by the head of Marie's bed; incapable of speaking a word, I seized my love's hand and watered it with a torrent of tears; never had sorrow so filled my soul.

When this storm had passed, I raised my bowed head, but I regained the rationality that had left me, only to understand fully the horror of my situation and the extent of my helplessness.

Illusions, misguided hopes, had always hidden from me Marie's true state. She found contentment in constantly deceiving me about her condition. When I spoke to her of our future happiness, she shed tears which I believed to be of joy. If I mentioned her sufferings, she was quick to change the subject of our conversation; unmindful of her illness, she used all her strength to distract me from my troubles, and while she pined away with cruel grief, it was still she who consoled me.

What was my amazement when, resting my gaze upon that dear hand which I pressed in a transport of despair and love, I saw it was withered to a terrible thinness!

The flash of knowledge that came to me was as a bolt of deadly lightning. The body of my love was wasted away by her illness—her face alone had not undergone its ravages and had kept, despite its tired look, the signs of unwavering strength; perhaps the power of her spirit revealed itself wholly in her eyes, or perhaps the burning of the fever caused the blood and the vigor which remained in her weakened body to flow to her face.

Thus the sad truth was revealed to my gaze. This, then, was the effect of those long days under a burning sun; of those still longer nights, passed in pain, without sleep or rest, unprotected, and in the ever-increasing torment of ceaseless wakefulness.

However, Ovasco, witnessing this scene, said to me: "My good master, you cannot leave this place; let me go to Detroit; I will soon return with the man whose help is so necessary."

When he saw that I hesitated to accept this offer of his devotion, which his state of illness rendered imprudent, he added: "Oh, I feel better; the thought of saving my dear mistress gives me strength."

"Faithful servant," I replied, "it is my life, too, that you will save."

I do not know if an extraordinary effort of the will can deaden the cruelest pain and suddenly revive a dying strength; but I saw Ovasco, after receiving my embrace, cross the river in a canoe, and at once cross the prairie beyond with the speed of a deer.

Here Ludovic broke off; his melancholy features were clouded by an ever-deeper sadness; and after a moment of silence he resumed in these words:

Alas! I have told you of our mischances up to that day; the misfortunes I must now relate to you are indescribable.

The day following Ovasco's departure, I experienced all the emotions aroused by illusory joy: I saw a considerable band of Indians arrive at Saginaw, whose costume and appearance were in all points similar to those of the Cherokees. I had no doubt that these were Nelson's companions, and, persuaded that he was among them, I hastened to meet them. But I recognized not one face when I came close to them, and soon was certain that these Indians, though belonging to the Cherokee tribe, were not those we awaited.

As I watched them, I witnessed a scene which led directly to a terrible revelation for me.

The arrival of the Cherokees had thrown the whole tribe of Ottawas, who occupied Saginaw and its environs, into a state of turmoil. They knew how disastrous to them was the presence of these newcomers in a territory which even now barely furnished the means of existence to its inhabitants. The majority hid their resentment. But some had not the prudence to do so.

"You are taking our land," said an Ottawa to a Cherokee chief.

"Are not the forests of Michigan," replied he, "big enough to hold us all?"

"No," answered the first, "we are already crowded in this country, and you shall not raise your houses here!" As he said this he made a threatening gesture. "Wretch!" cried his adversary. "Then you do not know Mohawtan?" And seizing his tomahawk he instantly stretched the Ottawa at his feet.

This act of violence created a great uproar among the Ottawas—I saw it with a feeling of horror. However, the words of the Cherokee evoked memories in my mind, and I recalled that George, in telling me of Nelson's persecution in Georgia, had spoken of an

Indian chief named Mohawtan, renowned for valor, who had been the first to give a sign of resistance to oppression. I asked him a question on this subject; I added that I was a friend of Nelson, the Presbyterian minister, the defender of the Indians. At mention of Nelson's name, the Indian's face took on an expression of mingled kindliness and wonder. "You are Nelson's friend!" he cried, with emotion.

"Yes," I answered, "and you will soon see him in these parts: I do not know what delay keeps him from us so long; he should have preceded me here. His daughter Marie, whom I love, is there, in that cabin. She is weak and ill, and I am half dead with anxiety. I am alone here, without friends, a prey to my torment, between two Indian tribes which I see are ready to engage in a fatal struggle. I pray you, take pity on my sad fate. Nelson, Marie's father, was your protector. His son George was no less devoted to your cause."

"George!" repeated the Indian, looking at me fixedly, "George! the bravest of men—and the most unfortunate!"

Not understanding these mysterious words, I pressed Mohawtan for an explanation. After a pause of several moments, he said: "An insurrection of the black population has been in preparation for a long time in the Southern states. When the Negroes of Virginia and the two Carolinas learned that the Americans in New York had burned the churches of the colored people, it was the signal for the outbreak of the revolt. A great conspiracy was formed, whose central point was Raleigh, in North Carolina.

"Only a month had passed since the cruel persecution of the Cherokees by the Americans, which had led a great number of them to exile themselves from Georgia. Those of our tribe who had not emigrated did not hesitate to support the Negro movement. I was of this number, and one of the chiefs of the tribe. The Indians gathered near Raleigh, in order to arrange a common plan of action with the chiefs of the insurrection. A council was held, and the extermination of our common enemies was resolved upon.

"They agreed that, upon a signal given at night, the Negroes of the countryside would come out of their cabins, and carry the fear of death into their masters' dwellings; while the Indians, gathered at a certain spot, were to attack Raleigh, and make themselves masters of the city and the city militia.

"The appointed day approached, but the chiefs would not listen to each other; each aspired to the honors of command, and found the obscure role of follower unworthy of him. Alas! the respect our fathers showed for the words of the old men and the voices of wise men is lost! In the meantime, George arrived from New York, where he had taken up the defense of the colored people. His name recalled to us the good deeds of his father. We received him as a friend: the nobility of his bearing, the loftiness of his sentiments, the superiority of his mind, impressed us all. He listened to our plans and consented to lead us. 'My rightful place,' he told us, 'is among the black men, but I am too proud of commanding such warriors as you to decline such an honor: besides we all fight for the same cause, that of freedom against tyranny. Moreover,' he added, 'although the vengeance my brothers will wreak, cruel as it may seem, is legitimate, I would prefer to avenge myself with the sword and not the dagger.'

"At the fixed hour, in the middle of the night, the flames of a beacon lighted at the country's highest point gave the signal agreed upon. But—it was incredible—the Negroes, for whose sake the insurrection was to break out, and who had been filled with courageous zeal upon the eve, remained inactive. Whether through stupidity or fear, all those unhappy men, who groan beneath the weight of the harshest oppression, made not one effort to become free; they did nothing they had promised, and not a white man was massacred in the countryside.

"But the Indians were faithful to their pledge. When the hour came, George gave our band the order to advance on Raleigh. But doubtless we had been betrayed—for hardly had we emerged from the forest which borders the road when we met a body of the militia, twenty times more numerous than we. Despite the inferiority of our forces, we engaged in battle. Ah! how can I tell you of George's bravery? Alas! did such heroism deserve so grievous an end?"

Here Mohawtan stopped; his emotion was extreme, and I saw that an Indian can weep; I understood the meaning of that tear and the silence that preceded it. The Indian told me of George's exploits, his intrepidity, his daring, his desperate efforts. "The son of Nelson," added Mohawtan, "seeing that he must succumb to greater numbers, said to me in a determined voice, 'Friend, save your life—but take this paper; it is for my father. If ever you see him again, you will give him George's farewell.' After these words, he was kindled with new ardor; he had recognized a mortal enemy in the fray. I heard him cry out boldly, 'Fernando! Cowardly assassin of my mother, die—I am avenged!' Alas! he soon was smitten by a fatal blow himself."

Here again the Indian ceased speaking; as for me, I heard him in the daze which comes over us with a new misfortune when the measure of our woes is already full. Mohawtan continued thus: "I tried to avenge the death of so dear a friend, but I was alone against an army: I must needs fly. Hardly escaped from peril, I looked back at the place where I had last seen George; but I could distinguish nothing more. At that moment the moon showed itself above the horizon with a red and bloody face. I knew then that it was a portentous night.

"The next day I learned of the shameful inaction of the Negroes. The governor of North Carolina made a proclamation to announce the victory of the militia over the Indians. He praised the prudence of the Negroes and ordered severe measures against us. Then what remained of our tribe made up their minds to go into exile. Informed of our plans, the United States government hastened to support them; for all that this country wanted was our lands. They even sent an agent to help in our retreat. Following the same route as the first emigrants of our tribe, we went first to Pittsburgh, then to Buffalo; there we were told of the halt our compatriots had made at that place; their meeting with Nelson, and their embarkation with him for Michigan. At Detroit we heard of their departure for Saginaw, going upstream. Desiring to reach the same place, we wished to go by the same way, but they told us that navigation in those parts was slow and difficult. We came to Saginaw overland.

"Friend," said Mohawtan, taking my hand, "fear nothing from our tribe. Nelson's daughter is here; what help does she need? Speak, command us, and each will obey."

His tale had distressed me more than I could express. George, Marie's brother, George, my dearest friend, was no more!

"Come," said Mohawtan, "here is what George confided to my care at his last hour." The Indian gave me a paper which bore Nelson's name.

I was overwhelmed with grief; however, accepting the Indian chief's generous offer, I begged his help in finishing our cottage. In an instant all the hands of the Cherokees were put at my disposal;

I showed what had to be done, and returned to Marie's side, bringing into our poor dwelling one more sorrow.

I applied all my efforts to hiding the trouble in my soul. I told Marie of the obliging zeal of the Indians who were working for us, and I left her for not a single instant. Three days passed, during which it seemed to me she gained a little strength. The next day Ovasco was due to return, then we would receive the aid we so desired, and Mohawtan came to announce joyfully that one more day would be enough to finish the work on our dwelling.

Thus, in the midst of my grief, I once more set out to hope!

However, toward evening of that fair day, the sky became filled with thick mists; although no wind blew, the tops of the pines shuddered queerly; a heavy oppression weighed on the forest; one could hear strange murmurs high in the air, while a gloomy stillness overhung the earth: everything presaged a storm.

I was seated beside Marie's pillow, trying to ease her sufferings with evidence of my love—I spoke to her of our coming happiness. She remained silent a long time, but, suddenly making a sign for me to listen, she said in a calm, resigned voice: "My love, stop deceiving yourself. My illness is a mortal one. Remember the day of our arrival in this place: at the instant when the moon, on fire, appeared like a bloody phantom, I was seized by a pain which has never left me. It is this pain which consumes me. No power can fight it. It is the decree of destiny, which it is folly not to believe. It is strange how my reason went astray; I, a poor colored girl, scorned by all, debased, degraded, had hoped for the greatest happiness ever given to a mortal! As though the unworthiness of my birth would not follow me to the tomb! Alas! my expiation is harsh! [. . .]

"Ah, what torture it is to be sleepless! Sometimes I thought slumber was about to overwhelm me, [. . .] but at the very moment when I had attained the goal, [. . .] a cruel stab of pain would plunge me again into the abyss."

"My God!" I cried, hearing these sad words, "I saw your pain, but, oh, my beloved, how far I was from thinking it so cruel! Why have you hidden the truth from me for so long?"

"Alas, my love," replied Marie, "need I throw you into despair by asking for help which you could not give? Yes, I feel the life ebbing from me, but I swear to you, Ludovic, all these ills are nothing compared to the torment my soul feels. My torment is the idea of the happiness that is escaping me, and that I have seen so close to me; it is that of giving up forever a hope so foolish, yet so dear! And then the grief which surpasses all others in my heart is seeing to what degree of wretchedness my disastrous lot has reduced you!

"Ludovic, forgive me for speaking thus to you: it is because soon——"

She broke off: I saw her gaze become confused; her eyes, wandering aimlessly, suddenly became fixed; then, an extreme restlessness having succeeded this moment of repose, her thoughts were roused to wander in delirium.

While this heart-rending scene was filling my soul with bewilderment and despair, I heard, without, the first sounds of the storm borne upon the air; far-off rumblings, at first faint, then increasing by degrees, announced the approach of the tempest; already the winds whistled loudly and the oaks of the forest began a murmuring among their motionless trunks.

Marie regained her senses, and raising herself on her couch said in a stronger voice "Listen, Ludovic, [. . .] Heaven has given me strength for a short while—let me speak of those whom I love, who are far away. My father! George! Alas! [. . .] I shall not receive my father's blessing—[. . .] oh, that he might know at least that his daughter remained pure and worthy of him until her last sigh! [. . .] And George—Ludovic, why have you not spoken to me of him for two days? We do not know his fate—I believe it is not happy! His heart is so good and his soul so great! He remained among those wicked people who hate us! [. . .] Perhaps you will see him again—but I shall die far from him! [. . .]

"And you, my beloved," she said, trying to turn toward me, and holding out her hand to take mine, "what can I leave to you in memory of me? Alas! nothing but sorrows! [. . .] Must my ill fortune follow you after I am no more? [. . .] To be happy you must first forget me. [. . .]

"My love, you will find me very weak before my last hour, but—I beg you—tell me once more that you have loved me tenderly, and that you forgive me." [. . .]

Overcome with grief, I pressed my beloved's face to my breast: "Forgive you!" I cried, "Angel of innocence and goodness!" And sobs stifled my voice.

As the word "forgive" left my lips, Marie's face took on an expression of gratitude; then she fell back upon her couch, as if all her wishes had been fulfilled. I saw her consciousness and strength declining with frightful rapidity. It was midnight. The fever redoubled—Marie fell into a terrible delirium.

At that moment all the fury of the tempest was unleashed without. The thunder crashed in the heavens; a boisterous wind lashed the forest; the waters of the storm fell with a violence against which our frail shelter was powerless to protect us. [. . .]

I was in an ecstasy of silent terror, of instinctive despair and religious hope, when Marie's eyes fell upon me, and she said, in a moment of lucidity, the last ray from a mind about to be extinguished: "My love, you are praying for me—ah, thank you! My God, I must indeed be guilty, for now you see the wrath of the Heavens!"

This passing gleam of reason was succeeded by a crisis yet more violent than the first; an extreme agitation overcame her senses; she uttered incoherent words, phrases broken by sighs—these words left her lips: "Accursed race, base blood, inexorable destiny"; finally she repeated my name twice, and, though delirious, she wept. She said no more.

I clearly saw that for Nelson's daughter life was drawing to a close. Nature itself, whose great cataclysms sometimes reveal the mysteries of the future, seemed to have warned me that the sacrifice had been consummated; the storm had announced each phase of her agony. [. . .]

Silence succeeded all the din of the thunder, the echoes, and the torrential rain; silence a thousand times more terrifying than all the voices of the storm and of pain—for there is still hope in the depths of pain if it can moan—and even as outdoors, all was silence around me.

Here Ludovic's voice failed. For long he had struggled to repress his tears, which at this moment flowed in abundance. The traveler wept with him, moved by the tale. Ludovic resumed:

I shall not try to depict the horror of my situation; there are griefs which fill the heart of a man for which language has no words. [. . .]

In the first moments I experienced a sort of content in the very extremity of my sorrow. The complete isolation in which I was plunged, while adding to the dread of my position, spared me one of the heaviest burdens of grief: the condolences of the world. In great misfortunes, one must weep alone; one then suffers too much for another soul to understand. Words of concern, and a few tears—these are all that the tenderest friendship can give; a remedy fitting for ordinary troubles, but how can one demand a broken heart from a friend?

However, at the moment when I congratulated myself on being alone to suffer without interruptions, I knew all the weakness of mankind. Such is the infirmity of our nature that the unhappy man, taking refuge in the secret joys of his grief, cannot bear for long an excess of the most cherished sorrow.

After enjoying my solitary tears, I fell into so great a prostration that I began to regret my distance from the world of men.

But the world I had fled could not hear me. I moaned; no voice answered mine. I reeled; no friendly hand was held out to support my weakness—then I must live upon bitterness and despair; then, in the presence of that dear being, a moment ago palpitating with love and now inanimate, death with its terrible mysteries revealed itself to me in all its horror. When I contemplated those adored features, where I searched in vain for a sign of life, my eyes were dimmed, my reason wandered; all the memories of that frightful night passed before my imagination, a thousand phantoms appeared to me; I thought I heard Marie's voice lamenting. I answered her, "My beloved, it is I! It is your love!" But her features were immobile—I sought for life on those pale lips, but lately so sweet, and found there only the chill of death. [. . .]

On the day following that fatal night, I was torn from my lethargy by a helping hand—it was that of Nelson. On entering the cabin he believed he saw two corpses. Alas! Why was it only an illusion? Would to Heaven he had not revived the little life in me that was about to be extinguished in grief.

Nelson entered followed by the Canadian whose dwelling we occupied, and who had left on the day of our arrival for Fort Gratiot. The vessel bearing Nelson and the Cherokees, having been unable to surmount the rapids opposite the fort, had made a halt; and since the violence of the current had been increased by the melting snows, they had resolved to wait a few days until there should be a more favorable moment. The place where the Indians disembarked was precisely that where the Canadian from Saginaw had gone. The latter, having met Nelson, informed him of my arrival with Marie. Told of the straits we were in, Nelson entreated the Canadian to lead him to us; and whether because the presence of the Indians gathered around Fort Gratiot had spoiled the chance of hunting wood pigeons, or because Nelson's prayers had touched the heart of the hunter, he consented to return; and after five days and five nights of uninterrupted travel through forest and prairie, they arrived to witness the last tragic scene of the frightful catastrophe.

First I gave thanks to God, who had sent me help in my exhaustion—but I soon realized that to console unhappiness it is not enough to have the same sorrow; there must be the same feeling of sorrow.

Nelson suffered a terrible blow on seeing the extent of the tragedy; but his stoicism overcame his grief. I could not believe that the mind could ever be so powerful over the heart, and that such coldness could be found in real sorrow—a few tears flowed from his eyes; soon I must needs weep alone. [. . .]

You see that cottage at a little distance from the one where I received you. The other day you were about to step over the threshold when I stayed your steps. You admired its elegant construction and gracious proportions; and you told me that there one could live happily with a beloved object; oh, I too believed in that happiness! That was the home prepared with such care; Marie's refuge, the roof which would shelter our pure and mystic joys—but since Heaven did not wish my plans to be accomplished, nor that dwelling to contain our felicity, I made of it a tomb.

When we transported the dear remains to that place, I had to bear new agonies, new heartbreak. I have drained the cup of bitterness. I watched the earth little by little swallowing up its prey, and when all had been blotted from my sight, my soul seemed to fall into yet deeper solitude. [. . .] Then, falling face down, I worshiped God. Thus began a ritual which, since then, I have repeated each day in the cottage consecrated to my grief.

"Oh, my beloved," I cried, ending my prayers, "you have preceded me by only a few days into the gloomy sanctuary! I feel it in the emptiness of my heart. I can live no longer, I shall soon rejoin you, beloved souls without whom I cannot live: Marie, angel of my days, without whom I can only wander here below from misery to misery; and you, George, my dearest friend, George, noblest of men, tenderest of brothers, who, faithful to the duties of a loving friendship until your last hour, went before your sister into the realm of shades, where now you are reunited. Ah! do not bemoan my absence—soon I shall be near you; cruel death has separated our bodies, but our souls shall bind themselves to each other with a bond never to be broken."

Thus I spoke, and I saw a new shade of sorrow come over Nelson's face.

"What words are these?" he cried. "George? my beloved son! Great God! Must my sacrifice be everything?"

My grief had led me astray: I revealed all to Nelson and did not regret the indiscretion of my despair; for the moment was appropriate for telling George's father all the immensity of his misfortune. Prayer and grief had lifted his soul toward Heaven; and the religious man is always strong. A thought which rises from the earth and reaches God is like a mighty column by which the weakest may uphold themselves.

For an instant Nelson bowed his head as though the blow had crushed him, and for the first time I believed that his moral strength would be overcome by his misfortunes. But he raised his head, revealing two tears surprised into flowing from his eyes; then I gave him George's letter. Nelson read it, and since that day I have reread it many times, so that I recall its exact words:

"My father," wrote George, "if this letter is given to you, it will tell you that I am living no longer. Do not grieve—I shall have suffered a death worthy of you and myself. I shall not be so cowardly as to attempt to take my own life—but it will be sweet to die fighting our oppressors. I know, my father, how men will judge me, if my name should survive in their thoughts. I shall be called a factionist and a rebel. They persecuted me during my life, and will tarnish my memory. But their condemnation will not strike my soul. I do not know if my blood is tainted, but I am sure of the purity of my heart; I shall appear before God with confidence. I have taken a fatal resolution, which gladdens me. I shall conquer my enemies, or I shall not survive our defeat. Alas! I have little hope of success. The black population is doomed to the eternal scorn of the whites; the hatred between us and our enemies is irreconcilable. An inner voice tells me that this enmity will end only with the extermination of one of the two races; I know not what yet sadder presentiment warns me that the struggle will be fatal. The tragic issue I foresee does not trouble me. I am ignorant of God's designs; but I know the duties whose source is within me; my conscience teaches me that it is always noble to give one's life in serving a holy cause." [. . .]

This letter added a sharper sting to my sorrow and filled even fuller the well of my tears.

Nelson contemplated the ground for some time with immobile gaze; then, raising his eyes to Heaven, "Oh, my God," he said in a mournful voice, "Lord, who to test me hast sent me the cruelest griefs that can tear a father's heart, I bow to Thy all-powerful decrees; I am sore afflicted, yet shall I make no murmur against Thy providence, for Thou art still just, though Thou art stern. I accept these hardships as expiations, and to avert Thy wrath, I shall strive to accomplish good works in Thy name."

At that moment a sound was heard outside the cottage. I went out: there were the Cherokees with Mohawtan at their head. "We come," said the latter, "to see if yesterday's storm has damaged the cottage, and we will help you to bring Nelson's daughter here."

"Nelson's daughter!" I cried in despair. "She is at rest there now!" He saw my flowing tears. Soon Nelson appeared. Mohawtan easily recognized him; the two friends embraced. The Indian, embracing Nelson, felt his paternal grief; he glanced into the cottage and saw the funereal task we had finished.

However, a terrible struggle was about to take place between the Cherokees and the Ottawas. The murder Mohawtan had committed cried for vengeance; it was a pretext for the Ottawas to drive out of their territory a tribe whose presence was an intrusion. Mohawtan asked: "Will you side with us?" I made no reply, for I was indifferent to all things. But Nelson, always filled with the religious zeal which had brought him to these parts, said, "No, I shall not take part in an unjust quarrel. Mohawtan, I am your friend, but why should I be an enemy to the Ottawas? Because they are defending their country, or because they have a horror of spilt blood? My mission upon earth is more noble and pure. If Heaven grants my prayers and aids my efforts, these threats of war and extermination shall not be fulfilled.

"A heavy obligation is imposed upon me," he added, turning to me; "I must do violence to my grief. My friend, the chances to do good are few; a good deed is the surest consolation in unhappiness. My task will be easily accomplished if I can penetrate the souls of these savages with words of the religion of peace."

Nelson followed Mohawtan and the Indians. They directed their steps to a place about three miles away, where the Cherokees were assembled to hold council.

I did not try to follow Nelson. I saw plainly that he had a secret proclivity in his soul which made him wish to fight the blows of fortune, sooner than try to heal the wounds of his heart.

Thus, despite the coming of Marie's father, I was soon alone. [. . .]

Despair having entered my soul, the idea of suicide offered itself, and I accepted it as the sole remedy of my misery. I made preparations for my death in a sort of moral exaltation, as I had formerly built dreams of happiness. I left a letter for Nelson in which I begged him to lay my corpse in Marie's tomb, and, my mind filled with my fatal resolution, I left the cottage.

"My good master!" cried Ovasco, falling upon my neck. It was the evening of the fourth day since his departure. The faithful servant had come with all haste. An old man bent with age, whose robes told me he was a priest, accompanied him.

The presence of Ovasco and this stranger I felt to be an intrusion; they hampered the execution of the designs I had just made; and the soul cannot remain in suspense over such a project. I said to Ovasco: "All is over!" and to the priest, "Your presence in this place is no longer necessary." Both understood me; Ovasco abandoned himself to the most violent grief; the old man gazed at me with penetrating eyes. Doubtless he perceived my trouble and divined my despair to its very depths in my heart, for he said to me with kindness: "My friend, I am very far from the town; be so good as to grant me hospitality for today." He added in a low voice, as though to himself, "I shall not leave this place, for there is great suffering here." Saying these words, he fell on his knees and prayed to God.

However, Ovasco, who did not know that the termination of

my ills was at hand, began to recount, in order to distract my sorrow, the circumstances of his journey. On reaching Detroit, he went to the only doctor in that city; the latter, knowing in what far-off region his aid was asked, bargained for his services, and put so high a price on them, demanding advance payment, that Ovasco could not meet it.

At that time there lived in Detroit a Catholic priest by the name of Richard; he was a Frenchman who had been banished in 1793, at the time when, in order to save civilization, religion and virtue had been forbidden. Arriving as a young man in the United States, he had grown old in his land of exile; everybody praised his wisdom, his knowledge, and his charity. The feelings of respect and veneration he inspired were universal, and the population of Michigan, of which three-quarters was Protestant, had nominated him several years earlier as their representative in Congress. Led to his house by the advice of the people, Ovasco presented himself, and invoked his aid as one prays for help from a superior power. The good old man shook his head, weighed down by the years, and said, "The poor unfortunates! They are very far away! Let us go with haste to their aid. I know," he added, "a little medicine—I have often been consulted in that wild land where the secrets of the art are almost unknown—and then, when I do not know how to cure the body, I apply myself to the wounds of the spirit."

On hearing this tale of Ovasco, I felt no little emotion penetrate my heart, and I could not think without remorse of the indifference I had shown toward the good old man.

"Forgive me," I cried, going to him, "I am most unhappy!" I threw myself into his arms; I experienced a thrill of admiration and awe upon touching those white locks which the wilderness had rendered still more striking. "And you—in spite of the weight of years—have braved this solitude!"

"My friend," said the priest, simply, "did you not come here yourself with joy?"

I maintained a sad silence.

"A generous passion," went on the old man, "a pure love led you to this lonely refuge. My friend, it is love which has led me also to your side—love, the source of all virtue and good. Oh, yes," he added, "I understand your misfortunes, since you have lost her whom you love. This white head would deceive you if it led you to believe that I am more virtuous than you. I too would be weak in the face of misfortune; it seems to me that my heart would break if I were forbidden to love God and to do good to my fellow men—you see, my only advantage over you is in loving something which cannot perish."

There was something tender and moving in the old man's voice. I believe that the languages of the Protestant and of the Catholic differ from each other as the mind differs from the heart. Then I opened my soul to him; he listened to me with an attention mingled with pity. But when he knew the plan I had formed of cutting short my days, I saw his eyes fill with sudden flame.

"Why," I asked him, "why prolong a wearisome, miserable life? What purpose do I serve on earth?"

"Unhappy wretch!" he cried, with a gesture of righteous anger. "Who are you to call Providence before the judgment seat?" And the octagenarian's eyes flashed lightning about him.

He went on gently, "My friend, you are my brother. I see you unhappy and about to commit a great crime: I shall not leave you."

The saintly old man was skillful at reaching my heart. I told him the story of my unhappiness. I told him my childhood dreams, my youthful fantasies, my illusions at every age. The tale of my misfortunes touched him deeply. He heard me in silence, and seemed to meditate profoundly; a whole day passed in which he never ceased to show the tenderest interest in me; little by little he calmed the storms in my heart, and when he saw me capable of listening to the voice of reason, he addressed these words to me:

"My dear son, you have made great mistakes; and your misfortune is the expiation of your errors. Society has struck you without pity, because you were its most dangerous enemy.

"All your griefs came to you through pride and ambition.

"You believed yourself called to great things, and instead of waiting for Providence to choose you to accomplish His plans, you imprudently threw yourself into an abyss of immoderate desires. I readily believe that you aspired to elevate yourself in serving your country. But ambitions like yours are too difficult to satisfy. The unhappiness of a whole people is not too much to satisfy one such ambition. Must the social structure crumble every day, to furnish bold and powerful hands the wherewithal to build glory and splendor on its ruins?

"Very rarely do the real ills of society supply nourishment to ambitious passions—great glory can still be found—it is pure glory which is lacking.

"History lists the famous names of all those, kings or despots, warriors or lawmakers, who have in turn for fifty centuries stirred up the world—but how many names does it transmit as great and pure as the holy, the immortal name of Washington?

"Beware, my dear son, of these restless upheavals: they are not without their loftiness, but they engender pride.

"The most useful men to society are not those who do such great things—great events take place as God sees fit, much more than through man's efforts, and the men who take part in them are sometimes less motivated by love of country than they are ardent in pursuit of a little celebrity.

"The path they follow is full of pitfalls.

"The poor laborer, whose whole ambition pursues his harvesting, does little good, but he cannot do evil; his horizon is bounded by the furrow he plows.

"When Mirabeau's vast passions burst into the political arena, what barrier held them? What glory glutted that power, famished for fame and renown?

"As for the literary fame you sought, how few geniuses in the world of letters enjoy a desirable glory! Tell me which is better—to die unknown, or to have written those impious pages where Byron makes game of God and humanity?

"Pride leads us astray again when it drives us to seek in this world a nonexistent happiness. We pity the man who is content with his modest lot; we think it enough for him, but have vaster desires for ourselves. However, my son, there is very little difference between one man's happiness and another's. What man is there so poor that he has not found in his life a bit of bread to nourish him, a woman who loves him, a God who hears his prayer? That, indeed, is all a man's life.

"The evil here below comes from the wish to fill with great happiness a heart that can hold but little. And it is again a fever of pride which, filling man with illusions, makes him scorn the paths to happiness followed by the greater number.

"Doubtless, the world has many vices, and it is still far from the perfection it will attain through the law of Christ! I know that, for an ardent, impetuous soul, all in society is a hindrance and an obstacle. But do not deceive yourself, my friend; the shackles that impede you, the chains that weigh you down, are easy and light upon the multitude—most men do not feel the noble impulses that move you, those sublime transports of enthusiasm; the common condition is mediocrity, and society makes laws to protect itself against the need for glory that threatens its repose, and the flashes of genius that tire its eyes.

"Moreover, is this enthusiasm lasting even in those who experience it? Let me tell you, my dear child, that the immense happiness you hoped to enjoy in this solitude with the worthy object of your love was but another fantasy, and perhaps the cruelest of all.

"In the age when passion burns, the life of two beings in love is all tenderness and exchange of generous sentiments. [. . .] They enjoy a happiness whose source is in themselves, and owe nothing to the world.

"But this time of fever in the soul is fleeting. It is a fugitive hour of enchantment in the long day of life. When that hour is fled, man's passions, like the ocean's waters after the storm, find their normal level. The great thoughts that exalted his soul, the noble sentiments that made his heart leap, seem only brilliant pictures or beautiful memories. He returns to the habits and exigencies of real life.

"Alas! Those most deeply in love lose a part of their goodness with age. The soul seems to dry up with the body, and all is parched by the years, even the fountain of love in a good heart!

"Your unhappiness is great, my dear son, but tell me, what would have been your fate if, after attaining the prize you strove for, you had seen that happiness, so much desired, vanish like a new chimera?

"A terrible catastrophe forestalled that ordeal—and you curse American society, whose prejudices, in exiling Marie, have led her to the grave. Your plaint is justified. It is true that the Americans pitilessly persecute an unhappy race. Yes, prejudice which dooms three million men to slavery or scorn is unworthy of a free, enlightened people. But need you seize upon the occasion of this irregularity to direct imprecations to Heaven? My friend, man's very iniquity alone is enough to make me believe in God's justice.

"The passions that aroused you against the state of society at the same time fascinated your eyes by showing you a perfect state in the primitive life. I have dwelt for a long time among the Indians; I know not what their forebears were; but, stripped of their primitive state which perhaps had some grandeur, the Indians of our days possess neither the advantages of a wild life nor the benefits of a civilized one.

"Guard yourself against the false notion that the individual worth of each man is better appreciated among the savages than in disciplined countries.

"If people in an advanced culture lay too much stress on the influence of wealth, the savage peoples give too much importance to physical strength.

"All European and American societies, with a few rare exceptions dominated by a number of mediocre minds, are governed by superior intellects. In the opinion of civilized men, a robust physique counts for little if it does not enclose a great heart; with the Indian, on the contrary, moral strength is powerful only in its union with that of the body, and the greatest soul amounts to nothing in a feeble frame.

"The life of the savage is a life of egoism. In these forests, where nature is so beautiful, its most touching voices are stifled. Vainly do the infirm, the wounded, or those whose reason is wandering call on the help of their fellows. These latter scorn the voices of the unfortunates who, having lost bodily strength, do not deserve to exist.

"In civilized countries, not all those in misfortune receive aid, but all may hope to receive it—and how many wounds are healed by public charity! How many lamentations are hushed by religion and good works!

"Finally, my friend, is this wholly material existence of the Indian, whose body alone is active, in accordance with the destiny of mankind? Do you not believe that he whose mind dominates his body approaches more nearly the divine nature from which he springs, the supreme intelligence of which he is a spark?

"My dear son, all has been error and exaggeration in the judgments you have made. Your first impressions of America were much too favorable, and you ended by judging it with unjust severity.

"This people, which does not have the charm of brilliance, is nevertheless a great people; I do not know if there will ever be a single nation in which so many happy lives can be found. Nothing here pleases you because nothing leaps to the eye, neither light nor shadow, great heights nor abysses: it is for this reason that the majority live so well here.

"Perhaps in your turn you will accuse me of basking in illusion: but I have founded on this people a hope which makes for the happiness of my old age. On the one hand I see the multitudinous Protestant sects in the United States; the dissensions which daily divide them; the inconsequence and frivolity of some, the absurdity of others. Then I consider Catholicism, always one and immutable in the midst of changing societies and multiplying sects; drawing people to itself through conversion while the most favored of the other communions remain stationary; reanimating itself with new vigor in this land of liberty, like an old man who, after long exile, returns to his fatherland. I cannot help but believe that the Catholic religion is the cult to come in this country—and this thought spreads a gentle light over my latter days."

When the priest had thus spoken he arose. "My friend," he added, "do not remain in this place. Beware of the gloomy counsels of solitude and unhappiness."

"Father," I cried, "you have kept me from a great crime—but do not demand of me a sacrifice beyond my strength. As long as one drop of blood flows in my veins, it will feed my sorrow. And who, if I desert this wilderness, will watch over this cottage, the sacred monument of my grief? Can you not see the greedy American plowing under these bones to fertilize his fields? Ah, I cannot allow such a profanation!"

Seeing that my resolve was unshakable, the old man left me, saying, "Remember, my child, that you have a tender friend not far from here; you might, one day, come to me—but, my dear son," he said, pointing to his head, whitened by the winters, "do not wait too long."

Thus speaking, the old man went his way, bearing my blessings and leaving a profound impression on my soul.

I was still unhappy, but I was reconciled with Heaven, for I had seen on earth the image of God in a venerable old man. I was the less alone since religion had entered my soul; and the sight of calm and resigned virtue had revived my courage.

The following day was one of great rejoicing among the two

Indian tribes who were reunited in that place. The boat carrying the Cherokees left by Nelson at Fort Gratiot had just arrived at Saginaw, and, thanks to the generous efforts of Marie's father, the Ottawas had buried the hatchet. The whole Cherokee nation was once more together; the Ottawas consented to give them asylum on their land. A treaty of alliance was concluded, and good will seemed established between the two tribes. Nelson settled himself in the midst of these savages, and redoubled his zeal to maintain the union between them and to teach them the virtues of Christianity. He tried to draw me near him; but I did not wish to leave my solitude and the tomb of Marie.

17

Epilogue

So spoke Ludovic; more than once during the tale the traveler had felt the flowing of his own tears. "Oh, how your misfortune moves me!" he said to the hermit. "And for all these years you have lived alone in this wilderness?"

"I did not always stay here," replied Ludovic. "I tried to leave, but in vain; I soon had to return."

At first the abundance of my tears and the violence of my grief made me think that my life would soon be consumed; but that last hope eluded me, and I had no more strength to shed tears than still was left to me for living. Then I led a wretched life here: I was overwhelmed by the length of the hours whose course was hastened by nothing; I wandered at random in the surrounding forest; I sought new lakes, virgin prairies, unknown rivers; I hunted wild animals which provided my nourishment. Sometimes, in the midst of my adventurous excursions, I would stop suddenly; leaning against the trunk of a tree I would meditate for long hours; all my sad memories came to me in solitude. These dreams of misfortune ended by disturbing my reason, and I would become deeply depressed. When my mind would free itself from this lethargy, it seemed to me, as I recalled my adversities, that my entire life had been a terrible dream—but soon I would find myself faced with the dreadful reality. A hundred times a day I would leave my cabin; a hundred times return with my griefs, the vexations and weight of my isolation.

Then the thought of the world of men passed through my mind. Since a fatal blow had broken my life, I had reflected much upon the errors of my youth; I felt how many were the delusions in my first projects. I had once judged the world by values which had vanished—the dreams of my youth were still present in my spirit, but my reason opposed them. I understood that to belong to society one should not envisage things from the immense and limitless standpoint where I had at first placed myself; that it was better to see but a narrow corner of the world than to gaze vaguely and confusedly at the whole; that, in a word, human intelligence and power have bounds which they should not try to overleap, on pain of becoming sterile.

Freed from the illusions which had lured me from my path, could I not return among men? I no longer deluded myself upon the sum of happiness which the world could offer—besides, I put far away the thought of the felicity of which I had formerly dreamed, but I felt within myself all the stirrings of a pure and upright soul. "Why," said I to myself, "could I not find, in contact with my fellows, a little of that simple, tranquil happiness given by a clear conscience? Should I not encounter consoling sympathy wherever there are virtuous men?"

In this state of mind I would doubtless have returned to Europe if, at the same time that I was overtaken in America by my frightful misfortune, another misfortune, no less cruel, happening to my family, had not opposed the idea of going back to France for fear of new anguish: I learned that my father was no more.

Then I remembered Nelson: not far from my dwelling that worthy minister of the Presbyterian Church worked with ardor at the religious instruction of the Indians. I thought I could join my efforts to his and, with him, succeed in civilizing the Ottawas and the Cherokees.

Having rejoined Marie's father, I undertook the execution of my plan; I tried to teach the Indians the principles which are the bases of all civilized societies. I showed them the advantages of an agricultural life, the benefits derived from the industrial arts; but they all replied that it is nobler to live by the hunt than by labor, and while admiring the miracles of industry, not one of them wanted to be a laborer. Though my theories were scorned, I saw that Nelson effected several salutary reforms in the Indians' customs, with the aid of religious dogma, to which the Indians submitted without any argument. I realized then that, if religion is the best philosophy of enlightened peoples, it is the only one an ignorant people can understand; and it seemed to me that Nelson understood better than I the weaknesses in human intelligence. I would have tried to imitate him if, on bringing up the subject of religion, I had not found myself in opposition to his principles: I was Catholic and he Presbyterian. Derived from different doctrines, our efforts would have been contradictory, and instead of strengthening the unity of the Indians, we would have sown the seeds of trouble and division among them. My lack of success in this first attempt did not discourage me: I had tasted a new experience which strengthened my reflections in the wilderness.

Forced to leave Nelson and the Indians, I thought of the old man who had come to me in my solitude and whose devout voice had halted me at the edge of the abyss. I went at once to him. I found him surrounded by the veneration of those among whom he passed his days. This instance of man's righteousness revived my courage.

I formed several relationships among people; I associated myself with several philanthropic enterprises and resolved to make a place for myself in politics. I entered wholly into practical life, but I soon perceived that I would not find in it the well-being I sought there.

Since I had seen that the works of man are ever unfinished, the principles of justice and truth ever offended by passion and self-interest, the most generous undertakings thwarted by a thousand obstacles, and the noblest institutions flawed with imperfections, my reason had taught me that such must be the spectacle offered by a society composed of humans. Yet this sight shocked my eyes and wounded all my instincts.

A witness of the calm and peaceful happiness enjoyed by the old man who had saved me from crime, I resolved to study his life. The serenity of his soul, the tranquillity of his spirit, seemed of inestimable value to me. Could I not, by emulation, become as happy as he? Yet, in looking closely at this man before whose virtue I had bowed as before the image of God himself, I believed I could see pettiness in his greatness. This priest, sublime in his charity, who passed half his days in doing good works, spent the other half in devotional practices which seemed narrow, over-meticulous, and childish to me. Doubtless I was wrong. Within myself, I acknowledged my error: when the work is so great, can the means be trifling? However, my feelings were stronger than my arguments.

After seeing virtue diminished by the shortcomings of intelligence, I found it otherwhere corrupted by usage and social needs.

I saw a man of evil ways given a place of honor by his fellow citizens, because he had political talents; another became a person of importance in the state because he had a private fortune. A young girl, the joy of her worthy and respectable parents, was married off by them to a rich old man!

I realized clearly that this was the way of the world. At times the good seems dependent on empty formality; at others, vice is part of virtue itself; but the evil seemed to me no less sad because I could see its causes.

Everywhere I found the same imperfections. The benevolent societies of which I was a member followed the purest charitable inspirations; but for each wound we could heal, a thousand remained without remedy. Is this, then, the whole of man's power? I approved of those who were not discouraged by such miserable results; but I felt myself incapable of imitating them. In vain I followed all the ways of a practical life and attempted to interest myself in society; I experienced nothing but boredom and disgust.

Then I looked at myself with calm firmness; I would not accuse society of injustice, nor rail against the wretchedness of mankind; but, in examining the past, the memories of my youth, my long adversity, and my present feelings, I realized a truth, the last, sad fruit of my life experiences: it was that, while seeing my mistakes, I still placed myself under the yoke; that, from the tenderest age, I had entertained illusions which had never ceased to be dear to me, though I had abandoned them. The first strayings of my spirit had drawn me into a fantastic world where I dreamed long chimerical dreams, and since the veil had fallen from my eyes I could judge the world sanely but could find no pleasure there.

I knew that one must expect to find much evil among men, and I could not bear a world where all was not well. I clearly perceived the impossibility of achieving the first goal of my ardent desires, and renounced its pursuit; but the reasonable goal, toward which it is wise to aspire, had no attraction for me; in seeing the happiness one might procure here below I felt myself incapable of enjoying it. Through having lived so long outside society, I had become unfitted for it, and my imagination had for so long fed on dreams of an ideal perfection that it could no longer enter upon the ordinary paths of humanity. I bore the yoke of habit, despicable and powerful.

The disgust inspired in me by the world aroused no hatred in me, and I realized that others could love that imperfect society in which I could not live.

I understood the happiness of that benevolence which is resigned to seeing the ills it cannot cure; the happiness of that virtue, often narrow in its views and powerless in action, which is still happy in its good intentions; that of a superior intelligence ruling mankind, stooping when need be to the level of vulgar minds and the littlenesses of life. But, in admitting the existence of this happiness, I had no wish for it, because I had conceived the idea of a happiness greater, purer, and more complete; I lacked it because I was powerless to attain it. I rejected the other, which seemed unworthy to me.

In vain I told myself a hundred times that having renounced the chimeras I must forget them, and look only at the realities among which I wished to live. It was impossible for me to put away the brilliant pictures whose falsity I had recognized.

A very short time sufficed to show me that the sickness within me was without remedy; I did not persist in fighting it: I recognized its extent and submitted. Without passion, without despair, I returned to this wilderness, the only place which suited my state of mind. I could live no longer among men; and this solitude offered my heart at least the interest of my most grievous memory, and also the dearest of my life.

Now I present the strange spectacle of a man who has fled the world without hating it, and who, though retired into the wilderness, never ceases to think of his fellow men, whom he loves, and far from whom he is forced to live. It is very sad to feel the need of society, and to have had the unhappy experience of being unable to live in it. The chief source of all my errors was my belief that man is greater than he is.

If man could comprehend the generality of things, could rally all human activity around a single principle, and establish on earth, by an act of his will, the empire of justice and reason, he would be God, no longer man. [. . .]

My second error was in believing unworthy of man the secondary role which his limited nature assigns him. The noblest passions, the most generous sentiments, can stir within the narrow circle bounding his power: the result is small, but the attempt is great. Never arriving at perfection, man ever aspires to it: that is his greatness. This is the aim of man on earth. I see this aim more clearly than any man whatsoever, yet less than any man am I able to attain it. Unhappy is he who, having a proud conception of the power of man, trains himself to the pursuit of immense goals, vast plans complete results; all his efforts will break down before the limited faculties of man, as before an inevitable calamity.

Here Ludovic stopped. "And so," the traveler asked him, "since your return to the wilderness you have passed your days here in perpetual isolation?"

"Yes," replied Ludovic. "At first, the nearness of Nelson and the Indians he was teaching was a chance for me to have some contacts, which I accepted without seeking them out, but soon this last tie was broken.

"The peace which reigned between the Ottawas and the Cherokees was troubled. The winter following my return to Saginaw was very rigorous. The lakes were covered with thick ice which killed off all the fish in their waters. Deprived of this means of existence, the Indians had no other resource for living than the game of the forest, which was soon almost entirely slaughtered.

"Then the Ottawas remembered that their tribe had formerly been sole ruler of these parts, and they saw, with reason, in the arrival of the Cherokees among them, the principal cause of their distress. Their wretchedness doubtless augmented their resentment. Nelson made vain efforts to avert the storm that he saw was about to burst. One day, the Ottawas, assembled from all parts of Michigan at a single place, not far distant from the settlement of the Cherokees, gave the signal for extermination, and, after a terrible struggle, Nelson saw the unfortunate companions of his exile massacred almost to the last man.

"Nothing can depict the perfidy and cruelty in war of these men who are so humane and upright during peacetime.

"This frightful event brought trouble to Nelson's heart; for his dearest wish had been to die among the Indians after having taught them the truths of the Gospel. But when the poor people for whom he had given up everything were lost to him, his stoicism was shaken, and one day he left the wilderness in order to return to New England, his birthplace, where he resumed his former way of life, as I hear. In leaving here he made vain efforts to take me with him. I shall never leave Saginaw. Since that day my life has gone on, uniform and monotonous. I have marked out my grave next to that of Marie."

"Oh, how I pity you!" said the traveler. "How sad you must be!"

"Yes," replied Ludovic, "my misfortune is cruel, but I bear it with courage. My greatest regret is in thinking that no one can understand my grief, and thus I excite the pity of no one. Otherwise, this bitter life is not without sweetness; every day I visit the monument, the object of my adoration. Each time that I pray, bowed in religious ecstasy, I think I can hear, above my head, a joyous concert of celestial voices, to which sad and mysterious notes respond, seemingly from the tomb: there is much harmony between the sadness of the earth and the joys of Heaven. I have no doubt when I hear them that Marie is already among the angels, and that her dear shade sends me these sweet illusions to beckon me to the delightful feast of immortality."

These last words of the hermit plunged the traveler into a profound reverie.

The next day the latter took leave of his host. I am told that shortly thereafter he left New York for Le Havre. On seeing the shores of France, which he had thought never to see again, he wept with joy. Returned to his dear fatherland, he never left it more.

Appendixes

A. NOTE ON THE SOCIAL AND POLITICAL CONDITION OF THE NEGRO SLAVES AND OF FREE PEOPLE OF COLOR

The existence of two million slaves in the midst of a nation where social and political equality have attained their highest development; the influence of slavery on the habits of free men; the oppression it imposes on those unfortunates subjected to servitude; the dangers it holds even for those for whose benefit it was established; the color of the race which furnishes the slaves; the phenomenon of two populations who live together, in contact but never mingling with each other; the serious conflicts which this contact has already engendered; the more serious crises to which it may give rise in the future: all these elements combine to show how important it is to know the fate of the slaves and of the free colored people in the United States. I have attempted in the course of this work to present a picture of the moral consequences of slavery upon the colored people who have become free; I would now like to offer a glimpse of the social condition of those who are still slaves. This study will lead me, naturally, to an examination of the characteristics of American slavery.

After outlining the structure of slavery, I will try to discover whether this social sore can be cured; what is the opinion of the American public on this point; what means they propose for freeing the blacks, and what objections are opposed to them; finally, what is the probable future of American society in this respect.

I

Condition of the Negro Slave in the United States

It would seem that nothing is easier than to define the condition of the slave. Instead of enumerating the rights he enjoys, would it not suffice to say that he possesses none? Since he is nothing in society, has not the law done everything in declaring him a slave? However, the subject is not as simple as it appears at first glance;

just as, in all societies, many laws are necessary to assure the exercise of their independence to free men, so one sees that the lawmakers must take many steps to create slaves—that is, to deprive men of their natural rights and their moral faculties, to change the state in which God created them, to substitute for their perfectible nature a condition which degrades them and keeps in perpetual chains a body and soul intended for freedom.

The rights which may belong to a man in any decent society are of three sorts, political, civil, and natural. Legislation endeavors to guarantee the enjoyment of these rights to free men, and uses all means to deny them to slaves.

As for political rights, the simplest common sense shows that the slave must be entirely deprived of them. One cannot allow participation in a society's government and the making of laws by those whom that government and those laws are charged with oppressing relentlessly. On this point, the task of the legislator is as easy as his path is clear; political rights, whatever their extent, constitute in all countries a sort of privilege. Not all free citizens enjoy it; it is all the easier to deny it to slaves: sufficient not to ascribe such rights to them.

Thus all the laws of the American states where slavery flourishes are silent on this subject; their silence is sufficient exclusion.

It is no less indispensable to deprive the slave of all his civil rights.

Thus the slave cannot marry. How could the law allow him to form a tie which his master would have the power to break by capricious will? The children of the slave belong to the master, like the increase of the herd: so the slave cannot be invested with any paternal power over his children. He cannot own anything, because he is the possession of another; he must therefore be incapable of buying or selling anything, and all contracts by which property is acquired and kept are equally forbidden him.

American law generally confines itself to declaring the nullity of contracts to which a slave is party; however, there are cases in which the law lends the support of a penalty to its prohibitions: thus, the law of South Carolina, in pronouncing null the sale or purchase made by a slave, decrees the confiscation of the objects which were the matter of the contract.[1] The Code of Louisiana contains an analogous arrangement. In Tennessee the law con-

[1] Beaumont's references to the statute laws and Black Codes of South Carolina, Louisiana, and Tennessee are here omitted. [Translator's note.]

demns the slave guilty of such a transaction to a flogging, and condemns the free man who has made the transaction to a fine.

Whatever the rigor and general scope of the prohibitions condemning the slave to nonexistence in civil life, one may imagine that the lawmaker enacts them without much trouble. Here again, it is a matter of rights that are all completely covered in the law. As a matter of fact, these rights were recognized in principle before they were sanctioned by the law; but, without having created them, the law did proclaim these rights, and found it a simple matter, while recognizing them in free men, to deny them to those it wished to despoil.

Up to this point, the lawmaker proceeds along a path comparatively free of obstacles. He has obviously done a great deal, since now neither fatherland, society, nor family exists for the slave; but his work is not yet done.

After having relieved the Negro of his rights as an American citizen, as a father, and as a husband, he must now take away even his natural rights; here is where the serious difficulties begin.

The slave is in chains; but how is one to eradicate his love of liberty? He is now unable to use his intelligence for the service of the State; but how is one to blot out his intelligence, which he might possibly use to break his bonds? He cannot marry; but, whatever name one may give to his relations with a woman, those relations exist, they cannot be denied; they comprise part of the wealth of the master, since each child born is one more slave; how can it bc managed that there should be mothers and children, fathers and sons, brothers and sisters, without family affection and family interests? In a word, how can a slave be made nonhuman?

The difficulties of the lawmaker increase as he goes beyond the denial of civil rights into the denial of natural rights, leaving the domain of fiction to penetrate into reality. His first care, in declaring the Negro a slave, is to class him among objects: the slave is movable property according to the laws of South Carolina; unmovable in Louisiana.

However, the law declares in vain that a man is a chattel, a piece of goods, merchandise; he is a thinking, intelligent thing; vainly the law reduces him to matter—he contains indestructible spiritual elements: it is essential that these faculties be stifled before they can develop. All laws relative to slavery forbid the education of slaves; not only are the public schools closed to them, but their masters are forbidden to allow them the most elementary instruction. One South Carolina law imposes a fine of one hundred pounds sterling on the master who teaches his slaves to read; the penalty is no greater if he kills them. Thus perfectibility, the noblest potential of human faculties, is attacked in the slave, who thus finds himself powerless to accomplish toward himself the duty, imposed on every intelligent being, of striving ceaselessly toward moral perfection.

The law endeavors to degrade the slave; but an instinctive dignity makes him hate servitude; a still more noble instinct makes him love liberty. He is chained, but he breaks his chains, and he is free—that is to say, in a state of open rebellion against the society and the laws which have enslaved him.

All the Southern states agree in outlawing a runaway Negro. South Carolina's law says that any person can seize him, arrest him, and flog him forthwith. The law of Louisiana says literally that one is permitted to shoot fugitive slaves who do not stop when pursued. The code of Tennessee declares that it is legal to kill a slave who, when summoned in the name of the law, [does not come forth]. This law adds that the slave, in such a case, may be killed with impunity by anyone whatsoever, and in whatever manner it pleases him to employ, without fear of being brought to justice. These same laws reward those citizens who recapture the escaped slave; they encourage informers and pay for the information. The law of South Carolina goes further: it decrees a terrible punishment for both the runaway slave and all persons who have helped him escape; in such a case it is always the death sentence.

All the powers of society are employed to recapture the escaped Negro. When, having reached the boundaries of the slave states, he sets foot on the soil of a state where there are none but free men, he may for a moment believe he has regained his natural rights; but his hopes are soon dashed. The North American states which have abolished slavery reject fugitive slaves, and deliver them over to the master who reclaims them.

Thus society marshals all its severity and most stringent rights to seize the slave and to punish in him the most natural and inviolable feeling of mankind—love of liberty.

Now we see the slave once more in chains; he has been punished for his sinful attempt for freedom; henceforth he will not try to break his chains; he will work for his master, who has succeeded in crushing him. But here the obstacles and problems of the legislator and the slave owner are multiplied again. In the slave they have stifled two noble qualities: moral perfectibility and love of liberty; but still they have not destroyed the whole man.

In vain the master forbids his Negro all contact with civil society; in vain he attempts to degrade and brutalize him; there is a point where all these prohibitions and attempts come to a halt; and that is where the interests of the master begin. Now, the master, after having bound the limbs of his slave, is obliged to unbind them so that he may work; in brutalizing him he still must preserve a little of the intelligence of the Negro, for it is his very intelligence that makes him valuable; without it the slave would be worth no more than any other livestock; finally, even though the Negro has been declared a material thing, he maintains personal relationships which are the very reason for his servitude; and the slave, to whom all social life is forbidden, finds himself nonetheless forced, in serving his master, to enter into relationships with a world in which he is actually nothing, where he exists only for others, but where he is made to shoulder the moral responsibility belonging to intelligent beings.

Here again, the man is still a man, by the will of the very ones who have tried to annihilate him. Thus, whatever the degradation of the slave, he must have physical freedom in order to work, intelligence in order to serve his master, social contact with him and with the world in order to carry out the duties of servitude.

But if he does not work, if he disobeys his master, if he rebels, and if, in his social contacts, he commits offenses, what is to be done? He will be punished; how? Following what principles? With what punishment?

Here, especially, arise difficulties by the score for the legislator.

The law having made a master of one and a slave of the other, creating two beings of an entirely different sort, one feels the impossibility of establishing the relations of the slave with the master or of the slave with free men, on a basis of reciprocity; then, in deviating from this rule, the sole equitable basis of human relationships, one falls into complete arbitrariness, and must violate every principle. Thus the crime of the master who kills his slave is not equivalent to the crime of the slave who kills his master; the same difference would exist between the murder of any free man by a slave and that of a slave by a free man.

The laws of all the American states decree death for the slave who kills his master; but a number of them impose only a simple fine on the master who kills his slave.

Assaults or violence by the master against the Negro are authorized by American law; but the Negro who strikes his master is punished by death. The law of Louisiana pronounces the same penalty upon the slave guilty of a simple assault upon the child of a white man.

The same distinctions are found in the relation of slaves to free persons. Thus in South Carolina, the white who wounds a Negro incurs a fine of forty shillings, but the Negro slave who wounds a free man is punished by death. If the Negro wounds a white man in defending his master, he incurs no penalty; but he undergoes punishment if he inflicts that wound in self-defense.

There is no law punishing the injury inflicted by a free man upon a slave. So slight an offense is not worth curbing; but the law of Tennessee decrees a flogging for the slave who permits himself the smallest spoken insult to a white woman. These are not anomalous differences; they are the logical consequence of the principle of slavery. A strange thing! They attempt to make a brute of the Negro, and yet inflict punishments on him more severe than on the most intelligent being. He is less guilty, since he is less enlightened, and they punish him the more. However, it is necessary: it is obvious that the scale of offenses cannot be the same for the slave and the free man.

The scale of penalties is no less different, and, on this point, the task of the legislator becomes still more difficult of accomplishment.

Not only may the gradations of penalties established for whites not apply to slaves, since society fears those it oppresses more than those it protects, but also, as we shall see, it is necessary to change the very nature of penalties for the slave.

Penalties applied by American law to free men are of three kinds: the fine, temporary or perpetual imprisonment, and death: the first affecting a man's property, the second his liberty, the third his life.

One can see immediately that no fine could be imposed on a slave, who, possessing nothing, can suffer no damage to property.

Imprisonment is also, naturally, a penalty inappropriate to the slave's condition. What does loss of liberty mean to one in servitude? However, one must make a distinction here. If it is a matter of temporary imprisonment, the slave will not fear it; he will see nothing in it but a material change in his position—always seized on hopefully by a wretched being; moreover, he will prefer idleness to hard labor from which he gains nothing. In fact, this would be a penalty only for the master; deprived of his slave's labor, his loss would be the greater the longer the duration of the punishment.

If it is a matter of life imprisonment, one might think perpetual confinement would be a heavy punishment even for a slave with no liberty to lose. But here another obstacle arises: perpetual confinement deprives the master of his slave: to impose this punishment on the slave is to ruin the master.

The objection to the death penalty is even greater. It destroys the master's property. Thus, all penalties decreed by law for punishing free men are inapplicable to slaves; death itself, that tool of all tyrants, here fails the slave owner.

However, one finds in American laws relative to slaves many instances of provision for death or life imprisonment. Sometimes these penalties are applied in courts of justice, but these cases are very rare; it is only when the slave has committed a serious offense against the public peace; then outraged society demands reparation; it seizes the Negro, condemns him to death or life imprisonment, and, since by this act it deprives the master of his slave, it pays him the slave's worth. "All slaves," says the law, "condemned to death or to life imprisonment shall be paid for from the public treasury. The sum shall not exceed three hundred dollars." Here interests of a peculiar nature conflict and exert a deplorable influence upon the courts of justice. The master, before giving up his slave to the tribunal, looks carefully into the crime, and gives notice of it only if he believes it to be a capital crime; for, the indemnity being paid only on this condition, he has no wish to hand over his slave unless the latter is to be condemned to death. On the other hand, society, paying for the right to do justice, exercises this right only with extreme reserve; it avoids shedding blood not through humanity but through economy; and, while it is to the interest of the master that society be inflexible in punishing his slave, society's interest lies in being indulgent to the slave. The master is prompt to give up his slave in but one instance: that is when the slave is old and sick; he then hopes that the death sentence upon the infirm Negro will net him an indemnity equivalent to the price of a sound Negro; but society guards against this fraud, and, in order not to pay the indemnity, will acquit the Negro. The slave, whose misery moves neither society nor the master, finds protection in the calculations of greed.

The preceding explains that singular Louisiana law which declares that the penalty of imprisonment for a slave may not exceed eight days, unless it be life imprisonment. "With the exception," it says, "of cases where slaves shall be condemned to perpetual imprisonment, juries convoked to judge the crimes and offenses of slaves shall not be authorized to imprison them for more than eight days."

The reason behind this provision is easily to be seen. Temporary imprisonment, depriving the master of the labor of his slaves and causing him loss without compensation, is in his eyes the worst of all punishments. Life imprisonment deprives him, it is true, of the person of his slave, but, at the same time, society pays him the price.

One may now conceive the impossibility of often imposing death or perpetual imprisonment on slaves; for such punishments, inflicted in great number, would ruin the slave owner or society.

However, there must be punishment for the slave—severe punishments, of which use may be made at any time. What should they be?

This is how necessity leads to the use of corporal punishment, that is, punishment which is immediate, applied without loss of time, without expense to the master or to society, and which, after inflicting cruel suffering on the slave, allows him to return quickly to his work. These punishments are the whip, the brand, the pillory, and the mutilation of a limb. Once more, the legislator finds a difficulty relative to this last punishment; for the limbs of a slave must be left intact and sound.

These are, in fact, the punishments proper to slavery; they are its indispensable auxiliaries, and without them it would perish. American laws have been forced to have recourse to them. In Tennessee, aside from the death penalty, there are but three punishments: the whip, the pillory, and mutilation.

The punishment for bearing false witness is worthy of remark: the guilty slave is put into the pillory, one ear first having been nailed to the post; after an hour of exposure, the slave has that ear cut off; then they nail up the other likewise, and an hour later that one is cut off like the first.

Yet the pillory, mutilation, and branding are not the customary penalties in the slave states; they require some care in their application, cause inconvenience and loss of time. The whip alone entails none of these troubles; it lacerates the body of the slave without endangering his life; it punishes the Negro without harm to the master: it is, in truth, the customary punishment of servitude. And so the American slave laws constantly call for its application.

We have just seen that the legislator must perforce attribute to the slave a criminality different from that of the free man; we realize that no penalty applied to a free man is suitable for slaves, and that to punish the latter one must have recourse to the cruelest severity.

Now, the crime of the slave having been defined and the nature of the punishment determined, who is to administer his punishment? On what principles will he be tried? Will he be surrounded, during the trial, by those guarantees which the laws of all civilized nations give to the unhappy accused?

Let us glance at American laws, and we shall see the legislator led by necessity to the successive violation of all principles. The first rule in criminal cases is that no one may be judged except by his peers. One can see the impossibility of applying this maxim of equity to slaves; it would be placing the fate of the masters in the hands of the slaves: thus, in every case, free men make up the jury charged with trying slaves; and here the accused Negro has to fear not only the bias of the free man against the slave, but the antipathy of the white against the black.

It is an axiom of jurisprudence that the accused is presumed innocent until he is declared guilty. I find in the laws of Louisiana and South Carolina contrary principles:

"If a black slave," says the Louisiana law, "discharges a firearm at some person, or strikes him, or wounds him with a lethal weapon, with the intent to kill, the said slave, if duly convicted of any of the said acts, shall be punished by death, provided that the presumption, as to his intention, shall always be against the accused slave, unless he prove the contrary."

Yet another salutary principle, consecrated by all wise legislatures, is that in criminal cases the penalties must be fixed by law. However, American law generally leaves the punishment of the slave to the discretion of the judge; at one time the law says that, a case being settled, the judge shall have administered the number of lashes he considers fitting, fixing neither maximum nor minimum; at another time, the law allows the judge decreeing punishment to choose among the penalties whichever he pleases, from flogging to the death penalty, exclusive of the latter. Thus the slave is at the mercy of the judge's whim.

But there is another principle even more sacred than the preceding: that no one can do justice on his own behalf, and that whoever has been wronged must appeal to the magistrates appointed by law to judge between plaintiff and accused.

This rule is formally violated by the laws of South Carolina and Louisiana, relative to slaves. In the laws of these two states one finds a provision which confers upon the master the discretionary power to punish his slaves, whether by blows of the whip or stick, or by imprisonment; he weighs the offense, condemns the slave, and applies the penalty; he is at once litigant, judge, and executioner.

Such are and such must be the laws of repression against slaves. Here the principles of common law would be disastrous, and regular forms of justice impossible. Should all the misdeeds of the Negro be brought before a judge? The life of the master would be taken up with lawsuits; besides, the sentence of a tribunal is sometimes questionable and always slow. Should not a terrible and inevitable punishment be forever suspended over the head of the slave, and fall upon the guilty, in obscurity, at the risk of striking the innocent?

Justice and the courts are then nearly always alien to the repression of the slave's offenses; everything is between the master and his Negroes. As for those who are docile, the master peacefully enjoys their labor and their brutishness. If the slaves do not work zealously, he whips them like beasts of burden. These transient chastisements are not registered in courts; they are not worth the expense of an inquiry. Anyone consulting the court records will find a very small number of cases relative to Negroes; but, if he goes about the countryside he will hear cries of anguish and distress: these are the sole evidence of sentences carried out on slaves.

Thus, for the establishment of slavery, a man must not only be deprived of all political and civil rights, but even despoiled of his natural rights, and the most inviolable principles must be trampled underfoot.

A single right is left to the slave: the practice of his religion; religion teaches men courage and resignation. However, even on this point the law of South Carolina shows itself full of prudent restrictions: thus, Negroes cannot pray to God except at certain set hours, and may not attend the religious gatherings of the whites. The slave must not listen to the prayers of free men.

What finer testimony could exist in favor of man's liberty than this impossibility of organizing slavery without outraging all the sacred laws of morality and humanity?

II

Types of Slavery in the United States

I have shown what are the severities and cruelties employed to found and maintain slavery in the United States. Yet I think that among these rigors and cruelties there is nothing which is peculiar to American slavery. Bondage is the same everywhere, and entails, no matter where it is in force, the same iniquities and tyrannies.

Those who aspire, while admitting the principles of slavery, to lighten the yoke, to give the slave a little liberty, to offer some bodily comfort and spiritual light, appear to me endowed with more humanity than logic. In my opinion, slavery must be either abolished or maintained in all its severity.

The mitigations allowed the slave only render more cruel in his eyes those rigors which are not suppressed; the benefits he receives become for him a sort of incitement to revolt. Of what use is it to teach him? So that he may the more keenly feel his misery? Or, when his mind has been developed, that he may make more intelligent efforts to break his chains? When slavery exists in a country, the bonds should never be loosed unless the lives of master and slave are in peril: the master's through the slave's rebellion; the slave's through the master's punishments.

All the oratory delivered on the barbartiy of the slave owner, in the United States as elsewhere, makes very little sense. Instead of blaming the Americans for their bad treatment of slaves, one should reproach them with slavery itself. The principle being admitted, the consequences people deplore are inevitable.

There are others who, wishing to justify bondage and its horrors, boast of the humanity of American masters toward their slaves; these people lack both logic and truthfulness. If the slave owner were humane and just, he would cease to be a master; his ownership of Negroes is a perpetual violation of all the laws of morality and humanity.

American slavery, which rests upon the same bases as all bondage of man to man, has, however, several distinct characteristics which are peculiar to it.

Among the peoples of antiquity, the slave was attached to the person of the master rather than to his domain; he was essential to luxury, and one of the visible evidences of power. The American slave, on the contrary, belongs more to the domain than to the person of the master; he is never a mark of ostentation, but only a useful tool in the master's hands. Formerly the slave labored for his master's pleasure, rather than to increase his wealth. The Negro serves only the material interests of the American.

Jefferson, who in other respects is not an upholder of slavery, has attempted to prove that the Negroes enjoy a happy life compared to the Roman slaves; after painting the kindly customs of

American planters, he cites the example of Vedius Pollio, who condemned one of his slaves to become the prey of the eels in his fishpond, to punish him for having broken a crystal goblet.[2]

I do not know if Jefferson's argument is valid. It is true that an American would be less severe to a slave who broke an article of luxury; but would he be so indulgent to one who destroyed something useful? I do not know. It is a fact, however, that the law of South Carolina condemns to death the slave who causes damage in the fields.

I believe, however, that the life of the Negroes in America is not subject to the same dangers as that of slaves among the ancients. In Rome, the rich held the lives of their slaves cheap; they regarded them no more than a bit of extra luxury, or a fashionable trinket. A whim, a fit of temper, sometimes a depraved instinct of cruelty, was sufficient to snap the thread of several existences. These passions are not to be met with in the American slave owner, to whom the slave has the material value of a useful object, and who, lacking violent passions, feels for the Negroes who work for him only the wish to preserve them.

The slave owner in the United States does not lead a brilliant social life on his estate, and never shows himself in the city with an escort of slaves. The exploitation of his land is an industrial enterprise; his slaves are his agricultural machinery. He cares for each of them as a manufacturer cares for the machines he uses; he maintains and tends them as though he were keeping a factory in good running order; he calculates the strength of each, works the strongest without respite and rests those who might be damaged by longer use. This is not a tyranny of blood and torture; it is the coldest and most intelligent tyranny ever exercised by the master over the slave.

However, from another viewpoint, is not American slavery harsher than the bondage of antiquity?

The calculating, practical spirit of the American master leads him on to two distinct goals: the first is to get as much work out of his slaves as possible; the second, to expend the least possible in maintaining him. The problem is to keep the Negro alive on very little food, and to work him hard without wearing him out. One can see the embarrassing alternative facing the master: he wishes his Negro never to rest, but fears that continuous labor will kill him. Often the American slave owner falls into the error of the industrialist who, having strained the mainsprings of a machine,

[2] Jefferson, *Notes on the State of Virginia.*

sees them break down. Since this greedy scheming kills off men, American law has of necessity prescribed the minimum daily rations a slave shall receive, and visits severe penalties upon the master who infringes upon this ordinance. However, these laws show up the evil without remedying it: by what means could the slave obtain justice for the more or less tyranny to which he is subjected? Generally, any complaint he makes calls down new rigors upon him; and if by chance he should come before the judge's bench, he would find as judges his natural enemies, all friends of his adversary.

Thus, I feel I am right in saying that in the United States the slave need not fear murderous violence, of which the slaves of the ancients were so often victims. His life is protected, but perhaps his daily existence is more wretched.

Here I will point out one more dissimilarity: the slave of antiquity often served the vices of the master; his intelligence was trained to this immorality. The American slave never has to perform such offices; he rarely quits the fields, and his master's habits are pure. The Negro is stupid; he is more brutalized than the Roman slave, but he is less depraved.

III

Can Black Slavery Be Abolished in the United States?

One cannot speak of slavery without recognizing at the same time that its institution in a nation is both a blemish and a misfortune.

The sore exists in the United States, but one cannot impute it to the Americans of today, who received it from their ancestors. Even now a part of the Union has rid itself of this plague. All the New England states, New York, and Pennsylvania have no more slaves. Now, could the abolition of slavery come about in the South as it took place in the North?

Before examining this important question, let us begin by admitting that in the United States there is a general trend of opinion toward freeing the black race. A number of moral principles combine to produce this effect.

First, religious beliefs, which are spread over all the United States. Several sects show ardent zeal for the cause of human liberty; the efforts of religious men are unceasing and their influence, almost imperceptible, nevertheless makes itself felt. On this subject, one wonders if slavery could last very long in the heart of a Christian society. Christianity means the moral equality of man. Once this principle is admitted, it is difficult not to arrive at the idea of social equality, whence it appears impossible not to go on to political equality. The legislators of South Carolina are well aware of the whole range of the moral principle which is the germ of Christianity; for in one of the first articles of the laws organizing slavery, they have taken pains to declare in formal terms that the slave who receives baptism shall not be made free by this act.

One can no longer deny that the progress of civilization is breaking down slavery day by day. In this respect, Europe itself influences America. The American, whose pride will not admit the superiority of any other to himself, suffers cruelly because, in the opinion of other nations, slavery has besmirched his country.

Finally, there is a moral reason, perhaps more powerful than any other in American society to encourage the freeing of the blacks, and that is the more and more widely accepted idea that the states where slavery has been abolished are richer and more prosperous than those where slavery still flourishes; and that idea has a basis in fact, of which they are finally taking note; in the slave states free men do not work, because work, being the symbol of slavery, is in their eyes degrading. So in these states the whites are idle; the blacks alone perform labor. In other words, the most intelligent, energetic part of the population, most capable of enriching the country, remains inert and unproductive, while the business of production is the work of another part of the population, uncouth and ignorant, doing its work without enthusiasm because it gains nothing from the labor.

More than once I have heard the Southern slave owners deplore the existence of slavery for this reason, and avow themselves in favor of its destruction. So one cannot deny that public opinion in the United States is tending toward the complete abolition of slavery.

But is abolition possible? And how can it be effected? Here I must review the diverse objections which are presented.

First objection: There are people who maintain that the slavery of Negroes is based on fact and not on principles. The African race, they say, is inferior to the European race; the blacks are therefore by their very nature destined to serve the whites.

I shall not discuss here the question of the superiority of the whites over the Negroes. It is a subject on which many fine minds are divided; I would need, to fathom it, more knowledge than I possess concerning it. I shall therefore present only brief observations on this point.

In general, the question of superiority is decided by a single act: a white and a Negro are placed side by side, and the declaration is made, "The first is more intelligent than the second." But here is a primary source of error; the confusion of race with individual. If I presuppose that the intellectual superiority of the present-day European is a constant fact, the difficulty is not resolved.

In fact, could it not be that the intelligence of the Negro is potentially equal to that of the white, and that it has degenerated through accidental causes? Since in maintaining a certain social status the black race has submitted for several centuries to a degrading condition transmitted from generation to generation—to a totally material existence, destructive of human intelligence—must it not result that for succeeding generations a progressive alteration in the moral faculties, which, arrived at a certain degree, takes on the appearance of a special characteristic, is considered as the Negro's natural state, though it is but a deviation?

This question, whose outline I have barely sketched, is treated in great detail in a two-volume work entitled *Natural and Physical History of Man*, by Richard.[8]

Having indicated the error into which one may fall by likening two races which for a long succession of centuries have followed different paths—the one toward moral perfection, the other toward brutishness—I will add that the comparison of individuals among them is hardly less defective. After all, how can one expect of the Negro, whose intelligence since his birth has never been awakened, the same mental development which in the white man is the result of an early and liberal education?

This question will receive great clarification from the experiment now being made in the American states where slavery has been abolished. In Boston, New York, and Philadelphia there are public schools for the children of the blacks, founded on the same principles as those for the whites; and I found that the opinion everywhere was that the colored children show an aptitude and a capacity for work equal to those of the white children. For a long time they have believed in the United States that the Negroes had not even sufficient wit to make business deals; however, at this moment there are, in the free states of the North, a large number of colored people who have made for themselves great fortunes in commerce. For a long time it was even thought that the Negro was destined by the Creator to bow his head eternally to the soil,

[8] The title of this work is given by Beaumont in English. The work could not be identified. [Translator's note.]

and that he lacked the intelligence and skill necessary for the mechanical arts. But a rich industrialist from Kentucky said to me one day that that was recognized as a mistake, and that Negro children who had been taught the trades worked just as well as the whites.

The question of the superiority of the whites is still, however, not entirely unclouded. Even supposing that superiority to be undeniable, what result will follow? Must one conclude, because he recognizes in the European a degree more of intelligence than in the African, that the second is destined by nature to serve the first? But where does such a theory lead?

Among the whites, intelligence is also unequal. Should servitude be the punishment of anyone less bright than average? And who is to determine the average intelligence? No, the moral worth of man is not entirely of the mind; it is above all a quality of the soul. After proving that the Negro comprehends less than the white, one must prove that he feels less keenly than the white; that he is less capable of generosity, sacrifice, and courage.

Such a theory does not stand up under scrutiny. Applied to the whites alone, it seems ridiculous; applied only to Negroes, it is more odious because it inflicts upon an entire race of men the most frightful misery.

Therefore we must set aside this first objection.

Second objection: There are other people who say: "We need the Negroes to cultivate our soil; the Africans alone can perform heavy labor under the broiling sun without danger; because we cannot do without slaves, we must maintain slavery."

These are the words of the American planter, who, as may be seen, reduces the question to that of his personal interest. True, the prosperity of the country is combined with that personal interest, if it were true to say that the land of the Southern states could be cultivated only by Negroes.

There is great divergence of opinion on this point in the Southern states. It is true that the closer to the tropics, the greater becomes the danger of working in full sunlight. But how great is the danger? Will habituation dispel it? At what degree of latitude does it begin—at that of Virginia or that of Louisiana? At the 40th parallel or the 31st?

Such are the controversial questions which are receiving many answers in America. In traveling through the Southern states I often heard it said that if the slavery of the blacks were abolished the agricultural wealth of the South would come to an end.

However, in Maryland today something is happening which is

sufficient to shake the faith of those who make such assertions. Maryland, a slave state, is situated between the 38th and 39th degrees of latitude; it holds the central position between the Northern states, where there are only free men, and those of the South, where slavery flourishes. Now, a few years ago it was universally believed in Maryland that Negro labor was indispensable to the cultivation of the land; and any voice expressing a contrary opinion was suppressed. However, at the time when I visited that country (October 1831), opinion had already changed entirely on this point. I can do no better in telling of this revolution in public thought than to report textually what was said to me in Baltimore by a man of fine character who held a distinguished place in American society:

"There is not a person in Maryland," he said, "who does not now desire the abolition of slavery as frankly as he formerly wished to maintain it.

"We have realized that the whites can devote themselves without any inconvenience to agricultural labors which it was believed could only be performed by Negroes.

"The experiment having been made, a large number of free laborers and white farmers established themselves in Maryland, and then we discovered another no less important fact: that, as soon as there is competition of labor between the slave and the free man, the ruin of the slave owner is assured. The farmer who works for himself, or the free laborer who works for hire, produces half as much again as the slave who works for his master without personal profit. The result is that the worth of free labor is half as expensive. Thus, such produce as was worth two dollars when we had only slave laborers cost actually only one dollar. However, what the slave produced had to be sold at the same price, so there was a loss; the slave owner gained half as much as before, yet his expenses were the same; that is, he had to feed his slaves and their families, take care of them in their infancy, their old age, and their illness; while his slaves still worked less than free men."[4]

I cannot leave this subject without repeating what was said to

[4] There is only one branch of agriculture in Maryland for which one can still use slave labor without loss, and that is tobacco growing. This crop, which demands much minute care, requires an immense number of hands; women and children are sufficient to the task; the important point is to have a large number of them, and Negro families, generally numerous, fulfill this condition. However, though Negroes are still of use in this field, they are not indispensable; tobacco culture is done equally well by whites. One can only say that, performed by slaves, it is still profitable, while in other industries slave labor is so no longer.

me concerning Negro slavery by a man justly famous in America, Charles Carroll, who, among all the signers of the Declaration of Independence, has longest enjoyed the result of his glorious deed.

"It is a false notion," he said, "that the Negroes are necessary for the cultivation of certain crops—such as sugar, rice, and tobacco. I am convinced that the whites could accustom themselves to it easily, if they undertook to do so. Perhaps at first they might suffer from the change wrought in their habits; but they would soon surmount that obstacle, and, once used to the climate and work of the blacks, they would do twice as much as the slaves."

When Mr. Carroll told me this, he was living on an estate where there were three hundred blacks.

I do not conclude from all this that the objection raised against white men working in the South is entirely devoid of foundation; but still, may one not suppose that several of the Southern states which up to now have considered slavery a necessity will recognize their error, as has Maryland today? Every day, communication between the states becomes easier and more frequent. May not the moral revolution which has taken place in Baltimore spread in the South? The Southern states, formerly purely agricultural, are beginning to be industrialized; factories in the South will have to compete with those in the North, that is, to produce as cheaply; they will then find it impossible to use slave laborers, since it has been shown that these cannot successfully compete with free laborers. Wherever the free worker appears, slavery falls. Lastly, it has been conclusively proved, economically speaking, that slavery is detrimental when it is not a necessity, and that it has been so judged by those who formerly believed it indispensable. But quite other objections than those of the more or less profit to whites of Negro labor have been raised against abolition.

Third objection: Suppose the principle of abolition be accepted, how shall it be put into execution?

Here two methods are presented: to make all slaves free from this moment on, or to abolish slavery only in principle, declaring free the children born to slaves. In the first case, slavery would vanish at once, and, on the day when the law was passed, there would be none but free men in American society. In the second, the present is excepted; those who are slaves will remain so; only the future is affected; they work for the following generation.

These two methods, one as simple as the other in theory, meet common difficulties in practice.

First, in order to declare the slaves or their descendants free, justice demands that the government pay their value to their possessors; indemnity is the first condition laid upon enfranchisement, since the slave is the property of the master.

How effect this redemption?

It is said that the American government is in a most favorable position to accomplish this; for the public debt of the United States is canceled: now, the revenue of the Federal government is annually 159 million francs. Of this sum, 74 million are absorbed by expenses of Federal administration; so 85 million remain, which were previously devoted to wiping out the public debt, and which could now be used for the redemption of the Negro slaves.[5]

I have often heard this means proposed for the accomplishment of general enfranchisement; but here, how many obstacles crop up! First, the point of departure is faulty: it is true that the United States has no more public debt to pay; but while paying it off, the country has considerably reduced the taxes which were the source of its revenue. Therefore it is inaccurate to say that the Federal government annually receives 85 million which could be applied to the redemption of the Negroes.

But let us suppose that this sum is at its disposal, and see whether it is possible to hope that it will be put to that purpose.

There were in the United States at the last census, taken in 1830, 2,009,000 slaves; now, supposing the average value of each Negro to be reduced to one hundred dollars, because of the number of women, children, and old people, the redemption of 2,009,000 slaves at that price would cost more than a billion francs.[6] To that sum must be added the price of at least 200,000 slaves born since 1830,[7] whose redemption would add 11,000,000 francs to the preceding billion. Supposing that the Federal government could and would apply each year to the redemption of the Negroes an annual sum of 85,000,000 francs, it could with this sum redeem only 160,000 slaves a year; it would take fourteen years at that rate to redeem all the slaves living today. But that is not all. The 2,009,000 slaves living at this moment increase each day, and supposing their annual increase to be proportionate in the future to that

[5] *National Calendar* (1833), s.v. "Public Revenues and Expenditures."

[6] $200,900,000, or 1,064,770,000 francs.

[7] I say at least 200,000; for the slave population in the whole Union increases by 30 percent every ten years. Four years have already passed since the last census, which stated that there were 2,009,000 slaves.

which it has been until now, it will be augmented annually by about 60,000; 47,000,000 francs would thus be used up each year, not to diminish the number of slaves, but only to prevent their increase; and these 47,000,000 francs are more than half the sum destined for redemption.

It is evident that the extent and duration of the pecuniary sacrifice which the government of the United States would have to impose upon itself would be out of all proportion to its efficacy. Is it imaginable that the American government would ever undertake such a task at such expense? I do not know whether a self-governing people would ever make a sacrifice as enormous as this except in a case of urgent necessity. The masses, skillful and able to cure their present ills, have little foresight for the ills of the future. Slavery, which could really become a source of trouble and disturbance for all the Union, affects in fact and measurably only a part of the United States: the South. How can one expect the North to set aside for the sake of the Southern states, through a vague foreboding of uncertain danger to them in the future, considerable sums toward the redemption of the Southern slaves, which might gain immediate and actual advantage to themselves if invested for the profit of all? I believe that to hope for such a sacrifice from the Federal government of the United States is to misunderstand the rules of self-interest and to misjudge the American character and the principles on which democracy works.

But the exorbitant price of redemption is not the only obstacle. Let us suppose this difficulty overcome.

Fourth objection: The Negroes being freed, what will become of them? Is the matter ended with the breaking of their fetters? Will they be allowed to stand free beside their masters? But if former slaves and masters find themselves face to face, with almost equal powers, should not disastrous conflicts be feared?

Obviously it is not enough to ransom the slaves; some means must be found after their enfranchisement to make them disappear from the society where they have been slaves.

On this point two systems have been proposed. The first was made by Jefferson,[8] who wanted a portion of American territory assigned to the Negroes, after the abolition of slavery, where they would live apart from the whites. One is struck at once by the defects and unwisdom involved in such a system. Its immediate consequence would be the establishment of two distinct societies

[8] *Notes on the State of Virginia*, p. 199.

on the soil of the United States, composed of two races, who secretly hate each other and whose enmity thenceforth would be openly avowed; it would mean the creation of an enemy nation next to the United States, which now has the good fortune to have neither enemies nor neighbors.

But since Jefferson outlined this strange proposal of separating the Negroes and the whites, another proposal has been made, without such disadvantages. A colony of freed Negroes has been founded in Liberia on the coast of Africa. Philanthropic societies were formed for the establishment, supervision, and maintenance of this colony, which is already prospering. At the beginning of 1834, it contained three million inhabitants, all free Negroes or freedmen emigrated from the United States.[9]

Certainly, if universal liberation of the blacks were possible, and they could be all transported to Liberia, it would be an unmixed blessing. But could the transportation of the freed slaves from America to Africa be accomplished on a large scale? Aside from the expenses of redemption, which I am assuming have been covered, those of transportation alone would be considerable; it has been reckoned that the cost of transporting one Negro would be $30 (160 francs), which means that for two million Negroes the sum would be 60 million dollars added to the preceding $200,900,000. Thus, the deeper one goes into the problem, the more are the obstacles.

Now I shall once more assume that these first difficulties are solved; I shall suppose that on one hand the government of the Union is ready, in order to free the Negroes of the South, to make the immense sacrifice I indicated without opposition from the Northern states, which up till now have small interest in the question; I shall suppose, moreover, that a practical means of transporting the freed population out of American territory exists; these obstacles removed, it still remains to overcome the most serious of all; I refer to the will of the Southern states, in which the slaves are living.

Fifth objection: According to the American Constitution, the abolition of slavery in the Southern states could not come about except through an act originating in those sovereign states; or at least, if the freeing of the blacks were attempted by the Federal government, it would be necessary to have the consent of the par-

[9] On the origin and progress of this colony, see the *American Almanac* (1834), under "Colonization Society," pp. 92 ff.

ticular states involved.[10] Now, I do not know how the Southern states may think or act in the future, but it seems to me beyond doubt that in their present condition of mind and interests, all would be opposed to the enfranchisement of the Negroes, even on condition of the preliminary payment of indemnities.

Certainly the sudden transition of the Negroes from the state of slavery to that of liberty would be a moment of dangerous crisis for the slave owners.

It is vain to say that on receiving their liberty the slaves would have no more grievances against society or against their masters; I reply that they have their memories of tyranny, and that the common condition of the oppressed is to submit while they are weak and to avenge themselves when they become strong; and the slave will become strong only on the day when he becomes free.

It is unlikely that the Americans of the slave states would willingly undergo the perilous risks involved in freeing the slaves with a view to sparing their grandsons the danger of a conflict between the two races.

They would do so even less willingly since, aside from the dangers attendant upon the measure, their material interests would suffer. All the wealth, all the great fortunes in the Southern states have been based, up to now, on the labor of the slaves; a pecuniary recompense, however large, would not replace the master's lost slaves; it would place capital in his hand for which he would have no use. Later, doubtless, new enterprises, new methods of exploitation would follow; but the suppression of slavery would be, for the present generation, the source of an immense disturbance in their material interests.

One wonders if it is possible that an entire generation would willingly undergo such ruination for the greater good of future generations. No, it is doubtful if they would impose it upon themselves even in the face of actual danger. Nothing is more difficult to conceive of than a large mass of men giving up their material

[10] See the Constitution of the United States. The powers of Congress are limited to the cases stated in the Constitution. Among these cases, enumerated in Section 8 of Article 1, the right to abolish slavery in the states where it is established is not included; several articles of the Constitution even formally recognize slavery, among others Article 4, Section 2, Paragraph 3. Finally, the Tenth Amendment says: "The powers not delegated to the United States by the Constitution, nor prohibited by it to the States, are reserved to the States respectively, or to the people."

well-being in order to avoid peril. The present peril is still only an evil to come; the sacrifice would be a present evil.

But, one may say, these objections are to a great extent avoided if, while declaring free the still unborn children of slaves, they maintain in bondage those slaves born before the act of abolition. In this hypothesis, those who abolish slavery keep their slaves, and the generation to suffer from the enfranchisement will have known no better state.

This system no doubt weakens the objections but does not entirely destroy them. Would it not be offering the slaves a basis for insurrection to declare their unborn children free while keeping their fathers in servitude? Great efforts are made to persuade the Negro slave that he is not the equal of the white man, and that this inequality is the basis of his slavery; what becomes of this fiction in the presence of a contrary reality? How can the Negro slave be expected to obey while his child is invested with the right to resist?

It would be attributing an exaggerated egoism to the Southern Americans to suppose that in keeping their rights intact they will destroy those of their children. It would be just as surprising should they make a great sacrifice in the interest of generations far in the future, as if they should sacrifice for their own interests those of their immediate descendants; for paternal feelings are almost egoism.

One may be sure, then, of finding the fathers as reluctant to take a measure ruinous to their children as to take a step ruinous to themselves.

However, here one might cite the example of the Northern states of the Union which have abolished slavery for the future, that is, for the unborn children, leaving enslaved all those who were so before the law was passed; and one might ask why the Southern states do not do the same.

The answer to this is simple. First, slavery was never established in the North on a grand scale. When Pennsylvania, New York, and the other Northern states abolished slavery, there were among them only a very small number of slaves. To give but one example, New York abolished slavery in 1799, and, at that time, there were only three slaves per hundred inhabitants: the Negroes could be freed, or their unborn children declared free, without fear of any regrettable consequences. The slave owners formed only a negligible part of the population; then, the nearly universal aim was that there should be no more slaves, that nothing might degrade labor, the source of wealth. In abolishing the slavery of the blacks for the sake of the future, the Northern states made no sacrifice; the majority, finding this abolition profitable, imposed the law upon the lesser number whose interests were contrary.

Now, how can the Northern states be compared with those of the South, where the slaves are equal, sometimes even superior, in numbers to the free men, and where, besides, the majority if not the whole of the population has reason to desire the maintenance of slavery?

One can see that the dissimilarity is complete up to this point; but may one not hope for some future change in the situation of the Southern states, and may one not agree that, though they have an interest today in preserving slavery, they may hereafter have an interest in its abolition? I am firmly convinced that sooner or later that abolition will take place, and I mentioned above the reasons for my conviction, but I believe as firmly that slavery will endure for yet a long time in the South; and in this regard it seems expedient to sum up the material differences which make any comparison impossible between the future of the South and what has happened in the North.

It is indisputable that the cold of the Northern states is unfavorable to the African race, while the heat of the South agrees with them; in the former they pine away and decrease, while they prosper and multiply in the latter.

Thus, the black population, which tended naturally to diminish in the states where slavery has been abolished, finds, on the contrary, in the climate of the Southern lands, where slaves are today, a cause of increase.

In the North, slavery was evidently detrimental to the greater number; the inhabitants of the South are still in doubt as to its necessity. Slavery in the North has always been a superfluity; for the South, at least until the present, it is profitable. For the men of the North it was adventitious; in the South it is part of the way of life, tied up with custom and every concern. In suppressing it, the free states had only to make a law; to abolish it, the slave states would have to change their social conditions completely.

The energy and the taste for work of the Northern men, the religious zeal of the New England Presbyterians, the strictness of the Pennsylvania Quakers, and also a very advanced civilization, all tend toward the rejection of slavery. It is not at all the same in the South; the Southern states have beliefs but are not passionately religious; several of them, such as Alabama, Mississippi, and

Georgia, are half barbaric, and their inhabitants are, like all men of the South, inclined by the climate to indolence and idleness. Thus slavery is not, up to the present, opposed in the South for any of the reasons which in the North have led to its downfall.

The Southern states are then a long way still from the enfranchisement of the Negroes.

However, as they cling to the present, they are terrified of the future. The progressive augmentation of the number of slaves among them is a fact well calculated to alarm them. Already in South Carolina and Louisiana the blacks are more numerous than the whites, and the cause of their increase is more serious still, perhaps, than the fact itself. Slave trade with foreign countries being forbidden throughout the Union, not only by the federal government but also by the individual states, it follows that the numerical increase of the slaves can result only from births; the number of whites in the Southern states not increasing in proportion to that of the blacks, it is manifest that within a given time the black population will become greatly superior in number to the white population.[11]

While they see the peril brewing, the Southern states of the Union do nothing to avert it; each opposes or favors the increase in number of slaves according as it is actually desirous of having more or less. In Maryland, in the District of Columbia, in Virginia, where free labor is beginning to penetrate, they free many slaves and sell as many as they can to the more southerly states. Louisiana, South Carolina, Mississippi, Florida, which have found until now immense profit in the exploitation of their land by slaves, are not freeing them and attempt unceasingly to acquire more. It frequently happens that, afraid of the future, these states make laws to forbid the purchase of Negroes from other parts of the Union. As I was traveling in Louisiana (1832), the legislature had just passed a decree to prohibit all purchase of Negroes from adjacent states; but generally these laws are not acted upon. Often the lawmakers are the first to offend against them; their private interests as proprietors make them buy slaves whose purchase they have forbidden for the

[11] As a matter of fact, the Southern states such as Louisiana, South Carolina, and Mississippi, where there is the greatest increase of blacks, buy slaves in neighboring states, Tennessee, Kentucky, Virginia, and Maryland. This is a cause of increase independent of births. But what proves that this is not the sole cause of increase is that the number of slaves is growing also in the neighboring states; and even those where it is diminishing, such as Virginia and Maryland, show no decrease in proportion to its former increase.

general good. In short, when one considers the intellectual movement stirring the world, the opprobrium which stigmatizes slavery in the opinion of all peoples; the rapid conquest which the ideas of liberty over the servitude of the blacks have already made in the United States; the progress which enfranchisement is continually making from North to South; the necessity in which, sooner or later, the Southern states will be of substituting free for slave labor, under the threat of being inferior to the Northern states; in the presence of all these facts it is impossible not to foresee a more or less imminent epoch in which slavery will have completely disappeared from North America.

But how will this enfranchisement be accomplished? What will be its means and consequences? What is the future of the masters of the freed slaves? That is what no one dares to determine in advance.

The fact is that in America the very race of the slaves is a more serious problem than their slavery. American society, with its Negroes, is in a totally different situation from the ancient slave-owning societies. The color of American slaves changes all the consequences of liberation. The freed white man retained almost no mark of the slave. The freed black has almost no characteristic of the free man; in vain will the blacks receive their liberty; they will still be regarded as slaves. Custom is more powerful than law; the Negro slave has been considered an inferior or degraded being; the degradation of the slave will cling to the freed man. His black color will perpetuate the memory of his servitude, and seems an eternal obstacle to the mingling of the two races.

These prejudices and aversions are such that, in the most enlightened Northern states, the antipathy separating one race from the other remains the same, and, what is worthy of note, several of these states have decreed in their laws the inferiority of the blacks.

One may easily conceive that in the slave states freed Negroes would not be treated exactly like freed white men. Thus one reads without surprise an article of a Louisiana law which says that free people of color must never insult nor strike the whites, nor pretend to equality with them; but that, on the contrary, they must everywhere make way for them and only speak or reply to them with respect, on pain of punishment by imprisonment, according to the seriousness of the offense.

It is equally little surprising to see that, in the slave states, all marriages between whites and free people of color or slaves are forbidden. But what seems perhaps more extraordinary is that even in the Northern states marriages between whites and blacks were for a long time forbidden by law. Thus, the law of Massachusetts declared null such a marriage, and imposed a fine upon the magistrate who performed it. This law was abolished only in 1830. However, while the interdiction is not in the law, it remains the same in custom; an insurmountable barrier is always interposed between the whites and the blacks.

Though living upon the same soil and in the same cities, the two populations have a distinct civil existence. Each has its own schools, churches, and cemeteries. In all public places where the two necessarily must be present at the same time, they do not mingle; but separate places are designated for them. They are thus classified in courtrooms, hospitals, and prisons. The liberty enjoyed by the Negroes is not, for them, the source of any of the benefits obtained in society. The same prejudice which heaps scorn upon them forbids them the practice of most professions. One cannot form an exact idea of the difficulties the Negro must overcome in order to make his fortune in the United States; he is met with obstacles everywhere, and nowhere with support. Thus, domestic service is almost forced upon the greatest number of free Negroes.

In the political sphere the separation is even wider. Though in theory they are allowed to hold public office, they do not do so; there is not a single example of a Negro or mulatto filling a public post in the United States. The laws of the Northern states generally recognize that political rights equal to those of the whites belong to free people of color, but nowhere are they permitted to enjoy them. The free colored people of Philadelphia, wishing, a while ago, to exercise their political rights on the occasion of an election, were ejected with force from the room where they had come to cast their votes, and they had to renounce the exercise of a right which in theory was incontestably theirs. Since then they have not renewed their legitimate claim. It is sad to say, but the only course open to the oppressed black population is to submit and to suffer the tyranny without complaint. Recently, men animated by the purest intentions and most philanthropic sentiments have tried to accomplish the fusion of the blacks with the whites by means of intermarriage. But these attempts aroused all the Americans' proud susceptibilities and terminated in two insurrections, of which New York and Philadelphia were the scenes, in July 1834.

Each time the enfranchised Negroes evince the intention, directly or indirectly, of making themselves the equals of the whites, the latter at once rise up together to repress so audacious an attempt.

These actions occur in the most enlightened and religious states of the Union, where slavery has long been abolished. Who can now doubt that the barrier between the two races is insurmountable?

Generally the free Negroes of the North bear their misfortunes patiently: but is it credible that they would submit to such humiliation and injustice if they were more numerous? They form an insignificant minority in the North. What would happen if, as in the South, they were numerically equal or superior to the whites?

What is happening today in the North gives a preview of the South's future. If it is true that the generous attempts made to transport the freed Negroes from America to Africa can never lead to any but partial results, it is unfortunately all too certain that one day the Southern states of the Union will contain in their midst two inimical races, distinct in color, separated by invincible prejudice, the one returning hatred for the other's scorn. There, it must be realized, is the great canker in American society.

How can this great political problem be resolved? Is a war of extermination inevitable? How soon? Who will be the victims? The Southern whites being in possession of the civilizing forces, of the habit of power, and certain, moreover, of finding support in the Northern states, where the black race is diminishing, must one conclude that the Negroes will succumb in the struggle, if a struggle there will be? No one can answer these questions. The storm is visibly gathering, one can hear its distant rumblings; but none can say whom the lightning will strike.

B. NOTE ON AMERICAN WOMEN

The most striking trait in the women of America is their superiority to the men of the same country.

The American, from his tenderest youth, is devoted to business; hardly has he learned to read and write when he becomes a merchant. The first sound in his ears is the chink of money; the first voice he hears is that of self-interest; he breathes at birth the air of industry; and all his early impressions persuade him that a business career is the only one becoming to a man.

The lot of the young girl is not the same; her moral education goes on till the day she marries. She acquires knowledge of history and literature; she generally learns one foreign language (ordinarily French); she knows a little music. Her life is intellectual.

This young man and this young girl, who are so dissimilar, are united one day in marriage. The first, continuing in his habitual course, spends his time at the bank, or in his shop; the second, who becomes isolated on the day she takes a husband, compares the actual life which has fallen to her lot with the existence of which she had dreamed. As nothing in this new world before her speaks to her heart, she lives in daydreams and reads novels. Having little happiness, she is very religious, and reads sermons. When she has children, she lives in close contact with them, cares for and loves them. Thus pass her days. In the evening the man comes home, full of care, restless, overcome with fatigue; he brings to his wife the fruits of his labor, and already dreams of tomorrow's speculations. He asks for his dinner, and offers not a word more; his wife knows nothing of the affairs that preoccupy him; in her husband's presence she is still isolated. The sight of his wife and children does not tear the American away from the practical world, and he so rarely shows them a sign of tenderness and affection that a nickname has been made for those households where the husband, after an absence, kisses his wife and children—they are called "kissing families." In the American's eyes, the wife is not a companion; she is a partner who helps him spend for his well-being and comfort the money he earns in business.

The sedentary and retired life of women in the United States explains, with the rigors of the climate, the poorness of their complexions; they do not leave their houses or take any exercise, and they live on a light diet; almost all of them have a great number of children; it is not astonishing that they grow old so fast and die so young.

It is a life of contrasts; exciting, adventurous, almost feverish for the man, sad and monotonous for the wife; it flows on uniformly until the day when the husband announces to his wife that they are bankrupt; then they have to leave, and recommence the same existence elsewhere.

Every American family, then, contains two worlds: the one entirely material, the other wholly moral. Whatever the closeness of the bond that unites the couple, there is still a barrier between them, separating the soul from the body, and mind from matter.

C. NOTE ON AMERICAN ANGLOPHOBIA

To say that the Americans hate the English is to render their feeling imperfectly. The inhabitants of the United States were under the domination of the English, and with the memory of their independence is mingled that of the wars that were its price. These struggles recall the time when there was profound enmity against the English.

The advanced civilization of England also inspires very pronounced feelings of jealousy in all Americans. However, while rivalry is evident at one minute, one sees that at the same time they are proud of their descent from so great a nation as England, and one finds in their souls the sense of filial piety which holds colonies to the mother country long after they have become free.

The memory of old quarrels fades day by day; but the jealousy grows. The material prosperity of the United States has taken a marvelous leap, which England looks on with an uneasy eye; and America cannot conceal from herself, in spite of her rapid progress, that she is still inferior to England. This feeling of the two peoples is quite justifiable in principle, but national pride, which the London press, like that of New York, incites to envy, has aggravated the situation.

The English papers are full of scorn for the United States, which they represent as a totally uncivilized country. "Just compare," says an English magazine published in London, "the morality of England with that of America! As though any parallel could be established between an overpopulated country where six million individuals are engaged in commerce and manufacture, and in which one's eyes are assailed by objects which invite theft; and America, where there is nothing to steal except grass and water; where the soil is the only means of livelihood; where each man must be his own tailor, carpenter, etc.; where the only knowledge necessary for living is how to plant corn and potatoes, and where the height of luxury is to make them into pudding; where the sight of a mirror is so rare that the population of a whole province flocks to see it," etc. [. . .] Every day one can read similar invective in the English papers. The irritation they cause in the Americans is quite natural, and their resentment is in exact proportion with the injustice of the English toward them.

Another cause leads to a similar effect. Englishmen traveling in America are very well received there, for three reasons: the first is that the Americans are naturally hospitable to foreigners who speak their language; the second—though they are jealous of England, they feel true pleasure in receiving individually each Englishman who visits them, in whom they see but a member of the nation from which they are descended; the third, they wish to be judged favorably, they and their country, by the English, precisely because they are rivals; they therefore take pains to be polite, to prove that America is not uncivilized; and since they sincerely believe there are very noble things to be seen in their land, they make it their duty to parade before the insular Briton's eyes all the moral and material wealth of the United States.

However, full of his preconceptions and able, moreover, to find without bias that America is inferior to his country, the Englishman on his return home writes up his "Transatlantic Voyage," which is nothing but a satire, continued in one or two volumes; sometimes he does not even disguise proper names, and holds up to the ridicule of his fellow citizens the respectable people who gave him hospitality. Even the most reserved are unjust and offensive. The work is published in England, and soon arrives in the United States, where its appearance strikes American vanity like a thunderbolt.

The rivalry existing between the Americans and the English is not only industrial and commercial. These two peoples have a common language, and each claims to speak it better than the other. I believe both are right. In England the upper class has a refinement of speech unknown in America, except in a small number of most unusual drawing rooms; and in the United States, where there is neither an upper nor a lower class, the entire population speaks English less well, perhaps, than the English aristocracy, but quite as well as the middle class, and infinitely better than the lower class.

D. NOTE ON BLUE LAWS

[In America] the observance of Sunday is not limited, as it is with us, to a ceremony; it lasts the whole day. Everyone, after the church service, retires to his home, and then one sees neither carriages nor men, women, or children on the streets. To prevent the passage of carriages they close the streets around the churches by means of chains hung across them, two feet from the ground. One would think, from the silence everywhere, that the city had been abandoned by some enemy who had left nothing but corpses behind. The law of New York State says that on Sunday all amusements, such as riding to hounds, shooting, gambling, horse racing, etc., etc., are forbidden. No innkeeper or wine merchant may sell spirituous liquors, and no shopkeeper may sell any merchandise.

It seems certain that a great number of Americans, shut up at home on Sunday, apply themselves very little to the Bible, and profit by the shelter that hides them to do things which are not at all pious; some abandon themselves unbridled to their passion for gambling, the more disastrous in America since the most innocent public gambling is prohibited; the gambler clandestinely takes the most dangerous risks; others get drunk on liquor; a great many, among those of the working class, go right to bed after the service. The same may be observed in England—owing to the same cause. Protestantism, which enjoins silence and reflection on the Sabbath, and forbids any sort of celebrations, considers only the condition of the higher classes of society. This wholly intellectual observance of the holy day is fitting for cultivated minds, and is designed to edify souls capable of meditation; but it offers nothing to the lower classes. You will never succeed in making the man who labors physically all the week spend all day Sunday thinking. You refuse him public amusements; retiring indoors he will abandon himself unchecked to the grossest pleasures.

I have mentioned the austerity of the Puritan customs, and how Sunday is observed. The amusements lost to that day are not found again on any other day of the week. In certain states they are not concerned with the natural disinclination of the inhabitants for diversions and games; the law simply prohibits them. Connecticut law absolutely forbids theatrical performances as contrary to good morals, without any exception for the big cities like Hartford and New Haven. In New Jersey horse races are not permitted; they are the occasion—so they say—of assemblages, gambling, wagers, luxury, disorder, and derangement of good habits, all immoral consequences. In Boston, it is forbidden to play the barrel organ in the streets; it would frighten the horses, they say. In New York, the law prohibits all such public diversions as one sees in Paris on the Champs-Elysées, such as seesaws, balloons, and running-at-the ring; all these things are a waste of time, and a public disturbance. In Massachusetts, there is a law according to which people who travel on Sunday may be arrested, and penalized by a fine. Those whose need to travel is urgent must ask for an authorization to travel on the holy day. The driver of a public conveyance who goes on the road without obtaining this permission loses his license for three years. The law of New York contains a similar disposition, but less severe.

E. NOTE ON THE INDULGENCE OF AMERICAN SOCIETY TO BANKRUPTS

I do not know if in any country there is a greater commercial prosperity than in the United States; yet among no other people on earth are there so many bankrupts. There are two main reasons for this phenomenon; on one hand, the commerce of the United States takes place under the most favorable conditions imaginable: an enormous, fertile countryside; gigantic rivers that furnish natural means of communication; numerous well-situated ports; a people whose character is enterprising, whose spirit is calculating, and whose bent is nautical; all these circumstances come together to make the Americans a commercial nation. This is the source of their wealth; yet for the very reason that success is a probability, they pursue it with frantic ardor; the spectacle of quick riches intoxicates speculators, and they race blindly toward their goal; this causes their ruin. Thus, all Americans are merchants, because they all see in trade the way to wealth; they all become bankrupt because they want to become rich too quickly.

A short time after my arrival in America, as I entered a drawing room where the elite of society in one of the largest cities of the Union was gathered, a Frenchman who had lived a long time in this country told me: "Above all, don't go and say anything offensive about bankrupts!" I followed his advice and it was well for me that I did: for among all the wealthy people to whom I was presented there was not one who had not failed once or twice in his life before making his fortune.

All Americans being businessmen, and all having failed more or less often, it follows that in the United States bankruptcy means nothing. In a society where everyone commits the same offense, the offense is one no longer. Indulgence toward the bankrupt comes from the fact that his is a common misfortune; but above all it arises from the extreme ease with which the man who has failed can recoup. If he had failed irrevocably, he would be left to his own misery; one is much more indulgent to an unfortunate man when one knows that he will not always be so. This feeling, which is not generous, is nonetheless part of man's nature.

One may now understand why there is no law penalizing bankruptcy in the United States. The electorate and the legislators are all tradesmen and subject to failures; they do not wish to punish the universal crime. Such a law, if made, would remain unapplied. The people, who make the laws, execute them or refuse to execute them in the courts, where the jury represents the people. Under these conditions, nothing protects American business from fraud and bad faith. Anyone can engage in business without keeping any books or registers whatever. There is no legal distinction between the businessman who runs into bad luck and the imprudent bankrupt who is a spendthrift and a fraud. Businessmen in every circumstance recognize the common prerogative.

If the Americans are indulgent toward bankruptcy, [. . .] it does not follow that they approve of it. Even those who continually fail in their obligations are loud in their praise of good faith.

F. NOTE ON POLYGAMY AMONG AMERICAN INDIANS

The basis of the story of Onéda is entirely true.[1] Polygamy exists among all the savage tribes of North America; each Indian has as many wives as he can get. These women really live in a state of servitude; they prepare the Indian's food, take care of his clothes, and do not leave his hut while he is hunting or on the warpath. The relations between the Indian and his wives are completely material; nothing moral or intellectual enters in. It is by no means rare to see three sisters serving as wives to the same man. The condition of Indian wives is as wretched as can be imagined; they have none of the prerogatives proper to wives in civilized societies, nor any of the sensual pleasures given them by the customs of the Orient, where they are slaves.

I said that the Indian has as many wives as he can get; it would perhaps be more accurate to say that he gets as many as he can feed; for the lot of the Indian family is so hard that parents readily give their daughters to anyone who can keep them alive. In this, all depends on the man's skill as a hunter; a famous hunter ordinarily has a large number of wives because he can provide them all with a means of existence.

The marriage of an Indian with his wives is accomplished with no ceremony, and sometimes is dissolved a few days after its formation. However, this happens infrequently; the Indian who breaks such a tie so easily would injure himself in the eyes of his tribe and would find no other family inclined to make an alliance with him.

One can imagine that this life of fatigue, wretchedness, and

[1] See above, pp. 95–98. [Translator's note.]

opprobrium would discourage and sicken Indian women; indeed, suicide is very frequent among them.[2] The anecdote I have introduced into the text of my book seemed to me one of the most striking examples of the despair into which the unhappiness of these poor creatures can plunge them. I added, after the tragedy, funeral ceremonies which are not a mere creation of my imagination. It is a fact that on the death of a friend the Indian manifests great sorrow; he blackens his face, fasts, and no longer paints himself with vermilion, abstains from any decoration in his dress; he makes incisions in his arms and legs, and all over his body; often the outward signs of his grief last a very long time. Major Long tells of having met an Indian who, for fifteen years, had refrained from painting his face with vermilion, commemorating the loss of a cherished friend, and he announced the intention of continuing the privation for another ten years. The Indian measures the show of his grief by the degree of affection inspired in him by the deceased.[3]

Tanner recounts in these terms the "festival of the dead" or *jebi-naw-ka-win*: "This feast is eaten at the graves of the deceased friends. They kindle a fire, and each person, before he begins to eat, cuts off a small piece of meat, which he casts into the fire. The smoke and smell of this, they say, attracts the *jebi* to come and eat with them."

G. NOTE ON AMERICAN SOCIABILITY

I could cite a thousand examples of the extreme sociability of Americans; I will limit myself to one. When, in the course of the year 1832, M. de Tocqueville and I left New Orleans to go overland to Washington, we crossed Lake Pontchartrain on a steamboat. Arriving at Pascagoula, where we were to take the stage, we found all the seats occupied, which was a great disappointment to us, since

[2] See *Account of an Expedition from Pittsburgh to the Rocky Mountains, Performed in the Years 1819 and '20 under the Command of Major* [*Stephen Harriman*] *Long, Mr. T. Say, and Other Gentlemen of the Exploring Party*, compiled by Edwin James (London, 1823), II, 394, and John Tanner, *A Narrative of the Captivity and Adventures of John Tanner . . . during Thirty Years Residence among the Indians in the Interior of North America* (New York: C. & H. Carvill, 1830). [The latter work has been published in a new edition, at Minneapolis, by Ross & Haines, in 1956.]

[3] See *Account* of Long's expedition, I, 281, and Tanner's *Narrative*, p. 288.

we had good reason not to want any delay in our departure; two Americans, quite unacquainted with us, seeing our predicament, got down from the carriage, offering us their seats in such a simple and obliging fashion that it was difficult for us to refuse. In numerous other cases, my companion and I had found the same sort of thing true of the Americans. Anyone who judges the men of this country by his first impressions risks odd misconceptions. Ask a question of an American and he will answer, monosyllabically, "Yes," or "No," without looking at you; or even not answer you at all. You will conclude that he is unsocial, and you will be wrong. He will be quite silent, but he is thinking about the question you have asked him; he reflects profoundly on it; if his memory seems to serve him ill, he consults another's, and—half an hour after your question, which perhaps you have forgotten—he will present you with his answer; not a haphazard answer such as you might receive anywhere in the civilized world, but a veritable dissertation, with numerous parts, divided into chapters and paragraphs. Most assuredly the man who thus comports himself is, if you like, not particularly polished in his manners, but he certainly is sociable, because mutual kindliness is the first condition of sociability. How many Europeans, for instance, upon such an occasion, will cut short your inquiry, or will reply at once, with the utmost urbanity, that it is completely impossible to give you an answer!

American sociability is based primarily on business customs; they have continual need of one another; business matters compel their perpetual intercourse; indeed, among them it is an accepted principle that men must at all times help each other. Their very equality upholds this principle; every American has the same good will toward all other Americans that members of the same class in our country have toward each other. This type of sociability, whose value the European feels acutely, sometimes loses part of its appeal here. They say that a New Englander sees nothing in his social relationships but a chance for doing business. When he meets a newcomer, he asks himself this question first of all: "Isn't there some deal I can make with this fellow?"

The American's sociability should not be confused with his hospitality. *In a general sense* Americans are not hospitable; true hospitality requires a leisure with which a man of business is not familiar. I say *in a general sense* because there are a number of exceptions to this rule; and I have had personal experience in these matters; but here I am presenting over-all impressions, which of course apply only to the majority.

On this point we must distinguish between the Southern and the Northern states. All the Southern states are slave states—this fact has tremendous influence on the customs of the Southerners. The slaves work—the free men are idle. The Southerners thus have a leisure lacking to the Northerners; they can receive guests without neglecting their business. Nearly all of them live far from each other, and away from cities; a friend's visit, or the passing of a stranger, is a happy event in a lonely dwelling place and, far from disturbing the rural family, is an occasion for rejoicing. For people with no occupation any pastime is valuable. One might say, indeed, that in the city one *sees* people, while in the country one *receives* them. From these conditions several results follow: the relations between people in the South, being less mercenary, are more agreeable than those among people in the North; the latter, expecting profit from their slightest social contacts, have a general kindliness; the former, less calculating, are more sincere; among the Northerners there is a sort of legal rigidity; among the Southerners, who are less stiff, there is more freedom and spontaneity. Since the existence of a slave population establishes an inferior class, all the Southern whites consider themselves a privileged class; they believe they are superior to other men (the Negroes). The exercise of their rights as masters over their slaves encourages the notion of their superiority and develops a feeling of pride; white skin is regarded in the South as a sign of true nobility. So the white people behave toward each other the more considerately and benevolently since they live side by side with men toward whom they feel nothing but contempt. Thus, in Southern manners something of aristocracy has crept in, and the result shows in extraordinary courtesy and in a more distinguished sociability than that found in the Northern states.

H. NOTE ON AMERICAN CRUDENESS

One must not accept the exaggerations the British retail on this subject; Mrs. Trollope says: "For myself, it is with all sincerity I declare that I would infinitely prefer sharing the apartment of a party of well-conditioned pigs to being confined to [a Mississippi steamboat] cabin."[1] These are *crude* insults. It is quite true that

[1] *Domestic Manners of the Americans,* Vol. I, ch. ii. [Translator's note.]

with their habit of chewing tobacco, which necessitates spitting, the Americans shock anyone who is accustomed to refinement in manners; it is no less true that their complete lack of gallantry is disagreeable to women; and one is completely disappointed if one expects among them any elegance of manners or any urbane behavior. But here the critic must hold his peace.

Americans do not flatter women, but they respect them, and this feeling of respect, which is not displayed overtly, is much deeper in them than it is in our civilized land of gallantry.

On the steamboats of which Mrs. Trollope speaks one finds an unpolished society, it is true; it is made up of tradesmen going from Ohio or Kentucky into Louisiana or the lands on the right bank of the Mississippi; but they do not present the disgusting spectacle implied by the English author. These steamboats are generally large, clean, and elegant; there are more than two hundred of them, incessantly plying up and down the great river. The food served aboard is abundant and wholesome, and the cost of a passage is incredibly cheap; one can go from Louisville to New Orleans for twenty-two dollars, meals included; the distance is twelve to fifteen hundred miles. Having made this voyage, I can speak of it with knowledge; one is so comfortable in the passengers' saloon that one can work, or write, or read there as one might at home.

Besides all this, American crudeness has its good side, too; our polished manners, our refinements of speech, are often but agreeable outward dress concealing egoism. Self-interest doubtless exists as much among Americans as among us, but in the United States there is less hypocrisy in manners.

I. NOTE ON EQUALITY IN AMERICAN SOCIETY

A great number of writers, notably English ones, have remarked that the laws of the United States guarantee an equality which is not found in reality; that there, as in several European countries, there is an aristocracy full of arrogance and contempt for the classes beneath them; and that the Americans, who have perfected the theory of equality, do not put it into practice. I must say that in traveling about the United States I received a quite different impression. I found not only political equality, set in motion by the cooperation of all citizens of the country, but I could see social equality everywhere, in money matters, in the professions, in all their customs.

There are few great fortunes; the hazards of trade which build them up sometimes knock them down; and at any rate they do not survive the equal division decreed by the inheritance laws.

The professions, whose diversity is so great, cause no dissimilarity in position among those who practice them. I am not speaking here only of Pennsylvania, where the Quaker influence has made equality among the professions an almost religious dogma, but of all the states in the American Union. Everywhere, any profession, employment, or trade is considered as an industry; shopkeeping, literature, the law, civil service, the ministry, all are industrial careers; those who follow them are more or less happy, more or less well off, but they have equality among themselves; what they do is not the same but it is of the same nature. From the domestic serving his master, to the President of the United States serving the State; from the mechanic whose brawn turns the wheels, to the man of genius who creates sublime ideas, all perform an analogous task and "do their duty." This explains why white domestics in America *help* their master, and do not *serve* him, in the ordinary sense of domestic service. It is also one of the reasons for the way trade is carried on in the United States: the American merchant certainly makes as much profit as he can; I even believe that he often cheats his customers; but in no case will he accept a penny more than he has asked, were he the wretchedest of all innkeepers. The laborer one employs, the porter one hires, the domestic who serves one in a hotel, all ask their *lawful* wages, the price of their work, and no more. To accept more than is their due, they feel, is to receive alms, and is consequently degrading. One may now understand why the President of the United States receives in Washington, on a footing of perfect equality, the firstcomer who wishes to speak with him, and begins by shaking hands with him; he acts the same way with all his fellow citizens when he travels in the different states of the Union. I have often heard men who fill eminent positions—such as Treasurer, Governor, Secretary of State—speak quite as a matter of course of their brother the *grocer*, their cousin the *salesman*, etc.

As further proof of the existence of practical equality in the United States, I will cite but two facts.

One day, as I was going to visit one of New York State's county jails, accompanied by the district attorney, the latter, as we walked together, told me the circumstances of a crime of which I was going to see the perpetrator; he painted the outrage in the darkest colors, adding that he himself had sentenced the guilty man. I arrived at the jail filled with the most sinister impressions, and was feeling a sort of horror at sight of the criminal, when I saw the district attorney go up to him and shake hands.

At another time, in a brilliant salon, where was gathered the best company of one of the largest cities of the Union, I was presented to a very well-dressed gentleman with whom I chatted for a few moments; soon after I asked who this man was. They said, "He is a very fine fellow—the county sheriff." I wanted to know what a sheriff was, and I learned that that means the executioner.[1]

How does it happen that, in the face of these actualities, which occur and recur continually in a thousand forms, there are still people who deny that Americans practice equality?

The reason lies in the misunderstanding of certain facts, and in a few appearances which to superficial observation seem to be realities.

Among the same people, where the living conditions are uniform, you may find men constantly basing their respect for others on riches, and attaching great importance to their birth. They don't say: "This man is worthy of respect because he is honest and just; the other is distinguished by his mind and his eloquence." They say: "So-and-so is *worth* $10,000—and such-and-such is *worth* only half that."

In the midst of this people, where democracy dominates society, one sometimes sees quite aristocratic instincts revealed. According to law, children divide their inheritance equally; but a father can dispose of his goods at his pleasure—giving everything to one child alone and disinheriting the rest. It very often happens that, exercising his right, an American endows this first-born with a considerable sum, not to reward him for better conduct than that of his brothers, but to make him a senior member of the family, giving him a position which flatters the pride of the head of the family.

These same Americans, who can be seen mingling with men of all conditions, often childishly value the antiquity of their origin and the nobility of their forebears. There are those who will endlessly reiterate their genealogies; sometimes they will stretch the truth to prove their illustrious descent. It is not uncommon that one

[1] In truth, the functions of the hangman do not entail in the United States the same degradation as among us; since they respect the laws here, they also respect those who enforce them; besides which they try to dignify the enforcer of the law by giving him additional important functions, with nothing degrading about them; a sheriff is a pillar of public strength.

who really belongs to an aristocratic family affects a sort of scorn toward those who show the same kind of pretension without justification. "Look at that gentleman," an inhabitant of ——— once told me, "who is so proud of his great fortune; he is a mere parvenu —his father was a cobbler."

The Americans, whose customs, in accord with their fundamental law,[2] recognize no nobility, nevertheless pay court to noble titles. A stranger is sure of receiving a welcome that is enthusiastic, very warm, merely warm, or cool, according to whether he is a duke, a marquis, a count, or no one in particular. A title immediately attracts the Americans' attention and draws their homage; the question of whether or not the man who bears it is worth the least thing is only secondary. Their political institutions and social conditions not permitting them to take titles of nobility, they cling by every possible means to trivial aristocratic distinctions. I am not referring here to the title of *gentleman,* which the least important coachman and lowest innkeeper will take; but to the fact that whoever achieves —by trade, the law, or any other profession—a position slightly superior to that of the majority never fails to add to his name the title *Esquire.* Many adopt a coat of arms, which they put on their seal rings and their carriages; in Maryland, one of the most democratic states, there are ardent democrats who add the name of their estate to their family name.

What can one conclude from these facts? That there is no real equality in the United States, and that there is an aristocratic tendency in their customs? No, indeed. What is happening here is not a progress of the present toward the future; it is a reminiscence of the past.

When one studies either the institutions or the customs of the Americans, one must never forget that their ancestors were English. This origin exercises on their laws and on all their way of life an influence which is doubtless constantly waning, but which will never disappear entirely. Now, there are two things which in England are most important in judging a man: his birth and his fortune. There is the true source of the respect Americans have for birth and fortune. It is a tradition, handed on from age to age, an old memory, an antique prejudice, which struggles alone against all the power of law and mores. The struggle is not serious; the love of titles, the taste for armorial bearings, family pretensions, are the play and competition of vanity; wherever there are men, their pride makes

[2] See Article 7, section 9, of the Constitution of the United States.

them seek distinction; but the best proof that with the Americans these distinctions lack a solid basis is that they do not hurt the feelings of the general populace. All power in the United States comes from the people and returns to the people; one has to be democratic there or be treated as a pariah. The ways of democracy do not please everyone, but all must accept them; some have tried to assume more aristocratic ways, to adopt less vulgar customs, and to create a class superior to the only existing class; some are pained at the idea of shaking hands with the shoemaker; to others it is distressing that a lackey cannot be found who will consent to mount behind their carriage, no matter how well he is paid;[3] some find it deplorable that public affairs are conducted by the ignorant mob; others are indignant that political functions are most often entrusted to mediocre men: but they all have to swallow these vexations and emotions. Those who manifest such sentiments soon incur public disapproval and must forever renounce any political aspirations in their country. Popular election is the only road to power; when election day comes, the voice of the masses is heard, and shatters all these little barriers of resistance and hostility against popular power.

I was surprised to see an English author who has written with some skill on the customs of the United States, [Thomas] Hamilton, fall into the errors I have just pointed out, and claim that there is no more equality practiced in the United States than in England. Among other arguments in support of his opinion, he reports an evening spent by him in a New York drawing room, where people of diverse professions were assembled. "Now," he says, "a lady near whom I was seated was as shocked as I was at seeing quite ordinary women in a distinguished salon. 'That young person,' she observed to me, 'is certainly pretty, but she is the daughter of a tobacconist; that other girl dances well, but she has had no education,' etc." Mr. Hamilton concludes from this that in the United States conditions are not equal; however, he might have replied to the lady who made such observations to him, "These common and vulgar ladies are your equals, since you are together in the same drawing room."[4]

Social and political equality in the United States is never seriously infringed except with regard to the black race. But here the

[3] No white domestic will stoop to such service.

[4] See Hamilton, pp. 65, 66. [Beaumont's note.] This quotation actually is a free paraphrase; see Thomas Hamilton, *Men and Manners in America* (2 vols.; Edinburgh: Blackwood, 1833), I, 111–13. [Translator's note.]

American does not believe he is violating the principle of equality, since he considers that the Negro belongs to a race inferior to his own; and on this subject it must be noted that in the slave states, where the inequality between the blacks and whites is most marked, the equality among the whites is perhaps still more perfect. As I said above, a white skin is the mark of nobility for them, and they treat each other with the regard and honor habitual among the members of a privileged class.

J. NOTE ON AMERICAN THEATERS

There are three theaters in Philadelphia: two of a high order, where tragedies and comedies are played; the third, quite inferior, is devoted to gross buffooneries.

The two great theaters are open only during the winter, when the evenings are long; the third is never closed. Even during the winter the first two are sparsely attended. The public which goes to the theater is generally thus composed: first, strangers who go because they do not know where else to pass their evenings; prostitutes, drawn by the presence of the strangers; young Americans of dissipated character; and finally a few shopkeepers' families, who acquire a rather questionable reputation in American society for frequenting the theater. Persons more distinguished in fortune and position do not make theater-going a habit; only something out of the ordinary will attract them there—for example, the presence of a celebrated guest actor. On such occasions, many go to the theater, not because they like it, but because it is fashionable. In truth, no one in the United States likes the theater, and nearly everyone who is seen there goes only through idleness. They pay no attention to the play. Americans in France who attend a play are quite astonished at the silence which reigns among the spectators, and the emotions aroused in them by the play. In America the audience does not know what is being played; they chat, they argue, they fidget about, they make it an occasion to drink together; the interest of the play is entirely lost to view.

The doctrine of the Quaker founders of Pennsylvania formally forbids the theater; since the Quakers are no longer in the majority they no longer make the laws, but part of their customs remain. One can say as much of the Presbyterians in New England; they have deviated, in Boston, from the rigidity of their principles in establishing theaters; but the population has neither the taste nor the habit of theater-going. I do not speak here of New York, whose American inhabitants seem no more desirous than in other cities for the pleasures of the theater. Plays are given more frequently there, it is true, but then there are twenty thousand foreigners in New York to whom the theater is almost a necessity. Quite a number of theaters could prosper in New York without leading one to the conclusion that the Americans of that city love the stage.

K. NOTE ON THE PRESENT CONDITION OF THE INDIAN TRIBES OF NORTH AMERICA[1]

In 1700, Beverley wrote: "The original nations of Virginia are extinct, though several towns still bear their names."[2]

Today one can find no trace of these savages; they are gone, to the last man. The French in Louisiana entirely destroyed the great nation of the Natchez.

In 1831, crossing the New York counties which border on Lake Ontario, I met several tatterdemalion Indians, who, walking beside the road, begged from travelers. I wanted to know what tribes these Indians belonged to; I was told that I was looking at the last of the Iroquois.

The country I was traversing was, indeed, the fatherland of the Six Nations: at each step one came across vestiges of the former masters of the land, but they themselves had disappeared.

It is easy to show in a few words the various causes to which may be attributed the great destruction of the savage nations.

It was the English, says Beverley,[3] who taught the savages to set a price on their furs and to use them for trade. Before that time

[1] This is Section 2 of an Appendix entitled "Note on the Past and Present Conditions of the Indian Tribes in North America." Section 1, "Past Condition," has been omitted. [Translator's note.]

[2] Robert Beverley, *The History and Present State of Virginia* (London, 1705). [The actual text reads: "The Indians of Virginia are almost wasted, but such Towns, or People as retain their Names, and live in Bodies, are hereunder set down; All which together can't raise five hundred fighting men" (new ed., by Louis B. Wright, Chapel Hill, University of North Carolina Press, 1947, p. 232).]

[3] *Ibid.*, p. 310 [p. 227 in 1947 edition].

they had estimated the value of these furs in terms of their usefulness to themselves. Beverley says elsewhere[4] that at the time when he was writing (1700), the savages of Virginia already were making use of cloth from Europe to cover themselves in winter. "We are already far from the time," say Cass and Clark, in 1829, in an official report (p. 23, Legislative Documents No. 117), "when the Indians could provide their own food and clothing without having recourse to civilized man's industries."[5] Lawson, Beverley, Du Pratz, Lahontan, and Charlevoix agree in saying that, since the beginning of the colonies, there has been a stupendous trade in whisky with the Indians.

Anyone who meditates on the few facts I have exposed will find in them the causes we seek of that ruin. Before the arrival of the white men, the savage procured for himself everything of which he had need; he considered the skins of animals only as a covering; his forests were enough for him, he found there everything necessary to his existence; he desired no more than that; he lived there in a sort of abundance, and multiplied.

From the time of the white man's arrival, the Indian formed new tastes. He learned how to cover his nakedness with stuffs from Europe. Fermented liquors revealed a source of hitherto unknown pleasures, singularly appropriate to his uncivilized disposition. He was offered murderous weapons which he was quickly taught to use; and as his nomad habits, his hunter's life, and the prejudices implicit in them forbade his manufacturing the precious things which had become necessary to him, he grew dependent upon the Europeans, and became their lackey. But as a hunter, he was a poor man; in exchange for the goods he coveted he had nothing to offer but the skins of wild beasts. [. . .] From then on, he had to hunt not only to supply himself with food, but also to procure those objects of barbarian luxury. Game became scarce; soon it could be obtained only with firearms, and it must be killed in order to procure these weapons. The remedy increased the ill; the ill rendered the remedy more difficult to find. Bear, deer, and beaver could no longer be caught, say Cass and Clark (p. 24), except with muskets. Little by little the savage's resources dwindled; his needs grew. Wretchedness unknown to his fathers assailed him from every side; to escape it he either fled or died. As he had never tilled the soil, so that he left no lasting monument to his existence in the country he inhabited,

[4] *Ibid.*, p. 230 [p. 161 in 1947 edition].

[5] The original quotation could not be found. [Translator's note.]

all traces of him were lost in a few years, even his name barely survived him; it was as though he had never been.

This destruction was inevitable from the moment when the Indians persisted in keeping to their way of life as hunters.

Among all the savage tribes which covered the face of North America, only a very small number are known at present who have tried to adapt their ways to the ways of tillers of the soil, who produce what they consume: these are the Chickasaws, the Choctaws, the Creeks, and especially the Cherokees. These four nations occupied the southern United States; they lived in the states of Georgia, Alabama, and Mississippi. In 1830 their number stood at 75,000 individuals. At the time of the War of Independence, a certain number of southern Anglo-Americans, having taken the side of the mother country, were obliged to exile themselves, and sought refuge with the Indians I am speaking of. These Europeans soon exercised great influence over the savages, intermarried with them, and brought among them our ideas and skills.

On February 4, 1830, Mr. Bell, reporting for the Committee on Indian Affairs in the House of Representatives, estimated the population of the Cherokees east of the Mississippi at approximately 12,000 souls. Of this number, about 250 individuals belonged to the white race—men and women who had entered into Indian families. There were also 1,200 black slaves, brought in by the Europeans. The remainder were pure-blooded Indians and a mixed race. Mr. Bell adds that intelligence and wealth are concentrated in the half-breeds; as to the rest of the population, they are in all respects like their brothers of the wilderness. Like them, he says, they have an invincible tendency to indolence; like them they are improvident and show the same inordinate passion for strong liquor.

Assuming that this account is accurate (which there is reason to doubt, when one notes the ardor with which Mr. Bell speaks throughout the report against the rights of the unfortunate indigenous race)—assuming, I say, the accuracy of the picture, one is led to think that if this imperfect civilization had had time to develop, it would finally have borne much fruit.

Even though the North American Indians, in their former state, had all adopted the same way of life and lived as hunters, the political structure did not take the same form with all of them. In the South, public authority was concentrated in a few hands; in the North, the entire people took part in the government: these differences may be remarked even today. Now, as then, most of the Indian nations of the South obeyed a single chief, or a very strong oligarchy. Since the men who composed the chosen few among the Cherokees and exercised unlimited authority were civilized, and interested in bringing civilization to the nation at whose head they were placed, it seems incontestable to me that they would sooner or later have achieved their aim, if they had been allowed the time to complete their work. But this was not to be: the land on which these unfortunate Indians lived was situated within the boundaries of the states I have named; today those states claim the land as their heritage, and the Union favors their plans by offering to the Indians who wish to leave the land free transportation to the vast country on the right bank of the Mississippi (Arkansas), where they may live beyond reach of the tyranny of white men. The more civilized portion of the Indians refuse to lend themselves to this scheme; but the bulk of the nation, who preserve most of the wandering habit of a hunting people, agree to it easily, and, placed anew amid an immense wilderness far from the center of civilization, would revert to their former savagery. Thus the American government daily destroys what the Cherokee government was trying to accomplish; while the latter draws the savages toward civilization, the Federal government pushes them back into barbarity. There is no doubt as to the result of this struggle: it is easy to foresee that in the very near future these unhappy Indians, transported to the right bank of the Mississippi, will have abandoned the plow for the ax and musket and will once again seek to provide their entire subsistence by the huntsman's unproductive labor.

The Chickasaws, the Choctaws, the Creeks, and the Cherokees are the only tribes who have manifested any propensity for an agricultural mode of existence. All the others have clung with strange tenacity to the ways of their ancestors and, though lacking their spirit or resources, still persist in living as they did.

If one looks comprehensively upon all the Indians who now inhabit North America, one can easily see that they have all clung to the way of life they followed two hundred years ago. Like their fathers, they gain their whole subsistence from the hunt; they lead, for the most part, the kind of life which was depicted in 1606 by Captain John Smith; however, immense changes have occurred among them. What are these changes? What is their cause?

The Indians had no laws; they were governed only by their traditions, customs, emotions, and habits; the more stable and regular these were, the more strong and peaceful was society.

It was in changing the opinions, in altering the customs, and in modifying the habits of the Indians that the Europeans wrought the revolution of which I am speaking.

The proximity of Europeans exercised one direct and one indirect influence upon the Indians—both of them fatal.

The Indian, despite his pride, feels in the depths of his soul that the white race has gained over him an incontestable advantage, and the Europeans, though he scorns them, nevertheless powerfully influence his opinions and conduct: as bad luck would have it, the only Europeans with whom the savages usually come in contact are precisely those who are the most depraved among the whites.

There has always been a flourishing fur trade with the natives. The Europeans who follow this trade are mostly unscrupulous, lackpenny adventurers, who find in the unfettered freedom of the forest a compensation for the hard labor they undertake. These foreigners show the natives of America only the vices of Europe and, what is more deplorable, familiarize them with those European vices which, being most analogous to their own, are the more easily adopted by them. They do not teach them the polished depravity of our upper classes; the Indian would not understand this and would not be endangered thereby; but they exhibit civilized man as more violent, more defiant of law, more ruthless—in a word, more savage—than the savage himself. However, to the Indian these European savages seem to be educated, wealthy, and powerful. And so in the Indian's conscience there is incredible confusion: he does not know whether the vices, which he understands only too well and despises, may not be the very causes of the superiority he admires; and, if they do not produce it, at least they seem to him no obstacle in the way of acquiring it.

However pernicious this direct influence of the whites may have been on the life of the savages, their indirect influence has been even more malignant.

I have mentioned how the coming of the Europeans made the lot of the Indians more unhappy than before, and how, while diminishing their resources, it increased their needs; but I could not give any idea of the extent of the evils to which, in our days, these poor people are a prey.

Among the Indians of the Northwest particularly, say Clark and Cass in their official report, only excessive labor can provide the Indian with the wherewithal to feed and clothe his family. Entire days are spent in hunting unsuccessfully, and, in the meantime, the hunter's family must eat roots and bark or perish. Many of these Indians die of hunger each winter. [. . .]

Tanner tells us that they teach young boys and girls, from their earliest youth, to bear the most rigorous abstinence.[6] They encourage them in their attempts by appealing to their pride. Being able to bear a long fast, he says, is a much envied distinction. Religion itself makes the fast holy; it is in the dreams of a fasting man that the future is revealed. Such customs, opinions, and mores speak for themselves and make it unnecessary for me to add anything more.

It is in these frightful conditions of misery that one may find the greatest single cause of the moral and political upheavals which have taken place among the North American Indians. It is in rendering the Indian a thousand times more miserable than his fathers that the Europeans have made him other than he was.

I have shown that, though the savages were not attached to the land as farmers, love of their fatherland was not unknown to these barbaric peoples; they only directed it to fewer things. This feeling was even more of a need to them than to other men, and produced in them, as everywhere else, admirable effects; the life of a hunter tends to isolate the individual from his kind, to reduce society to the family unit, and, inhibiting communication between men, to destroy civilization in the seed. The attachment the Indians feel for their tribes, on the contrary, tends to draw great numbers of them together, and allows them to pool what little intellectual attainments their hunting life allows them. This instinctive love of their country tends no less to develop the feelings than the minds of these savages; it substitutes a kind of larger and nobler egoism for that narrow one born of self-interest. We have seen to what sublime virtues it has sometimes given rise. The Indians thus united, moreover, exert over each other the control of public opinion, an always salutary control, even in the heart of an ignorant and corrupt society; for the majority of men, whatever their elements, always have a preference for what is just and upright.

Today, national spirit as such no longer exists among the indigenous Americans; one finds with difficulty a few feeble traces of it. Indians who lived in the wide-open spaces are today confined within the limits of European dwellings; some die of starvation and wretchedness, others have retreated and are widely dispersed, always driven on by civilization. Among these savages, the ragged relics of a once powerful people, some wander at random in the wilderness; reduced to individuals or families, they feel themselves

[6] *A Narrative of the Captivity and Adventures of John Tanner* (New York: C. & H. Carvill, 1830), p. 288.

freed of any obligation toward their kind, from whom they expect no aid; others have been absorbed into other nations met with on their way, but whose ways and memories they do not share. Among even these nations, which contact with Europeans has not yet destroyed or forced to flee, the social ties have weakened. Hardship has already forced the men who belong to them to live separately, the more easily to find a way to support their lives; necessity has weakened in their hearts that feeling for their fatherland which, like all other feelings, needs for its preservation to be combined with a sort of well-being. Pursued each day by fear of death from hunger and cold, how can these unfortunates trouble themselves with the general interests of their country? What does national pride become in a poor wretch who is dying in the anguish of poverty?[7]

The same cause which has weakened the love of their land among the Indians has altered their customs, distorted their feelings, and modified their entire outlook.

We have seen what touching rites the Indians living two hundred years ago accorded to their dead, with what superstitious veneration they surrounded their ashes; there is nothing that introduces more morality among men and prepares them better for civilization than respect for the dead: the memory of those who are no more never fails to exert a great and beneficial influence upon the actions of the living. Our ancestors form a greater and more perfect generation of men than that surrounding us, and in their presence we are forced in some sort to live better. Only in the bosom of a fixed and peaceable society can there be respect for the dead. The Indians of our day have become strangers here; many of them have been forced to flee the country where lie the bones of their forebears and to change the customs that their fathers bequeathed them. Absorbed in the needs of the present and fears for the future, the past with its memories has lost all power over them. The same cause acts upon the tribes who have not yet left their territory. The Indian ordinarily has only his family as witnesses to his last moments; often he dies alone, perishing far from the village, in the heart of the wilderness where he must lie hidden to secure his prey. A little earth is hastily strewn over his remains, and everyone departs without loss of time, in order to find the wherewithal to sustain their own always precarious lives.

One may see, from John Smith, Lawson, and Beverley, with

[7] One may see in Tanner's *Narrative* that Indians band together for hunting purposes much more than from any national spirit.

what kindness the Indians received strangers two hundred years ago, and with what charity they aided each other. These hospitable manners and kindly virtues were part of the kind of life led by the savages and one can still find traces of them today; rarely does the Indian close his door to one who asks shelter or refuse to share his meager means with one less fortunate than himself. Tanner recounts how he and his family, being near death from want, met an Indian whom he did not know and who belonged to a different tribe.[8] The Indian received Tanner in his cabin and bestowed upon him all that he needed. This is still the custom, adds Tanner, among those Indians who live far from white men. In another instance, the head of a family having died, all the Indians volunteered to hunt to provide for the family's needs. Later, Tanner tells how, having gone a great distance from any Europeans, he cached his furs in a place where he knew he could find them on his return. If the Indians who lived in that far-off region, he said, had seen his cache, they would not have been tempted to break into it; the skins were not, to their eyes, so costly as to lure them to theft.[9]

However, it is not always thus; often one finds, in the wilds of America as in our civilized countrysides, a grudging welcome which formerly one need not have anticipated here. Thievery increases; growing need gradually erodes the simple primitive virtues which arose naturally from the social conditions of the natives.

Religion forms the strongest social tie yet discovered by man. The savages of our day have kept a few of the notions their fathers had, mingled with their belief in God and the immortality of the soul; but these notions become more and more confused.

This is easily explained: among all peoples, but particularly among uncivilized peoples, their rites form the more substantial and lasting part of their religion. Indians who lived two hundred years ago had temples, altars, ceremonies, and priests. The savages of today have neither the time nor the power to build monuments or create permanent institutions; they do not live long enough in the same place, nor in great enough numbers, to observe the periodic cycles of certain ceremonies; nor to make the choice of certain prayers. Besides, man, to be concerned with the affairs of the other world, needs in this one to enjoy a certain physical and spiritual tranquillity. Today's Indians lack this tranquillity: in this respect as in all others, they have become much more barbaric than even their fathers.

[8] *Narrative*, p. 45.

[9] *Ibid.*, pp. 65, 89.

The vestiges of religion are hardly recognizable among them except for incoherent superstitions kept alive by immediate feelings and the needs of the moment. If an Indian is ill, he imagines someone has laid a curse on him and sends gifts to a so-called sorcerer to induce him to keep him alive.[10] If an Indian is hungry, he prays to the Great Spirit to show him in a dream the place where he may find game. He molds an image of the animal he wishes to kill, and after chanting magic songs, he pierces it with a sharp instrument. The tribes have no more priests, but only soothsayers, and they make use of them only in case of sickness or hunger.[11]

I have said that the way of life followed by the natives of North America prevented them from making any considerable progress in the arts. However, some of the Indians have raised considerable buildings. In some instances there reigned among them a barbaric luxury which attested to ease and leisure; there is no more of this today. Not very long ago, say Clark and Cass, one sometimes saw Indians wearing robes of beaver fur, but such a thing is unknown today. The exchange value of such clothing procured to the savage who possessed it the means of clothing his entire family. Seeing the Indians of today dressed in wool and provided with our weapons, one is tempted at first to believe that civilization has begun to penetrate among these barbarians. This is an error. All these things are of European make; they bear witness to the perfection of our skills without having taught the Indian anything. The latter, in what they produce themselves, are inferior to their ancestors; in becoming more nomadic and poor, they have lost the wish to build large and durable constructions. The savage hastily fixes a sort of den and, as long as it affords him temporary shelter from the rigors of the weather, he is content: I would say that in his farming there is an analogy—without a fixed domicile, the Indian today does not know where to plant his field of corn and has no idea if he will have the time reap the harvest. He concentrates more and more, therefore, on hunting, and the rarer becomes the game, the more he considers it his only resource. Thus it is that the coming of a farming people has rendered the natives of North America even less inclined to be farmers than they were before. All men who lead a roving and precarious life tend to improvidence; chance necessarily plays so great a part in their lives that they are tempted to abandon everything to it willingly; but never has the Indians' improvidence, the natural

[10] See Tanner, *Narrative*, p. 166.

[11] *Ibid.*, pp. 174, 285.

result of their social conditions, shown itself in a more uncivilized way than in our times. [. . .]

Among the Indians of former times, in all the nations of the continent, there were regular political powers. There were monarchies in the south, republics in the north; everywhere there was more or less well-organized public power; and it was rightly that John Smith said: "These Indians are barbarians, nevertheless they often show more obedience to their magistrates than do civilized peoples."

Today things are much changed; most of the nations of the south still bow to a single chief,[12] but his authority is often disregarded. The chain of traditions on which it was founded being broken, the customs which served as its support having been modified, the men to whom it applied being fewer and more nomadic than formerly, to a servile obedience has succeeded a spirit of wild independence which can produce nothing but disorder. In the North the trouble is still greater than in the South. Absolute monarchies are powerful in themselves, for in them authority rests its own strength long after its prestige has disappeared. But when disorganization creeps into the heart of a democratic republic, society disappears in some sort at once; its ties are broken; individuality appears everywhere: thus it happened to the wandering tribes of the North. When we refer to the accounts that William Smith, Lahontan, and Charlevoix give us of the Iroquois, the Hurons, and all other men speaking the Algonquian language, we find that at the time these authors were writing, in each tribe a number of chosen men and all the old men exercised a powerful control over all the actions of the natives and lent to individual weakness the protection and support of society. Evidence of this type of government is barely recognizable in our times. [. . .] In national councils it is might and not right which makes the laws; the wisdom of experience is disregarded, and youth dominates. Today, say Clark and Cass, one can say that no government exists among the tribes of the North and West. Custom and public opinion alone maintain a kind of barbaric social community. Formerly the old men, or civil chiefs, possessed real authority; but it is long since this has been so: one can hardly find a trace of that order of things. When the Indians assemble to debate on their com-

[12] See *Travels* of Major Long, to the Rocky Mountains, first expedition, vol. I, pp. 223, 228. [For complete reference, see above, p. 223 n.2.] The organization of the southern and northern tribes differs completely, say Lewis and Clark. Among the first, authority rests in the hands of the few; among the second, of the many.

mon affairs, they form pure democracies, in which each claims equal right to give his opinion and to vote; though these deliberations are generally conducted by the old men, it is the young men and warriors who really exercise the power. No measure can be securely adopted without their assent. In such states of society, where the passions reign, the tomahawk would soon put an end to any attempt to direct or restrain public opinion. Experience, say these same authors, has shown us the expedience of getting all the young warriors present to sign treaties. It is above all necessary to be sure of the consent of the majority of the Indians.

However, it is not rare that, among the savage tribes I have been discussing, certain individuals come to exercise more influence than others over their fellows. But that influence has no lasting foundation; it is acquired, so to speak, by chance, is exercised haphazardly; and occasionally it reaches no more than a few members of the tribe.

The Indian who leads a band of warriors has no control over those who accompany him, says Tanner; he exerts only a personal influence upon them.[13] "Under such circumstances," he writes, "they chose me for a leader; since we had no other aim than to procure meat, and they knew me to be a good hunter, they were right to act thus."[14]

The men making up these savage tribes are too scattered to be able to acquire the habit of communal obedience. They are beyond all control by the very fact of their wretchedness. Nothing can be expected of them, and they have nothing to lose: it is therefore difficult to discover among these northern Indian nations anything resembling a society. The individual finds no protection but in himself, as in the state of nature. Tanner's whole book is as full of acts of violence and brigandage as of misfortune and misery. Nowhere can one find authority standing by to mediate between the strong and the weak, between the attacker and the victim. The Indians have lost the very notion of this guardian power. When a northern Indian is the victim of some crime, he seeks vengeance if he is stronger, and runs away if he is weaker; in neither case does the

[13] *Narrative*, p. 125.

[14] *Ibid.*, p. 172. [Page 162 in new edition (Minneapolis: Ross & Haines, 1956). The actual text reads: "Wah-ka-zhe . . . determined that . . . his band should, for the winter, be guided by me. As we had in view no object beyond bare subsistence, and as I was reckoned a very good hunter, and knew the country better than any other man of the band, his course was not an impolitic one."]

thought of a social power occur to his mind. In this, as in all the rest, personal judgment takes the place of custom and law. [. . .]

Two hundred years ago, the natives of North America formed tribes of hunters. A fixed domicile, ancient customs, respected traditions, assured means of subsistence, tranquillity in body and mind which was the result of easy circumstances allowed them to enjoy, in the social state of hunters, all the conditions of well-being and greatness which that social state permitted.

Today, seemingly nothing has changed. The same tribes still live by the hunt and have preserved all the usages inherent in that way of life. Nevertheless the Indians of today are nothing like their fathers.

The Europeans, scattering the Indians among wildernesses strange to them, disrupting their traditions, confusing their memories, breaking their habits, altering their mores, have forced them to the tragic end of the hunting life. It is thus that contact with civilized, educated, and agricultural men, has rendered the Indians more nomadic and uncivilized than ever they were before.

L. NOTE ON THE NEW YORK RACE RIOTS OF 1834

The events which took place in New York in July 1834 furnished the text of Chapter 13 of this work, entitled "The Riot." I think I should place beside the story, whose basis is entirely true, the exact account of all that happened.

The principle of slavery had been abolished in the State of New York in 1799; but the Negroes who had ceased to be slaves had not become the equals of the whites. The color of these freed men was a constant reminder of their origin. However, the black population, possessing liberty, aspired also to equality. That is the main point in the quarrel between the two races in the northern United States.

As long as the freed Negroes show themselves submissive and respectful to the whites, as long as they hold themselves to a position of inferiority, they are assured of support and protection. The American then sees in them only those poor unfortunates whom religion and humanity command him to aid. But as soon as they announce their claims to equality, the pride of the whites is aroused, and the pity inspired by misfortune gives way to hatred and scorn.

The Negroes, being very few in the Northern states generally, submit without resistance to all the exactions of white American pride. There is no struggle, because the oppressed accept abuse and tyranny. The serious clash, of which New York was the scene last July, is explainable only by the concurrence of quite extraordinary circumstances. There are only 44,870 colored persons in New York State, as against 1,913,000 whites, and in the city itself 13,000 colored people to 200,000 whites; neither the Negroes nor the Americans, therefore, could have thought of fighting each other; the first because they were too few and the second because they were too many. However, there is among the white population itself a group working to establish the complete equality of the Negroes. This group, composed of sincere philanthropists, religious men, ardent Methodists and Presbyterians, attacks with indefatigable zeal the prejudices separating the Negroes from the whites. They are called "abolitionists," because they are trying to abolish slavery wherever it exists, and "amalgamists," because by means of mixed marriages they want to bring about the mingling of the two races. They have organized a society called the Anti-Slavery Society, and founded a newspaper which supports the Society's doctrines. This Society has the strength supplied by deep conviction, an honest aim, and generous passions, but its numbers are small.

For a long time the claims they raised in favor of the unfortunates of whom they are the patrons roused little irritation among Americans of opposite opinions; but, toward the beginning of the year 1834, they were no longer listened to with indifference.

First, it cannot be denied that the repercussions from the emancipation of the blacks in the English colonies were felt throughout America, even in the heart of states where the Negroes were free. It is easy to see that the colored people, who have gained as yet only half the rights to which they aspire, were strongly stirred by the social revolution taking place so near them for the benefit of beings who resemble them in every way. This effect has been felt not only by the Negroes but also by their white advocates. These, instead of restraining the jubilation of the black population, encouraged it, not perceiving that their endeavors for the black race, supported by the white Americans when they amounted to no more than vain words, would stir up the most violent passions as soon as their realization seemed possible. Seeing this movement, as yet only moral and intellectual, the Americans felt the necessity of nipping it in the bud; and many, who until then had listened patiently to the abolitionists' theories on the equality of the blacks, switched suddenly from tolerance to hostility. Several successes on the part of the Negroes and their supporters added to the bitterness of this opposition.

Intermarriages are certainly the best, if not the unique, means of fusing the white and the black races. They are also the most obvious index of equality. For this twofold reason, unions of this sort arouse the rancor of the Americans above all else.

Early in the year 1834 a minister of the Anti-Slavery Society, the Reverend Doctor Beriah Green, performed in Utica the marriage of a Negro to a young white girl, and there was a sort of popular uprising in the city, following which the reverend doctor was hanged in effigy on the public street.[1]

Shortly afterward, Methodist and Presbyterian ministers in New York City married whites with colored people: this victory over prejudice encouraged the Negroes and roused the strong indignation of their enemies.

The month of July, 1834, arrived; the Americans celebrated the anniversary of their Declaration of Independence. For them this is always the occasion for long speeches on liberty and on the inalienable rights of man. The Negroes listened to some of these speeches, and their supporters did not omit on this occasion to remind them that the people of the black race have a liberty as sacred and rights as inviolable as the white men.

On July 7, an American, a friend to the Negroes, published in a newspaper a letter in which he announced that, in spite of a prejudice he scorned, he proposed to marry a young colored girl.[2] That same day a meeting of colored people was held in Chatham Street Chapel and speeches were made, the texts of which were the equality of whites and Negroes and the abolition of slavery in the entire Union. By an unfortunate coincidence, the members of the church music society, who customarily met in the same place, wished to occupy it at the same time the African gathering was in progress. Thence arose a regrettable conflict which was quickly over, but it added still more to the irritation of the two groups. At the same time a pamphlet against slavery was being circulated; at the head of the pamphlet there was a little engraving of a slave dealer tearing a slave from the arms of his wife and children and driving him away with blows of a whip: nothing was neglected which might arouse the indignation of the Negroes and the zeal of their friends. Another meeting

[1] See the *National Intelligencer*, February 4, 1834.

[2] *New York Commercial Advertiser*, July 7, 1834.

in Chatham Street Chapel was announced for the following day, July 9; the whites who sided with the Negroes promised to attend.

Then a very sharp feeling of annoyance became manifest in public opinion. The press showed itself unanimously hostile toward the colored people and bitterly derided the whites who so far forgot their dignity as to associate with wretched Negroes. The papers called the Negroes "the colored gentlemen," and the Negresses "the ladies of color"; they heaped sarcasm upon the white philanthropist who had published his intention to marry a colored woman. While the plans for the Chatham Street Chapel meeting were in progress, a powerful opposition was organized, and there was every indication that an unpleasant encounter would take place on that occasion. It is to be noted that at the time when these events took place the heat was excessive in New York. The 9th, 10th, and 11th of July were, in America, the hottest days in the year 1834. The temperature is not unconnected with popular agitations.[8] On the appointed day (July 9), a great crowd surrounded Chatham Street Chapel; but the police, foreseeing a clash, had called off the meeting, which did not take place. However, in the crowd there was a certain number of people who had been drawn there solely in the hope of a fight, and who could not bear to go away without having done some mischief. It was the theater hour; they found out at that moment that at the Bowery Theater there was an English actor, named Farren, who was accused of having spoken ill of the American people. "To the Bowery! To the Bowery!" cried several voices; soon the crowd surged toward the theater, which, a moment later, presented a scene of nothing but trouble and confusion. When this deed had been accomplished, the agitators turned their minds again to the idea which had set them in motion.

Among the most zealous of the friends of the Negroes was an American named Arthur Tappan. They knew that he received colored people in his house, and he had even dared sometimes to appear in public in their company. A voice shouted, "To Tappan's house!" and the crowd immediately rushed there. The factionists smashed the windows, burst in the doors, and, finding no one at home, took the furniture, threw it into the street, and set it afire. The police arrived meanwhile; a struggle followed, in which the people were by turns the winners and the losers; at two in the morning the fighting stopped: so passed the day of the 9th. The next day

[8] One American paper reported the names of a great number of persons who died of the heat on July 10.

the rebellion took on a still more serious character. It was found that the people planned to destroy Arthur Tappan's shops on Pearl Street and to attack the home of Dr. Cox, a Presbyterian minister devoted to the Negroes and their cause. Indeed, on the evening of the 10th, the crowd swept down on Dr. Cox's church, hurled missiles at its windows and doors, and withdrew. From there they went to the minister's house; but Dr. Cox and his family had left New York, having been warned of the danger that threatened them. Then the factionists began to demolish the house and were already at work when a detachment of the militia arrived, sent by the authorities; the insurgents, entrenched behind barricades made of overturned carts and wagons, put up a resistance. But after a half-hearted struggle, they yielded. On the same day, another church, belonging to the colored people and situated in the neighborhood of Laight Street, had been the object of the same attacks and outrages. The insurgents had tried to demolish it; a huge crowd had also gathered near Chatham Street Chapel, but dispersed peacefully upon the assurances of the proprietors of that edifice that they would never allow meetings to be held there having the abolition of slavery as their object. At midnight order was restored; but graver trouble was brewing for the next day, July 11.

It would seem certain that if, on the 10th and 11th, the authorities had taken energetic measures, the seditious movement would have had no consequences. It would have been enough to order the militia to meet force with force and use all their weapons against the insurgents, without any exceptions. [. . .]

However, the group which demanded these energetic reprisals was not the strongest or most numerous. If the riots had been of a purely political nature, the majority would have been sure to arm itself immediately with all its powers and to crush the attacks or the resistance of the minority. But on this occasion the New Yorkers were divided between two opposed ideas. On the one hand, their respect for the law and their desire for peace and order made them feel the necessity of stopping the insurrection. On the other hand, the fate of the victims did not excite their interest at all. Indeed, the majority sympathized at heart with the violent actions of the lesser number; nevertheless, respect for principle, and even a sense of shame forced them to oppose these actions. This strange situation explains the slackness of the measures taken by the authorities against the insurrection.

From early morning on the 11th, numerous detachments of the militia were marched about; but it was known that they had received no order to fire on the people in case of renewed unrest. It was not, as has been said, the absence of the governor which made the use of firearms against the rioters impossible. The mayor of New York had the incontestable right to order this action; but he did not believe he should do so.

The first violence committed by the rioters was upon Arthur Tappan's shops. They flung a hail of stones through the windows of the building and were preparing more serious assaults when the arrival of the militia made them take to their heels. Toward nine in the evening, Dr. Cox's church, which had been attacked the day before, was assailed again by a furious mob; a thousand missiles were hurled against its walls; the police arrived but were repulsed by the people. At the same time, another group of rioters was giving free rein to more criminal and impious violence. In Spring Street, the church of Dr. Ludlow was invaded. (The doctor's devotion to the cause of the Negroes invited the hatred of the factionists.) Windows were broken, doors smashed in, walls demolished; the ruins and fragments of the church served as a barricade behind which the rebels took up their position; a serious engagement took place between the people and the militia; the alarm was rung, the whole city was aroused; after several successes and reverses on either side the victory rested with the militia. The insurgents withdrew, but only to try more destruction elsewhere; they went to Dr. Ludlow's house, broke the doors and windows, and committed all sorts of violence. At the same time a church belonging to the blacks, and situated on Center Street, gave way to the popular frenzy. The rumor had got about that a few days before, the minister of this church, the Reverend Peter Williams, as much to be respected for his virtues as for his religious spirit, had married a colored man to a white woman.[4] Thenceforward the fury of the crowd grew to its full measure. The doors and windows were torn out, smashed, demolished, to the accompaniment of cheers from the onlookers; everything they could find inside the church was seized and thrown into the street. Soon the adjacent houses, occupied by colored people, were attacked and broken into; the furniture was sacked, pillaged, and burned; the same acts of violence were repeated in several other parts of the city. Other churches were profaned; all property belonging to colored people was declared outside the law. Their persons were respected no more than their property; wherever a colored

[4] *Mercantile Advertiser* and *New York Advocate*, July 12, 1834.

man appeared he was immediately attacked. However, as all were terror-stricken, they hid themselves. Then the populace, ingenious in its senseless fury, demanded that all the inhabitants should light up their houses. They were thus forced to show themselves. Obeying the commands of the people, a Negress appeared in the window after illuminating her house. A hail of stones fell upon her. Several colored families, fearing the same fate, kept their windows dark, but the people, concluding from this that Negroes were there, attacked and destroyed their houses.[5]

It is only fair to say that in the face of this impious vandalism the immense majority of Americans, and even those who had sympathized the day before with the vandals, were struck with disgust and horror. All those in the city who had property to protect experienced a feeling of fright. There was a general spirit of reaction, not in favor of the Negroes, but against their oppressors. Everyone realized the danger of allowing a factional and sacrilegious populace to continue longer in control of the city. It was known that the insurgents intended to continue on the following day their acts of violence and to destroy from top to bottom the churches and public schools of the blacks. The mayor of the city gave the strictest orders to the militia. The press addressed pitiless words to the rebels. Those who showed the least tendency to sedition should be killed "like dogs," said one paper on July 11 (*The Evening Post*). The militia marched, full of zeal, against the insurgents. Forthwith the sedition was put down for good. The following day the mayor of the city gave an account of his actions to the City Council. He declared that up to the last day of the disturbance he had judged sufficient to repress it the means which events had proved were inefficacious; this naïve admission of an error whose consequences had been so deplorable seemed quite satisfactory. The mayor had merely followed the shifts of public opinion. When the rebellion broke out, it was fondly hoped that rigorous measures were not necessary to combat it; it affected only the colored people. They clung to that hope as long as possible. Everybody was grateful to the magistrates for having shared the common illusion.

The struggle being ended, each party tried to evade the responsibility for it. The majority of the population had risen up to repress the factionists: at the moment when the rebellion took on a character alarming to the city, the greater number attempted to lay

[5] *Mercantile Advertiser* and *New York Advocate*, July 12, 1834.

the blame for the riots and their consequences on the victims. The insurgents were undoubtedly at fault for placing themselves above the law, but had not the Negroes and their supporters provoked them? One paper went so far as to demand that Mr. Tappan and Dr. Cox, whose ruin was caused by the riots, be accused of disturbing the public peace.

Those whose feelings were not so severe against the supporters of the blacks were at least indulgent toward their enemies. The press admirably seconded this tendency and furnished arguments to those whose reactions had been merely emotional.

The true cause of hostility against the Negroes, as I have said before, was the offended pride of the whites, at the pretensions to equality shown by the colored people. Now, a feeling of pride does not justify hatred and revenge. The Americans could not say: "We have allowed the Negroes to be attacked in our cities; we have allowed their private homes to be invaded, their churches to be profaned and torn down, because they had the audacity to wish to be our equals." This language, which would have been the truth, would have shown too much cynicism.

This is how the press helped the Americans out of their embarrassment: The advocates of the Negroes, it said, who wanted colored people to be the equals of the whites, demand the abolition of slavery in the whole Union; now, this is asking something contrary to the Constitution of the United States; in fact, the Constitution guarantees to the slave states the preservation of slavery as long as it pleases them to keep it; the interests of the North and the South are distinct. Those of the South rest on slavery. If the North works to destroy slavery in the South, it is doing a thing which is hostile and contrary to the very union of the states. Therefore, to favor the emancipation of the Negroes is to be an enemy of the Union.

The natural conclusion of this reasoning is that every good citizen in the United States should keep the blacks in servitude, and that the real enemies of the country are those who oppose slavery. The factionists who abandoned themselves for three days to the most iniquitous and impious violence were, fundamentally, animated by noble sentiments, while those who by their philanthropy toward an unhappy race had excited the just indignation of the whites were traitors to their country. Such are the consequences of a sophism.

Doubtless the Southern states could abolish slavery themselves; but since when have the Americans of the North lost the right to call attention to the evil of a vicious law? They destroyed slavery among themselves; and they are forbidden to wish for its destruction among their neighbors! They are not making a law, they are expressing a wish; if this wish is criminal, what becomes of the right of discussion, of freedom of speech and expression? Will this right cease to exist because it is used to attack the most monstrous of institutions? The Americans allow the vilest pamphleteer to write publicly that their President is a wretch, a swindler, an assassin; and an honorable man, moved by a profound conviction, cannot tell his fellow citizens that it is sad to see a whole race of men condemned to servitude; that nature revolts on seeing the child torn from its mother's breast, the husband separated from the wife, man beaten by man, and all in the name of the law! Finally, because there are still slaves in the South, must the freed Negroes be crushed without pity who, in New York, aspire to the rights of free men?

On July 12, the day after the insurrection, the Anti-Slavery Society published the following declaration:

1. We entirely disclaim any desire to promote or encourage intermarriage between white and colored persons.

2. We disclaim, and entirely disapprove, the language of a handbill recently circulated in this city, the tendency of which is thought to be to excite resistance to the Laws. Our principle is, that even hard laws are to be submitted to by all men, until they can by peaceable means be altered.

3. We disclaim, as we have always done, any intention to dissolve the Union, or to violate the Constitution and Laws of the country; or to ask of Congress any act transcending their constitutional powers; which the abolition of slavery by Congress, in any State, would do.[6]

All this proves that in the United States, under the rule of popular sovereignty, there is a majority whose actions are irresistible, which crushes, breaks, annihilates everything which opposes its power and impedes its passions.

The events which have just been related roused a lamentable echo a few days later in the city of Philadelphia. On August 11, 1834, without cause or pretext, the whites attacked the Negroes; a sharp conflict ensued which lasted half a day. The agents of au-

[6] *New York American*, July 14, 1834. [Beaumont's reference.] The disclaimer is signed by Arthur Tappan and John Rankin; its text is given above as it appears in the Washington *Daily National Intelligencer* of July 17, 1834. [Translator's note.]

thority displayed great energy against the rebellion, which was put down; but it threw the black population into a state of dejection. Two days later one of the papers reported that during the two days just past, steamboats going from Philadelphia to New Jersey had not ceased carrying a great quantity of colored people who, fearing for their lives in that city, determined to seek refuge elsewhere. Tents could be seen on the New Jersey shore, where the Negroes found temporary shelter while waiting to hire themselves out in a place where their lives and liberty would be assured.*

Thus the Negroes, freed by the North, are forced back by tyranny into the Southern states, and find refuge only in the midst of slavery.

* *Philadelphia Gazette*, August 14, 1834.